Fisher of Me.

a story of
faith, fish, and the sea

by Terry Cross

TUMBLAR HOUSE
'Bona Tempora Volvant'

Arcadia
MMX

Printed in the United States of America

ISBN 0-9842365-5-4

Fisher of Men. Copyright © 2009 by Terry Cross

Visit our Web site at www.tumblarhouse.com

For my Wife
and my Sister
and my Mom

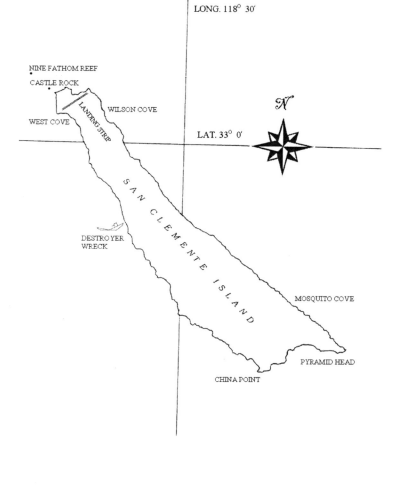

LONG. 118° 30'

NINE FATHOM REEF
CASTLE ROCK

WEST COVE

WILSON COVE

LANDING STRIP

LAT. 33° 0'

𝒩

SAN CLEMENTE ISLAND

DESTROYER
WRECK

MOSQUITO COVE

PYRAMID HEAD

CHINA POINT

Chapter 1

The man shivered, not because of the coolness of the ocean water bathing his bare skin, but because of a sudden, strong feeling that he was being watched.

That was odd, Simon Andrews thought, as he blew his snorkel clear and took his first look in months at the underwater world. Diving conditions were perfect, with no wind or current to speak of and water visibility of over fifty feet. Convincing himself that he was probably imagining things, Andrews kicked away from his boat, stopped after swimming only a few yards, and raised his head out of the water to take in the scene before him. His sloop, *Time Out,* hung slack on her anchor line against a backdrop of San Clemente Island's chaparral-covered hills. Andrews lifted his new underwater camera up to his faceplate and snapped a shot.

Two days of sailing and motoring had brought Andrews to this magical place. He had spent the night at Catalina, rounded the west end of San Clemente Island by noon today, and finally stopped when he came within sight of the partially submerged destroyer wreck. From the *Time Out's* bow he had clearly seen his anchor hit the bottom twenty-five feet below, and he had grabbed his fins, mask, and snorkel, and had tumbled over the side into the blue Pacific.

This was the life, Andrews told himself, taking in the underwater scene before him. Selling Porsches in Newport Beach was lucrative but stressful. A week by himself on the backside of San Clemente Island was just what the doctor ordered.

Twitch.

Andrews' eyes darted in the direction of a fleeting movement on the bottom. Goose bumps scampered across his skin as again the feeling of being watched swept over him. He scanned the ocean bottom for a possible cause of the feeling. Ribbons of feather boa kelp, ten-feet long and lined with fringe, swayed like grass skirts in the gentle surge. Various fish, though fewer in number than what Andrews expected to see, swam in and out of the kelp's protective curtain and seemed to be going about their normal fish business.

It was just as he suspected. He badly needed some time to unwind.

Andrews was ready for his first dive. He hyperventilated by taking ten long breaths. He held the tenth one, jackknifed his body, and sliced downward through the water, reaching the bottom with a few strong kicks of his swim fins.

That wasn't bad, he thought, considering that he hadn't been in the water for two months. He felt comfortable, and he figured he could stay down for at least half a minute before he had to surface for air. He knelt on the sandy bottom and began framing imaginary pictures with his new camera.

Twitch.

Another fleeting movement caught the corner of Andrews' eye, but this time he mentally chronicled the movement's location. Whatever it was, it was behind him and only a few feet distant. He placed a finger on the camera's shutter release and eased his body around in hopes of not scaring away a good picture. He saw nothing but the swaying bushes of feather boa and the noticeable lack of fish. Puzzled, he continued to look through the camera's large viewfinder, sensing that some photogenic, undersea creature was probably right in front of him but hiding in plain sight.

Too late, Andrews spotted the source of the movement. As the ocean floor opened up and engulfed him, his underwater scream was captured and carried upward in a swirling cloud of bubbles that broke silently on the surface.

Debris and sand that had been stirred up soon began to settle back to the bottom. A calico bass peeked out from its hiding place in the feather boa. A fresh afternoon breeze rippled the ocean surface, and the *Time Out*, secure at anchor, swung her stern another degree towards shore.

Chapter 2

"It's a seventeen footer!" Storm Hancock yelled through Farallon Island wind and rain, ignoring the worsening conditions while keeping himself focused on the huge shark swimming barely an arm's length below him. Storm lay stretched out on a slippery, wet, pitching plank suspended like a painter's scaffold from the side of the research vessel, *Nemo.* At the moment, it was all he could do just to stay on the plank. In fact, he was about one second away from completely aborting the attempt.

But this was a seventeen footer, Storm reminded himself, and as he searched the huge fish for recognizable markings, he became convinced he hadn't seen this particular great white before.

"Come on, big fella'," Storm whispered to the shark as he wrapped his feet tighter around the edges of the plank.

"Cooooooooome on."

"Underwater video says we got a female!" a voice called out through the rain.

"A female?" Storm yelled back. "Everybody be extra careful!"

The scientist part of Storm knew full well that he couldn't justify his last statement. He had no hard data, just feelings, but he was right. Women were nothing but trouble, and a shark this big was trouble enough already even without being a female.

"Bring the bait closer!" he yelled to the college student who dangled a twenty-pound salmon from a rope near the *Nemo's* stern.

As many times as Storm had attempted this maneuver, the thrill had only increased. He inched his chest further out over the end of the plank, and he tightened his grip on the two-thousand-dollars-worth of monitor that finished off his research budget.

"Coooome on, big gal," he whispered.

The great white moved closer to the dangling salmon, and Storm's senses heightened to surreal awareness. He heard the electric whine from motors moving the underwater video camera built into the *Nemo's* hull. On one side of his peripheral vision he saw the dart-tag harpoon bobbing with the *Nemo's* motion and ready to be hurled by the student holding it. On the other side he saw the student dangling the salmon and coaxing the great white ever closer. In his mind's eye he visualized the student who was video-taping the whole scene from atop the *Nemo's* flying bridge.

"Coooooome on."

Everything happened at once.

The great white lunged forward, and Storm felt the dart-tag harpoon whiz by his ear. He flung his upper body downward and pressed the monitor hard against the great white's back. The shark took half of the salmon in one bite and lunged again. It engulfed the rest of the salmon, and now its teeth became caught in the stout hemp rope holding the bait. The student handling the rope let it go, but the end of the rope was still made fast to a cleat, and the *Nemo* pitched wildly as the huge fish thrashed in its struggle to break free. Storm wrapped his arms and legs around the plank and hung on. He envisioned nothing worse than falling into the water next to a great white that was going berserk. The next second, the shark's massive tail swept upward and slammed into the plank, breaking Storm's grip and catapulting him into the air. He came down hard, landing with his legs straddled across the monster's back. The shark's sandpaper skin grated Storm's hands as he grappled to stay on top. He opened his mouth to yell for help, but he couldn't take in enough dry air to make a sound. He wound up not having to, because his safety harness suddenly dug into his body and jerked him upward. Faster and faster he rose until he was dragged over the *Nemo's* rail like a sack of potatoes to tumble in a heap with all four of his students.

The great white, meanwhile, had finally freed itself, and the *Nemo* again rocked with the gentle rhythm of the waves.

In the sudden calm, Storm lay motionless. He listened to the quiet slap of the waves against the *Nemo's* hull. He heard the wind lessen, and he felt the rain fall soft upon his skin. He opened his mouth and discovered that the raindrops tasted sweeter than he remembered.

"Life is good," he said, and he wondered how many paths taken and not taken had combined to bring him to this time and place. The students unpiled themselves from on top of him, and he took stock of his body. Several areas promised to hurt in the morning. He tried moving his arms and legs. Everything seemed to be working. Finally, he pulled himself to his feet.

"Well, that was a first," he said to his student crew. "Does anyone know how we did?"

The student who had been video-taping from the flying bridge said, "The monitor looked like it was stuck on good."

"Really?" Storm said in amazement. "I thought maybe I'd chucked it in the drink."

The student who had nearly harpooned Storm's ear said, "The dart's in clean, right at the back of the dorsal fin."

"You guys are still gunning for more grant money," Storm said with a grin.

"That's nothing!" remarked the student who had been below deck aiming the underwater video. "We've got three seconds of Dr. Hancock's face underwater while he's riding a great white!"

The students whooped and gave each other high fives, but Storm didn't mind them celebrating at his expense. After slogging out here in rotten weather weekend after weekend, they deserved it. "Let's get out of the rain," he said, and he led the group into the *Nemo's* main cabin. Dry towels stashed for such an occasion were passed out, and then Storm said, "I'm pleased to announce that the initial fieldwork of this project is officially over."

Groans and cheers filled the cabin.

"And the real work is about to begin."

That statement was met with groans only.

"But now, I would like to propose a toast."

That got their attention, Storm told himself, since everyone on board understood that alcohol was strictly forbidden aboard the *Nemo*. With dignified solemnity he opened the *Nemo's* ample refrigerator and retrieved a cardboard shoebox that was tied shut with white string. Milking the students' growing curiosity, he took his time opening the box and taking out a foil-wrapped object, which he just as deliberately unwrapped.

"Is that your mom's fruitcake?" one student asked with hope sounding in his voice and who was obviously aware that Mrs. Hancock's fruitcake was famous in local biology circles and that those who tasted it were a select few.

"Arrrrr, matey, it be that," Storm replied out of the side of his mouth while he scrunched one eye shut. "And it be soaked in rum, by gum."

Storm cut the cake into five equal pieces and passed them out. He held his piece up and announced, "To the magnificent, mysterious *Carcharidon carcharius* and to a job very well done." And also to my next endeavor, whatever that is, he added silently as he touched his piece of cake to the others in the toast. He broke out a bottle of sparkling cider to wash down the cake, and then he excused himself and made his way outside and up to the *Nemo's* flying bridge. He had a decision to make. It was still raining, and the wind had come around to the northwest. That was fine with Storm. The wind shift put the *Nemo* in the lee of the nearby Farralon Islands. He turned on a weather radio and confirmed what he had already sensed was coming. It was only going to blow harder the rest of the day. If they tried for the *Nemo's* home port in Bodega Bay, they'd wind up battling straight into the teeth of a gale the whole way. If they ran for San Francisco, they'd have a following wind and sea, but they'd be bucking the tide when they hit the Potato Patch. That was the local name for the sand bar guarding the bay's Golden Gate entrance, and that fierce outgoing current slamming head-on against the incoming seas would turn the place into a regular washing machine.

From the flying bridge Storm methodically swept his gaze from bow to stern over every inch of the custom vessel, *Nemo*. He mentally ticked off the modifications he had done to make her one of the most seaworthy boats for her size that had ever been built. She could take them home in worse weather than this, he decided, but why should she have to? He climbed down from the flying bridge and entered the cabin where his crew was excitedly planning how to best edit the underwater video, and obviously not for its scientific content. He said, "We're going to ease in tight to the island and drop the hook until this thing blows over. You'll have to put up with my cooking one more time, but we'll get a safe night's sleep, and we can head for Bodega first thing in the morning."

That was the right thing to do, Storm told himself as he watched the students break up their meeting and proceed to their assigned duties to get the *Nemo* underway. Granted, he had a plane to catch tomorrow afternoon, and now his schedule would be a lot tighter than before. He might have gone on to San Francisco if he'd been alone, but with the students he'd just play it safe.

Hah! Safe! Storm thought, remembering his recent ride on the back of a shark. That little fiasco sure hadn't been very safe. It had all happened too fast, and he hadn't seen it coming. He'd been right to follow his instincts and not let anybody but himself out on the plank. He'd also been right about the female great white.

She'd been nothing but trouble.

Storm still had a plane to catch. His students had survived another night of his cooking, and now the *Nemo* skimmed across the ocean as smoothly as an iceboat on a frozen lake. Her twin V-eight engines hummed in tune with each other, turning twenty-eight-inch props that could push her at over thirty knots. If the conditions held, Storm and his student crew would make the run from the Farallon Islands to Bodega Bay, be in port before the afternoon northwester blew in, and he'd still have time to catch his plane.

Everyone was up on the flying bridge. Storm was giving each student a trick at the wheel. His policy was that everyone should know how to drive the boat. He figured that someday it would come in handy. Besides, it was just plain fun to let someone else drive while he enjoyed the ride.

Storm had poured his heart into rebuilding the *Nemo*. At one time she had been the *Princess,* a forty-two-foot sports-fisher bought as a tax write-off and used mostly to host cocktail parties. She eventually wound up being impounded by the police, and when Storm discovered her moldering in a Redwood City dry dock, he saw, under her coating of grime, a jewel waiting to be polished. He picked her up pennies on the dollar and began her resurrection into a custom research vessel. Another marine biologist with grant money to burn might have first decked her out with the latest scientific gadgetry, but Storm had concentrated on making her seaworthy. She had already been so ruggedly built that some of her sisters had served in Vietnam, but Storm had made her even more rugged. He had replaced her picture windows with smaller windows that could be dogged down. Her doors and hatches were likewise reinforced. In theory, green water could sweep her to the flying bridge, and she would stay watertight. If she did ever fill up, Storm was counting on the flotation foam he'd crammed into every spare nook and cranny to keep her afloat.

A student tapped Storm on the shoulder and pointed aft. In the boat's wake, sleek animal forms broke the surface in flat arcs and were gaining on the *Nemo*. Storm trained his binoculars on the speedy animals, and he recognized the distinguishing black-and-white markings that made them look like miniature killer whales.

"Dall's porpoises!" Storm announced, loudly enough for all to hear, and he handed his binoculars to a student and scampered down to the *Nemo's* stern for a closer look. Storm had only seen Dall's porpoises one other time in his life, and the one thing that had impressed him about them was that they were fast.

Very fast.

The leaders of the pod of porpoises caught up with the *Nemo* and branched off to either side. They were close enough that Storm could hear the water make a tearing sound whenever their dorsal fins broke the surface. They seemed to be keeping up easily, and for all intents and purposes Storm decided that they looked like they were having fun.

Now stop that idiocy, he thought to himself. Storm couldn't stomach it when people projected human attributes onto dumb animals. He was a scientist, after all, and his purpose was to observe nature as it actually presented itself and not how he wanted it to be. That was one reason he didn't frequent ocean theme parks with their trained seals, and trained dolphins, and whatever else they trained. He considered that sort of activity to be a bunch of unscientific, anthropomorphic fluff.

The porpoises continued gaining on the *Nemo* until some of them were cutting in front of her bow. Even though Storm assured himself that they were undoubtedly exhibiting instinctual behavior that just happened to involve the *Nemo*, they still looked like they were playing.

He raised his hands above his head. One hand he held with his forefinger and thumb two inches apart. His other hand he held with his thumb straight up. The student at the wheel picked up the signal, and Storm heard the *Nemo's* engines increase a little in speed. The porpoises seemed to be game, and they too increased their speed.

Storm raised his thumb again and pumped his hand up and down. The engines roared, and the *Nemo* surged ahead. One by one, as Storm had expected, the porpoises began falling behind. He didn't want to tax the *Nemo* needlessly and was about to give a signal to slow the engines, but he stopped himself. A solitary porpoise, larger than the rest, was still in the chase. With every arcing leap a puff of vapor sprayed from its blowhole, and it gained a few more feet on the speeding *Nemo*.

Storm heard the porpoise's rhythmic breathing. It had a determined quality. He surprised himself by saying, "Come on! You can do it! Come on!"

"Now stop that anthropomorphic baloney!" Storm chided himself aloud, but he still couldn't help but appreciate the beauty and strength of the leaping mammal.

Maybe it would be all right if he just whispered.

"Come on," he encouraged quietly.

The porpoise now streaked so closely alongside the *Nemo* that Storm could have reached down and touched it. It held its position, racing a foot below the surface. Storm watched, mesmerized, as lines of compressed water streamed back along its sleek body. Then, without losing any speed, and as if to say, "Isn't this fun?" the porpoise rolled its body slightly to one side and looked Storm right in the eye. Storm looked back, even more fascinated than before, and he caught himself wondering what the porpoise might be thinking.

Chapter 3

Terry kept a wary eye on the group of men to her north. She didn't want them edging any closer.

"It's outside," the grey-bearded surfer next to Terry called, interrupting her thoughts, and he dropped flat to his surfboard and dug for the horizon. Terry snapped her gaze seaward. She caught only a glimpse of what the greybeard was referring to, but that was enough. She dropped flat to her own surfboard and paddled swiftly across the ocean surface towards the oncoming giant.

A hundred yards up the coast, as if they too had heard the greybeard's warning, a pack of at least thirty more surfers also paddled furiously.

They were all at "Trestles," the world-famous surf break at Camp Pendleton Marine Base in Southern California. Terry didn't know the greybeard by name, but his close proximity told her that he was of a similar mind set. Like her, he would rather ride a less-than-perfect wave with only one other person nearby than fight for a perfect wave in the middle of a mob. That was fine with Terry. She was twenty six, but the majority of her regular surfing buddies were men over fifty. They were just easier and more fun to be around. Whenever she paddled out into the younger crowd she seemed to cause problems. Maybe it had to do with her exotic combination of Asian and Polynesian features. Maybe it was the way her wetsuit clung to her feminine form like a coat of black paint. Maybe it was because she had grown up surfing in Hawaii and was the equal of most any Trestles surfer, male or female. What Terry did know for sure was that the guys in the water who were under thirty seemed to be clueless about how to behave around her, and the guys under twenty seemed to be clueless about most everything.

Terry and the greybeard paddled over a watery rise and saw before them a majestic blue wall, a hundred yards further out, speeding toward them in regal silence. They paddled even harder. To their north, where the wave would hit shore first, three from the pack turned around to catch it. Shouting obscenities at each other, the three surfers collided and tumbled down the wave face in a tangle of bodies, leashes, and surfboards.

"Ah, yes, the brotherhood of surfing," the greybeard crooned over his shoulder in a voice imitating W. C. Fields.

The wave, now empty of surfers, writhed down the coast like a giant anaconda. The greybeard and Terry were now far enough outside to catch it. The greybeard stopped paddling and eyed Terry with a wild look. She was closest to the wave's onrushing curl, and for the faithful few who still remained loyal to surfing etiquette, the wave was hers to ride, or to give away.

"Go!" she yelled.

With a grin, the greybeard spun his board around, paddled furiously, and was gone. Terry swept over the top of the wave, looked seaward, and her heart raced. Before her loomed the wave of the day, maybe the year. To her north, in front of the pack, its mountainous face was already feathering white at the top. The pack churned the water into foam in a futile attempt to paddle out to it, but it was no use. They were too close in to shore, and they were about to pay the price. Terry, however, had a chance to catch it.

Maybe.

Southward and seaward she sped, throwing everything she had into paddling for this one wave. The northern section of the wave exploded in front of the pack, engulfing it in an avalanche of whitewater. A horizontal vortex spewing white spray from its barreling mouth bore down upon Terry. She stopped paddling, spun her board around, and now had to make a split-second decision. On the one hand, she would have to be insane to take off so late and so close to the curl. On the other hand, waves like this didn't come every day.

She paddled for it.

The wave lifted Terry high. Its lip pitched forward, but Terry was already up on her feet, digging her bare toes into the thick wax spread across her board for traction. Time seemed to stop as she plunged down the wave face. At the last possible instant, she pulled the board's nose up, carved a sweeping turn across the bottom of the wave face, and streaked southward on a razor-straight line midway up the surging wall of water. High overhead, the wave's massive lip heaved out and over her, and Terry shifted her weight forward to gain speed. She rocketed into the forming tube for one, two, three full seconds as she experienced the surfer's ultimate thrill, and then the tube backed off momentarily, giving her the slightest opening. Terry aimed her board upward and shot high into the air over the wave's top. She splashed down safely behind the wave, which continued on its unstoppable jaunt down the coast in defiant indifference to its brief human encounter.

"Wow," Terry exclaimed quietly, climbing back onto her board. She hadn't ridden a wave that radical since leaving Hawaii. As she sat on her board and reflected on the ride, the water around her smoothed as if it had been oiled, which often was the case after a large set. Terry took advantage of the calm to look skyward and say, "Thank You." She meant to offer a prayer of thanks after every good wave if there was time and if she remembered. This time, she had remembered, and saying that simple prayer seemed to be the right thing to do. She opened her eyes and drank in the scene around her. Life was indeed good. She had her health, her family, her job, her faith....

Her faith? Hah! Where was that going? Terry asked herself. Was she really that much of a Christian? She had certainly thought so ten years ago in Lahaina. She had even stood up in front of the entire congregation at Maria Lanakila Church to profess her faith. But now, things seemed different. Had life just been simpler back then, or had she developed a deeper understanding of what it actually meant to be a Christian? Terry didn't know, but either way, she sensed that a storm was brewing inside of her that was only going to increase in fury.

"I'm just not an evangelizer," Terry lamented, gazing up into a summer blue sky. She brought her gaze back to sea level and watched the pack to the north regrouping and preparing to battle it out for the next set of waves.

"And those boneheads wouldn't listen to me even if I were," she added in frustration.

Terry's eyes chanced upon the prominent Christian fish symbol adorning the deck of her surfboard. That should count for a little bit of spreading the gospel, she rationalized, but it wasn't nearly enough, especially if she considered all of the good things in life she'd been given. She really should be doing more, but what...?

Some of the pack paddled to catch a wave, and their activity brought Terry back to the present. She had a choice to make. Her big ride had brought her partway in to shore. She could call it a day and let a smaller wave take her the rest of the way in, or she could paddle back out into the lineup. She didn't take long to decide. She would go in. She had surfed well, and she hadn't gotten hurt. It was time to call it quits. She turned her board toward shore to catch an oncoming wave but surprised herself by letting it pass by unridden. It was as if a voice inside of her was calling for her to paddle out just one more time. It wasn't an audible voice, but more like an idea that wouldn't fade away. Not exactly knowing why, she began to paddle out again. "Just one more time," she told herself. Besides, the calm after the set was holding, and the paddle out should be easy.

"This is just ducky!" Terry complained aloud, ten minutes later and berating herself. She should have gone in. She had gotten greedy. It was the old sucker ploy. Her one-more-time-easy-paddle-out had turned into a paddling nightmare. Big set after big set had thundered in, piling up mountains of white water in front of her. She might as well have been trying to paddle up Niagara Falls. To add insult to injury, when she finally did reach the lineup, the waves died down again to nothing and stayed that way.

Forever.

Terry sat on her board, waiting for anything that might take her back to shore.

"Just one more time," she told herself, fuming. The greybeard had gone in long ago. The pack was even further away. She was all alone, and she was becoming impatient.

She waited.

"Hellooooo!" A barely audible cry carried across the water.

Terry sat up high on her board.

"Heeeeelp!"

Now fully alert, Terry scanned the horizon. A hundred yards further out to sea she saw what looked to be someone waving to her. What anyone could be doing that far outside she could only guess. She dropped flat and sped seaward like a bullet, finally stopping a few yards away from a young man treading water. He looked to be in his twenties and probably Hispanic, judging from his bronze skin color and facial features. Terry eased herself into the water and gently pushed the empty board towards him. "How are you doing?" she asked, trying to sound calm.

The man grabbed the board and clambered up onto it. "I'm getting a little tired," he answered matter-of-factly.

And cold, too, Terry reasoned, noticing the purple tinge of his lips. And wasn't that just like a macho-man anyway, she thought, continuing her observation of him. Here he was with no wetsuit, no swim fins, and wearing only Marine-issue swim trunks. He was two-hundred yards out to sea, slowly freezing to death, being swept away by a rip tide with the next stop Japan, and all he could say was, "I'm getting a little tired."

It was all so typical.

Terry swam the board and her passenger back to the beach, taking her time to avoid being caught by any bigger waves. On the way in she gave her captive audience an in-service lesson about waves, rip currents, and the advantage of wearing swim fins the next time he went for a dip in big surf.

When they finally reached water that was only knee deep the man stood up, faced her, and quietly said, "Thanks a lot." He was no doubt aware of the gaggle of marines on the beach that had flagged down a passing lifeguard jeep and were now gesturing animatedly in his direction.

He must be terribly embarrassed, Terry thought. "My pleasure," she answered, and she smiled at him and waded toward shore but in a direction away from the marines. She found her backpack where she had left it on the sand, and she peeled off her wetsuit, leaving her clad in a skin-tight one-piece swimsuit. Over that she put on baggy shorts and a sweatshirt, and she was ready for the long walk up the trail to the parking lot. She ducked under the railroad trestle that gave the beach its name, and her sandaled feet reached the paved part of the trail.

It had been a good go-out, Terry reflected. The summer of '82 had started slow, surf-wise, but was now shaping up nicely, and she could use a few more sessions like today. She walked at a comfortable, purposeful pace up the trail, meeting a steady stream of surfers hurrying in the opposite direction. As one particular group of five young men approached, the conversation among them abruptly ceased, and Terry suddenly felt like a side of beef at a butcher's convention. Steeling herself, she gave the young surfers the slightest, "hello," in reply to which two of them grunted something unintelligible. Moments later, she heard them all barking like a pack of hyenas, solidly confirming her assessment of all male humanity under the age of twenty.

Terry loaded her board and backpack into her car and soon was headed south on the freeway. She passed Oceanside and cut over to old Highway One to cruise the rest of the way down to Leucadia where, until a year ago, she had lived from the time she and her family had moved to the mainland. They had left Hawaii to help her uncle, who had been ill and dying, and had wound up owning a half acre of land with a house at one end and a sandwich shop at the other. Terry had come to love Leucadia's laid-back atmosphere, which was one reason she was heading south today instead of north to her apartment in Redondo Beach.

It was too bad they couldn't have built the aquarium here instead of there, she mused as she pulled into a parking lot next to a rainbow-shaped sign proclaiming, "Mama Ho's Natural Store." The store building itself was a 1950's wooden house that had been modified to serve food. Terry remained in her car and watched warily while a station wagon, its dented exterior a patchwork of body filler and primer paint and its roof rack piled high with surfboards, lurched to a stop right next to her.

The station wagon's doors flew open, and three young men burst out and tromped into Mama Ho's with all of the grace of a head-on train wreck. Terry killed another minute before exiting her car, and then she leisurely climbed the wooden steps to Mama Ho's front deck where a bulletin board fluttering with advertisements now underwent her scrutiny. Of the dozens of flyers, she tore down one about palm reading and another one about tarot cards. By then, she figured that a transformation would have probably taken place inside of Mama Ho's. She cracked open the front screen door, peeked inside, and saw the three young men standing at the order counter. A plump, olive-skinned woman behind the counter was handing one of them change.

"*Mahalo aikane,*" the woman said, smiling at the young men. They turned away from the counter, saw Terry standing in the doorway, nodded politely and smiled. Terry smiled back, entered the rest of the way in, and closed the door gently behind her. It was just as she'd figured. When Mama Ho turned on that matronly Polynesian charm of hers, these boys didn't have a prayer.

"*Aloha,* Kanani," Mama Ho called across the room. "How were the waves?"

"*Nui nui,* " Terry answered, enjoying the dropped-jawed look on the faces of the three surfers.

Mama Ho hustled out from around the counter and gave Terry a hug. She sent the young men a wink and said loudly, "I'll get these boys the best walnut-oat burgers this side of the Pacific, and then I'll fix you up something special. Also, you got a couple of calls."

Terry took a seat at the table furthest away from the surfers while Mama Ho rushed back behind the counter and dove into action. Minutes later, Mama Ho served the three surfers and then rushed back behind the counter again. She held up a ripe papaya for Terry to see and then launched into another flurry of activity.

"That's OK, Mama," Terry protested.

"OK, nothing!" Mama Ho said over her shoulder. "You got all that cold water. You got all that exercise. Now you're going to get some calories." A blender whined, ending all conversation momentarily, and then Mama Ho breezed out from around the counter and placed a tall glass filled with a thick golden liquid in front of Terry.

"The best papaya smoothie in the world, and I want you to drink the whole thing."

Terry took a sip. It was delicious. "You didn't sneak in any cod-liver oil, did you?"

"Doesn't it taste all right?" Mama Ho asked in wide-eyed innocence.

"It tastes fine."

Mama Ho beamed. "Then you'll just have to guess about the fish oil."

Mama Ho pulled a chair up close to Terry and said loudly enough for the young surfers to hear, "Since half the fun of surfing is telling someone about it, why don't you tell me all about your big waves?"

Terry recalled her outing in detail. When she finished the part about saving the Marine, Mama Ho took Terry's hands in her own, closed her eyes, and said, "We thank you, Lord, for all your mercy."

"Yes," Terry thought heavenward, "We do thank you, but shouldn't I have done more? I told the Marine to get swim fins, but shouldn't I have told him about you?" Terry glanced over at the three surfers who had been quietly eating their meal. They were intently watching Mama Ho, who still had her eyes closed.

How easily she speaks of God's goodness, Terry thought, seeing the effect that Mama Ho had on the youths, and she wondered how she could do the same without people thinking that she was some kind of religious whacko.

Mama Ho stopped praying, produced a piece of paper from an apron pocket, and studied it. She said, "Let's see. First, Sheriff Jim called. He said he had something about that diver that disappeared last week. And Dr. Frank called to tell you that some fishermen brought in a live white shark."

Terry was indeed interested in any news about the diver. Part of her job as Public Relations Ambassador for the newest aquarium in California was to investigate any ocean-related mishaps that might wind up alarming the general public. It was her responsibility to transform that alarm into informed respect. She told herself that on her way back to Cal Ocean USA, she would pay a visit to Sheriff Jim Palmer. The capture of the great white was another matter.

"I hope Sheriff Jim has something good," Terry said, "because so far I haven't heard anything."

"Are you going to go and see that shark tonight?"

"Nope. No need to. It'd probably be dead by the time I got there. Captured great whites go into some kind of shock, and then they go belly up. I've got two days off, and I'm spending them here. The shark will wind up on ice, and I'll be back in plenty in time for the post mortem. So, where's Dad?"

"He's out back, working too hard, as usual." Mama Ho hustled back behind the counter, pulled something out of the refrigerator, and hurried back to Terry. She handed Terry another papaya smoothie. "Give him this, and tell that old man that he's '*pau hana.*'"

Terry stepped out the back door of the store onto a wooden deck and took time to admire the garden. Vegetables of all kinds grew in neat plots artistically separated by gravel paths. All of that was surrounded by fruit and avocado trees, creating a park-like setting where store patrons could eat or walk or just sit and enjoy the tranquility. At the far end of the garden, draped in modesty from another era, stood another 50's vintage house which the Ho family had transformed into their home. Terry surveyed the scene until she spotted a straw hat bobbing up and down amid tomato plants. She tip-toed down the deck's wooden steps, but when her feet grated on the gravel path the straw hat popped up, revealing Tommy Ho underneath it. "Terry! I heard the surf was booming," he said, smiling broadly at his daughter.

"It sure was," Terry answered. She handed him the smoothie. "This is from Mama, and she says to tell you that you're 'finished working.'"

Tommy took the drink and led Terry over to a bench resting in the shade of an avocado tree. He removed his hat and hung it on the hand of a three-quarter-life-size statue of Saint Francis. "Did I ever tell you about the time I was surfing Makaha?" he asked as he sat down.

Terry laughed, because he had told her this story several dozen times, and each time he somehow came up with a new version. "Let me guess," she said. "You were all alone and unassisted."

"That's right. There I was, alone and unassisted...."

Tommy stood up, handed Terry the papaya smoothie, and struck a dramatic pose. "'One had to have his wits about him, for it was a battle in which mighty blows were struck, on one side and in which cunning was used on the other side—a struggle between insensate force and intelligence.'"

Tommy paused in his speech as if waiting for a response.

"I've got you today," Terry said. "That's Jack London and The Cruise of the Snark."

Tommy snatched the smoothie back from Terry and sat back down. His face painted a picture of amazement. "Terry Kanani Ho, how did you know that?"

"That's easy, Papa. I am my father's daughter."

"Yes you are," Tommy said, and then his smile changed into a frown. "Did you get the message from Sheriff Jim?"

Terry heard the concern in her father's voice. "I did. What are you thinking?"

"Just that it reminds me of that other missing guy, the lobster fisherman. We never did learn what happened to him. I'll tell you, Terry, as much as I love that ocean, it bothers me how good she keeps a secret, especially when somebody disappears without a trace. She's a lovely lady, but she can be a dangerous one."

That evening, Terry joined her parents at their weekly Bible Study. She was asked to read aloud the night's scripture verses. She read from her own Bible that was dog-eared from use. She read from the Gospel of Mathew.

> Now Jesus, walking by the Sea of Galilee, saw two brothers, Simon called Peter, and Andrew his brother, casting a net into the sea; for they were fishermen. And he said to

them, 'Follow me, and I will make you fishers of men.'

As Terry continued reading, the words blew like a strong wind stirring a tempest within her heart. She finished the reading, closed her Bible, and thought heavenward, "I've already told you. I don't know how to be a fisher of men."

For the next twenty minutes the group discussed what Terry had just read. Terry added the least to the discussion, but she listened attentively, hoping to glean what she could on how to share her faith, and maybe, upon honest examination, on how to get around sharing it without feeling too guilty.

Chapter 4

Storm's return flight from Hawaii began a gradual descent towards LAX. At twenty-thousand feet, while passing over San Clemente Island, the Boeing 747 began lurching like a covered wagon crossing the prairie, and Storm reminded himself perhaps for the hundredth time how very much he hated flying. Why couldn't they have just given him a mask and fins and asked him to dive down a hundred feet holding his breath? That would have been more to the liking of someone who just wanted to study sharks, work with his graduate students, and stay out of the spotlight. But, no, they had asked him to fly to Hawaii, give a talk in public, and fly home again.

The plane staggered as if it had been punched in the stomach by a giant hand, and Storm searched for a way to get his mind off of his own stomach. He placed his hands against the window next to his seat, and then he pressed his forehead against the back of his hands. With his hands serving as a cushion to protect him from getting his nose smashed during the airplane's violent lurching, he peered out the window.

As he expected, the air outside his window looked perfectly calm, confirming to him why he much preferred to be immersed within the ocean over being bounced across the sky in the bowels of a mechanical bird. When the ocean looked calm, it was calm, with no pretense of being anything other than what it was. The things he did for grant money, Storm thought, as a sudden wave of nausea swept upward from his stomach. He said a silent prayer to no one in particular that the plane wouldn't fall out of the sky, and he concentrated harder at looking out the window. He could see the northwest end of San Clemente Island. There was Wilson Cove, where an old friend of his could be working at this very moment. And there was Castle Rock, where he had first seen a great white shark.

The picture in his mind of the great white was as fresh as when he had seen it, and this whirlwind trip to a world seminar on sharks was an indirect result of that first encounter. The talk he had given at the seminar seemed to have gone well. At least, no one had thrown any rotten tomatoes. For that, he figured he should be thankful, but he found himself feeling surprisingly unfulfilled.

"Would you like to be down there right now, Dr. Hancock?"

Storm pulled himself away from the window to see who could be addressing him as "doctor." He was never comfortable with the title. He'd always figured that doctors were people who made their living helping sick people to get well. He would have preferred another label, but such was life. Before him, smiling, stood a flight attendant. He recognized the cover of the magazine in her hand. So that was how she knew to call him "doctor." That particular magazine issue contained an article about him and his study of great white sharks, and Storm remembered how surprised and flattered he'd been that someone outside of the scientific community had bothered to take an interest in his work.

Storm considered the flight attendant's question. Would he like to be down there right now? Yeah, anywhere had to be better than being in a plane, and the water down there would be a heck of a lot warmer than at the Farallon Islands where he'd just completed the field work of his shark study. Of course, it wasn't nearly as warm as the coral reefs of Hawaii that he'd just left, but the kelp forests of 'Clemente were just as pretty in their own way.

"I've always said the diving at San Clemente Island is as good as any in the world," he answered, smiling.

The attendant opened the magazine to a photograph that showed Storm stretched out full-length on a plank suspended from a boat a few feet above a huge shark in open ocean. She said, "My son's crazy about sharks, and when he saw this picture, he said he wanted to be a marine biologist just like you. I'd really be grateful if you'd autograph it for him." She held the magazine and a pen out to Storm.

This was a first, Storm thought to himself, but if other people could sign autographs, why couldn't a marine biologist?

"I'd be glad to," he said, taking the pen and magazine. "Let's see. What should I write?"

"Could you write something to Todd?"

"To Todd? Sure." Storm spoke as he wrote. "To Todd, best of luck, and remember to never, ever turn your back on a *Cacharidon carcharius*. Best wishes, Storm Hancock." He handed the magazine back to the attendant, who beamed at what he had written.

"I can't thank you enough. Uh, carcar, kacare...."

"Great white shark," Storm explained. "Todd will know."

The "fasten seat belt" sign lit up, and the attendant thanked Storm again and hurried to her duties.

An older, grayer form of Storm met him at the airport. Anyone seeing Storm and his father for the first time would probably have put the two together. Athletic and tan, but with no obvious pretense of trying to fit into any mold, their outward appearance would have qualified them both as poster boys for the Southern California Beach lifestyle. Storm's father welcomed him with a handshake, and soon they were battling the worst traffic in the nation as they headed south to the small beach town where Storm had grown up. They conversed easily, as friends do. Storm's father said, "Aren't you about finished with your shark-tagging project?"

"Now we're just waiting for the monitors to come in," Storm answered. "If everything goes perfect we'll get all ten of them back and filled with good data. Of course, that never happens. Something breaks, or gets eaten, or just plain quits working at the worst possible time. You name it; it happens."

"So you've utilized all your monitors?"

Storm chuckled at that question. "Utilized" wasn't exactly the right word. "Annihilated," "obliterated," and "wrenched clean out of sight" better described what happened to his precious monitoring gear when the goal was to attach it to uncooperative great white sharks in open water. "Yeah," he answered. "I've utilized all of them and also all of my budget."

"And now the real fun begins when you get to analyze all that data."

Storm thought of the hours that were going to have to be

spent deciphering everything the monitors had recorded. Of course, he would have lots of student help, but still....

"Oh yeah, fun," he answered.

"And then what?"

"That's a good question. You got any ideas?"

"Oh, no. It's just that your mom's wondering...." Storm's dad's voice trailed off.

"When I might find a decent girl of my own and settle down to a real job." Storm finished the sentence.

"Well, yes. Something like that. You'll no doubt hear more about it when we get home," Storm's father said with a smile in his voice.

Storm had learned long ago that his father was not in the least bit worried about his marital status and that he got a huge kick out of his mom's matchmaking efforts.

When they finally reached the family home in Laguna Beach, Storm's mother had lunch waiting for them on the rear deck. Storm told his parents about his trip and the autograph session on the airplane. His mother said, "I'm thankful you've found something you like to do. Though, I must say I'm still not thrilled when you share the water with sharks."

Storm didn't reply, and his father just grinned at him. They both knew where this conversation was heading.

Storm's mother stood up and began picking up the lunch dishes. "I don't suppose you've found a girlfriend."

"Nope. Haven't looked," Storm answered flatly. He didn't want to help carry the conversation any further than it had to go. What he really wanted to do was walk, no, run, down to the beach. He heard waves breaking, calling, and there were few pleasures that he enjoyed more than bodysurfing in the Southern California ocean on a warm, summer afternoon.

His mother said, "Storm, you're thirty two, and that's old enough to get some responsibility."

"I am somewhat aware of my age."

"Then you should know you're old enough to spend a little less time with fish and maybe meet up with a girl you like."

"It just so happens that I like fish," Storm replied matter-of-factly. "Now, if there happens to be an intelligent girl out there who also likes fish, maybe she'll like me too, but, as I said before: I'm not looking."

"Which means, you're not finding."

Storm let out a huge sigh and stood up with a look of utter defeat on his face. In a serious voice, he said, "You're absolutely right. There's something I've been meaning to tell you and Dad, and I guess there's no better time than right now."

Storm's mother stopped gathering dishes.

"It's like this," Storm continued. "I've decided to become a Roman Catholic priest, so you see, I really don't need to be looking for a girlfriend."

The plates in Storm's mother's hands fell back to the table with a crash. She stood open-mouthed and speechless until she saw Storm's father grinning from ear to ear.

"Why, you two...!"

Storm was already in full retreat. He called behind him, "I'm heading for the beach! If I meet a mermaid, I'll ask her to marry me on the spot!"

"I heard that, Storm!" his mother called toward his retreating back, "and I'll hold you to it!"

Wearing only swim trunks, and carrying a pair of swim fins, Storm trotted down to Crescent Bay. It was only a block away, but the sun-baked asphalt of the street caused Storm to hurry to keep the bottoms of his bare feet from burning. He stopped upon reaching the relative coolness of a concrete stairway that led the last ten feet down to the beach. In front of him curved a quarter mile of white sand nestled between two prominent rocky points. Crescent Bay was Storm's backyard, and the memories of his growing up washed over him in waves of pleasant familiarity. He had first skin dived the bay at age seven, and by age twelve he could breath-hold dive to fifty feet at Dead Man's Reef and surface again with a fish on his spear. Using scuba gear, he could find his way around the bay at night as well as most divers could in the daytime. When surf was up, as during the big south swell that he'd just missed while flying to Hawaii and back, or in today's fun, smaller surf, he bodysurfed the bay with a fluid grace that could elicit spontaneous applause from people on the beach.

Storm ran down the steps and across the sand. He put on his swim fins at the water's edge and entered the cool water. He didn't wait for a lull in the waves but powered straight out, diving under the lines of incoming whitewater until he arrived just outside of where the waves were breaking. A dozen other bodysurfers shared the lineup with him, intently watching the horizon. Crescent Bay didn't break as viciously as the famous "Wedge" a few miles up the coast, but she broke hard. Over the years she had crushed Storm's six-foot frame into a pretzel shape more than once, and even on small days he treated her with respect.

"Outside!" one of the bodysurfers called.

Storm looked seaward and assessed the oncoming waves. There were three waves in the set. He swam over the top of the first two and waited for the third. At just the right moment, he stroked hard for shore. The wave lifted him high, and then he fell down the wave face in classic bodysurfing form with his arms and body making the shape of an inverted cross. He penetrated the water's surface a split second ahead of the curl, arrowed his body seaward, and was already swimming towards the surface when the wave broke at a harmless distance behind him. With technical precision he bodysurfed several more waves until the cool water caused him to shiver. He rode one last wave straight in, on his belly as a seal would do, all the way to shore, somersaulting out of the wave to land standing up in knee-deep water.

He took his fins off and strolled towards the concrete stairway. The good bodysurfing session had reminded him of younger days. He lingered again at the top of the stairway and let the sun warm him while he looked fondly back at the bay. There was no doubting it. Crescent Bay had the prettiest water, the prettiest waves, the prettiest sunsets, and yes, he thought reluctantly, even the prettiest women. It had been near these very stairs that he'd met the last person to break his heart. Why he'd gone to that church party at his Mom's urging he'd never know. The last thing that he had planned on doing was getting romantically involved, and then look what had happened. He wasn't a Christian, and he couldn't honestly say that he ever planned to become one. One day, out of the blue, she had told him that there was no use in their going any further with the relationship, because they would be "unequally yoked." Now, a full two years later, Storm felt surprised at how painfully the memory still burned.

"Unequally yoked?" Storm thought cynically. Whatever happened to "love bears all things" and all of those other so-called-Christian catchphrases? Whatever happened to just trying to work things out? Maybe it was all just talk. One thing for sure was that if a woman could create that much heartache, it was no wonder that he continued to immerse himself ever-deeper into his beloved ocean.

Storm watched the waves roll into the bay. Now there was a real lady, he told himself. Sure, she might seem coldhearted at times, but at least she didn't build you up just to cut you down. He probably was better off liking fish in spite of what his mom said.

He took a last, longing look at the bay. Try as he would, he couldn't shake off a gnawing feeling of emptiness. He decided that the waves were getting bigger, foreshadowing what could turn into another big south swell. He turned and trotted up the hill, all the while trying to understand the workings of his heart.

Terry had planned her drive north from Leucadia to miss the worst of the Southern California morning traffic rush. Her plan didn't work, and her drive was terrible, but she eventually arrived in one piece at the Marine Division of the Los Angeles County Sheriff's Department in Port San Pedro. She entered the unattractive building and recognized the uniformed woman seated behind a front counter. "Good morning. Would it be possible to see Sheriff Palmer?"

"He told me you might show up this morning," the woman answered, as she opened a gate in the counter for Terry to pass through. She escorted Terry to an open office door and said, "Terry Ho is here."

A hulk of a man, in his fifties with salt spray in his hair, stood up from his chair behind a massive, cluttered desk.

"Terry!" he boomed in a voice that proclaimed the joy of living. "You got my message, huh? How's your mom and dad? How's the job treating you? How are you doing, anyway? You're looking better than ever. Have a seat."

Terry laughed inwardly at Sheriff Jim's greeting that hadn't given her a chance to even say "Hello." It was so easy to be around him, almost as easy as being around her parents. Was it just because he was older? She tried to picture him sitting on a surfboard, but it didn't work. He would look better sitting on a horse, because he reminded her of Marshall Matt Dillon on the old reruns of Gun Smoke. Though he was only a fictional character, Matt Dillon was Terry's kind of rough-and-tumble gentleman hero. Maybe that was why she liked Sheriff Jim. She liked heroes, and she liked gentlemen, rough-and-tumble or not. She reached to shake his offered hand and watched her own hand disappear within his massive paw. She took a seat in one of the two uncomfortable-looking chairs on her side of the desk and said, "Let's see. Yes, I got your message. Mom and Dad are fine. My job is challenging, but I'm loving it, and I'm running late, so what do we have?"

The swivel chair behind the desk groaned in protest as Sheriff Jim sat down heavily. "I wish it was more," he answered, running his hands back through his graying hair, "but here it is. The missing man's name is Simon Andrews."

Terry's body tensed as her mind shot back to last night's Bible study and the storm brewing in her heart. The name "Simon Andrews" brought up thoughts about Simon and Andrew, which brought up thoughts about her failure to be a fisher of men.

Sheriff Jim must have noticed something unusual, because he asked, "Did you know him?"

"No, I didn't know him. His name just brought up a memory."

"That happens a lot in this business. Anyway, we got one Simon Andrews, age thirty six, no known health issues, vacationing by himself on a sailboat on the backside of 'Clemente."

"Who called it in?"

"A commercial abalone diver. He said he'd seen the boat anchored for a week before he realized he hadn't seen anybody on board, so he decided to check it out. He found some food going bad, some full scuba tanks, a wet suit, but he didn't find any fins, mask, or snorkel, and that's when he took a look under water."

"This guy sounds pretty sharp," Terry replied. "You said he was a commercial abber?"

"Yeah, but he's one of the more-careful of the bunch, so he's still got most of his brain cells."

A period of silence followed, which Terry understood to be Sheriff Jim's flair for the dramatic. She finally asked, "And did he find anything?"

"I thought you'd never ask," Sheriff Jim answered with obvious relish. "He found this." From a desk drawer Sheriff Jim took out a plastic bag containing a dented-and-scratched *Nikonos* underwater camera. He handed it across the desk to Terry, who held it gingerly, as if she might somehow damage it further. "We know the camera belonged to Andrews from a receipt we found on board," Sheriff Jim continued. "We developed the film, and it looks like he took only two pictures."

"Assuming that Andrews took the pictures," Terry added.

"I think we can assume that," Sheriff Jim said, as he reached back into the drawer and pulled out a four-by-six print that he also handed to Terry. She looked at the picture of the *Time Out* floating serenely at anchor. The scene looked much too idyllic to lead to a diver disappearing from the face of the planet.

"How could anything bad happen on a day like that?" she asked.

"It's hard to figure," Sheriff Jim replied, and he pulled another photograph from the drawer and handed it to Terry. "We had this one blown up. I was hoping you'd tell us what it is."

Terry studied the eight-by-ten print, turning it a couple of times before she was sure it was right-side up. An unfocused, mottled blob of dull red and green took up most of the foreground. In better focus in the background was obviously some kind of kelp. She finally said, "It looks like someone got a tie for Christmas and threw it overboard."

"That's as good a guess as I've heard so far," Sheriff Jim said, "but just pretend that I'm a complete idiot, and tell me what else it could be."

"Well, in the background there's definitely some *Egregia*."

"Some who?"

"Uh, grandpa whiskers?" Terry ventured.

The look on Sheriff Jim's face changed from blank to blanker.

"Feather boa?" Terry tried again.

"Feather boa!" Sheriff Jim exclaimed, looking relieved. "Yeah, he said he found the camera on the bottom right next to some big bushes of feather boa."

Terry stood up and edged towards the door. She was running late. She said, "If you can spare a copy of this, I can ask around at work."

"That'd be great, because right now I've got a whole lot of nothing."

"Maybe I should talk to the ab' diver?" Terry suggested.

"There's not much more to tell, but come to think of it, maybe you should get to know him. Those abbers can teach you things about the ocean that you'll never learn in school." Sheriff Jim scribbled something down on a piece of envelope and handed it to Terry.

"Cap Hanson," Terry read.

"Yeah, his real name is David Jones Hanson, but he goes by 'Cap'. It's got something to do with Davy Jones' Locker. Anyway, as divers go, he's the best, and while you're at it, get to know Smitty too."

"Smitty?" Terry said, amused. "Is that a person, a parrot, or a dog?"

"It's a person. He's Cap's sidekick. Anything Cap doesn't know, Smitty does."

"'Sidekick' makes it sound like we're talking about the Wild West."

"Those abbers are a bunch of characters, and that's a fact, but I'm pretty sure you'll like Cap and Smitty," Sheriff Jim replied in a fatherly voice that reminded Terry of her earlier conversation with her dad. She asked, "Did you ever find out anymore about the lobster fisherman?"

"Nothing new. They found his boat with a trap line in the winch and the trap snagged on the bottom. He must have gone over the side to free it and...." Sheriff Jim shrugged his shoulders.

The lack of a proper explanation gnawed at Terry's wellbeing, and she said, "It's only two events, and you can call it women's intuition or whatever, but this latest disappearance has a familiar ring to it. Is it just me, or are we looking at some kind of pattern here?"

"Maybe, and maybe not," Sheriff Jim said, turning his palms up apologetically. "Anyway, like I say, let me know if you find out anything at all."

"I will," Terry answered. She backed out of the office, and as an afterthought she added, "God bless."

"Well, God bless you, too."

Chapter 5

Traffic was never a problem at San Clemente Island, unless too many abalone boats happened to tuck into the same sheltered cove at night. It was a typical summer morning with shafts of sunlight slicing through a lifting fog. The ocean surface, rippled by a breeze, caught the sun's rays and reflected them back as if from a million moving mirrors. Showing off her new coat of green paint, the *Emerald* glistened like her namesake.

"An emerald danced upon a sapphire sea, upon a sapphire, diamond sea. And when she danced, no other jewel was ever as pretty as she."

Such were the rhyming words of the lone man aboard the *Emerald* as he watched the sunshine duel with the fog for supremacy.

To the casual observer, the *Emerald*, all twenty-three feet of her, wouldn't appear to be nearly enough boat to cross sixty miles of open ocean from Newport Beach to San Clemente Island. Her captain and lone crewman knew better, however, and they felt safer aboard her than they would if they were aboard many of her luxurious Newport Bay sisters. The big yachts could usually be seen turning around at the harbor mouth, but not the *Emerald*. She set course toward waters that would never dampen their pampered teak decks.

The *Emerald* was a commercial abalone boat, built from the keel up for the sole purpose of helping a certain eclectic cast of characters pry the delectable shellfish from the ocean floor. The would-be poet on board her was Smitty, actually Francis Armistead Smith, named Francis for the Catholic saint, and Armistead for a Confederate War hero. Although Smitty wouldn't describe himself as either a saint or a hero, he did fancy himself as somewhat of a poet, even if he didn't look the part. In truth, the way Smitty looked was like someone named Smitty ought to look. With his faded-blue Dodgers baseball cap, a perpetual stubble shading a weathered face, and a gap in his smile in the place of two front teeth, the name fit him like a glove.

Name and looks aside, Smitty had found his niche in life. Until eight years ago, he had been one of those souls falling through the cracks, and then he and Cap Hanson had discovered each other. Since that providential meeting, Smitty had become the cook, dive tender, mechanic, and entire loyal crew of the *Emerald*. He had also become family, and he lived in a granny unit behind Cap's San Pedro home.

The day brightened, and Smitty turned an experienced eye forward to watch another coil of air hose slither off the bow, leaving only a few feet out of the three hundred that had been there at the beginning of Cap's dive. Out of habit, he checked his watch and said, "Thirty all day, sixty for sixty, ninety for thirty, and a hundred for twenty five." That was the mantra Smitty repeated whenever Cap was underwater. It was the depths in feet and the time in minutes a diver could stay underwater before having to worry about the bends. The numbers were a fact of life, and Smitty repeated them at least a dozen times a day. On this dive Cap had already been down ninety feet for over twenty-five minutes. If he didn't surface within the next five minutes, he would have to make a decompression stop on the way up.

It shouldn't be long now, Smitty thought, putting the finishing touches into the day's hamburger lunch. He added a pinch of paprika, a dab of Worcestershire sauce, a handful of raisins and, "Voila!" he remarked. "A culinary masterpiece!"

Smitty hung his upper body over the *Emerald's* side and used the blue Pacific to rinse the gooey hamburger mixture from his hands. The crumbs of hamburger had sunk only inches before huge opal-eye perch sucked them up in a feeding frenzy. Smitty laughed at them and said, "You moochers don't let nothing get by, do you? And that's why you never get fried up for dinner." He was referring to the fact that the *Emerald* didn't have a head, and the opal-eye were regular customers.

Smitty completed his washing, looked forward, and his light mood turned sour. The last coil of air hose slid into the water, became tight as a guitar string, and pulled the *Emerald* forward against the current until the anchor line began to sag.

"Ahhhhhh!' Smitty growled.

Smitty knew exactly what the tight air hose meant. No doubt, Cap had just seen some abalone, and he was dragging himself, the kelp that was tangled in his hose, and the *Emerald,* all in an attempt to reach those abalone. It also meant that Cap was going to have to make at least one decompression stop to spend time breathing excess nitrogen out of his system. If he didn't, and he surfaced too quickly, bubbles could form in his body tissues and fluids and leave him paralyzed, or worse.

"Hurry up down there, Cap!" Smitty grumbled. He put a pressure gauge on the big, green oxygen bottle strapped to the deck. He cracked the valve open and squinted at the gauge. Satisfied, he removed the gauge and replaced it with a twenty-foot hose that had a scuba mouthpiece at one end. He opened the valve, took a test breath, and continued to grumble as he lowered the mouthpiece into the water to be ready for Cap. He hated it when Cap had to decompress. Maybe the pure oxygen he'd just put over the side would help. He didn't know for sure. The U.S. Navy thought that it did, and that was good enough for him.

The sun rose higher in the sky, warming the air to a surprisingly pleasant temperature, but Smitty's mood continued to grow sourer by the second. For something to do he stepped aft to the transom and scrutinized the gasoline-powered air compressor supplying the air for Cap. It sounded smooth enough for the moment. On further analysis he spied a drop of water jiggling at the bottom of a small glass bowl connected to the carburetor.

That would have to do for now, Smitty told himself. The bowl had separated the water out of the gas just like it was supposed to, but he'd want to empty it as soon as Cap was up.

Since he could do nothing at the moment for the compressor, he looked around for something else to worry about, but it was no use. He had the *Emerald* in shipshape perfection, so he resigned himself to sitting down on the *Emerald's* engine cover to soak up the rare island sunshine.

The *Emerald's* stern suddenly reared up into the air like a startled horse.

"Holy, jumping catfish!" Smitty cried out, as the stern kept rising until it tumbled him off the engine cover. He half fell, half slid all the way forward into the *Emerald's* cockpit area. He lay on his side, rubbing a throbbing elbow and watching in disbelief as the stern of the *Emerald,* now several feet out of the water, swayed from side to side like a snake charmer's cobra. Smitty pulled his way up from the floor until he could look forward through the cockpit's windshield. One more foot, and the *Emerald's* bow deck would be under water, and it was all because of Cap's air hose pulling down so hard.

Smitty had seen a lot of strange things on the water, but this took the cake. He hung on, frozen in indecision, and then the *Emerald's* stern dropped like a stone and smacked back into the water.

There followed a strange quiet.

"The compressor!" Smitty's mind screamed. "The drop of water!"

Smitty scrambled to the stern, grabbed the compressor engine's starter cord and yanked it once, twice.

Nothing happened.

He held the throttle full, extended the manual choke, and pulled the cord again, once, twice.

Again, nothing.

"You lousy piece of...!"

Smitty watched as a drop of gas fell from the bottom of the carburetor. That meant the engine was now flooded.

"Calm down and talk it through," he said aloud. Years of tinkering with recalcitrant engines now became crucial to his next move.

"Full throttle, choke off."

The engine fired on the first pull. At the same time, the *Emerald's* stern jerked upward again, throwing Smitty into the cooling fins at the top of the compressor and splitting his chin. He ignored the pain and raced for the radio.

"Mayday! Mayday! Mayday! This is the *Emerald!* I'm off the destroyer wreck at 'Clemente, and got a diver down! Mayday!"

Smitty turned up the volume and ran for the bow. He didn't have a clue what was going on. He just knew that Cap was in trouble, and he needed help.

The radio came to life.

"*Emerald*, this is the *Mermaid.* We're on our way."

"*Rainbow* here, Smitty. Hang on."

From a half mile away, the distinctive roar of Old Henry's diesels carried across the water. That meant the *Cyclops* was coming.

"This is Coast Guard San Pedro to the boat in distress. Please say again your situation."

Smitty wasn't answering anybody. He was on the bow furiously hauling in Cap's air hose, which was now slack. Coil after coil of hose piled on the deck, and then Smitty came to a broken end. The hose didn't look cut. It looked like it had been pulled apart like so much twine.

Smitty didn't know what to do. He saw two ab' boats, similar to the *Emerald,* hurtling around the point of the island. They were the *Mermaid* and *Rainbow*. From the other direction chugged the fifty-foot *Cyclops* and Old Henry.

Smitty scanned the water, trying to pick out something, bubbles, anything, from among the floating tops of the kelp forest, but there was nothing to see.

Terry entered a carpeted tunnel dimly lit by a shimmering glow from the tunnel's far end. Every employee and volunteer at Cal Ocean USA laid claim to a favorite attraction, and Terry's favorite was the California Bay. It was her special thinking place, especially on Mondays when the park was closed for maintenance. She exited the tunnel and stepped into a large viewing area. In front of her, windows three stories high framed a vast tank filled with underwater flora and fauna. Her reaction was the same as at the moment she had first seen the California Bay. It was as close to being in a kelp forest that one could get without actually being there.

Terry approached the windows slowly, giving herself time to enter into the visual illusion of being under water. She gazed deep into the tank and thought about Simon Andrews, the lobster fisherman, and the mysterious photographs until she became aware that another person had entered the room and now stood next to her.

"It's beautiful, isn't it?" the stranger whispered, as if to speak louder would be some kind of desecration.

Terry recognized the woman's voice. "It is truly beautiful, Doc'," she answered to Cal Ocean's chief ichthyologist. "What's astounding is that the real ocean is even more beautiful."

"Yes, and even more mysterious," Dr. Frank replied.

Terry certainly agreed with that last part, especially in light of the recent events. She continued to stare at the scene before her, letting it engulf her ever deeper when suddenly, in the gloom at the farthest recesses of the kelp forest, a ghostly shadow glided in and out of view.

What was that? Terry asked herself.

There it was again, a sinister shape following the California Bay's perimeter to Terry's left. The haunting figure glided closer and into better light. Terry observed the pointed snout, the enormous unblinking eye, and the powerful all-business body that tapered radically to end in a huge crescent-shaped tailfin. She noticed how the creature seemed to cut effortlessly through the water. It disappeared behind some kelp and then swam into full view.

"This is incredible!" Terry remarked.

The great white shark passed so closely to Terry that its pectoral fin brushed the window in front of her.

Terry shook her head in disbelief. "How...?"

"Watch what happens next," Dr. Frank replied.

The shark glided to Terry's right, and Dr. Frank said, "Do you see the hose coming down the side of the tank?"

Terry spotted a black hose that entered the tank from above, came down the side, and disappeared somewhere below. Just before the great white reached the hose, a curtain of tiny bubbles rose from the bottom. The shark swam through the bubbles, seemingly paying them no mind.

Terry spun around to face Dr. Frank, who said, "Here's the deal. We had a white shark that was sinking fast, and I'm calling everybody I know. A friend of mine calls a friend of his, who leaves a message with some shark man named Hancock, who gets back to him with some wild idea he'd just heard about in Hawaii. I don't have anything to lose, so I call a dentist friend; we set this up, and the shark's still alive this morning."

"Dentist friend?" Terry said. "Wait a minute. What are those bubbles?"

"Nitrous oxide, otherwise known as laughing gas."

Terry listened, dumbfounded.

Dr. Frank continued, "When you stop to think about it, the idea's not all that crazy. Fish use their gills to absorb dissolved oxygen gas from the water, and we just added a little something extra to the oxygen."

Terry turned back toward the tank. The shark swam away into the gloom, seemingly healthy and content.

"So, you've 'narked'... your shark?" Terry said with hesitation, using the diving vernacular for a diver suffering from nitrogen narcosis.

"Essentially, yes. I could be wrong, but if I'm right, that shark has 'rapture of the deep.'"

"If I wasn't seeing this with my own eyes, I wouldn't believe it. Maybe I still don't. Anyway, congratulations. So, what's next?"

"What's next is we're stuffing a yellowtail with as many vitamins, antibiotics, and anything else we can cram in it, and we're going to dangle it in front of him and hope he eats it."

"You're the fish expert, but my Mama always said that the best thing for someone feeling poorly is cod liver oil."

Dr. Frank seemed to accept the home-remedy advice. "Cod liver oil might not be a bad idea. I'll ask the yellowtail crew to pack some in."

Terry pulled the photograph that she'd been given by Sheriff Jim out of her briefcase and handed it to Dr. Frank. "Here, maybe you can help me with this."

Dr. Frank studied the photograph, turning it first one way, then the other. "I'll bite. What is it, besides being out of focus?"

"No, no. I want you to tell me."

"Is it supposed to be alive?"

"Maybe."

Dr. Frank answered tentatively, "I suppose it could be a big kelp fish, some kind of *Heterrostichus*. The color's kind of funny though. Is it from around here?"

"It's from the camera of that latest diver lost at San Clemente Island."

"Really?" Dr. Frank said, more as a statement than a question. She studied the photograph even more intently and finally said, "I have absolutely no idea what this is."

Chapter 6

Ninety feet down, Cap Hanson had been on a routine abalone dive, routine in the fact that he wasn't finding any abalone. The few that he had come across were all slightly below the commercial legal size limit. He'd mostly found scars, the circular marks on the rocks where abalone had been removed by other divers or perhaps even himself. The only thing not routine about this dive was that it was going to be one of his last, because the Southern California abalone fishery was well into the painful process of being shut down.

Maybe it was all for the best, Cap told himself. He gripped a boulder with one hand and pulled some slack in his air hose with the other. It wasn't like the good old days when he'd have a hundred-dozen legal abs' by noon. Besides, he knew what the problem was. The islands had been fished so hard for so long that there just weren't enough legal-sized abalone left to provide for a decent living. Some folks even said that the white abalone, the prized shellfish that he was hunting on this dive, might become extinct.

And here he was, still fishing hard.

Like all of the commercial ab' divers, Cap used hookah gear, breathing compressed air from a scuba regulator mouthpiece and hose that connected via his weight belt to three-hundred more feet of air hose. At the end of it all churned the compressor on board the *Emerald*, providing the air for Cap and doted over by the watchful Smitty.

As usual, and despite Cap's focused efforts to the contrary, by this time in his dive his hose had become thoroughly entangled with the stalks of the thick kelp forest. Instead of swimming, he was now reduced to dragging himself hand-over-hand across the bottom. When the time came to surface, he would have to drag himself to the *Emerald's* anchor line and haul himself up. In a tight spot, he could always disconnect his air hose or drop his weight belt and be instantly free from the tangle, but he would also lose his air supply. Those options were reserved for only the most desperate of situations.

Cap studied his decompression meters and grimaced. He always wore two, just in case, and both of them told him that he needed to surface immediately if he didn't want to have to decompress.

Surface? Cap thought in grim humor, as he struggled against the intertwined snarl of kelp and hose. How could he surface when it was all he could do to just move? He reasoned that the anchor line was somewhere behind him. He contemplated turning around to look for it, but just then he spotted a rock covered with large white abalone.

And wasn't that always the way? Cap asked himself rhetorically. So often, just when his decompression meters were telling him to go up, only then would he find abalone.

Cap muscled his way across the rocky bottom, pulling his hose, the kelp, and the *Emerald*. The rock was large, the size of a Volkswagen beetle, covered with enough white abalone to make up for the lean pickings he had found so far on this trip. He stopped within arm's reach of the rock. He couldn't stretch the hose any further. He would have to hold himself to the bottom with one hand and gather abalone with the other. If he lost his grip, the pull from his hose would snap him back a good twenty feet, and he'd probably be forced to use what strength he had left to work his way back to the surface. He chose a big abalone and slipped his custom ab' iron that he torched from an automotive leaf spring underneath the abalone like he'd done countless times before.

Twitch.

Cap hesitated before popping the abalone off the rock. What if he just left it alone? What if this abalone, overlooked by him and his fellow divers for all these years, was the very one to keep the species alive and healthy?

Cap pulled his ab' iron carefully back out from under the abalone. He gave the abalone a friendly tap and smiled as it sucked itself down even tighter to the rock. That was it, then, Cap thought to himself. He was finished diving abalone.

He continued to hold tight to the bottom and looked around

the surrounding kelp forest to get his bearings, and especially to find the anchor line. He spotted it only fifty feet away, in the same direction that his hose was trying to pull him. That was good.

Twitch.

Cap let go of the bottom, and the tension on his hose zoomed him towards the anchor line like an underwater bungee jumper. At the same instant, the water around him exploded into a whirling maelstrom. Liquid hands wrung his body and dragged him in the opposite direction back towards the rock. He slammed into the rock out of control. His regulator ripped from his mouth, and his mask was wrenched from his face. Then, the pull from his air hose rejoined the tug of war and yanked him back towards the anchor line.

Cap tumbled to a stop on the bottom, ninety feet down with no mask and no air. He needed to see, but the salt water stung his eyes and was filled with swirling debris. He swept his hand along his weight belt, found the regulator hose, followed it to the end, and shoved the regulator into his mouth.

Thank God, it was still working.

He held the regulator there with both hands and breathed hard and fast. He prayed that, whatever was happening, the worst was over.

The water around him erupted again, flinging him forward with such violence it seemed as if it were trying to tear itself apart. Something huge and heavy smashed him in the side, crushing the wind out of him and rolling him end over end. He clamped his jaws shut with all of his might to keep the regulator in his mouth. His air hose jerked him upward, then downward, and then it wrapped across his chest and pinned him to some massive, writhing thing. The air became harder to breathe. "Don't let it stop! Don't let it stop!" Cap prayed for the air to keep flowing.

The air quit altogether.

"Oh, God!"

Cap's arms and chest were pinned under the wrap of air hose. He fought to reach the air hose disconnect, but every time he got close, the violent movement beneath him jerked his hands away. By chance alone, his hand banged against the lip of his weight belt buckle. His fingers curled around it and pulled. The weight belt fell free, giving slack to the hose that pinned his body. He wriggled out from under it and shot upward like a missile.

He had ninety feet to go.

Cap had not gotten a deep breath before the air had quit, and he realized quite soberly that his chances for survival hung on very slender threads. If he could ascend the ninety feet without air, which was doubtful, and if he could locate the anchor line, and if Smitty had the oxygen regulator waiting at twenty feet, then he could stop there and hold on and decompress. If any of those things didn't happen....

Cap powered upward through the kelp, and at the same time he angled his ascent in what he prayed was the right direction to the anchor line. Through the burning salt water his unprotected eyes saw the surface shimmering above him. He saw the oxygen regulator sparkling in the sun. He saw his field of vision narrow into a long dark tunnel. Cap had seen the dark tunnel several times over the years, and now it told him three things. He was going to pass out. He wouldn't get to the oxygen regulator. He was going to get the bends.

The long dark tunnel collapsed into total blackness.

"Oh, God ...!"

Drawn to the commotion ninety feet beneath the *Emerald,* a great white shark diverted from its open-water cruising and nosed into the kelp bed. It was young, only a six footer, but the monitor placed on its back by Storm ten days ago had barely affected its movement. During that time it had traveled a long way on only a little food. It chanced onto an inattentive kelp bass and snapped it up.

Twitch.

The young great white saw a fleeting movement, approached it warily, and was inhaled.

Chapter 7

A dark object broke the surface fifty feet in front of the *Emerald's* bow. "Cap!" Smitty cried, and he flung himself into the water. Cap's body bobbed on the surface lifelessly like a doll. Smitty raced towards him, tearing his way over, under, and through the surface kelp. He finally reached Cap and cradled him in his arms.

Thank God that Cap had floated on his back, Smitty told himself. An unconscious diver in a wetsuit floated either flat on his back or flat on his face. The latter was lethal. Cap's eyes were closed, and Smitty feared the worst. "Cap?" he said, praying that he'd get a response.

Cap opened his eyes, and the fear that Smitty saw in them filled him with both hope and dread. He knew that he and Cap were both thinking the same thing.

Cap was alive, but for how long?

"I can't move my legs," Cap said, which told Smitty that Cap was already slipping into the deadly grip of the bends.

"Don't you worry none," Smitty said in what he hoped was a convincing voice. "Help's on the way, and you're gonna' be fine."

Smitty was not at all convinced that Cap would be fine. Over the years he had been around other bent divers, and he had watched helplessly as one of them had died. It now all boiled down to a matter of time.

The *Cyclops, Rainbow,* and *Mermaid* arrived together. Old Henry ran to the bow of the *Cyclops* and yelled, "Put him on the *Rainbow!* She's the fastest! I'll tell the Navy you're coming!"

They lifted Cap aboard the *Rainbow* and made him as comfortable as possible on a makeshift bed of abalone nets, and then the *Rainbow* sped away.

Hope now flickered in Smitty's heart. The *Rainbow* was indeed fast, and the shoreline flew by as the *Rainbow's* captain took her full throttle through shortcuts in the reefs that only an ab' diver would know. On the other side of the island, not far around the west end, lay Wilson Cove, the port for the military facility on San Clemente Island. There, the Navy operated a decompression chamber. If Cap could only be placed inside of the chamber quickly enough, the bends process could be reversed.

The *Rainbow* churned to a stop at the pier at Wilson Cove. Two medical corpsmen were waiting with a stretcher. With them was a young Navy doctor that Smitty recognized. He remembered the time that he and Cap had brought in another diver who had been worse off than Cap was right now, but because of that young doctor's effort and skill, the diver had survived. If anyone could pull Cap through, he could, Smitty thought hopefully.

As they strapped Cap to a stretcher prior to running him up a ramp to the top of the pier and into a building containing the chamber, Lieutenant Rory Russell met Smitty's eyes with a look of recognition. "I never thought we'd see Cap Hanson in the chamber," he said.

The chamber resembled a rounded cube of steel with an oval-shaped door that had a wheel in its middle. They carried Cap through the door and placed him on a bunk, then, all but Cap and Russell exited the chamber.

"Take us down easy to one-six-five," Russell said, "and do something about Smitty's chin." Russell closed the door from the inside, and one of the corpsmen dogged it tight with the wheel. The rushing sound of a mixture of compressed oxygen and helium filled the outer building as the air pressure in the chamber was increased to simulate a hundred-sixty-five-foot dive under water.

Now, there was nothing to do but wait. One of the corpsmen cleaned Smitty's wound and closed it with a butterfly suture, then Smitty and the *Rainbow's* crew paced the room, from time to time peering into the small window in the oval door. Smitty felt like his whole life was lying in there on the bunk. Finally, Lieutenant Russell's voice, made comical sounding because of the helium mix of gases inside of the chamber, came over the intercom.

"We have a situation."

Smitty's heart sank.

"Cap says he was supposed to radio his wife on shore this morning and remind her to feed the neighbor's dog. If you could make that call for him he'd be much obliged. Also, you can tell Smitty that Cap's going to be fine."

The day suddenly brightened further, as if the sun had finally won its battle with the fog. Smitty said, "I sure could use a walk around outside."

"You can go outside," one of the corpsmen answered. "Just stay within arm's reach of this building, unless, of course, you want to wind up in the brig."

The crew of the *Rainbow* departed, but only after Smitty had nearly wrung their hands off shaking them in appreciation. He was shown a small room with bunks. He waited there, and outside the building, and at the chamber door.

The afternoon sun slipped lower in the sky. Storm tossed the local newspaper onto the deck table, grabbed his duck feet and headed back to the beach. He still had time to catch some waves before sunset, and this would be his last chance before heading back to Bodega Bay. The swell turned out to be dropping, instead of increasing, but at least he could go for a relaxing swim. He trotted down to Shaw's Cove, the next beach south from Crescent Bay, and found the lifeguard still on duty and in a heated argument with three teenagers dressed in scuba gear. Poorly dressed, particularly one of them, Storm noted, and that was the source of the argument. One of them was wearing only the Farmer John bottom part of a wetsuit, but he was carrying enough weight on his weight belt for a full suit, and that wasn't the worst of the problem. Instead of being part of a proper quick-release weight belt, the weights were strung onto a piece of rope tied with a knot around the kid's waist. That could prove deadly during an emergency, especially considering the diver's obvious inexperience. To top it off the kid didn't have any kind of buoyancy vest, and Storm was in full agreement with the lifeguard, who seemed determined that anyone equipped like these guys wasn't going to scuba dive at his beach on his watch. The lifeguard finally won the argument, and the disappointed divers trudged up the stairs from the beach while vocalizing loudly their disgust at the lifeguard.

The lifeguard grinned at Storm and said, "Now that those valley boys are safe, I can finally go home."

Storm put his duck feet on and entered the water. There were hardly any waves to catch, so he started a slow swim around the point back to Crescent Bay. The newspaper article he had just read bothered him. Another person had gone missing, presumably while diving at San Clemente Island. Storm had never thought of the water there as being overly dangerous. Sure, a diver could get in trouble anywhere if they tried hard enough. Take these three kids for example. That lifeguard had probably just saved somebody's life, and they didn't even know enough to appreciate it. Heck, all it took was a little common sense. Then Storm remembered his ride on the back of the great white. How had common sense landed him there? Maybe common sense was more of a subjective relativity than a verifiable reality. He told himself that he would research the subject someday, and maybe even try writing about himself.

Storm took his time rounding the point, enjoying the cool Laguna water at the end of a warm day, and when he finally reached Crescent Bay he stopped in waist-deep water and caught a few small waves before coming in. It was a weekday. The sun was setting, and there were just a few people on the beach when he left the water. He strolled to the concrete stairs and stopped to take one last look at the beach. His attention immediately riveted to two suddenly-recognizable scuba divers exiting the water at the south end of the bay. They looked hurried and agitated, and Storm felt a wave of adrenaline race through his body. He ran down to meet the divers as they strode quickly across the sand. The kid with the rope weight belt wasn't with them.

"Where's your friend?" Storm demanded.

"We…we don't know!" One of them stammered.

Storm's worst fears swarmed over him. "Where'd you see him last?"

They pointed towards Shaw's Cove. "There, on the other side!"

Storm ran. He had crossed the rocky point separating the two beaches a thousand times, and his bare feet knew the way. On the point's far side he came to a cloud of bubbles streaming to the surface not ten feet away from the rocks. He pulled his fins on and jumped in. The water was only twelve feet deep but looked dark because of the low light from the setting sun. Storm took a deep breath and dove into the bubbles. On the sandy bottom he found the third diver fighting for his life. The teenager was kicking wildly for the surface, but his weights kept dragging him back down. His regulator swayed uselessly on its hose behind him in free flow, and his entire body contorted as he yanked desperately on the rope around his waist in a futile attempt to break it. It was obvious that he was in full panic and had only seconds to live unless Storm found a way to help him.

The kid's scuba tank had a handle attached, and Storm reached for it. He couldn't hope to haul the panicked kid to the surface, but maybe he could drag him across the bottom to where the cove's rocky point swept down to the bottom. Storm grabbed the handle and swam hard for the rocks. The diver spun around and tried to climb Storm like a tree. Storm fought himself free and grabbed the handle again, kicking towards the rocks with all his strength. The kid again tried to climb him, but this time Storm steered him into the rock face, and the would-be-drowning-victim clambered up the rock to the surface and air and safety.

Storm surfaced with his heart and head pounding. He had done everything on one breath. He was cut, bruised, and bleeding. His eyes were burning from the salt water, and a purple sea urchin spine protruded from his right knee, but it was all worth it. The kid was safe on the rocks and had learned a valuable lesson he wouldn't soon forget.

Storm swam leisurely back to the beach while trying to fit what had just happened into a logical context. This kid could have easily become a statistic added to those other missing divers, he figured, but a fortuitous combination had led to a logical outcome. Storm's awareness and experience, the kid's youthful vitality, and some exquisite timing had come together to save the kid's life.

Yep, Storm told himself. Most questions could be answered if one looked hard enough for a logical explanation. The question of divers disappearing at San Clemente Island should prove to be no exception.

Chapter 8

"Do you have a question about the ocean? Stay right where you are, because here with all the answers is K-EBB's very own, Terry Ho."

"Hello again, everyone," Terry said, smiling at the camera, "and welcome to, 'Ask About Our Ocean'. Our first question comes from ten-year-old Samantha. She writes, 'Is it true that every seventh wave is a big sneaker wave?'"

Terry's monitor showed footage of the Banzai Pipeline in Hawaii superimposed electronically on the blank wall behind her.

"Samantha, the only way that a wave can sneak up on you is if you're not watching for it. When you're at the water's edge, especially if the waves are big, you should never turn your back to the ocean. As far as the seventh wave being the biggest, the next time you're at the ocean, count the waves as they come in, and you'll find out for yourself whether or not that theory holds water. Thanks, Samantha."

"Our second question is from Mr. K. Robins." As usual, Terry didn't mention the questioner's town address on the air, but this question, coming from Marina Del Rey, begged a question of its own. How many people would have the same first initial and last name of one of her least-favorite politicians and also live in the same town as he did? Not many, she figured, and judging by the question's content it could easily be from United States Congressman Kevin Robins.

Terry struggled to keep her composure, because not only was Robins an arrogant, condescending sexist, he had the gall to end his public addresses with the words, "God bless America," as if he were some kind of pious choirboy.

If Robins was a Christian, then she could fly like a duck, Terry told herself, and yet he used words in public that she herself should be saying, but didn't.

Which meant they were both hypocrites, she thought

cynically.

Terry smiled at the camera and said, "Mr. Robins writes, 'Some people say that technology has the power to destroy the planet. What would you say to them?'"

Maybe she should have let his question go for somebody else's, Terry considered, now that it was too late and she had already accepted the challenge. No doubt, Robins was hoping to trap her into saying something that he could use to his own political advantage.

Well, fine, Terry thought angrily. Let him hope. She plastered on her sweetest smile while behind her photographs of hydraulic gold mining now played on the monitor. "Mr. Robins, if the misuse of natural resources causes the extinction of species until all that's left are cockroaches and sludge worms, would that qualify as a destroyed planet? Of course, I'm using exaggeration to make a point, but let's look at some facts. Since the time of the Gold Rush, at least twenty species of animals and thirty species of plants are believed to have disappeared from California. Hopefully, this trend can be stopped, because once a species is gone, it's gone forever, and any commercial, medical, or aesthetic value is also gone with it."

The monitor now played majestic scenes of Yosemite National Park. Terry continued, saying, "The challenge for you and me, Mr. Robins, is to encourage our elected leaders on the local, state, and federal levels to find the balance between a healthy economy and a healthy environment. If that balance is not found, the earth we leave to our grandchildren could be a poorer place."

Terry purposely didn't close with, "Thank you, Mr. K. Robins," as she normally would have done. She considered saying, "Love you; mean it," but chose instead to just freeze on her smile until the red light on the camera facing her winked out.

The anchor man to her right finished the segment by saying, "Thanks, Terry, and you at home can ask Terry about our ocean by writing K-EBB, or ask her in person at Cal Ocean USA right here in Redondo Beach."

In his spacious Marina Del Rey condominium Kevin Robins accidentally pushed the wrong button on the remote control of his television, replacing Terry's picture with the Three Stooges.

"Hah! That's appropriate!" He said, laughing. He figured out his mistake, rewound the segment of "Ask About Our Ocean" that he had just recorded, and watched it again.

"You'll never make it in politics, Ms. Ho," Robins preached to the television after he had again listened to Terry answer his question. "That wasn't bad for an amateur, though. You never really answered my question, and you managed to stay on both sides of the issue at once."

For the briefest instant, Robins considered if Terry demonstrated potential worthy of being molded to serve his purposes, but then he decided that she would be of better use by merely being manipulated. Of course, it was all for the common good, he reminded himself, as he turned off the television and opened the wet bar that was built into his desk. As for Terry's opinion on the environment, he couldn't care less, but she was gaining in popularity, and it helped him to know where popular people stood on the issues.

Robins poured himself a brandy, eased himself down into a deep, leather chair, and raised his glass in a toast. "To Ms. Ho. May your head always stay in the clouds."

It really was a shame that she was such a bleeding-heart environmentalist, Robins conceded. She wasn't entirely stupid, as pretty a little thing as she was, but balancing jobs and the environment was a lot harder to do than say. She could talk about saving whales and redwoods all she wanted, but the man on the street voted for the guy who could bring home the bacon.

Robins didn't consider himself to be anti-environment by any means. He was simply pragmatic. The environment, and especially the ocean, represented industry, transportation, recreation, and national defense. Those issues translated into jobs for his constituents and, more importantly, votes for him. Still, it never hurt to give at least the appearance of appreciating the ocean for purely aesthetic reasons, and to that end he had taken up scuba diving with enough visible display of passion to get himself noticed. The unforeseen consequences of this undertaking had served him better than he'd hoped. He had not only become somewhat of an adventurer in the public's eye, he had kept the whale-and-tree huggers, like Ms. Ho, guessing as to his real priorities.

Robins turned his attention to his latest special interest and his newest true love. On top of a pile of blueprints in the middle of his desk sat a handcrafted model. He picked it up and held it in one hand while he ran the fingers of his other hand over its smooth curves.

"You are a beautiful piece of work whether you win me another term or not," he crooned to it. "And no matter what happens, you'll keep some of the nature nuts out of my hair."

The model that Robins cradled so tenderly was of a two-man submersible of his own inspiration that could be used for either research or defense. The dual purpose in itself was extraordinary, but that was only the beginning, as Robins had so often quoted in his sales pitch to gain funding to build the prototype. What was really unique about her was her propulsion system and shape. While the majority of research submersibles were propeller-driven, hydrodynamic nightmares that, as Robins was fond of saying, "sucked juice like a Casino sign in Las Vegas," his own vessel represented an innovation in underwater shape and propulsion. She was, in essence, a mechanical tuna, sporting a tuna shape that cut effortlessly through water and powered by a mechanical tuna tail that produced twenty-percent more thrust than a propeller for the same amount of energy. The prototype vessel rested in its secret hangar, the whereabouts of which was known only to Robins and his tight-lipped production team. Robins was her most experienced pilot. She was, after all, his baby, since he had been responsible for her design and funding. If she had been a hard sell at times, he believed that once the voters understood her capabilities, he would reap the dividends at the ballot box.

Robins caressed the model as if it were alive. "The whale-hugging defenders of the seas will like you," he cooed to it, and as his gaze swept over the two openings in her nose that led to torpedo tubes he said, "And the real defenders of the seas will love you."

He carefully placed the model back on its stack of drawings and turned his attention to something that had potential to affect the timing of the submersible's grand unveiling. He was probably making too much out of nothing, he told himself, but he hadn't been elected to three consecutive terms by being careless.

He tore open a hand-addressed envelope. The note inside was brief to the point of irritation.

Congressman,
    No luck so far. Commander Logan isn't helping.
    Fishbeck.

Robins poured himself another brandy and walked over to a picture window that looked out onto the harbor lights of Marina Del Rey. He nursed his drink and let his mind wander far beyond the lights to the dark expanse that marked the Pacific Ocean. Unavoidably, he then thought about his father.

"You must be growing soft, Kevin," he grumbled, pulling his eyes away from the night. He gulped the remaining half of his brandy and let the burning in his throat help shove the memories back into the depths of his mind.

Robins suddenly felt tired and old. He walked back to his desk and crumpled into his chair only to find Reginald Fishbeck's note staring up at him. He really hadn't expected Fishbeck to find out anything, but he had hoped. Maybe there was nothing to find. People were always drowning somewhere for any number of reasons. It was just odd that they were also disappearing. He had plans for some upcoming events at San Clemente Island, and he didn't want any unknown surprises to spring up at the wrong time. He wanted some answers, but he also wanted things to stay quiet. He unlocked one of the desk drawers and pulled out a black book which he opened to the phone number of Fishbeck's father. He would cash in on some favors and maybe get a fire lit under the younger Fishbeck, but then he thought better. He closed the book and put it back in the drawer.

Before doing anything, he would first talk to Commander Logan.

It was two a.m. when the decompression chamber door finally opened, and Cap climbed out on shaky legs. Cap smiled at Smitty and said, "I think it's time to find a different line of work."

Smitty wrapped his arms around Cap. In all the years he had known Cap, this was the first time he'd ever hugged him.

"I'm all right, thanks to you," Cap said.

"Yes, he is," said Russell, "and it's time that we all get some real sleep. Smitty, if Cap complains of anything at all, you tell us. Otherwise, I'll see you at o-nine-hundred."

Smitty led Cap to the small room with bunks where they would spend the rest of the night. They turned the lights out, but Smitty lay awake. He was worn ragged by the day's events, but he was still too keyed up to sleep. He heard Cap moving in his bunk. Cap obviously wasn't sleeping either.

"Smitty?" Cap said quietly.

"Yeah, Cap."

"What about the *Emerald*?"

"Old Henry's got her."

"That's fine. Say, Smitty, you saved my life today."

"Nah, I didn't do all that."

"Yes, you did, and I won't forget it.

"You still ain't told me what happened."

"I don't know if I can. It was all so crazy and fast. Let me sleep on it, and we'll talk tomorrow. I can tell you one thing, though. There's something really big and nasty down there."

Chapter 9

Three weeks had passed since Storm's wild ride on the great white. Eight out of ten monitors had been recovered and now sat on tables in Storm's garage in Bodega Bay. The adhesive holding the monitors to the sharks' backs had broken down, and the monitors had floated to the surface and been found by fishermen, recreational boaters, and beachcombers, and had been turned in. Hopefully they'd each ridden on the back of a shark for a minimum of two weeks, but after that, who knew where they'd been? Scratches and dents were expected, but Storm was surprised at the condition of the latest one recovered. It was a mangled mass of metal, plastic, and flotation foam, and it was a wonder that it had been recovered at all. Its band of flotation material was strung out like a rag and barely hanging on to the monitor by a single, frayed thread of nylon webbing. The metal case containing the monitor's innards was crumpled and punctured in several places, and there was little doubt that the unit was a total loss.

Storm cradled the monitor as one would a wounded animal, carefully, with both hands underneath. As he peered into the wreckage from all angles, a glint of white surrounded by bent metal caught his eye. He placed the monitor remains on the table, probed into it, and removed a large, great white shark tooth.

"I wonder," he said aloud to himself.

From the tooth's size alone Storm had gotten a gut feeling. He maneuvered what was left of the monitor's metal case until he found its identification number, and then he checked it with his records.

"Grumpy!" he said triumphantly.

Storm's gut feeling had been correct. The monitor had been attached to the female seventeen-footer. His student crew had given all the sharks nicknames, and they had named the huge female "bronco" in honor of his wild ride. Storm, despite his disdain for anthropomorphic fluff, had secretly named her "Grumpy." From the films and pictures he had studied over and over, he would know Grumpy in a heartbeat if he ever saw her again.

He'd just as soon never see her again.

"Well, that's a done deal," Storm said, putting the wreckage in a cardboard box and turning his attention to another monitor. It looked to be in good shape. It had been found drifting far to the south almost at the Mexican Border. That, in itself, was interesting, considering that it had been placed on one of the smallest sharks to receive a monitor. Storm had almost passed on tagging the six-footer but then had decided to go for it. He had been right to do so, he now decided, having retrieved the monitor from so far away. Of course, just because the monitor was picked up way down south didn't mean that the shark had actually been there, what with the prevailing currents. It could have come off somewhere else and then drifted a while. Hopefully, the recorded data inside would reveal more.

Storm lifted the monitor and turned it round and round. It looked to be reusable. The only apparent rough treatment was a series of deep, parallel scratches along the metal casing and into the flotation foam. He looked at the marks from every angle and came up with no logical explanation for them. His phone rang. He answered it, threw it down, and ran for his car.

Chapter 10

Watchful eyes followed the progress of the dive boat *Hope* as she rounded the west end of San Clemente Island, skirted close inside of Castle Rock, and then chugged another twenty minutes south before gliding to a stop fifty yards offshore from the destroyer wreck.

A Navy MP in a jeep on shore turned to his companion. "Logan says to discourage any civilians in this sector."

"So, what do we tell them?" the second MP asked.

"Logan says to tell them we're going to blow the place up."

That sounded good to the second MP Besides being used as a training area for the Navy SEALs, San Clemente Island was used by the Navy to practice aerial-and-naval bombardment and also carrier landings. Dive boats, fishing boats, and recreational craft were constantly being asked to move to safer locations. The second MP said, "Well, we better tell them soon. They just dropped the hook."

The first MP reached for the radio in the jeep. "Should we just try to call them up?"

"No way," the second MP said with a grin. "We'll tell them in person. There might be some babes on board."

"Yeah!"

Terry was on board. She had been monitoring the scuttlebutt at her favorite scuba shop. That was one of her ways to take the pulse of the public concerning the strange disappearances. She was pleased to observe that, so far, there hadn't been much of a stir. The shop's dive master had invited her to help with a student dive at San Clemente Island, and she had agreed in a heartbeat. She always enjoyed helping with the dive classes, but her main motive for joining this particular trip was the opportunity to get a feeling for the backside of the island. She had never dived there. The backside was mostly the realm of ab' divers, lobster fishermen, and the Navy. A sport-dive boat rarely came to the backside, but today was special. Today's trip was the final exam for one of the more-expensive scuba courses in Southern California, and the dive master meant for his students to get their money's worth. Thirty-one divers and three instructors, including Terry, were on board.

Terry stood on the upper deck of the *Hope* and surveyed her surroundings. Inshore of the destroyer wreck a rocky beach blended gently upward into hills of chaparral. The water surrounding the *Hope* was as smooth as glass. The tops of the kelp splayed across the surface in all directions, indicating little to no current. From time to time, a pair of harbor seals popped their heads up from the water and took quizzical looks at the intruders. Terry tried to conjure up an uneasy feeling, or women's intuition, or anything else that could warn her of something amiss, but conditions were, in a word, perfect.

Such a tranquil scene, at an island named for someone who had met such an untranquil death, Terry's mind wandered. The story handed down through the ages was that Saint Clement, because he wouldn't renounce his faith in God, had been tied to an anchor and thrown into the sea. Could she have done that? Would she ever be called to do anything like that?

She wondered.

Terry watched carefully as a lone snorkeler, by far the first person in the water, powered out in front of the *Hope's* bow.

That had to be Todd, Terry told herself with a smile. She had come to know the gangly fifteen-year-old on the trip out. He had been too excited to sleep and had talked to her for over two hours while she had mainly listened.

Much like Mama Ho would have done, Terry thought, pleased with herself.

Todd had shared his dreams of becoming a marine biologist, and he had proudly shown her his autographed magazine with an article about Dr. Storm Hancock. Today he had hopes of seeing a shark, not necessarily a great white, but maybe a blue.

Listening to Todd hadn't been all that difficult, and Terry wondered if he wouldn't be the perfect person on whom to practice a little evangelization. He seemed to be receptive to her, and it would probably be a fairly painless endeavor. If he were a Christian already, then so much the better. She would merely reinforce his faith.

Terry continued to watch as Todd began to make free dives. She noticed that, for a beginner, he could stay underwater for a long time.

"Don't overdo it, Todd," she said to him mentally.

As Todd worked his way further away from the *Hope*, Terry came to a decision. After the day's diving was done, she would talk to him about Jesus.

Now, who were these guys?

An inflatable boat powered by an outboard engine sped out from around a nearby point and in seconds had pulled alongside the *Hope*. One sailor stood up and conversed with the *Hope's* captain. The other remained seated in the inflatable and appeared to be trying to get Terry's attention without looking like he was trying to get her attention. She scowled down at him, which caused him to begin what looked to be a concentrated visual inspection of a valve on the inflatable's hull.

Terry scanned the water again for Todd. He was now thirty yards in front of the bow, on the surface, and continuing to move further away. Terry did a slow visual circle of the water around the *Hope*. There were the two harbor seals. They were traveling faster than she thought possible, porpoising out of the water in great leaps. They must be playing, she thought, as she continued to watch them race away. The seals continued their amazing speed around the next point of land and out of sight, and two realizations suddenly sent fingers of ice water scampering down Terry's spine. The first one was that the hills on the shore looked exactly like the background in the photograph of the *Time Out*. The second one was that the harbor seals weren't playing at all.

They were in full flight.

Terry looked for Todd. Thank goodness; there he was, now fifty yards out, making free dive after free dive.

"Todd!" she yelled three times, but with his face in the water, and also because he was wearing a wetsuit hood, he obviously couldn't hear her. She bounded down the ladder to the lower deck and ran to where the sailor and the *Hope's* captain were talking. They looked at her in surprise.

"Didn't you say the *Hope* has a recall signal?" she asked urgently.

"Yeah, there's an underwater siren," the *Hope's* captain answered.

"Then I think we should use it right now."

Chapter 11

Storm forced himself to watch the repugnant spectacle unfolding before him. A wire rope had been looped twice around the tail of a great white shark and then hooked back onto itself. A dockside crane groaned as it lifted the giant fish from the deck of a fishing boat to hang full length above the pier at the Dunes Restaurant at Bodega Bay. People poured onto the pier, jostling each other to get closer to the magnificent fish. It was huge, a female, and among the growing crowd it was perhaps only Storm who was aware that the picture of her being presented was but a grotesque caricature of her real self. Suspended by her tail, swelled and misshapen, with her innards scrunched forward because of gravity, she now possessed all the sleekness of a cow. Her mouth hung open, gaping, adding to the falsehood as people poked and prodded her and posed for pictures and gawked at her rows of serrated teeth. Then Storm spotted what he was looking for but hoping not to find. A dart tag was affixed to the back of the shark's dorsal fin.

It was Grumpy.

Storm suppressed a cry of rage. How dare they catch his shark and treat her like this! He held himself back from shoving his way through the crowd and trying to cut her down. He didn't have a knife, and he probably couldn't have cut through the cable anyway. He breathed deeply and slowly, trying to calm himself as his immediate anger gave way to a growing sadness. There was nothing for it he figured, and he slipped into the throng and maneuvered his way closer to the shark. Conversations around him told him that people were just doing what people do, but it was a shame that they never got to see what a great white really looked like in the wild as it streamed majestically through the water. Storm figured that most of them knew about the sleekness of a dolphin, but few of them had ever seen the great white in its natural state. She was pure power and efficiency, sleek as any tuna, but in a harder, more predatory way. If the tuna was a speedboat, the great white was a torpedo boat.

It didn't matter what they knew. Grumpy never deserved to be hung up like a freak in a side show. If she was caught for her meat, as was hopefully the case, then why not just get on with it?

OK, Storm told himself. Maybe he was acting a little sentimental over a dumb animal, but still....

He turned to walk away. He didn't want to add to the spectacle any longer.

"It's a tiger shark," a beet-faced man in front of him said to a bored-looking kid slouching at the man's side.

Storm stopped. Should he even bother? No. Yes. He faced the man and the boy. "It's a great white," he said with a smile, trying to look friendly and not too condescending.

"That's what's been eating those people off Catalina," the man said.

Storm had heard nothing about mishaps at Catalina Island, so he figured the man was probably referring to the events at 'Clemente. How to put this and still sound friendly? "That's certainly possible, but it's not very probable," Storm said, still smiling. "There's never been a documented attack by a great white in those waters."

"Then what's happening to them?" asked the kid, showing perhaps the slightest flicker of interest.

"That's a good question," Storm answered honestly. "I bet there's some good books in the stores on the pier. Maybe you could read about the ocean and come up with some ideas yourself."

"It doesn't look so great to me," the kid remarked, looking at the shark with obvious disdain.

Another budding genius, Storm thought, but then he'd been lucky enough to grow up literally on the beach. Who knew where this kid had been? Storm thought of some kid he'd never met named Todd who now had his autograph, and he momentarily wondered what it might be like to raise children. It was probably harder than it looked. Another good reason to remain a bachelor.

The beet-faced man shrugged his shoulders at Storm, as if to say, "I can't tell him anything."

Storm didn't want to be pushy, but he couldn't pass up a teaching moment. "This is one animal you never want to turn your back on," he said, hopefully.

"Oh yeah? Watch this." The kid turned and faced the other way and said, "There, I turned my back on it." He faced forward again and said, "I want to go to the arcade."

"Wait just a minute," Storm said. He had spotted a wooden-handled string mop leaning against a dock rail. It was the type of mop found around old fishing boats, with its dried-out wooden handle, half of its yarn gone, and the remaining yarn frayed and shedding. Storm picked up the mop and approached the shark. She was still dripping blood and water and was so freshly dead that he could almost feel the power draining from her. It all seemed so pointless and tragic, but perhaps some little good could yet come from her dying. Storm shoved the free end of the handle into the great white's mouth. The shark's jaws slammed shut and snapped the mop handle in two as if it were merely a toothpick. Storm held the severed mop handle up for all to see.

"Wow!" the kid exclaimed, his eyes hanging as wide open as his mouth.

"Bingo!" Storm thought to himself.

Todd Everett was anything but bored. He hit the water moments behind the *Hope's* anchor and worked his way up current. He practiced his free dives, diving deeper and deeper each time. Today was checkout day on scuba gear, but there were two dozen divers ahead of him, and he figured that he had at least an hour before his own turn. He meant to spend that hour in the water.

Fifty yards in front of the *Hope's* bow he made his deepest dive yet. His capillary depth gauge read twenty feet, and for a few, magical seconds he hung suspended in the kelp forest midway between the surface and the bottom. He looked down and watched in amazement as a California bat ray, four feet

across from wing tip to wing tip, flew majestically through the
water below him. He could have stayed down longer, but he
heard the sound of an engine, and he surfaced quickly. A quick
look around showed him an inflatable boat alongside the *Hope*.
What were they doing? It didn't matter. He was diving.

Todd hyperventilated by taking deep, slow breaths,
blowing off carbon dioxide. This activity enabled his body to
resist the urge to breathe, thereby allowing him to stay under
water for a longer period of time. He dove again and stopped at
thirty feet. The bottom called up to him from only ten feet
deeper. He kicked easily back to the surface and gathered his
wind for his first forty-foot free dive.

Twitch.

Todd turned his head and caught the end of a fleeting
movement forty feet below.

Twitch.

This time he glimpsed something that reminded him of an
eel, and he wanted to see an eel almost as much as he wanted to
see a shark.

Twitch.

Todd was now absolutely positive that he was going to
make it to forty feet. He began a mental count of ten slow
breaths.

One, two....

Twitch.

...three, four, five....

The recall siren from the *Hope* pierced the air and the
water.

Rats! He thought.

...six, seven....

Twitch.

Todd shut out the sound and continued counting.

...eight, nine, and ten!

He took the biggest breath he had ever taken in his life,
jackknifed his body, and pointed his toes to the sky.

During the very last instant of Todd's huge, tenth breath,
one drop of the mighty Pacific Ocean—a mere one twentieth of
a milliliter of water, had soared up and over the rim of his

snorkel barrel, fallen the length of the barrel without touching the sides, cycloned down his windpipe, and hit him smack in the carina, that gathering of nerves where the bronchi branch apart and where all coughs are born.

Todd's head was all of three feet under water when his forty-foot free dive disintegrated into an air-gasping, rip-the-mask-off somersault back to the surface.

Holding his mask in one hand, he sculled high on the surface amidst a violent session of coughing. Finally, he recovered enough to put his mask back on, and then he saw people on the *Hope* waving for him to return to the boat.

"OK, I'm coming!" he yelled at them in frustration and embarrassment.

He knew he could have made it to forty feet.

Twitch.

Chapter 12

From forty feet below, the creature watched its would-be prey swim away. Minutes earlier, a harbor seal had escaped its ambush. The creature had been thwarted twice this morning, which meant that it hadn't eaten anything substantial in over a week. Now, all it could do was watch and wait for something else to come near, but as it sat hungry on the bottom, a memory trickled through the maze of the creature's primitive brain. The memory was of another time of hunger when the creature had drifted down through open water onto an unsuspecting sand bass. The memory was of that unusual incident when the creature had actually gone to the prey instead of waiting for the prey to come to it.

Then the creature did something that it was not used to doing when prey was near.

It moved.

Sand streamed from the creature's massive body as it lifted free from its hiding place and surged upward. Attack vibrations raced ahead of it, warning all other water creatures to either flee or hide.

The prey animal, however, continued along the surface at its plodding, noisy pace.

The creature plucked Todd from the surface as easily as a rising trout takes a mayfly.

A woman's scream pierced the air. "Right there! Something happened to him right there!"

Terry bowled through people that didn't move out of her way quickly enough. She reached the bow rail to see where the woman was pointing. Only a slick spot swirling on the ocean surface marked where Todd had been snorkeling only moments before.

"Jesus, help me!" Terry cried, for once not caring who heard her or what they might think. She fought her way back through the gathering people, grabbed her fins, mask, and snorkel from her gear bag, and bounded into the Navy inflatable. "Let's go, now!" she yelled.

The sailors started the inflatable's engine, and the boat sped the short distance to where Todd had last been seen. Terry dove into the water before the boat came to a complete stop. She powered down through the kelp canopy and grabbed a kelp stalk for an anchor. She looked in all directions, but there was only the kelp forest illuminated by shafts of sunlight. Her pounding heart drowned out any other noise. She searched the kelp, praying, hoping. A giant shape suddenly appeared out of the kelp. Terry's snorkel ground in her teeth as a black sea bass, barely a body's length away and looking like a creature from another time, cruised by her. Terry had never seen a black in the wild, let alone one that weighed five-hundred pounds. She watched, immobilized, until the huge fish swam out of sight, and she was left again with only the pounding of her heart.

She was out of air.

Terry picked her way upward through the kelp. She didn't dare get tangled up. Five feet from the surface she stopped. A facemask and snorkel nodded in the gentle surge. The curve of the snorkel had hooked around a kelp branch in a delicate balancing act. The slightest position change would cause it to dislodge and sink into the forest. The mask faceplate was cracked from top to bottom. Terry unhooked the mask and snorkel from the kelp and cradled it as if it were precious crystal. She surfaced to find the *Hope's* own small boat waiting. She handed the mask up to the dive master, who looked at it and said, "This is Todd's."

Terry prayed that this was all somehow a dream and that she would wake up in her bed in Leucadia. "Are you sure?" she asked.

"Sure, I'm sure," the dive master answered. "I sold it to him."

The dive master, the boat, the sky and water all seemed to swim around Terry as if reality had suddenly vanished. She offered neither resistance nor help as hands reached down and pulled her into the inflatable, and as she lay against the boat's rubber side, the fact bore into her that her dream was all too real.

The dive master and the *Hope's* captain insisted that no one else get in the water. The two inflatables circled the area over and over in a forlorn attempt at finding Todd. With each passing minute the water seemed to become more foreign and unfriendly, and for the first time in her life that she could remember, Terry looked at the water and felt afraid.

Chapter 13

"If we have any more questions, we'll call you." With that remark, the sheriff detective departed the *Hope* and left Terry as just one more in a boatload of people numb with shock.

Questions? Yeah, she had questions. What in the world had happened? And how much of it could she have prevented? And where was her loving God when Todd Everett was physically removed from the planet?

Terry drove to "Mama Ho's Natural Store" and pulled into the parking lot without any recollection of how she had gotten there. As soon as she stumbled through the front door her parents seemed to realize something dreadful must have happened. Tommy Ho shut the door behind Terry, and Mama Ho put up the "closed" sign. They waited on the remaining customers until the store was empty, then they joined Terry at one of the tables. Tommy Ho pulled his chair up close to Terry and faced her. Mama Ho stood behind Terry's chair and placed her hands on Terry's shoulders. No one said anything.

Finally, Terry broke the silence. "A kid lost his life today. There was something huge, a shark....something. One second, a beautiful young man was alive, and the next second he was gone."

Terry spent the next hour telling her parents all that had happened. After that, she walked alone in the garden, rehashing the morning's events over and over only to come to the same, useless conclusion. Another diver was gone, and she didn't have a clue why.

At suppertime Terry joined her parents at the table, but she couldn't eat, and she didn't engage in the conversation that was already unusually somber for a Ho family meal. Mama Ho took away Terry's untouched plate of food and replaced it with a papaya smoothie. "Kanani, you know you have to eat something," Mama Ho said gently.

Terry forced herself to take a sip of the golden drink. She

looked at Mama Ho and realized just how much she appreciated her. "Mama, I just want to know why this had to happen. I mean; he was just a kid."

"Honey, the best we can do is to know it must have something to do with God's plan."

"God's plan?" Terry answered indignantly. "It's God's plan that a fifteen-year-old kid can be swallowed whole, and I couldn't do anything to stop it?"

Tommy Ho reached across the table and lovingly wrapped Terry's hand into both of his own. "Kanani, do you remember the Marine? You saved a man's life that day. That was God's plan too."

"If that's God's plan, I don't understand it, and I don't like it."

"And for us poor, mixed-up people, we'll probably never understand," Tommy Ho answered tenderly. "But I do know I wouldn't want the job of holding the universe together. We'd better just leave it to him and do our best as he shows us."

"If he shows us!" Terry answered bitterly.

Late that evening Mama Ho found Terry still awake, sitting up in bed with her light on.

"You can't sleep, Kanani?"

"No, Mama. There's too many unanswered questions."

Mama Ho picked up a Bible from Terry's dresser. "Maybe you could find some answers in here, or at least some words that might help you sleep."

"Sure. Why not?" Terry answered. She reached out for the Bible more to placate her mother than for her desire to read it.

Mama Ho left, and Terry stared at the book in her hands. Did it really contain answers? Tonight she didn't have much confidence that it did. She closed her eyes anyway, slipped her thumb between two pages near the Bible's middle, and opened it. She opened her eyes to see the first page of the book of Jonah, and she chuckled without humor at the grim irony.

"Jonah?" she said heavenward. "You really want me to read Jonah?"

Terry listened for an answer but heard only the sound of crickets singing in the garden.

"Well, fine!" she said angrily, and she began to read. She knew the basic story about Jonah and the whale, of course, but tonight, perhaps because she really did want answers, she read the story as if for the very first time. She read slowly and carefully, and when she had finished, contrary to her mother's hopeful expectations, she felt no comfort whatsoever. In fact, she felt worse than before she had read it. Jonah had been called to spread a message of repentance and forgiveness. A great fish had swallowed Jonah, and perhaps a great fish had swallowed Todd. Jonah had survived, but young Todd had been lost. The city of Nineveh had turned from its old ways and had turned back to God, but what about Todd? Why hadn't she talked to him about her faith when she'd still had the chance?

Ok, maybe she was being a little unrealistic and too hard on herself, she reasoned, but still....

Terry laid awake deep into the night until she finally fell into a sleep troubled by unhappy dreams.

The next morning Terry drove to the house of Todd's parents in the small, inland town of Vista. Judging from the line of cars at the curb, and from what she could see and hear through the open doorway, the house appeared to be full of people. She rang the doorbell, and a fortyish-looking man came to the door. He seemed tired and sad.

"Can I help you?" he said, friendly enough.

"Hello, my name is Terry Ho...."

The door slammed in Terry's face.

"Who was that, Honey?" Terry heard a woman's voice ask on the other side of the door.

"It's one of those darned TV people," she heard the man answer.

"I was with Todd on the *Hope*!" Terry said, loudly enough to be heard through the door.

Silence.

The door opened. This time there was the man plus a teary-eyed woman. The man said, "What did you say?"

"I am so sorry. My name is Terry Ho, and I was with Todd just before the accident."

"Don't mind me, please," the man said, reaching out his

hand. "I'm Bob Everett, Todd's father. This is his mom, Liz. Things have been pretty rough around here."

Terry entered the house amid numerous introductions to the Everett's family and friends, and she was shown to a chair in the front room. She immediately noticed the large open Bible prominently displayed in the center of the coffee table. She leaned over for a closer look. The Bible was opened to Psalm 139.

"That was one of Todd's favorite passages," Liz Everett said. "It talked about being in the ocean."

"Then..., Todd was a Christian?" Terry asked. She felt as if a heavy weight might be lifting from her shoulders.

"Oh yes, certainly," Bob said. "And that's our only joy— that some day we'll all be together again."

Terry suddenly found herself weeping unabashedly in front of total strangers.

Liz handed Terry a box of tissues and wrapped her arms around her. "You go ahead and cry, dear. Goodness knows I've cried a lot today, and I'm going to have to cry a whole lot more."

Terry accepted the tissue gratefully. She felt embarrassed, relieved, sad, and glad all at the same time. When she was finally able to speak, she said, "I'm going to find out what happened to Todd. If it's the last thing I ever do, I'm going to find out."

After spending an hour at the Everett's home, Terry left and drove just out of sight from the house before she pulled off the road. She removed a small Bible from the glove box, opened it to the book of Jonah, and she read the story again. This time, when she reached the part about the great fish, she took from it a lesson about how strength can rise from the depths of despair. Even though he'd done it begrudgingly, Jonah had eventually wound up praying to God to make the best out of a hopeless situation. To Terry, that sounded a lot like what Mama Ho would do and what she should always be doing herself. She closed the book. The praying part wasn't so hard, but she still didn't see how any good was going to come out of any of this.

Terry pulled away from the curb and continued her drive to Leucadia. She felt relief that she was off the hook about talking to Todd, but she wondered how she would keep her promise to find out what had happened. Also, she prayed that, if the opportunity presented itself, she would have the courage to share her faith and not hold back in fear of what anyone might think.

At Mama Ho's, Terry worked in the garden until late into the afternoon. She usually enjoyed helping her father, but today she was mostly trying to escape the reality of yesterday morning. She cut the ripe ears of corn from their stalks and dropped them in a basket at her feet. The tall corn stalks, with their long tapered leaves, reminded her of the kelp forest that she had plunged into in her frantic search for Todd. If she closed her eyes she saw the kelp, the black sea bass, and the broken facemask.

"Terry, Sheriff Jim's on the phone."

Terry jerked as if awakening from a bad dream. She waved in answer to her mom and hurried into the back of the store.

"Sheriff Jim, Thanks for calling back."

"You're welcome, and I'm sorry. This must be pretty hard to take. I heard you were real close to things when they happened."

"They happened literally right in front of me. Somebody screamed, and I looked where they were pointing, but there was just a shiny spot on the water where Todd had been."

"A big shark took him. Isn't that basically the case?"

"I don't know. If it had been a shark you'd think that somebody would have seen a fin or something. Nobody saw anything. It was like the water itself just opened up and swallowed him."

"I know this doesn't seem like the right time to ask, but have you had a chance to talk to Cap Hanson and Smitty?"

"No."

"Maybe you should. I heard they had something happen to them pretty close to where you were yesterday. According to them, they ran into something big and nasty. Just talk to them sooner than later. I don't know, Terry, but I think somebody's hiding something."

"Who would want to hide anything?"

"I don't know for sure. It's just that when I get to asking around, I feel like I'm being stonewalled. It's like some people know more than they're telling."

"What people?"

"The people on the island."

"The island? You mean the Navy? Why would they hide anything?"

"I don't know. There's all kinds of secret stuff going on out there. Maybe there's a connection, maybe not. I'm not naming names yet, but something just doesn't set right. Just go see Cap and Smitty, and then get back to me."

Terry said goodbye to Sheriff Jim and walked slowly back out to the garden where Tommy Ho was still working.

"Well?" he said.

"He doesn't know anything either, Papa."

Nobody knows anything, Terry thought. Not her, not Sheriff Jim, only God.

Chapter 14

Commander Logan slammed the phone down so hard it bounced through its cradle, skittered over the edge of his desk, and swung from its cord like a pendulum. Another person was drowned, eaten, taken to Venus by little green men; he didn't know what, but it had happened at his island and on his watch. A sheriff was ringing his phone off the hook, and to top it off he was being asked to look the other way while Fish and Game did its own investigation. Logan leaned over his desk to reel in the phone, and he winced from a pain that shot up his leg. A helicopter crash had left him with his right femur spliced together by titanium rods and screws. The leg seemed to bother him more on foggy days and when he was angry, and today it hurt like the dickens. He dialed a number, and to the voice that answered he said, "This is Commander Logan. Put out a marine bulletin that the backside of San Clemente Island is closed from the Mile Towers to Seal Cove for a thousand yards out. It's off limits to all civilian boaters because of naval exercises. I also want it in every local boating-and-fishing rag, and I want it on with the weather."

With deliberate calm Logan returned the telephone safely to its cradle. That was still playing their game, he told himself, and if they didn't like it they could fire him.

Logan's official capacity at the island was Director of Civilian Affairs. To his thinking that was a glorified title for someone who held peoples' hands so they wouldn't do something stupid. In particular, he was responsible for keeping civilians safe when they visited or worked on San Clemente Island, and he was responsible for keeping the goings-on at the island safe from their curious eyes and ears. He also had to deal with the occasional abalone diver or commercial fisherman who decided to take a walk on shore, and there were always recreational boaters running aground or wanting to have a picnic in some romantic cove. Technically speaking, bad things that happened to civilians while they were in the water weren't his direct responsibility, but the water was around his island, and that was cause enough. He'd kept low key about the Porsche dealer and the lobsterman and the civilian plumber. The plumber's disappearance had never hit the papers, and he just hoped that someone had notified his next of kin like they'd promised. He hadn't done much about those events, and by playing them down, no real news had been made, especially with the rest of the madness that was going on in the world. But now things were different. A fifteen-year-old kid was gone, and he was still being told not to worry and to let some buffoon named Fishbeck from Fish and Game have the run of the island.

Logan didn't trust Fishbeck for a second. Maybe it was because Fishbeck's face bore the most constant unemotional expression that Logan had ever seen on a person, a live person anyway. Someone had theorized that Fishbeck was spying for politicians who wanted the base shut down now that the cold war was over. Someone else had suggested that Fishbeck was secretly counting goats. Logan was constantly being badgered by one environmentalist group that wanted the island's wild goats to be protected and by an opposing environmentalist group that wanted them all shot.

If Fishbeck was counting goats, fine. Logan didn't care. What really mattered was that another person was gone, and Fishbeck didn't seem to know any more about it than anybody else. In fact, if Logan hadn't made a couple of discoveries by his own initiative, they'd all know a whole lot less than they did. Logan figured that if they'd just turn him loose, he'd find out what was happening. He'd get the whole island working on it. He'd even get the goats working on it.

Logan stared at an unopened letter on his desk, and his leg throbbed again. He slipped a dagger from his desk drawer and sliced the envelope open.

Dear Commander Logan.
Pursuant to our previous conversation, the date for Ambassador Liu Xin's visit has been confirmed for October 4, of this year. I trust that you will provide the most

accommodating facilities available to insure him an enjoyable diving experience. I will be his official host, of course, but I am counting on your firm and capable support. It is not confirmed that Mr. Liu will be collecting live specimens, but the possibility is to be taken into consideration. His personal security officer, Yi Kim, should be arriving, via Hawaii, two days prior to Mr. Liu. I know that the exquisite diving around San Clemente Island will be an experience that Liu Xin shall never forget, and it will be one more step, albeit a small one, to bringing our two countries closer together. Please contact me regarding any concerns.

Your obedient servant,
Kevin Robins.

Logan picked up the phone, and he contemplated whether or not he could crush it with his bare hands. Your obedient servant, he thought. What a crock!

He had some concerns all right. A Chinese diplomat was coming to sightsee underwater, and he had a regular Bermuda Triangle going on. It was going to be just peachy if he wound up having to tell the Chinese that their man just got eaten by we-don't-know-what, but not to worry, because Fishbeck is hot on the case.

Forty minutes later, by refusing to give up in the wake of answering machines, the occasional human voice, and unending holds, Logan had Kevin Robins on the line. The congressman's voice oozed through the phone like molasses in summer. "Commander Logan, what an unexpected pleasure. What can I do for you on this fine, California day?"

Logan would have bet a month's pay that the congressman considered his call neither unexpected, nor a pleasure. "What you can do is cancel Liu Xin's trip until we find out what's going on. And if you really want to help, do something to get Fish and Game out of the way."

"Oh, I see," Robins replied in a voice that, to Logan, seemed balanced carefully between hurt and surprise. "Now, Commander, we don't want to act too hastily. If we cancel Liu's trip, it could be construed as losing face, and at a time when we're making great strides in improving relations with the Chinese. I wonder if you're underestimating just how much weight this friendly visit to your island can carry."

Logan's knuckles turned white as he did his best to crush the phone. "It'll carry a lot of weight if their man winds up eaten."

"Commander, I've done my homework on you, and I know I'm right when I say you wouldn't let that happen," Robins replied in soothing tones. "Besides, Fish and Game's Officer Fishbeck is personally keeping me apprised to his investigation. I'm almost certain that these curious incidents can be attributed to human error, and it all boils down to a matter of taking proper precautions and using common sense, two virtues in which a man of your training and caliber happens to excel."

The phone had successfully resisted Logan's effort to crush it. "Congressman, your Officer Fishbeck has been poking around here for weeks now, and he hasn't found squat. If you'll get him out of the way, I'll find out what's happening."

Robins chuckled, as if saying, without the use of words, that Logan was needlessly alarmed. "Commander, as a favor to me, let's give Fishbeck a little more time. He's a good man. In fact, the only person I'd rather have on the case besides you is him. Let's just let him do his job, and I'm certain that between the two of you, we won't have a thing to worry about."

The phone was still bouncing in its cradle when it rang.

"Logan!"

"Whoa! Is your leg acting up again?" said the voice on the other end.

"Oh, it's you. Sorry. I was just talking to someone who's trying real hard to get on my bad side."

"Anybody I know?"

"Probably. Listen, do yourself and me a favor, and never run for office."

"Don't worry. There's no chance of that. Anyway, on your guy, Fishbeck, here's what I learned. He graduated from Fresno State with a major in law enforcement. He's into guns, pistols mostly, and he's won some shooting trophies. After college he installed home security alarms, and then the rumor is that his father helped him get into Fish and Game with some kind of friendly deal. Last year he received a commendation for busting up a ring of abalone poachers up near Mendocino. I guess it was a big operation. Also, it looks like his father is hooked up pretty tight with Congressman Kevin Robins. Does that help?"

"Yeah, that helps a lot. Thanks."

Logan eased the phone back onto its cradle and massaged his leg. He needed to think and walk. One thing for sure was that he didn't trust Fishbeck or Robins any further than he could throw either one of them. He left his office and walked toward the pier, doing his painful best to not limp. The north end of the island was unusually quiet. It had been that way a lot lately since the post-Cold-War debates had begun in Washington about which bases were to be decommissioned. He neared the building that housed the decompression chamber, and he heard the clank of tools on metal. Curious, he walked around the building into a fenced-off area and let himself through a gate. He was just in time to see a pair of legs squirming their way into a concrete well built underneath the chamber's new air compressor.

"Hello!" he said loudly. "Who's under the compressor?"

"Lieutenant Russell," answered a voice from below. "Who's up there?"

Logan knew the young doctor only from brief contacts with him, but he had instantly liked him.

"This is Commander Logan," he called back. "Don't let me bother you." He turned to leave, but Russell called up to him.

"Sir, do you see an empty coffee can on the ground?"

"Yes, do you need it?"

Russell answered affirmatively, so Logan handed it under, and then his curiosity caused him to wait to see what happened next. There was the soft swish of fluid pouring into a can and then the sound of a wrench being applied to a bolt. Shortly thereafter, the coffee can reappeared, followed by Russell, squirming back out from under the compressor.

"You like getting your hands dirty?" Logan said with a grin.

Russell climbed to his feet. "Let's just say that this is the first new compressor we've had here in twenty years, and I want it broken in right. As you can see, they put the oil drain in a convenient spot."

"That's because this is a civilian-built compressor. If it'd been Navy-built, you wouldn't get to it at all."

They were both grinning now, and Logan's positive feeling about Russell grew stronger. He said, "What do you think about people going in the water around here and not coming back out?"

Just the look alone on Russell's face told Logan that he'd done some thinking about it already, and he hadn't liked his conclusions. "I think we need to find out what's going on before somebody else goes missing."

"That's a given, but how?"

"Well, Sir, I'm about two cents away from calling up an old friend of mine."

"Anybody I know?"

"Just an old school chum, but he knows sharks and fish and everything else that lives in the water, and he's just crazy enough to be smart, if you know what I mean. If anyone could help, it'd be him."

Logan reached into his pants pocket and felt some coins. There were at least two cents.

Chapter 15

Ruddy ducks bobbed like corks and tucked their heads deep into their feathers as a brisk wind whipped Bodega Harbor into a meringue of whitecaps. The slapping of steel halyards against aluminum masts and the cries of gulls and osprey blended into sweet music for Storm, who had been working since sunrise buttoning the *Nemo* up for a long winter's nap.

The *Nemo* wasn't entirely Storm's responsibility. She officially belonged to a coalition of universities, but because he had orchestrated her purchase and refit, it was understood that the *Nemo* was Storm Hancock's boat. Any person or school needing to use her ultimately wound up going through him. Along with that honor he had inherited the pleasure of keeping her shipshape.

This morning he was in no hurry to be finished with his work. The *Nemo* would probably sit idle for several months, and he wanted to leave her in tiptop condition. Besides, he enjoyed being aboard her. He didn't believe in luck, but it did seem that good things happened to him around the *Nemo*. The resounding success of his latest project was evidence. If you threw Grumpy's completely destroyed monitor out of the mix, all the sharks had sent back usable data.

Storm methodically rubbed polish onto the *Nemo's* stainless steel wheel. Yes, it had been a good project, and now that the fun part of it was over, he was already mulling over his next endeavor. Did he really want to join that behavioral study of reef sharks? Granted, it would be at the Galapagos Islands, which should be reason enough to get excited, but he knew what his real problem was. Even though he'd been planning the Galapagos trip for months, hoping to lose himself in yet another adventure, he was already anticipating the inevitable letdown that would come at the end of the project.

Storm's eyes lingered on his reflection in the steering wheel's curving surface. The image was distorted, like his own feelings of completeness. Try as he would to lose himself in his beloved ocean, a gnawing hunger still tugged at his heart.

"Hey, Storm!"

Storm poked his head over the cowling of the *Nemo's* flying bridge. The dock manager was standing outside of the marina office with his hands cupped around his mouth, hollering into the wind. "You got a phone call! It's some guy named Rory Russell from the Navy!"

"Thanks! I'll be right there!" Storm hollered back. He threw his polishing rag down and barely touched the rungs of the ladder as he dropped from the flying bridge to the main deck. He vaulted over the *Nemo's* rail to the dock and hustled up to the marina office.

"You can take it here," the dock manager said. He handed the phone to Storm and stepped outside for a smoke. Storm heard his old friend's voice for the first time in months.

"Hey, Stormy, how the heck are you?"

"Rory, you won't believe it. Just the other day I was twenty-thousand feet above you and thinking I should try to call you, but you called me first. I still can't picture you in the Navy. Do you like it, I mean, seeing the world and all?"

"I'm not seeing too much of the world, at least not yet. Mostly, I'm unbending ab' divers and patching up Navy SEALs. Those guys are always getting banged up."

"I'm still surprised, and I'm impressed. And how's married life? Are you still happy?"

"It can't be beat, but how about you? Have you found a steady girl yet?"

"Oh, no! Not me! You're talking to a man who's better off single. It gives me more freedom than the alternative. Speaking of which, when are you free that we can get together?"

"That's why I'm calling, Stormy. Is there any chance that you could come down here real soon?"

"How soon, is 'real soon'?"

"Say, tomorrow."

"Tomorrow? What's the rush?"

"Let's just say that there's a problem, and you're the man to call, kinda' like Superman, or Zorro, or somebody. Can you come?"

"Who's got a problem, the Navy?"

"You could say the Navy, or the abbers if you want. Could you come?"

Storm thought for a moment. There was an underwater film festival next week in Long Beach that promised to have some hot footage on the Galapagos Islands. He supposed that could be a good enough excuse to drop everything. "What exactly is the problem?"

"I can't tell you the whole thing over the phone, but it has to do with divers going missing."

"Going missing? You're not talking about what's going on at 'Clemente."

"Yeah, that."

"And you think you need me? I don't see a connection."

"I'm not even sure if I do myself. Listen, Stormy, there's something weird going on down here. For some reason it's been dumped in my lap, and I don't know what to do about it. I need your help."

Storm didn't need long to make up his mind. The few times that Rory had asked him for help there had usually been a good reason. He said, "All right. I'll come."

The relief was apparent in Rory's voice. "I knew I could count on you. Are your folks home this time of year, or are they out seeing the world?"

"They'd be home, and they'd love to see you."

"Then why don't we meet at your folks' house Saturday morning? That gives you three whole days to get here."

"Not much more than two, really, but that's fine. I just need to finish buttoning up the *Nemo* for the winter, and one more day ought to do it."

"When you see what's happening down here, you might not want to button her up too tight."

Storm hurried back to the *Nemo* and picked up the pace. Rory's advice not to button her up too tight had peaked his curiosity. Maybe whatever Rory had going on would be more exciting than a behavioral study of reef sharks.

Rory put the phone down and looked across the building to the decompression chamber. He was alone in the building, but the presence of another person was almost palpable.

Here we go again, he thought, wiping his moist palms on his pants. He walked across the building, looked through the open door of the chamber, and his heart raced. Yesterday he had deliberately closed his personal locker inside of the chamber. Now the locker door hung ajar. He didn't keep much in the locker, usually only a book to read in case he was stuck inside the chamber with a patient during a lengthy decompression. Two days ago he had gone to the locker to retrieve a book, and he had found two audiocassette tapes. The tapes had each contained a recording of a strange, watery sound. In black marker on each tape case had been written a date and a time. Yesterday he had gone to the locker again and had found an envelope containing photographs and news clippings.

Russell took a deep breath, climbed into the chamber, and opened the locker door. What he saw sent a wave of adrenaline rushing through him. Stuffed inside the locker was a bright-blue swim fin that he was sure he'd seen before. He pulled the fin out, and he shuddered when he saw its condition. Wicked-looking scratches ran parallel the entire length of the fin blade on both sides. In some places the hard rubber had been cut so deeply that light shone through. The whole thing looked as if it had been yanked out of a bear trap.

Russell turned the fin over and over, puzzling at what could have made the scratches. His only conclusion was that whatever had happened to the fin, it had been violent.

Chapter 16

Storm noticed how Rory clutched the sports bag he was carrying as if it contained the Holy Grail. He led Rory to the back deck where a table had been stocked with tea and cookies, courtesy of his mom. Rory placed the bag on the table, unzipped it, and pulled out a folder. "Here's the deal, Stormy. A few days ago things started showing up in my locker." Rory opened the folder and handed Storm three newspaper clippings. Storm glanced over them quickly. They were about the Porsche salesman, a lobster fisherman, and the most recent event about the teenager whose name had been withheld for privacy. The stories were all unfortunate, but none of them mentioned anything conclusive as to what had happened, and they could probably all be explained away without reaching too far out of the ordinary. The story about the teenager was by far the most sensational, what with the speculation about a shark attack, but the chances of such an actual event happening in local waters were statistically slim. Storm placed the clippings on the table and said, "Bad things happen to good people, but I still don't see how they concern me."

"Just wait," Rory replied. He pulled a color photo from the bag. "Simon Andrews was never found, but apparently they found his camera. If the note written on the back is correct, this is a picture he took on his last dive."

Rory handed Storm the photo. He studied it, turning it different directions, but about all he could discern for sure was that it had been taken underwater.

"What do you think?" Rory asked.

"It's out of focus."

"So it is," Rory agreed with a grim smile. "Here's something else."

Rory pulled the blue swim fin from the bag and handed it over. "This belonged to a plumber working at the island. He helped me put in the new air compressor. I didn't know him

well, but he seemed like a decent guy and a good waterman. He
went lobster diving one night and didn't come back."

"You knew him?" Storm said, not so much as a question,
but to acknowledge the personal turn the mystery had suddenly
taken.

Rory only nodded in reply.

"This thing's been through a meat grinder," Storm said,
holding the fin up and looking at the sunlight shining through
the deepest marks. He traced the scratches with his fingers.
They vaguely reminded him of the scratches on one of the
monitors. He passed it off as just a coincidence. He said, "I've
seen fins beat up, but never like this."

"What's alive that could do that?" Rory asked.

"Alive?"

"Yeah, like if it got tangled up in something's mouth."

"Are you kidding?"

"Just thinking out loud."

Storm searched his brain for a connection between the
newspaper clippings and the photograph and the scratches on
the fin, but he couldn't find one. Finally, he said, "I don't know
anything alive that could do that, in the water anyway."

"How about a great white?"

Storm shook his head. For the most part he had already
ruled out that possibility. "My gut feeling is no. The spacing
seems wrong, and great white teeth have serrations that should
leave tiny marks that I don't see here. I'd need a magnifying
glass to be sure."

"Well, if it wasn't a white, how about a black sea bass. Cap
Hanson once told me he'd bumped into one that could have
weighed a thousand pounds. He said its eye was as big as a
salad plate."

"A big black? Hmmm. I suppose that's possible. I'd have
to look at a black's mouth. Who's Cap Hanson?"

"This guy," Rory said, handing Storm a piece of paper with
a phone number and an address. "He's a commercial ab' diver,
and he's got a story you need to hear. I told him you'd meet
him Monday morning."

Storm's curiosity had been taxiing on the runway, but now

it was taking flight. He pointed to the bag. "Is there anything else in there?"

"We're just getting to the good stuff." Rory pulled out a portable tape player and a set of headphones. "The Navy doesn't have underwater listening devices at San Clemente Island, and you heard that straight from me," Rory said, holding up his right hand with his fingers crossed. He handed the earphones to Storm, who said, "You really think the fin was chewed up by something alive?"

"First, get a load of this, and then ask me again," Rory answered, and he hit "play."

Storm put on the earphones. He heard various crackling, whooshing, and snapping sounds. He looked at Rory and shrugged his shoulders. Rory let the counter on the tape player run to twenty on the dial before he shut it off.

"So, what'd you hear?"

"The only thing for sure was pistol shrimp," Storm replied. "It sounds like a castanet convention."

Rory rewound the tape to zero. He said, "This time, listen carefully when the counter hits sixteen."

This time, when the counter hit sixteen, Storm picked out a distinct sound that was somehow familiar. He rewound the tape and listened to it twice more before removing the earphones.

"Well?" Rory asked.

"It's cavitation. It's the sound of something moving through the water, or maybe something actually moving the water."

Rory nodded affirmatively.

"You know what it sounds like?" Storm continued. "It sounds like when you sneak up on a big calico bass, and you're just about to pull the trigger, and he flips that big tail of his, and he's gone. It's like that, only it sounds a lot bigger than a calico bass."

Rory popped the tape out of the machine and showed it to Storm. The tape case was marked with a date and time. Rory said, "This is exactly when that fifteen-year-old kid was taken."

Storm's curiosity was now blasting into orbit, and his behavioral study on reef sharks seemed to be ebbing away like the tide.

Rory put another tape into the machine and hit "play."

Storm put the earphones on again. He heard the same background noises as before, but then, without Rory's warning of when to expect it, he heard a distinct sound similar to the sound on the first tape. He took off the earphones.

Rory said, "That one was from the night the plumber disappeared."

Storm let out a low whistle and said, "I see what you meant when you said there's something weird going on, but here's what I want to know. Why did somebody go to a lot of trouble to get this to you?"

"I think something's being hushed up," Rory answered confidently. "When the plumber turned up missing, people on the island acted like nothing happened, and there was nothing in the papers, not one little bitty column. What if someone wants some help trying to figure out what's going on, but they need to be quiet about it? Maybe because I'm medical and out of the normal loop, they think I'm a safe contact."

Storm looked at Rory's bag and wondered if it contained a cloak and dagger. His behavioral study on reef sharks was even closer to being history. "Is there anything else?" he asked.

"There is one more thing." Rory took a folded paper out of his shirt pocket and handed it to Storm. "This was in the swim fin."

Storm unfolded the paper and read aloud the one-word message: "Jonah." He looked at Rory, who grinned without humor and said, "Weird, huh?"

"Cloak and dagger," Storm replied.

Rory said, "The question now is, what do we do?"

While Storm chewed on that one, Rory put everything back into the bag and shoved it across the table. "I'd be real happy to let you hang on to this."

Rory left, and Storm's mom helped him find a ruler and a magnifying glass, and then he shut himself up in his room. He worked nonstop until evening when his parents knocked on his door. He already knew what they wanted. He opened the door, smiling, and said, "Don't tell me. You're off to church."

"Why don't you join us?" his mom said. "It's going to be a good study. We're looking at Old Testament prophecies that have been fulfilled in the New Testament."

"Thanks, but if I went, I'd be the biggest hypocrite there."

"That's not true," his mom answered.

"You mean there'd be bigger hypocrites?"

"Of course I don't mean that, you rascal. What I mean is that no one understands everything completely. You just first have to try, and then you let your faith work on the rest."

"Mom, I am letting my faith work, and that's why I'm going to take a pass."

Late that night Storm was no closer to figuring out the mysterious scratches than when he had started. Finally, he just closed his eyes, walked his fingertips along the fin, and let his imagination run. First he imagined the fin being run over by a truck with snow tires, and then he imagined the fin being dragged through a pile of barbed wire. The one thing he didn't imagine was the fin being bitten by a great white shark.

He opened his eyes. Maybe it really was barbed wire, he reasoned. Maybe the fin had gotten tangled up in some kind of underwater-demolition training course. He finally dropped wearily into bed, knowing only that he didn't know.

The next morning, as soon as the fog had burned off, Storm grabbed his fins, mask, and snorkel and trotted down to Crescent Bay. He entered the water at the north end of the bay where the sand and cliffs met. He snorkeled straight out, following a line of underwater reefs that eventually disappeared out of sight below and left him in open water. He kicked out further until he was even with Seal Rock, and all that was below him was a green void. He hyperventilated and knifed straight down fifty feet to the base of Dead Man's Reef. There, he stood and looked up into a green gloom, the tips of his fins just touching the sand bottom, his body swaying in gentle surge. The water visibility was only thirty feet, which meant he couldn't see the surface. The loneliness he felt was something that couldn't be explained to someone who hadn't free dived in open water. Sunshine, air, and life were all somewhere above him out of sight. No one even knew he was there except God, that is, Storm told himself, if there really were a God.

Storm fought off the lonely feeling by concentrating on what his body was telling him. He still felt comfortable, and he decided he had time yet to spend on the bottom. Predictably, his thoughts drifted to Psalms, the book of the Bible that most always came to him on a deep dive.

That he would even know the name of a book of the Bible would come as a surprise to most of his friends and family. He was actually better acquainted with the Bible than many professed believers, having read the whole thing from cover to cover, and now being on his second, full read through. Far from being antagonistic to a belief in God, he was wide open to the prospect, and he had run a gauntlet from watching big-haired preachers on TV to a challenging reading of Thomas Aquinas. On the outside he avidly discouraged the well-meaning proselytizing of friends and family, but on the inside he was indeed interested in finding out for himself about God. He just wanted to find out on his own terms, in his own way, and at his own pace. He also wanted some hard, empirical data, and that data, so far in his search for truth on this particular subject, had failed to surface.

The cold and the gloom and the loneliness began to win over him, but he reasoned that if his favorite passage in Psalms were true, he wasn't really alone, and God was there with him even at the base of Dead Man's Reef.

Was it true?

He wondered.

Storm had been at the bottom for over a minute. An increasing concentration of carbon dioxide in his system suddenly hammered at sensory neurons located in the back of his brain. It was time to surface. He pushed off from the bottom and swept upward with a series of exaggerated scissor kicks and long glides. In a few seconds he passed the visibility barrier, and he saw the surface shimmering thirty feet above. Instantly, the feeling of loneliness vanished like a mirage, and he was reminded of the Bible verses he had read earlier that morning. They had spoken about having faith in something even though you couldn't always see that same something with your own eyes.

Could the scripture be saying that seeing wasn't actually believing? Storm asked himself.

That certainly wasn't a very scientific approach, he answered himself back. Yet, only a minute ago, when he had been fifty feet down while holding his breath, he had taken consolation in knowing that the surface was somewhere above him even though he couldn't see it.

The surface was now only ten feet away, giving Storm confidence to slow his ascent and finish the dive in contemplation. A deep, long, breath-hold dive was always somewhat of a spiritual experience. Maybe it was because it never failed to put him so in touch with his own mortality. One thing for sure was that as often as he had tried, he had never found the proper words to describe the feeling.

Storm hung motionless, eight feet underwater, suspended in blue-green ether, and deep in thought. Perhaps the morning's scripture was implying that the larger scope of creation was beyond human sensibilities. With that thought spinning in his head he spotted a mysterious-looking white object pulsating and wheeling through liquid space. He angled upwards and towards it to discover a jellyfish, shaped like a shallow bowl and illuminated bright white by the sun. With each swimming pulse of the bowl a fringe of tentacles lining the bowl's rim swayed simultaneously in a mesmerizing ballet. A closer examination revealed a quintet of small, brown crabs hitchhiking near the bowl's center. Storm marveled at this latest discovery until walls of a dark tunnel crept into his vision. He forgot the jellyfish, shot to the surface, and drew in great draughts of air.

It was several minutes before he had recovered enough to do anything more than just float and watch the world drift by. He'd better be more careful and not get so engrossed in the scenery, he told himself.

When he finally caught his breath, he snorkeled north towards two craggy rocks that jutted twenty feet above the surface. The two of them together constituted Seal Rock, and

Storm approached them with anticipation because of what he expected would happen next. Ten yards away from the rocks he stopped and waited on the surface, and it wasn't long before a trio of sea lions cruised up from below. Twisting and turning in their underwater flight, the sleek mammals displayed the essence of fluid movement. Storm tried to dive and swim with them, but they inevitably left him in the underwater dust. They always returned, however, and exhibited to Storm what might be described as playful behavior. He fought the temptation to attribute to them such anthropomorphic fluff, though he did allow himself a certain physical kinship with them, in as much as he and the sea lions were constructed of the same general set of organic molecules.

The minutes flew by in rapt fascination, and as much as Storm fought the idea, he finally couldn't get around it.

They were playing.

A young female rushed straight at him and snapped her jaws full of vicious-looking teeth a foot away from his face before swerving to one side and speeding off. The first time a sea lion had ever done that to Storm he had just about swallowed his snorkel, but by now it was an old trick. This time he stood his ground, and the sea lion unknowingly obliged him with the close look at her mouth that he wanted. That look convinced him a sea lion hadn't caused the mysterious marks on the fin, which meant there was nothing more for him to do now but set his course toward shore and hope he might learn something useful when he met with Cap Hanson.

Chapter 17

"The old fool!"

Twelve time zones around the world from Storm and Crescent Bay, Yi Kim hissed insults through his regulator. Thirty feet in front of Yi, with the help of Congressman Kevin Robins, Liu Xin maneuvered an anesthetized clown fish into a clear plastic bag.

Yi, Liu Xin, and Robins were scuba diving on a sheer coral drop-off named Ngemelis in the Palau Islands in the South Philippine Sea. Outside of the local native population, Palau was known mostly by adventuresome sport divers and a dwindling remnant of survivors of a bloody battle fought a generation earlier. For the Japanese, the islands had been a stepping stone to an expanding empire, but following the battle of Guadalcanal they had become a stepping stone leading back to Japan and the end of the war in the Pacific. Almost forty years later, the remains of the battle, in the form of coral-encrusted ships and planes, had become a scuba diver's dream. Liu Xin, at the invitation of Congressman Robins, had come to Palau to see and revere these artifacts of war and also to add to the "Seven Seas of Peace" aquarium in his hometown of Shanghai. Liu Xin had stated there was no more appropriate place to obtain specimens for the aquarium than the site of such bitter fighting. To that end, and with the help of Congressman Robins, he had come with his personal assistant to collect sea anemones and the colorful clown fish that lived symbiotically within the anemone's stinging tentacles.

Did the arrangement between the anemone and the clown fish exhibit Marxism or Maoism? Yi wondered cynically, as he watched Liu Xin waft another clown fish into captivity. One thing Yi was sure about was that they were wasting time here, especially his, because his agenda concerned bigger fish than the ones now swimming in the old fool's plastic bag.

Yi's agenda had sprouted two generations before he was

even born, taking root in the fertile ground plowed up by the Japanese occupation of Korea. Yi's grandfather had been active in one of the few Korean entities capable of going underground and offering organized resistance—the Christian Church. In retaliation, the Japanese had killed Yi's grandfather, but his grandmother had escaped to China while carrying Yi's mother in her womb. When Yi was born, his parents had resolved to teach him about his mixed heritage, and from the age that he had been able to reason he had been proud of the Korean blood flowing in his veins. He would sit transfixed at his grandmother's feet, listening to her tell about the church's brave resistance to the occupation. The stories had enkindled within his heart a fire of Korean nationalism. The stories had also told of a man being killed on a cross supposedly in redemption of the world. Yi had listened intently to those stories too, but mostly out of respect for his grandmother. He never told her how he thought her faith in God was a crutch that could only weaken the limbs of self-reliance, and that redemption came from being the strongest and not as a gift from heaven. What had happened to his grandfather was proof enough. For all of his grandfather's faith, the man on the cross hadn't saved him from the Japanese.

The end result was that Yi applied himself faithfully to the People's Republic of China, but his real reason for living was to see an undivided Korea with the western imperialists and their capitalistic puppets stripped of power.

But he couldn't help that happen while chasing the old fool around the world looking for fish! Yi vented silently, watching Liu Xin and Robins disappear behind a giant sea fan.

Yi bitterly recalled the day that he had taken up the sport of scuba diving. It had happened during the year he had been sent to the United States to learn English, and it pained him like a festering sore. The diving, plus his multilingual skills, had singled him out to be Liu Xin's personal aid on these meaningless trips.

Liu Xin was in the way politically and physically, and he had gone soft in Yi's eyes, looking to the West for ideas, criticizing the Party, and casting a favorable eye on growing dialogue between East and West. And Yi didn't believe that he was the only one who had seen this. He had heard questions being asked about Liu Xin's continued worth as a foreign ambassador and even about his allegiance to the Party.

The old fool was playing a dangerous game, Yi told himself knowingly. Of course, he understood why Liu Xin's worthless trips to collect fish were tolerated, even encouraged. Wherever Liu Xin unpacked his shiny, state-of-the-art scuba gear, his hosts were impressed that a citizen of backward, bamboo China could pursue such a modern and westernized sport. Liu Xin was conducting invaluable public relations damage repair for a country continually smarting over human-rights abuse allegations.

Yi swam away from the reef until he reached a blue emptiness that dropped away forever. The Ngemelis reef was thirty feet deep on one side and never-ending deep on the other. Even the diver with ice water in his veins couldn't linger for long over that drop-off without scurrying back to the safety of the mother reef.

Yi hung suspended in underwater space, gazing down into the deep blue, fighting the urge to flee back to the shallows. He thought about how a person could get lost in those depths. The easiest thing in the world was to let a vertical wall like Ngemelis suck you down deep into the surreal realm of nitrogen narcosis, where your exhaust bubbles tinkled like wind chimes, and the meaningless faces of depth gauges mocked the senses. Yi had seen it happen before. During one dive in the Philippines past two hundred feet, he had watched his fellow divers merrily lose themselves to the rapture of the deep, and only his cool head had kept them from swimming even deeper into oblivion.

Yi looked over to the reef to see Liu Xin and Robins capture yet another clown fish. He thought of the congressman's invitation to dive in America. That would be more wasted time, he raged silently. He had to free himself from the old fool once and for all. Perhaps the time had finally come to take measures he had heretofore deemed to be too drastic.

As Yi wrapped himself in thoughts even darker than the inky depths below, the thought suddenly occurred to him that he might escort Liu Xin on a deep, deep dive, perhaps at a place called San Clemente Island.

Chapter 18

Twitch.

The movement at the opposite edge of the underwater clearing tantalized her curiosity, and she was torn between her desire for a closer look and her instinct for self-preservation.

Twitch.

From a safe distance she saw it again, an eel-like wriggling among the dense ribbons of feather boa. Despite her increasing fear, she poked her head into the clearing, and then she bolted away into the cover of the kelp forest.

She was a sea lion, a *Zalophus californianus*, to be exact, the species most often seen as trained seals at Cal Ocean USA and other ocean aquariums and theme parks. A beach on San Clemente Island's ocean side had been her birthplace, and the bountiful waters around the island were now her home. A mother for the first time, she had embarked on a feeding foray this morning, and she had a pup of her own waiting for her at the rookery. For several weeks she had felt a new presence coming ever closer from out of the depths, and now it was here.

Officially, she was known as SC79-F12, given that designation three years earlier by a pinniped observation camp based on the mainland side of the island. She had been monitored from the first week after her birth, and because she had an endearing way of revolving while she swam, she had been nicknamed "Waltzing Matilda," which had naturally shortened to just "Matilda."

Twitch.

Matilda swept by closer, now farther away, slipping her muscular body in and out of the kelp stalks like a weaver's shuttle, always keeping a wary distance from the fearful presence.

Twitch.

She ventured closer than ever, cast a furtive glance, and the kelp curtain hid her again.

Twitch.

Matilda's curiosity became too great for her to resist. Like a living torpedo she streaked straight in at the mysterious movement. As she did, a cavernous maw exploded open in front of her with the sound of an underwater thunderclap. The vacuum formed by the sudden opening in the water engulfed Matilda and pulled her towards two ferocious jaws. She thrashed her flippers with every ounce of her strength to break the current's deadly grip. The giant mouth snapped shut, but Matilda was already rocketing for the surface, and she didn't slow her fear-crazed flight until she collapsed in exhaustion at the rookery.

Matilda hadn't escaped clean. Teeth, as long and sharp as ice picks, had carved wicked parallel grooves into her tail flippers, and now that she was finally at rest, pain from her wounds radiated throughout her body.

Over time, these wounds would heal, and Matilda now understood how dangerous this new island presence was and that somehow she must communicate her knowledge about it to her waiting pup.

Chapter 19

Terry drove slowly beneath a canopy of ancient sycamores. The street and the trees seemed to have aged together, presenting a surprisingly homey-looking neighborhood in the industrialized port town of San Pedro. Terry stopped a block short of Cap Hanson's house. She wanted to walk the rest of the way and have time to gather her thoughts. As she strolled, she read from a tour book, learning the city's history while absently negotiating the upheavals in the sidewalk caused by the roots of the old trees. She gave the commentary only a cursory reading, noting the main points: San Pedro, oil town, fishing town, deep-water port, originally named "Ensenada de San Andres," because it was discovered on the Catholic feast day of Saint Andrew, but the calendar was found to be wrong, and the town was renamed "Ensenada de San Pedro" for the feast day of Saint Peter.

Saint Peter?

The reading from the Bible study attacked Terry like a cat waiting to pounce. "As he was walking by the Sea of Galilee, he saw two brothers...."

Saint Andrew?

Terry's mind took the idea and ran with it.

Peter and Andrew?

Simon Peter and Andrew?

Simon Andrews?

Fisher of men?

Suddenly, Terry's left foot, instead of swinging forward to catch her next step, stubbed fast against an inch-high ridge in the sidewalk. Her body pitched forward, and only her athletic reflexes allowed her to run out of the fall and keep from falling face first on the sidewalk. She recovered her footing and caught her breath.

"You don't give up, do you?" Terry said, glaring up to the sky.

Without further incident she arrived at a modest house surrounded by a picket fence lined with abalone shells. Every shell had been cleaned and polished, bringing out swirls of magenta and turquoise and making each shell prettier than the one next to it. Terry let herself through an unlocked gate and followed a walkway past an old wooden dory overflowing with poppies. Against the dory leaned a huge, rusty anchor of the type seen anymore only on flags and tattoos. Terry paused as a folksy, familiar ambiance washed over her. It reminded her of what she felt when walking in the Ho garden. She approached the house slowly, letting each step invite her deeper into the feeling, and then she climbed wooden stairs bordered by a pair of running lights from some ancient, large vessel. She crossed a deep porch to the front door but saw nothing that looked like a doorbell button. She finally pulled an intricately woven knot of rope that served as the lanyard for a brass bell hanging by the door. The door opened to reveal a woman in her fifties, plainly dressed, but wearing a huge smile. The woman stuck out her hand and said, "Hi. You must be Terry. I'm Molly Hanson." A man appeared in the doorway behind Molly. He too, looked to be in his fifties. Molly said, "And this is my husband, Cap."

"Welcome, welcome," Cap said, shaking Terry's hand and leading her into the front room. Cap and Molly bustled around Terry as if she were a long lost relative until they were all well stocked with drinks and pastries and sitting down. All the while, Terry marveled at the surrounding decor of fascinating nautical objects. She figured there was probably an equally fascinating story connected to each one of them.

Cap returned her to her real reason for the visit by saying, "I guess what happened to me's been getting around. You're the second person in two days to come and see me about it."

"Really?" Terry asked, suddenly all ears. "And who was the other person, if you don't mind my asking?"

"Dr. Storm Hancock."

The name slammed Terry like a crashing wave. She remembered Todd Everett proudly showing her his autographed magazine. She remembered the slick on the ocean surface marking the last spot that Todd had been seen alive.

She remembered the broken face mask bobbing in the kelp. "Storm Hancock was here?" She said, struggling to keep her composure. "Did he say why?"

"He said he couldn't tell us all the details. Just that he's thinking about doing a special study, and he thought what happened to me might be important."

Important? Terry thought. Yes, it was important. Everything was important. "Did he happen to say how he found out about you?"

"Sure he did. It turns out the Navy doctor who saved my life is his old high school buddy."

Molly leaned over from her chair and placed her hand on top of Terry's left hand, a hand not wearing a ring. "Do you know Doctor Hancock, dear?"

Terry had been back aboard the *Hope*. "Excuse me?" she said absently. "I'm sorry. No, I don't know him, but I do know a little about his work."

"Oh, Honey!" Molly said passionately. "You should get to know him. He's a proper gentleman, and he's good looking to boot."

"Molly, Molly, Molly," Cap said, rolling his eyes. "You'll have to excuse my wife, Terry. She thinks she's Yenta the Matchmaker."

"Well, it's true," Molly said indignantly. "Don't listen to him, Terry. Dr. Hancock's a right fine fellow."

"Actually, I suppose I would like to meet him," Terry said, still fighting to pull herself back from the morning on the *Hope*.

"Hah!" Molly remarked triumphantly.

"Yeah, yeah, all right," Cap conceded. "Anyway, Terry, do you want to hear my tall tale?"

Terry had recovered enough to get back to the business of why she was there. "Yes, I do, and do you mind if I make a recording?"

"Him, mind?" Molly interceded. "There's nothing he likes better than spinning a good yarn. You get him and his buddies to telling sea stories, and the first liar doesn't stand a chance. Isn't that right, Cap?"

"Yeah, normally, but this story's true, and it's pretty hard to top."

"All the stories are true, Terry," Molly said with a smile, but a gravity in Molly's eyes told Terry that the stories, though enjoyable to hear now, at the time they happened were cause for a fisherman's wife to worry.

Terry removed a portable cassette recorder from her handbag, and she and Molly listened while Cap told of his wild dive that morning on the *Emerald*. He finished his story by saying, "Yeah, whatever it was, it almost got me, and I've got the souvenir to prove it." Cap lifted his shirt to show the black-and-blue marks where his ribs had been bruised.

"Wow! That is some story," Terry said after Cap had finally sat down. "What do you think it was that almost got you?"

"Maybe it was a big black sea bass. I mean a really big one. Or maybe I got tangled up with a gray whale. Sometimes they cruise through the kelp. I remember when the *Mermaid* got its hose tangled with one. They had a rough couple of minutes. One thing sure is I don't ever want to meet up with it again."

"You must have been terribly frightened," Terry said. She remembered her own fear when she had been holding her breath in the kelp forest, listening to the pounding of her heart while looking for Todd.

"I was excited. I'll say that. I try to stay all prayed up for that sort of thing, but I wasn't sure if the good Lord was going to pull me through this time."

"But we're glad he did," Molly said, and she got up, stood behind Cap's chair, and draped her arms lovingly over his shoulders.

Cap said, "What do you think it was, Terry?"

Terry struggled to maintain some semblance of scientific objectivity. Could it have been a big black? Could it have been a whale? She didn't know, so she said, "I don't even want to guess, but I am curious. What did Dr. Hancock think that it was?"

"He's like you. He didn't want to guess either."

Terry decided to go for broke. She pulled the mystery photograph from her purse and handed it to Cap. When he looked at it his eyebrows hopped upward in a double take. "This is exactly the same photo that Dr. Hancock showed me."

Terry's heart quickened. "Are you sure?"

"I'm positive."

"Do you know what it is?"

"I'll tell you exactly what I told him. I don't remember seeing this thing in the picture. My mask was gone, but I seem to remember a flash of color or something just when I was pushing off for the surface. I'm not sure if it was this thing here. You gotta' remember that I was in a big hurry to get topside."

Terry felt like she might burst out of her skin. "But Dr. Hancock had this photo. Did he say what he thought it was?"

"He didn't have a clue," Cap answered, and then he leaned forward, glanced around furtively, and whispered, "Terry, do you think there's something fishy going on?"

Terry laughed in spite of the squall roiling through her mind. It felt good to laugh.

Now it was Molly's turn to roll her eyes. "That is bad," she said in mock scolding. "Terry, can you believe this guy cracking jokes about something that cracked his ribs? Maybe it cracked his head too. Now, how about some lunch?"

Terry accepted Molly's invitation, and the next hour flew by when the front door opened and a salty looking character walked in as if he owned the place. Unbeknownst to Terry, the new arrival had just finished some overdue dental work. That, a clean shave, and a store-bought haircut had produced a rugged, but overall-handsome figure. Terry stood up and met him with an outstretched hand. "You must be the faithful Smitty."

Smitty's normally ruddy complexion flashed two shades redder with the praise of a pretty woman.

"Yeah, old Smitty's gone through some changes since that little adventure," Cap said after the introductions were finished. "In fact, I do believe he's getting religion."

"Is that true?" Terry asked, looking at Smitty.

Smitty seemed to weigh his words carefully before he

spoke. "Well, Miss Terry, that morning we almost lost Cap I was doing some mighty fierce praying. I guess my prayers were answered, so I'd better be keeping my part of the bargain."

"That's right," Cap said, "And you should see the single ladies in church. Some of them are looking at him pretty darn close."

"Ahhhhhh!" Smitty growled.

"You see? Cap's just as much a matchmaker as I am," Molly said, sending Terry a wink. "But it's true," she said gleefully, and she reached over from her chair and slapped Smitty hard on the knee.

"Ahhhhhh!" Smitty growled again, but Terry thought that he loved the attention.

An hour later, before Terry was completely out the front door, Molly pressed a piece of paper into her hand. "Honey, you get in touch with this man, and remember you're always welcome. Don't call first. Just come, and we'll put another plate on the table." Molly squeezed Terry's hand that held the note. "Bring a friend, and we'll put on two plates."

Chapter 20

Storm drove down Harbor Drive past Redondo Beach's King Harbor and pulled into Cal Ocean USA's parking lot. He was not at all sure why he was even there. Two days into a cloak-and-dagger mystery that someone was supposedly trying to keep quiet, he had received a phone call from some TV person named Terry Ho, who apparently had a copy of the photo from Simon Andrews' camera. She had asked to meet him today but not until noon, because she would spend the morning at church. As soon as he was off the phone from that strange conversation, Storm had called Rory for advice.

"Yeah, Mr. confirmed bachelor," Rory had said, laughing at him. "Go ahead and meet Terry Ho."

So, here he was, Storm groused, as he waited in an open plaza just inside the main entrance for his host to arrive. His only hope was that he wouldn't have to see an emasculated-and-caged killer whale named "Bubbles" or "Foamy" or something worse, if something worse were even possible. He passed the time by watching children run a gauntlet of water jets that fired randomly from out of a nautical-themed mosaic on the plaza floor. Had he been in a better mood, or not been about to meet someone, he would have liked to have tried that himself.

A woman carrying a clipboard walked with purpose in Storm's direction. She looked undeniably attractive, even to a confirmed bachelor. Her Cal Ocean uniform of a khaki-colored skirt and blouse modestly relayed the presence of a solid, but definitely feminine, body underneath. Her skin, a shade darker than her clothing, whispered to Storm of mystery in some exotic land. The ebony ponytail falling halfway to her waist completed a picture cut straight from a south-sea-island travel commercial.

This was not Terry Ho, Storm told himself.

"Dr. Hancock?" the woman said, walking up to Storm and

extending her hand. "I'm Terry Ho. Thank's for coming."

Storm's eyes were momentarily drawn to the small cross that Terry wore as a necklace. Centered in the V formed by her collar, glinting at the end of its delicate chain and resting against her smooth skin, the cross suggested a golden treasure cast up by the tide onto a tropical beach of dark sand. Storm's gaze shifted slightly to drink in the elegant line formed by her collarbones, and then he caught himself. Embarrassed, and hoping his ogling had been too brief to be noticed, he grasped Terry's outstretched hand and said, "My pleasure. Call me 'Storm.'"

"Have you been here before, Storm?"

"Nope. First time."

"Then you get the VIP tour."

Storm suppressed his feelings about the possible exposure to anthropomorphic fluff. "That sounds good to me," he said, trying to be positive.

Terry led the way through a spacious main gallery to a deck overlooking a large, open area laced with waterways and boardwalks. "This is our estuary," she said with obvious pride. "Here we have plant and animal communities in their natural habitat of the local intertidal environment."

Storm merely nodded in acknowledgement.

They walked along the estuary's curved boardwalks until they reached a pier jutting out into a waterway. A variety of shorebirds were visible walking and probing the shallows. As Storm and Terry watched, an egret standing on the bank darted its head downward and speared a fish with its beak.

"It really is very impressive," Storm said begrudgingly.

"Thank you," Terry said, smiling at Storm, and he felt a sudden flicker of uncomfortable excitement.

He concentrated on the birds.

"Storm, look there on the beach. Do you know that one?"

Storm searched to pick out what Terry was pointing at until he saw a small mound of feathers blending in almost perfectly with the pebbly sand. He said, "Well, it might be a killdeer, but it's kind of small. Maybe it's a young bird?"

"That is correct, and now I'm impressed," Terry said,

beaming at Storm. "It's a killdeer hatched from an egg from an abandoned nest."

"But hatching eggs in a theme park isn't any kind of long-term solution for species survival," Storm remarked.

"You're right. Ultimately, the answer is for everyone to view the beach as a wild ecosystem teeming with wildlife."

"I couldn't agree more, especially about the 'wild' part," Storm answered. He was wondering if this place wasn't so bad after all.

Terry led him through a huge, enclosed aviary and then to a small stadium. "This is where we have the mammal and bird show," she explained. "If animals can't be returned to the wild, we find a way for them to earn their keep."

"You only use animals that can't be returned to the wild?"

"That's right, and we always reinforce with the public that whatever behavior they are seeing is something the animals do naturally and that we've just worked it into a skit."

"Hmmmmm."

"We don't make the animals seem to be human, if that's what you're wondering."

Storm put on his best poker face. Not only was she physically attractive, she was amazingly perceptive.

He concentrated on the birds.

They returned to the main gallery where a tide pool touch tank had been descended upon by thirty enthusiastic fourth graders. Terry said, "This is what it's really all about."

"It certainly is," Storm agreed, "but I'm curious. I haven't seen hide nor hair of a trained killer whale. I thought that was a prerequisite for a place like this."

"We do have a killer whale, but she's not trained. Come on, and I'll show you."

From the main gallery Terry led Storm past a tunnel that led to something called the "California Bay," upstairs to a restaurant that spanned Harbor Drive like a bridge, and down the other side to an area advertised as the "Big Lagoon." They didn't stop at the Big Lagoon as Storm had expected, but instead passed through a door in a high wooden fence, behind which stood the skeleton of another grandstand that was under construction. They walked down a gently sloping tunnel illuminated by a green, shimmering light from its far end. Storm exited the tunnel and found himself eye to eye with eighteen feet of the fiercest predator in the ocean, lolling in full view against a wall of underwater windows that curved out of sight around a circular tank. As Storm looked at the killer whale, for all intents and purposes, the killer whale's eye appeared to be looking back at him.

"This won't be open to the public for at least a couple of months," Terry explained.

Storm approached closer to the nearest window, and he could see the surface rippling fifteen feet above. He turned to Terry. "How on earth did you catch her?"

"Actually, she caught us. She almost literally swam into the Big Lagoon from the ocean. It was as if she knew that we could help her. It turns out she had a fractured vertebra."

"Are you telling me that you X-rayed her?"

Terry grinned at Storm's amazement. "That's a long story in itself. The main thing is that she's going to heal up and could quite possibly be returned to the ocean."

"She probably has a name," Storm said, and he braced himself for "Foamy."

"Oh yes. She's our 'Betsy.'"

"Hmmmm."

"What's that?" Terry asked, all smiles.

"I was just thinking out loud," Storm answered carefully. With each passing moment around Terry, he found himself becoming more positive about their meeting. He could live with the name "Betsy" as long as he didn't have to say it himself. He had already ruled out killer whales as suspects for the marks on the swim fin, but he was still interested in a mouth that could swallow sea lions whole. Hoping for a look at Betsy's teeth, he moved to the window to his left and said, "OK, big gal, let's have a look at your action end."

As Storm moved, the killer whale moved with him, and instead of getting a good look at Betsy's mouth, he found himself again looking her in the eye. She seemed to be studying him. Storm chuckled and said, "No, big gal. I want to see those pearly whites of yours." He again moved left to the next window, and Betsy moved with him, again stopping with her eye even with his.

"Oooooooh kaaaay," Storm said, and he began to walk around the large circular tank. Betsy stayed with him, moving from window to window, looking him right in the eye. Storm began to jog, slowly at first, then quickly, and then he ran. For two complete circuits around the tank he ran as fast as he could, and Betsy stayed with him, all the while looking him right in the eye. Terry, meanwhile, watched the whole episode from one window.

Storm finally pulled up, huffing and puffing.

"That was fantastic!" Terry said excitedly. "She's never done that!"

"Hey, I hear about a game, and I want to play, that's all," Storm said. The words left his mouth before he had time to think about them.

But it was true. He had enjoyed running around the tank with Betsy, but that didn't mean he had to believe anything more than that.

Terry was all smiles. "Let me show you one more thing, and then let me buy you lunch." She led Storm through the tunnel to the California Bay. They entered the darkened viewing area and joined another group of fourth graders watching silently as the fluid scene flowed by in front of them. There were majestic king salmon, followed by wary striped bass, and a school of mackerel, and a great white shark.

"Oh.....my...." Storm remarked, and he plastered his face against the window along with the fourth graders. He watched enthralled as the shark cruised past him and disappeared into the far gloom. He turned to Terry. "I had heard something about this, but I didn't want to believe it until I saw it for myself. What's your fish doctor's name? Dr. Fred? Dr. Fran?"

"Dr. Frank," Terry answered, smiling. "I could arrange a meeting between you two. Now, how about trying our fast, fine, seafood cuisine?"

Storm was indeed ready to eat. They both ordered fish and chips in the fast-food Cal Ocean restaurant and carried their food trays to a table overlooking King Harbor. Storm wondered when they would talk about why he was really there.

Terry said, "Storm, we've both talked to Cap Hanson."

The French fry that Storm had just picked up fell from his fingers, spilling the little paper cup of ketchup on his tray.

Terry continued, "And we both have the photo from Simon Andrews' camera. I know you're beginning a study about something special, and my job is to see that the public gets the right information, especially if it concerns their safety." Terry paused for a moment and then said, "Did you know a young man named Todd Everett?"

An uncomfortable feeling seeped upward from the depths of Storm's memory, flirted with the idea of surfacing, but then submerged again. He answered thoughtfully, "No, I don't believe that I've ever heard that name."

"He was the teenage boy that was lost at San Clemente Island. He was literally snatched from the ocean surface right before my eyes."

Storm looked at Terry in a new light. She was exhibiting incredible composure considering what she had just told him. He said, "I'd read a little about that incident, but I hadn't heard any details."

"The day of that incident Todd showed me a magazine that you'd autographed."

The connection hit Storm like a wet mop in the face.

Terry waited while Storm sat in stunned silence. Finally she said, "There's something new and deadly in the water, Storm. I think it got Todd Everett, Simon Andrews, the lobster fisherman, and it almost got Cap Hanson."

And a plumber, Storm thought grimly to himself.

Terry dabbed her eyes with a napkin, and her voice trembled as she said, "I don't know what's going on, or how I'm going to find out, but I'm going to."

Storm avoided Terry's gaze while he mulled over his dilemma. She was obviously working on the same problem as he and Rory. Cal Ocean USA probably had the financial and technical ability to help her, and maybe him too, investigate what was happening. Also, she had revealed a passion for life that Storm appreciated, and that presented a real problem. He had only known her for a couple of hours, and he appreciated her way too much already. The last thing he needed right now was to be thrown together with an attractive young woman, especially one who happened to like fish.

But whatever was out there had gotten Todd!

Storm remembered how pleased he had been to autograph that magazine.

Finally, he looked Terry in the eye and said, "There's more."

Chapter 21

Terry stared out from the balcony of her Redondo Beach apartment and watched the sunset turn the ocean surface into a carpet of dusty rose. She had to admit, the grim focus of their meeting aside, she had enjoyed giving Storm a tour of the park. His enthusiasm had been refreshing, especially his spontaneous game with Betsy. Even more refreshing was how much respect he had shown her as a peer with similar interests and values. She also had to admit that she had found him to be rather attractive looking.

Terry was content being single, but she hadn't ruled out the possibility that something just beginning could develop into something long lasting. Despite her recent feelings of unworthiness, her objective was to remain open to whatever God placed before her. As for male friends, and perhaps even marriage, being a part of the ultimate scheme, she believed it would unfold at its proper time and place without her trying to rush things along.

Terry and Storm had talked late into the afternoon, picking apart everything they both knew about the mysterious events. They had first covered the possible explanations, and then they had covered the impossible. The only sure conclusions reached were that they had to do something, even if they weren't sure of their course, and they would pool whatever talents and resources that were available. Storm would see about getting the *Nemo*, and Terry would try to enlist the help of Cal Ocean USA. In both cases they would have to do some smooth talking, because as Sheriff Jim had stated: they had a whole lot of nothing to go on. They had also decided to meet again tomorrow night at Rory's home, hoping at that time to form more of a plan.

The glow of sunset dimmed until Terry could barely make out the dark curve of the horizon. She wondered how deep the water was ten miles out. How deep, how dark, and how lonely?

An onshore breeze picked up, causing her to shiver in the unexpected coolness.

The next morning Terry arrived at Cal Ocean USA and hurried to the California Bay to collect her thoughts. The only problem was that her thoughts weren't collecting. Try as she might to focus on the mystery of the missing divers, her thoughts kept drifting back to her visit with Storm. What she felt for him was something she hadn't felt about anybody for a long time. She wasn't exactly scared of the feeling. It was more like strapping yourself into a roller coaster that a part of you wanted to ride, but the other part of you didn't.

The California Bay didn't work its usual magic, which meant that she might as well go to her office. She managed to weave her way there without having to talk to anyone, and she attacked the pile of mail on her desk. The first letter she opened bore a Camp Pendleton return address.

Dear Terry,
    Second Platoon, "A" Company of the "Fighting Fifth" has chosen you as our inspirational mascot. We were hoping you would send us a picture. We watch "Ask About Our Ocean" every Wednesday night.
    Semper Fi
    Corporal Raul Santos
    P.S. We all got swim fins.

"Yes, Raul," Terry thought aloud, "You can have a picture, autographed even." She smiled without humor as she remembered her dad's kind words to her about how saving the marine's life had been a part of God's plan. OK, fine, she thought, but why hadn't the plan included Todd Everett? She put the letter in her "things to do" pile.

The face of Terry's student intern emerged from the other side of her office door. "Terry, I thought you were off today."

"I'm working on a special project in my spare time," she replied. That's a laugh, she thought. She didn't have any spare time.

"The chief says he wants to see you."

Terry didn't want to see the chief. "Does he know I'm

here, or can I just see him tomorrow?"

"He knows you're here, and he has that look."

"Rats! I mean, Thanks."

That look on the chief's face meant something was up, and Terry hoped whatever it was wouldn't interfere with her secret mission.

But how could it not interfere? How could anything not interfere? Terry remembered her promise to Todd Everett's parents. She wouldn't let anything get in her way. Not the chief, not Storm, not anything. She gamely tried to gather her wits during the short walk to Keith Stafford's office, but by the time she reached his office her wits had scattered to every point of the compass with no hope of retrieval. Stafford's secretary greeted Terry outside of his office door. "Rumors are flying that you're looking for some kind of new marine species," the secretary said, as if probing for confirmation.

That did it. Terry blustered past Stafford's secretary, sailed through his office door unannounced, flopped down in a chair in front of his desk, and considered herself fortunate not to have wound up on the floor. Meanwhile, the look on Stafford's face that Terry had been so worried about had blended into an even mixture of surprise, humor, and bewilderment.

"Terry, thanks for coming over so quickly," Cal Ocean's president said in a kindly tone. "Tell me. How's everything going?"

Terry fumbled over her words. "Going? Everything's going great...fine."

"I'm certainly glad to hear that. I wanted to see you, because an envelope came to me that was really supposed to go to you. I didn't realize it until I saw your name on the note inside."

Stafford handed Terry a large manila envelope. She opened it, took out a color photograph of sea lions sunning themselves, and a wave of fear rushed over her. The sea lion in the foreground was holding its tail flippers high in the air. Parallel, pink-colored lines ran the length of the flippers where the sea lion's dark skin had been peeled away to expose the flesh underneath. The wounds immediately reminded Terry of

Storm's description of the plumber's swim fin. At the bottom of the photograph a caption read, "SC79-F12-Matilda."

The startled look on Terry's face must have alerted Stafford, because he said, "Terry, you're up to something."

Terry didn't want to lie, so she didn't say anything.

Stafford pressed on. "Is it important enough that Cal Ocean should be helping you with it?"

As much as she wanted to, Terry wasn't prepared to answer the question. She said, "It could be very important, and yes, I'm going to need lots of help."

"And can you tell me about this important 'something?'"

"Not this second, but hopefully, very soon."

"Uh huh," Stafford answered. He drummed his fingers silently on his desktop and said, "And how do we help?"

"I may need some time away from the shop."

"How much time, and when?"

"I can't tell you that either."

"I see," Stafford said slowly. "You know, Terry, now's not a good time to be taking on outside projects. The volunteers are in full swing, and we have a slug of school programs starting up."

"Believe me. I know."

Stafford eased out from around his desk to stand in front of her. Terry understood that he was the proud father of two daughters close to her own age, and that he, more or less, considered her to be daughter number three. He said, "Terry, I want you to level with me. Are you all right?"

"Yes."

"Your mom and dad?"

"They're fine."

"Good. Good. Well, if anything changes, you'll tell me?"

"Right."

Terry left Stafford's office under full sail. On the way back to her office she read a handwritten note from one of the interns at the pinniped observation camp on San Clemente Island.

Terry,
  You asked for us to watch for anything unusual. The

marks on Matilda's tail fins are brand new. We've never seen
anything like them before.
 Hope this helps.
 Cathy.

Terry stopped in her tracks and leaned against a wall. Her
mind reeled as the real message of the photograph and note
sunk in. Yes, Cathy, she thought. Marks like those had been
seen before, and someone had disappeared. The awful morning
on board the *Hope* grated across Terry's memory like a
recurring nightmare. She remembered her promise to Todd's
parents. She turned around and marched back into Stafford's
office. "Chief, do you have a moment?"

"Twice in one morning I'm being blessed," Stafford
beamed in reply.

Terry closed the door behind her. "What we talk about
stays absolutely in this room?"

Stafford's smile sobered into seriousness. "Absolutely."

Storm arrived at Rory's house before Terry got there. Rory
greeted him with, "So, Mr. through-with-women, what do you
think of Terry Ho?"

"She's nice," Storm answered flatly.

"Nice?" Rory replied, and he grinned long enough that
Storm finally said, "What?"

"I know you, Stormy. If you say she's nice, what you really
mean is she's something special."

"Suddenly, everyone's a mind reader," Storm said irritably.
"Suddenly, everyone knows more about me than I do. She's
nice. Can't I say she's nice?" Storm felt foolish that he had
gotten upset so quickly.

"Sure you can," Rory replied, still grinning like a Cheshire
cat, "and that nice person is pulling up right now."

Storm didn't know how he should greet Terry. Thankfully,
the moment Terry entered the house, Rory's wife rescued him
from his plight by calling out, "There's something about San
Clemente Island on the news." Storm quickly gathered with
everyone around the television to see K-EBB's anchor woman
saying, "Recently there's been a series of bizarre diving

accidents off of our coast at San Clemente Island. Are the waters there safe? This morning we talked to scuba-diving Congressman Kevin Robins, fresh from a diving trip in Micronesia, and we asked him that very question."

Robins, dressed in a wet suit and sitting on the side rail of a small boat, now filled the TV screen. The background of hills and houses told Storm that Robins was anchored in the big kelp bed directly off of downtown Laguna Beach. Robins wore a facemask that, at the moment, was pushed up on his forehead. A tiny microphone could be seen clipped to the collar of his wetsuit.

"I always told my dive students that the best way to lose their mask was to wear it like that," Terry said cynically.

"He can afford a new one," Storm said. "Let's listen."

"Safe?" Robins said, cupping his hand over the tiny earphone tucked into his right ear. "If the island weren't safe, it wouldn't be one of my favorite places to dive."

The anchorwoman's face filled the screen. "But with the recent rash of mysterious diving accidents, will you continue to invite foreign dignitaries to scuba dive there?"

Again, the screen showed Robins, who gave a reassuring laugh and said, "Concerning those recent events, I have personally taken some proactive measures, and I am more than certain that all will be readily explained away. As for my continuing to share our fantastic, California, underwater treasure with the world, this upcoming October I have invited Mr. Liu Xin, a member of the Standing Committee of the People's Republic of China, to take a diversion from the Pacific Rim Economic Summit in San Diego and join me on an underwater excursion. Naturally, in light of safety concerns, you can believe me when I say that there's nothing down there to be afraid of."

Robins flashed a grin at the camera, pulled his mask down over his face, put his snorkel in his mouth, and tumbled backwards into the water. The picture switched back to real time and the anchorwoman. "And there you have it," she said. "According to Congressman Robins, the waters around San Clemente Island are safe and sound."

Rory turned down the TV volume and said, "Proactive measures? What the heck does that mean?"

"He jumped in the ocean wearing K-EBB's mike and earphone, if that means anything," Storm replied.

Terry doubled over laughing.

"And what's a Standing Committee, anyway?" Rory asked. "Do they stand up all the time?"

Terry, gasping for breath, managed to get out, "They're the people supposedly in charge of China when the government isn't in session."

Storm was impressed. "How do you know that?"

Terry sat up straight and wiped tears from her eyes. "Oh, that was good, and from one of my favorite people too. I know that, because I'm part Chinese, and I like to keep up on the old sod."

Rory said, "If this Liu Xin guy is coming, I bet the old sod would be real happy if something happened to him."

"Oh yes," Terry answered. "There's nothing they like better than an excuse to get mad."

"Maybe I've got some better news," Storm said. "We've got the *Nemo*. We just have to come up with the liability insurance and the supplies. Anybody got a few extra thousand dollars handy?"

"We have a sponsor," Terry said. "I told my boss, Keith Stafford, everything we're...."

"Everything?" Storm interrupted.

"It was that or nothing," Terry countered. I told him what we're doing, and he's willing to back us for a month without disclosing anything important to anyone. After that, it's put-up or shut-up time."

"One month," Rory thought out loud. "That doesn't seem like much time, considering we still don't have a plan."

"No, it's not," Terry replied, "but it's better than nothing."

"It's settled then," Storm said with finality and glad to be moving in some direction, even if it wasn't fully planned out. "I'll get the *Nemo* ready and bring her down, but I'll need a crew. Rory?"

"I've got two weeks leave, and I'm coming with you."

Storm turned toward Rory's wife. "What do you think about that?"

She answered, "We've discussed it, and it's all right, but thanks for asking."

Now Storm debated hard with himself. Should he, or shouldn't he? If he did, wasn't he just asking for trouble?

"Terry?"

"I can't leave right now."

Storm felt relief, disappointment, both, neither.

Terry said, "If I want to join you later, I have to spend the whole next week doing some heavy delegating, but I think I do know someone you should absolutely take with you."

"Really?" Storm said, surprised and curious. "And who would that be?"

"That would be Smitty."

Chapter 22

A naval gun pointed ominously at Old Henry and the *Cyclops*. The gun presented no danger, unless Old Henry somehow managed to entangle the *Cyclops'* wheelhouse with the gun's overhanging barrel. The gun, stubbornly clinging to the slanting deck of the destroyer wreck, would never fire again. The destroyer itself lay broken in two. The larger half showed above water as a length of capsized hull. The smaller half, with the gun, jutted from the water like a breaching whale. All was rust. From time to time, an abber' might board the smaller section and climb into the gun cab just for something to do, though the wreck, along with the entire island, was restricted territory and off limits to civilians for any purpose.

Old Henry didn't care much for restrictions, especially at the island, and he didn't care much to dive for abalone. He did it mainly for spite—to spite his increasing age, to spite conformity, to spite the Navy, to spite Fish and Game, and to spite anybody else trying to lay down rules for his life. He moved from cove to cove, living aboard the *Cyclops* and only leaving the island long enough to sell his abalone and to stock up on supplies at Avalon on Santa Catalina Island. He was a philosopher, a writer, and the abalone divers' spokesman in any legal matters concerning their livelihood. Swell permitting, this week he had scheduled to dive the destroyer wreck. It didn't matter to him that commercial abbing' was now officially banned. He could always find someone to sell the abs' to. If the Navy caught him, he would leave peacefully. That was the game, and he'd played it for years.

Today the swell was more than accommodating, and Old Henry had an easy time sneaking the *Cyclops* in close. Tucked in neatly behind the destroyer wreck, he figured he probably wouldn't be noticed. Even if he were, he figured the chances were pretty good that the Navy would leave him alone.

Old Henry didn't use a dive tender, but he didn't dive deep, rarely getting below thirty feet. Instead of a wet suit, he wore a dry suit. It was a baggy covering of rubber that sealed at the wrists, ankles, and neck, and it kept him warm and dry. Instead of swim fins on his feet, he wore tennis shoes. With this unconventional setup, and wearing forty pounds of lead to give him traction, he walked and hopped across the ocean bottom in a style reminiscent of an astronaut walking on the moon.

It had been a couple of weeks since that crazy incident with Cap and the *Emerald,* and the stir it had caused had completely left Old Henry's mind. He had made several uneventful dives in the area since then, and aside from some fuss he'd heard in the radio chatter about a dive class gone haywire, things were pretty much the way they'd always been. Besides, he had his own theory of what had happened. Cap had gotten tangled up with a whale. He'd seen it happen before, and it had almost happened to him once. A gray whale comes sliding through the kelp, gets a flipper or fluke wrapped around a diver's air hose, and then all hell breaks loose. The funny thing was that the diver never gets to see the whale. He just gets the living daylights beat out of him, and he darn near drowns, and he only learns about the whale afterwards when he's back on the boat. It was a rare event, and Old Henry was not worried about it happening to him.

In the brightening morning light twelve feet below the *Cyclops,* Old Henry hopped along from boulder to boulder. The rocks were thick with green and black abalone, most of which measured a few millimeters shy of the commercial mark, but he was finding enough good-sized abs' to keep the dive interesting. In an hour, two-dozen greens and blacks had swollen his net bag like Santa's sack, and he was considering ending his dive.

Using his unorthodox diving technique, Old Henry had several methods of surfacing. Usually he pulled himself up the anchor line. That was the most practical and easy way. Sometimes, if he wound up directly under the boat, he filled his lift bag with air from his regulator mouthpiece, and he let the bag float him up. He could also pull himself up the air hose if he had to. His last option was to drop his weight belt and then swim, but swimming was difficult without swim fins.

Old Henry's bag had grown heavy, and his mask had fogged from the heat of his exertion. He was contemplating his surfacing options when he came across an unusual rock formation. It was smooth and colorful but not covered with the normal overgrowth. As he peered through the fog on his faceplate at the strange mound, he couldn't recollect the likes of it before. He decided to clear his mask and take a better look. He took two steps backward, flooded his mask with sea water, and then blew it clear with air from his nose. There, that was better, he told himself, and as he puzzled on the scene before him, it slowly pieced itself together. He picked out the tail, the dorsal fin, the line of the mouth.

The eye.

Old Henry spun around and bounded away across the bottom. In his attempt at speed his little hops were more comical looking than effective. He tried to hop and fill his lift bag at the same time. A loop of his air hose snagged on a knee of rock and jerked him to a halt. He turned around to free the hose, and he saw.

It was coming.

Chapter 23

The crisp chatter of Smitty's socket wrench stood out against the stillness in the *Nemo's* main cabin. The only other sound was Rory, seated at the mess table, softly muttering to himself as he struggled to clean up the monitor that had ridden on the six-foot great white. Across the cabin from Rory, in the navigator's nook, Storm fought the urge to take a much-needed nap, closed his eyes anyway, and listened to his improbable crew go about their work. This wasn't bad, he told himself. Having Smitty on board gave him a cook and a mechanic, and with Rory he had a "doctor" doctor. Now, if he only had someone on board who knew something about electronics they could refurbish the retrieved monitors for him. Storm couldn't say why, but he had a feeling the used monitors just might come in handy. As if to emphasize that last thought, Rory's mutterings took on a new intensity.

Storm forced his eyes open just in time to see Smitty's head appear, seemingly up through the cabin floor. Smitty had been installing new sparkplugs which had originally been purchased for the *Emerald* but had been donated by Cap Hanson to the *Nemo's* twin V-eights.

"All right, Skipper," Smitty said animatedly as he clambered out from the hold. "The next time you give her the gun, you'd better hold on to your hat."

"Those sparkplugs should work," Storm said kindly, "from what I hear Cap paid for them."

"They'll work. You'll see. You'll have more giddy-up, and you'll get better gas mileage to boot."

"I won't complain if either one or both of those things happen."

Storm returned to his charts. Terry had certainly been right about taking Smitty on as part of the crew. Last night Smitty had impressed both him and Rory with his culinary ingenuity, and today he was all over the *Nemo*, checking her out from her

flying bridge to her bilge and from her bow to her swim step. If
something needed cleaning, he cleaned it. If it squeaked, he
lubricated it. Experience on the water had taught Storm that
something minor could quickly become something major, and
he was thankful for Smitty's attention to detail.

Storm traced the *Nemo's* route on the chart that overflowed
his table. He wanted to get down south as soon as possible, but
the main thing was to be sure to get there. He wondered if they
should try running at night to save time. Plenty of boats had
cracked up on this coast doing just that.

"You stupid piece of electronic slime!"

"What's that?" Storm looked up from his chart to see Rory
holding the shark monitor over his head with one hand, while
with the other hand he probed the monitor with a butter knife.

"I dropped a screw into the bowels of this thing," Rory
lamented. "And I'm going to have to blow it up to get it out."

"Ohhhh," Storm said, suppressing laughter.

Meanwhile, Smitty positioned himself to hover intently
over Rory's shoulder. Rory, still probing for the screw, now
held the monitor with both hands and had the butter knife
clinched between his teeth.

In forced seriousness, Smitty said, "I think you need to
dissociate the mammy tappers from the klinkershim rods."

A bead of sweat formed above Rory's left eyebrow and
threatened to trickle into his eye. Over the knife he said,
"Thank you. Thank you ever so much. Oh, Oh, I almost got...."

The butter knife clattered to the table and then to the floor.

"Unmitigated landfill fodder!" Rory cried, putting the
monitor down in disgust.

"Tsk, tsk. Such language," Smitty said in mock scolding.
"Skipper, you might oughta' take this lad behind the woodshed
and give him a talking to; maybe even whup' him some."

Storm grinned wide in reply. Having Rory around
reminded him of more enjoyable times. He watched in quiet
amusement as Rory and Smitty ganged up on the monitor, and
he began to wonder if he had been too involved with his work
for his own good. Maybe his mom was right. There was more
to life than sharks, and when you got down to it, who really

cared about them besides himself? His eyes strayed to the little brass plaque fastened to the wall above the table where Smitty and Rory were working. He'd come across it at an antique store and had liked it enough to tack it up. It had a nautical look to it and some words from Psalm 139.

Storm's thoughts drifted to his favorite Psalm, then to the Bible in general, a gold cross necklace, and finally to Terry and his last meeting with her at Rory's. She had been occupying his thoughts a lot lately. Too much, he told himself, and he refocused on the chart in front of him.

But why should she even concern him? he reasoned, not focusing on the chart at all. She probably had a dozen boyfriends from which she could take her pick. He was probably just one more fish on the stringer.

Still, one never knew.

Storm looked over at Smitty and Rory, and he had a sudden inspiration. He retrieved the plumber's swim fin from a storage compartment and took it to the mess table. Smitty and Rory watched as Storm turned the fin until the scratches on it lined up with the scratches on the monitor.

Smitty's eyes grew wide. "What does that mean, Skipper?"

What did it mean, indeed? Storm asked himself. Did it mean that whatever they were looking for wasn't afraid to attack a six-foot great white? He faced Smitty and Rory and answered honestly, "I don't know."

By mid-morning of the next day, Smitty announced that the *Nemo* was as ready as ever, and her crew took her out for a shakedown. A bumpy sea running from the northwest made for a good test, and in an hour of bucking and bouncing, the only problem showing itself was a radio-antenna bracket that had rattled loose. Smitty tightened the bracket, and the *Nemo* was back in port, secured and rinsed down before noon. Shortly thereafter, savory aromas wafted from the galley, causing Storm and Rory to find reasons to hang around close by. At Smitty's signal they scurried like children playing musical chairs in their enthusiasm to sit down for lunch. Smitty removed a roasting pan from the oven, and Rory remarked, "Man, oh man, that smells great. What are we having?"

"I call it 'mom's meat loaf.'"

"This is how your mom makes it?" Storm asked, ready to compare it with his own mother's favorable cooking.

"Well, not exactly," Smitty replied. "She died when I was ten. I just remember it was good, and I pretend this is how she would have made it."

Storm looked at Smitty and tried to fit in this new piece of the puzzle of what was turning out to be a most remarkable man. "I bet she was a good mom, Smitty."

"Probably so."

Storm tried to lighten the conversation. "I detect some spices in the air, maybe even a little Cajun influence. You wouldn't be a southern boy at heart, would you?"

Smitty continued to set a feast on the table while saying, "M-i...crooked-letter-crooked-letter-i...crooked-letter-rooked-letter-i...humpback-humpback-i."

Storm and Rory looked blankly at each other and then back at Smitty. "Uh, do that again?"

"Sure," Smitty answered, obviously enjoying his friends' bewilderment. He repeated the ditty twice more while he finished setting the table. Storm and Rory remained speechless, and Smitty said, "You sunny-Californy' boys don't know a southern state when it's spelled out for you in plain English? Let me do it again slowly. M...i...."

"I've got it!" Rory blurted. "It's Mississippi. Are you from Mississippi?"

"Born and bred in Biloxi," Smitty said proudly.

"And that's where you learned to cook so good?" Storm asked.

"Nope. That all happened after my mom died, and they shipped me off to my Aunt Emma's at Catalina. She was the cook for a cattle ranch on the island, and anything I learned about cooking I learned from her."

Smitty served the plates of food, which were consumed with gusto. Smitty sprang up to get everyone seconds. Meanwhile, Rory said, "Storm, you know what? I think that Terry girl has taken quite a liking to you."

"Nah."

"Yeah, really. Smitty, what do you think?"

"Oh, yeah. She's sweet on him. I seen it."

"You're both seeing things."

"She sure is pretty," Rory ventured.

"Whatever happened to those seconds?" Storm said loudly.

"Coming right up," Smitty said, taking Storm's plate. He piled the plate high with food and handed it back to Storm, but when Storm tried to take the plate from him, Smitty hung on to it, and with a Mississippi-syrup drawl, he said, "She sho' 'nuff is purdy ain't she?"

"Yeah, she's purdy. Now, gimme' that plate."

"It would be pretty if we ever got to see it!" Kevin Robins grumbled into his regulator. He gripped the anchor line and held himself easily against the gentle current as he waited impatiently for his host, the owner of the motor yacht *Write Off,* to join him in the water.

"Come on, Ramsey! Get the lead out!" Robins grumbled again. "Or, at least, try to get the lead on." Robins laughed inwardly at his unkind wit as he visualized Ramsey's struggle to buckle a weight belt around his ample girth.

Breathing through his snorkel and with his face in the water, Robins beheld a panoramic view of the Nine Fathom Reef. It was a majestic underwater pinnacle sweeping up from the depths to within fifty-four feet of the surface, hence the name given to it by the commercial abbers. On one side the reef sloped gently downward to twenty fathoms. On the other side it plummeted much deeper than the average sport diver would ever venture. The reef lay off the beaten track, showing on the charts only as an unnamed patch of shallow water. With strong currents, few abalone, and the abalone that were found being of low meat yield and wormy, the commercial abbers didn't waste their time there. The sport dive boats usually didn't visit either, because it was a long trip to the back side of San Clemente Island, and it was also just a plain spooky spot to dive. Most sports divers didn't care to jump into open water that far from shore.

The congressman and Ramsey had located the reef by

aligning the northwestern-most point of the island with Castle Rock and following that line out until the depth sounder jumped up suddenly to sixty feet. They had received those directions from a friendly dive tender on a boat called the *Emerald*. At first, they had passed the dive tender off as a rummy, but his directions had been right on. The reef was exactly where he'd said it was, and it was a beauty.

From Robins' vantage point the theme of the reef was purple, provided by the cauliflower-sized clumps of coldwater coral scattered like ornaments across the rocky substrate. An abundance of reef fish and invertebrates, plus high odds for encountering any of the large pelagic fish, added up to a spectacular diving spot. If the reef lacked anything, it was the kelp forest, but dozens of the smaller kelps thickly inhabited the reef, and the forest was just minutes away by boat.

Now that the *Write Off's* owner had finally joined Robins in the water, the two divers switched their breathing from snorkels to regulators and began their descent using the anchor line as a guide. In open water such as this a diver could suck a scuba tank dry in no time trying to swim against the current. It was better to go down the line, work the reef upstream by using handholds on the bottom, and end the dive with a leisurely drift on the surface back to the boat. That was the smart and easy way to dive, and Robins liked to do things the smart and easy way.

This truly was a beautiful place, Robins thought, breathing easily as he and his diving buddy touched down at sixty feet. He had dived Hawaii, the Caribbean, Palau, arguably some of the diving hot spots on the planet, but he believed this diving to be just as good or better. He figured what made those other places so hot was exactly that, the heat. People on a vacation wanted warm water where they wouldn't need wetsuits and weight belts.

They could have their wimpy warm water, Robins told himself as he took in the majesty around him. This was the best diving in the world.

Robins and his host first checked to see that the *Write Off's* anchor was secure, and then they explored the reef, staying between sixty and seventy feet. There was no need to go any deeper to see the best the reef had to offer. To do so would only decrease their bottom time, because their air would be used up faster, and they would have to surface earlier to avoid the bends.

Robins pulled himself along the bottom hand-over-hand and became more and more absorbed within the surrounding natural beauty. He moved carefully, mindful not to break the brittle coral clumps with his swim fins. He dismissed from his mind the recent strange events taking place in the waters around the island. He was, after all, miles away from where those events had happened.

Yes, sir, Robins told himself, he had promised that there was nothing out here to be afraid of, and here he was proving....

Robins suddenly pulled himself down hard onto the reef. The fragile coral crushed like glass beneath him, but he didn't care. He was being watched. He felt it as sure as he was breathing. The reef sloped gently away to his left. He scanned in that direction but saw nothing but blue water to infinity. He looked behind him towards Ramsey, whose bubbles were rising out of a depression in the reef twenty feet away. There was nothing unusual in that direction either. The feeling of being watched intensified, and Robins began to breathe faster. Sweat formed on his face behind his mask, and his faceplate began to fog. He looked desperately again over to Ramsey, who was yet in another hole. He considered banging his knife against his tank to signal Ramsey but then decided there wasn't time. He couldn't take the feeling of being watched for a moment longer. Whatever was down there with them, he was going to have to leave Ramsey alone with it. He let go of the bottom, put his feet down, and bent his knees for a solid push off, but then he relaxed, and his breathing immediately began to slow down.

An arm's length away, peering out of a rocky cavity the size of Robins' fist, were two small, intense eyes perched on either side of a mottled lump. Robins slowly brought his face close to the object and watched fascinated as two tentacles, each one coiled around a fragment of shell and holding it like a shield, lifted up and blocked the entrance to the cavity.

That hadn't happened, Robins told himself.

He backed away, the tentacles holding the shell fragments lowered, and Robins saw an octopus, no bigger than a large chicken egg, tucked inside the cavity. He was instantly enthralled. He had heard that the octopus was smart, some said smarter than a dog, but he had never seen anything like this. He drew his face close, and the tentacles holding the shells came up. He drew back, and the tentacles came down. A smile played across Robins' face. He would have to show this to Ramsey.

He turned towards his diving buddy, who had found yet another hole to climb into. He would have to swim over to Ramsey and lead him back to the octopus. Robins began swimming with purpose, and as he did, the proverbial call of the sea tugged hard at his heart, beckoning to him to let go of his rigid self-control and to just appreciate the ocean for itself.

Robins had heard that call many times but not so loudly of late, and he believed that he understood the basis for its hold on him. It was an inheritance from his father, a Navy Chaplain for twenty years who had started Robins on sea stories before he could even walk. Young Kevin had heard the stories, and once upon a time he had dreamed of becoming a sailor himself, that is, until that fateful day his father went to sea and never came home.

"Swept away," they'd told him, "in a typhoon while trying to save a mate in trouble."

The boy had been devastated, and with his father's death the stories and dreams had also died.

The call to Robins became fainter, and he hesitated in his swim to Ramsey. The argument arose within him that it had been the ocean, supposedly created by a loving God, but as cold-hearted as any siren that ever sang to Ulysses, that had taken his father away from him.

Robins stopped swimming. He looked across the reef to Ramsey, who had finally gotten his head out of holes, and he questioned their relationship. Was Ramsey really that much of a friend, or was he more like a useful tool? Robins decided what the answer was to that question, turned around, and swam in the opposite direction.

He would let the big sap find his own octopus.

Robins and Ramsey surfaced without difficulty, pulled anchor, and idled the *Write Off* to a shallow inlet close to the island and in line with Castle Rock. That was the other place that Robins wanted to bring Liu Xin. It was shallow, safe, full of kelp, and the things not seen at the Nine Fathom Reef could be seen there. Again, it would be miles away from where the strange events had taken place.

Robins let go the anchor, not trusting Ramsey to do it without getting his fingers caught in the chain, and he watched it hit bottom twenty feet below in clear water. After a lunch of sandwiches and beer from the *Write Off's* richly stocked galley, he and Ramsey made a leisurely dive where they didn't have to worry about the bends or being swept away by currents. They puttered around under water for the better part of an hour, and then they changed into dry clothes and cruised the *Write Off* around the point to Wilson Cove where they had made arrangements to meet with Commander Logan. To Robins' displeasure, Logan brought Officer Fishbeck from Fish and Game aboard with him. Robins poured them drinks—ginger ale for Logan, and fancy fizz-water for Fishbeck—neither beverage worth drinking in Robins' opinion, and then Logan cut to the chase, as Robins had expected he would.

"Congressman, I'm not criticizing Fishbeck. He just doesn't have squat to go on, so I can't blame him for not finding anything, but we still don't know what's happening out here. Seeing as how that's the case, I don't think it's a bright idea to expose a foreign diplomat to unnecessary danger."

"Commander, Commander," Robins cajoled, the charm seeping from his mouth like oil from a press. "Let us be frank with each other, but first, may I call you Robert?"

Logan's face took on a whole new dimension of disgust, which Robins thoroughly ignored. "Robert, I just exposed myself and my good friend here to this so-called danger."

Robins turned to Ramsey. "John, at any time today did you sense that you might be in danger?"

"Well, no Kevin, I...."

"There, you see?" Robins broke in, spreading his open palms wide for effect. "We just made two, fantastic dives, and we're still in one piece."

He placed a reassuring hand on Logan's shoulder. "Robert, Bob, I know you'll take every necessary precaution to insure Liu Xin's safety, and I'm confident that Officer Fishbeck will solve this little mystery in plenty of time. But, just to ease your mind, know that I'm in constant contact with Mr. Yi Kim, and I'm keeping him fully informed about the situation."

Logan stared at Robins as if he were from another planet. He said, "I can see there's nothing more to talk about, Fishbeck. Let's go."

With Fishbeck trailing behind him like a sad puppy, Logan left the *Write Off* without another word.

From the cockpit of the *Write Off* Robins watched Logan and Fishbeck stride away down the pier. The Commander gestured with his hands as he walked. He obviously wasn't happy.

Logan had no vision, and Fishbeck was an idiot, Robins told himself. With the end of the cold war it was Logan's job on the line and not his. As for the bumbler, Fishbeck, if he managed to stumble across something unusual, then all the better. Of course, the chance that Liu Xin could be exposed to any real danger was another matter. Then again, Robins could envision worse scenarios. He had been partly truthful when he'd said he was in contact with Yi Kim. Only yesterday, he had sent a message to Yi, explaining that there were unusual occurrences happening at the island and how unfortunate it would be if there were to be an incident involving Liu Xin.

Yi Kim, now there was an interesting fellow, Robins thought, as he pulled the *Write Off* away from the pier and shouted commands to Ramsey. He had first met Yi on a diplomatic mission to Hong Kong and had been with him again recently in the Palau Islands. Considering the short time they had been together, Robins believed he had come to know Yi quite well. He and Yi both seemed to tolerate a measured strain, short of direct confrontation, between their two countries. For himself it added up to votes, and for Yi? Well, maybe he didn't know exactly, but it was a sure thing that Yi had an agenda, maybe several, and he was holding them close to his chest. The biggest roadblock Robins saw to any close relationship with Yi was that Yi was a hothead, and those types often wound up destroying themselves and sometimes took others down with them. He would have to play Yi very carefully.

Robins jerked the *Write Off's* throttles backward, and he chuckled as Ramsey stumbled and nearly fell over the bow rail.

Chapter 24

Storm spread a chart across the mess table for Rory and Smitty to see. "Gentlemen, I suggest tomorrow we head south. I'm thinking we can make Newport Beach in three long days. The first day to Monterey, then Morro Bay, then Newport. It'd be all daytime running. I'd rather not run at night, though I am anxious to get there."

"Me too," Smitty agreed. "We gotta' figure out what tried to eat up Cap before Mr. Louie Sin gets there. You know, I read someplace they found fossilized white shark teeth on 'Clemente. They said that shark would have been fifty feet long."

"It's Liu Xin," Storm corrected, "but thank you for that comforting news. Anyway, how does that sound?"

Smitty placed a weathered hand on the chart. "Let's see, Skipper. The North Pacific high's really kicking in. That should give us some fair-to-middling weather for at least a week. We'll get some following seas in the afternoons when the northwesters blow, but that'll be all right. Still, it'd be better to round Point Conception before noon on that third day."

Smitty slid his hand down past the lower left-hand corner of the chart and continued, "There's a whale of a blow down south that's heading out towards Hawaii. It could send a hefty swell our way. It probably won't sneak past Conception and the Channel islands, but if it did, I've heard that bar at Morro Bay can get kinda' sketchy."

Smitty stepped back from the table, hooked his thumbs in his belt, and wrinkled his brow as if he were thinking hard. "Yeah, Skipper, if we leave bright and early tomorrow, I'd say three days running daylight would just about do it, Lord willing, that is."

Storm just nodded his head in silence. He'd learned soon enough not to be surprised by anything that Smitty said.

Rory grinned at Storm and added, "That all sounds good to me, Lord willing."

"Then it works for me too," Storm replied. He purposely didn't give them the satisfaction of saying, "Lord willing."

He continued by saying, "Let's get an early start, say...."

"Not too early, Skipper," Smitty interrupted. "The fog'll need some time to lift, and...."

"And Smitty needs his beauty sleep," Rory cut in, while Smitty grinned and nodded affirmatively.

"Then how about up at six and gone by seven?" Storm asked.

"That's good, Skipper," Smitty answered for himself and Rory.

That business settled, there was not much left to do for the rest of the day but to kick back and relax. The *Nemo* was already packed, fueled, and checked over. Any more supplies would wait to be loaded at Newport Beach. The afternoon was free for reading, fishing, or doing nothing. Storm just wanted to be sure to be on board at suppertime. He decided to take a walk around the docks. From the time he was a kid he had loved to walk among the boats and wonder where they had been and what stories they could tell if they could only talk. As he wandered aimlessly from dock finger to dock finger he read the boat names. He believed that the names were a window into the hearts of the boats' owners. His own boat's name, "*Nemo*," Latin for "no man," had been chosen because Storm considered himself to be a loner similar to the fictional captain in the Jules Verne classic. That is how he explained it anyway.

He strolled past the *Betty Ann* and the *Linda Lee,* and it occurred to him that many of the boat names consisted of two female names that contained a total of three syllables. He took the idea further, concluding that as you read the names you started on one note, stayed at that pitch for the second syllable, and finished a little higher in pitch on the third syllable. But if you were calling a boat on the radio you would finish on an even higher upward note. Of course, if you said the boat name more than once, the last time you would say the third syllable on a lower note.

His analysis was getting much too complicated to continue. One thing sure was that the best boat names rolled off the tongue like honey.

The foghorn on the north jetty began its plaintive wail. Storm turned a corner to follow a dock finger towards the harbor mouth, and he ticked off those particular boat names fitting his theory as they passed: *Billy Jen, Ginny Lou, Terry Lynn.*

Hmmm, Terry, he mused. Maybe he should call her to see if she had found out anything new. A sudden thrill passed through him. Yes, he would call her right now. He could use the phone at the marina office. He turned around to walk the other way, but then he stopped.

"Now, hold it right there," he told himself. That wasn't the real reason he'd be calling, and he knew it. He'd best just stick to the plan and call her tomorrow night from Monterey. He continued on his meandering course until he reached the end of the docks. He leaned against a piling and gazed out the harbor entrance. What was he supposed to be doing anyway? He didn't know what he was looking for. He didn't know where to look for whatever "it" was, and he didn't know exactly how he was going to look for it. The plan was only half baked at best, and they had a little more than a month to pull the whole thing off.

He stared at the whitecaps rolling endlessly into the harbor entrance. Perhaps their hypnotic movement would relax his mind enough for some clear thinking and maybe even some answers.

Instead, came the fog, at first just a few tongues licking the top of Bodega Head, and then came the onslaught, cold and wet, roiling over and around the Head and cutting the harbor entrance off from view. Storm chuckled without mirth. There were his answers all right, as clear as pea soup.

A small power boat materialized from out of the gray curtain and droned into the harbor. The large numbers and letters on the side of its cockpit identified it as a sea urchin boat. As a teenager, Storm had worked one summer on an urchin boat. It had been cold, unglamorous work, and the hookah gear alone had given him enough adventure to promise himself never to use hookah again, especially diving in kelp. But Cap Hanson had told him there was something down there that was even spookier than hookah. That didn't sound promising, and then there were Smitty's reassuring words about fifty-foot white sharks.

Storm felt suddenly very small and unimportant as the fog, like a huge gray mouth, swallowed up the urchin boat, and then everything else until Storm could only see the finger of dock he was standing on. He returned to the *Nemo* by the shortest possible route. When he finally spotted her through the fog he was surprised at how homey she looked. Warm light emanated from her windows, and he could see Rory seated at the mess table and Smitty bustling around the galley. Storm stood outside in the drifting wet, listening to the wail of the foghorn and puzzling as to why he had never before thought of the *Nemo* as being cozy. She was fast, seaworthy, practical, everything he wanted in a boat, but she had never been cozy, at least not up until now. It was probably just a function of the fog, his scientific mind reasoned, and he resisted the urge to think about how it might suit him to be married and settled down. He climbed aboard the *Nemo* and entered into a cabin filled with the good smells of food and the good talk of friends.

By seven the next morning the *Nemo* was under way, cruising smoothly at twenty knots over an ocean of blue-green glass. To her left, Tomales Point sloped gently to the sea. Dead ahead, the tip of Point Reyes jutted out in seeming defiance of the mighty Pacific. The foggiest, windiest point on the West Coast was unusually kind today, and Storm hoped it was a good omen for the rest of the trip. They passed the point in glorious sunshine and calm, waving to the tourists who waved back from the old lighthouse three-hundred feet above. From there they picked a line near to the coast while straightening out most of the curves, passing the Golden Gate on one of those rare mornings when it wasn't blanketed in fog. Again, they were blessed, with barely a bump when they cruised through the dreaded Potato Patch. Next, came Half Moon Bay and then the tall lighthouse at Pigeon Point. Finally, with the setting sun spilling a river of fire across the ocean surface, Monterey Bay seemed to open up her fluid arms in a welcoming embrace. Smitty had the wheel on the flying bridge. Storm said to him, "Let's try out your new sparkplugs."

Storm appreciated the way Smitty drove the *Nemo*, and he trusted him not to hurt her.

Smitty eased the throttles forward until the *Nemo* was hurtling across the bay at thirty knots. The spray from her hull captured the sun in drops of liquid gold that shot into the air like sparks. Off the bow, lights began to wink on in the old port of Monterey, creating a beckoning portrait of safe harbor. The harbor drew close, and Storm asked Smitty to slow the *Nemo* to idle, as much to be careful as to admire the moored fleet of double enders that are the signature of Monterey. The boats were patterned after *feluccas,* the sleek sailboats of the Mediterranean, except in the place of masts and lateen sails they sported outrigger poles for salmon trolling. The last few rays of sun bathed the brightly painted fishing boats, setting them ablaze with color, and as Storm and the *Nemo's* crew experienced the visual enchantment of Monterey, there was another sensation filling the air. The deeper that Smitty navigated the *Nemo* into the confines of the marina, the stronger became the smells of seafood, cotton candy, and caramel corn. Not one smell stood out, and yet they all stood out. Storm and crew breathed deeply of this aromatic concoction, and by the time the *Nemo* was tied to a pier the spell had been woven. Rory was the first to succumb, saying, "Instead of making Smitty cook tonight, why don't we eat out?"

"Yeah," Smitty agreed vigorously. "I want to try the clam chowder."

So, they did the famous Old Monterey Fisherman's Wharf. In the deepening twilight with a yellow moon rising they found the evening becoming hopelessly romantic. The only problem being that none of them had anyone to be romantic with. Rory said he wished that his wife were there. Storm wondered about Terry, and even Smitty seemed to have a faraway look in his eye. They dined on fish and chips and clam chowder, and then they walked the wharf with the rest of the tourists and revelers. Storm excused himself from Rory and Smitty to make his planned phone call to Terry. He found them again, locked in a serious discussion over whether to get the cinnamon-flavored candied apples or the ones that were covered with caramel. He said to them grim faced, "It got Old Henry."

Chapter 25

It was a somber boat that Storm woke up to the next morning. Rory was already up, nursing a cup of coffee in the galley and watching out the cabin windows at Smitty, who seemed to be aimlessly wandering the *Nemo's* decks. Storm poured himself a cup of steaming dark liquid from the pot on the stove, and he sat down at the mess table. He took a careful sip from his cup and grimaced.

"Is it too strong?" Rory asked.

"It tastes like some of the burro's in it that carried it down from the mountain."

Rory pushed a bowl of sugar across the table. "I admit it's not as good as Smitty's."

Storm scooped a full teaspoon of sugar into his cup and then tasted it. The coffee had maybe become drinkable. He looked out a forward-facing window. Smitty was on the bow, coiling the same piece of rope over and over. "Have you talked to him this morning?"

"Not much. He's taking the news about Old Henry real hard. Maybe you can find some extra things for him to do."

"I could, if he hadn't done everything already."

Storm prodded and cajoled his crew enough to get the *Nemo* underway. He figured that activity of any kind would be the best medicine for everyone, and he made sure that Smitty spent the most time at the wheel. There wasn't the usual laughter on the flying bridge. There was only the throaty singing of the *Nemo's* V-eights. Despite the glum mood on board, today's run to Morro Bay promised to be easy. They would be left with a long third day to Newport, but they could get an early run at Point Conception, as Smitty had suggested. Also, as Smitty had predicted, the northwester picked up brisk behind them, and a ground swell spawned from the giant storm off Hawaii grew all day. The *Nemo* had to slow down as she met the increasing hills of water off her starboard bow. She continued to slide over them easily in deep water, but her crew was all too aware about what these swells could become upon reaching the shallows of a sand bar.

It was late afternoon when they rounded the ancient volcanic core known as Morro Rock and stopped just outside the Morro Bay harbor mouth.

"Whoooeeee!" Rory remarked, as Smitty snuck the *Nemo* in as close as he dared to the breakers booming on the bar in front of them.

The harbor entrance was effectively closed.

Storm had been watching and counting. "During a set there's seventeen seconds between the big ones."

"I ain't liking the looks of this at all, Skipper," Smitty said.

"Should we push on to Port San Luis?" Storm asked.

"It faces south," Rory answered. "They'll be getting hammered."

"He's right, Skipper," Smitty agreed. "That place will be rougher than a cob."

"Then this is probably our best bet," Storm said. "What do you think, Smitty? Can we sneak her through?"

Smitty waited to answer as another huge wave passed beneath the *Nemo*, lifted her high, and then let her down before exploding only fifty yards in front of her bow. Smitty said carefully, "I still don't like it, Skipper. Maybe we oughta' just ease her back out into deep water until this thing settles down. We got fuel. We can idle on one engine. We could even drift if we wanted. It'd mean night watches and all, but we'd be safe."

"I'm with him," Rory said.

"Then it's unanimous," Storm said. "I say we spend the night outside. Now, what the heck is this guy doing?"

Running before the wind, parallel to the breakers, and on a course between the *Nemo* and the bar, a small sailboat had suddenly appeared. Storm had noticed the boat earlier, but had forgotten about her when he had seen the sandbar breaking. She had a reefed mainsail and jib set, one person visible in her cockpit, and she was pulling everything possible out of the stiff breeze blowing up her quarter.

"The *Marie*," Storm said quietly, reading the name written

in flowing letters on the sailboat's bow. Now there was a boat with only one female name. Maybe he'd have to rethink his initial analysis, but then he recalled that all those other names had been on fishing boats. Sailboats were obviously a different species.

The *Marie* crossed the *Nemo's* bow as another giant wave lifted both boats until they were looking down on the jetties forming the harbor entrance. The wave passed on, dropped the boats deep into a trough, and then exploded on the bar.

"He's going for it!" Smitty cried out.

Sure enough, the instant the last wave broke, the little sailboat turned hard across the wind to port, sheeted her sails in tight, and heeled over until her lee rail shipped green water. Her sole crewman, squeezing the *Marie* for every last drop of speed, leaned his body far to windward.

Automatically, Storm looked outside to assess the oncoming waves. He looked back at the *Marie*, which was flying across the water in the very essence of sailing. Again, he looked seaward.

"She'll never make it," he said with quiet finality.

The next wave bore down relentlessly, lifting the *Nemo* high before dropping her so deep into the following trough that all that could be seen of the *Marie* was her mast tip racing desperately away. The next moment, the giant wave exploded on the bar, and the *Marie's* mast tip vanished.

"Holy, jumping catfish!" Smitty cried. "Hang on!"

The *Nemo's* engines roared to life. She leapt forward like a wild beast and hurled herself across the forbidden bar. Then she shuddered from bow to stern as Smitty churned her propellers in full reverse. She came to rest in a cauldron of spume and foam. The *Marie* floated nearby, swamped and dismasted. Between the two boats Storm spotted a person swimming furiously for the *Nemo*.

Rory raced down to the aft deck, vaulted the transom rail, and stood on the swim step to await the stranger. Storm arrived at the transom rail a moment behind him. He glanced outside, and his heart sank. The rule of thumb was that in every thousand waves there would be one wave that was twice the size of the average, and the wave bearing down on them now looked like it could be that very one. "Hurry! Hurry! Hurry!" he yelled, though it was obvious the swimmer was giving it everything he had.

The rogue wave piled higher, and there was nothing more that Storm could do but watch, wait, and wish that a man could swim as fast as a Dall's porpoise. He suddenly remembered how his quiet encouragement had seemed, even if he had only imagined it, to have helped the porpoise swim so fast. He watched the wave loom ever higher.

"Come on! You can do it!" he shouted.

The monster wave feathered white at the top just as the swimmer reached the *Nemo's* stern. Rory jerked him onto the swim step and pressed both himself and the stranger hard against the transom. The wave began its curl. Storm reached over the transom rail and clutched a wad of each man's shirt. He dug his knees into the transom and yelled as loud as he could.

"Hit it, Smittyyyyy!"

The south swell now rocking Morro Bay had already been pounding Southern California beaches for hours. Congressman Kevin Robins emerged from the cockpit of a gleaming white submersible, perched himself on the side of her launch trailer, and rode there as her support crew hauled her the rest of the way out of the water. Robins was careful to present a dramatic profile just in case he might be in someone's viewfinder. Water from San Diego Bay glistened on the curves of the underwater craft, prompting Robins to run his hand along her smooth surface and coo, "You are one sexy baby."

He stepped lightly down from her trailer to the concrete launching ramp, struck another pose for good measure, and then walked around the sub, patting her affectionately as he looked her over on his post-dive inspection.

Protected from the raging swell by North Island, Robins had just logged his forty-fifth hour in the submersible. That made him her senior pilot by ten hours, though he still hadn't taken her out in open water.

But nobody had, he reminded himself, and it wasn't just him. Besides, they were still working the bugs out of her. He'd heard the rumors. He made it his business to know what was said behind other peoples' backs. How was he supposed to know he would get claustrophobia when the hatch closed over his head? He had never known the feeling before, and the craft had been specifically designed to promote a feeling of openness for her occupants. The entire top half of her body was formed of clear acrylic, and Robins had been as surprised as anyone, and had been terribly embarrassed by his unexpected ailment. His frustration at taking longer than scheduled to become proficient in her operation had only been enhanced by one other piece of scuttlebutt.

Because the sleek, underwater boat was shaped like a tuna and propelled like a tuna, it was only natural that the people closest to her had started calling her *"Charlie"* after the famous, canned tuna personality. The name had caught on, and Robins could live with it. What stuck in his craw was the other remark drifting like rotten plankton throughout the project— that crack about "Chicken of the Sea." He understood well enough that they weren't talking about canned tuna, but they were referring to him and his slow timetable about taking *Charlie* out into water other than San Diego Bay.

He'd show them "chicken" Robins thought bitterly, as he inspected *Charlie's* mechanical tail.

Actually, he'd shown them already. Through raw determination he had worked through the claustrophobia problem, and he was fully capable of taking *Charlie* on her first open-water dive. What everyone else didn't know was that a rummy dive tender's directions and Liu Xin's visit had altered his timetable. For Robins, there was a politically advantageous time to do everything, and *Charlie*, cruising majestically at the Nine Fathom Reef in front of a visiting Chinese diplomat, would play wonderfully on video. With luck he'd make the local news and maybe even the networks.

Robins inspected *Charlie's* nose and ran his fingers over the slight bulge delineating one of her two torpedo tubes.

Sheer genius, he thought in self-adulation, admiring the

direct products of his own imagination. Each tube could hold a slender torpedo that could be launched by a slug of air and then could propel itself a range of a thousand yards. To satisfy the nature lovers, an easy component replacement at the back of each tube transformed it into a sleeve that could house a mechanical arm for any number of uses.

Robins bent low to check the lower nose of *Charlie,* where resided a pair of directional thrust propellers used for backing up, hovering, and maneuvering. The propellers were housed in concave depressions that did little to mar *Charlie's* sleek lines. Robins ran his hand over the smooth lip of one of the recessions. They weren't too ugly he thought, just ugly.

Charlie's support crew signaled to Robins that *Charlie* was secure on her trailer and they were ready to shove off. Robins completed his walkabout, disgruntled that he hadn't seen his camera crew. He knew, of course, that they could be filming telephoto.

They'd better be working and for their own sake, he told himself, considering all of the hard-earned taxpayers' money they were being paid. But *Charlie* was almost dry anyway, and she photographed better wet. He gave the crew the go-ahead to haul *Charlie* back to her hangar. He cooed to her as she pulled away, "You're going to make a big splash, and I'm going to make some smart people eat their words."

Chapter 26

Bullets of spray stung the back of Smitty's neck an instant before a cataclysm of white engulfed the *Nemo*. In the teeth of such a maelstrom, the average person might have slammed the *Nemo's* throttles forward so hard that they broke, but not Smitty. He knew that even the best-tuned engine could sputter and cough when the throttles were thrown open too fast. Instead, it was with calculated cool, and with every cell of his body tuned in to the *Nemo*, that he swept her throttles forward, asking her for maximum power. In response, her engines screamed their fury, and the *Nemo* burst forth from the mountain of white water as if the ocean, having first tasted the *Nemo*, now spit her out. The *Nemo's* engines died to a whisper, and she glided to a stop and floated as serenely as a mallard in a millpond. Smitty leaped from his chair and ran aft. Water streamed from the *Nemo* in a hundred places, but miraculously, Storm, Rory, and the stranger were still onboard, wrapped like so many wet rags around the transom rail. Smitty dropped to his knees, first, to give thanks, and second, because his legs felt so weak that he didn't trust them to hold him up.

The *Nemo* had indeed survived. White water had engulfed her but not green water. That, and the fact the last person out of the cabin had dogged down the cabin door, had kept her from swamping.

"Are you hurt?" Rory asked, assessing the stranger for injuries as soon as he and Storm had helped him onto the *Nemo's* aft deck.

"I'm all right. I'm just wet," the stranger answered flatly. He looked back at what was left of the *Marie*. She had just taken her third great hit. The wind pushed her closer to the south jetty, and another large wave would reduce her to nothing more than so much flotsam.

"Do you want to try to save her?" Storm asked gently,

hoping the stranger would realize that such an attempt would almost certainly be futile and extremely dangerous.

The stranger's voice belied more sadness than any other emotion. "No. She's gone, but thank you."

A harbor patrol boat pulled alongside the *Nemo*. After it was determined there were no casualties, the *Nemo* continued on to one of the visitor docks in the harbor while the harbor patrol oversaw the final demise of the *Marie*. The *Nemo* was made secure to the dock, and her crew and guest gathered at the mess table to warm up with dry blankets and hot chocolate, compliments of Smitty. For the next few minutes several mugs were emptied and replenished without the stranger further acknowledging his rescuers' presence. He seemingly preferred instead to just stir his hot chocolate and then stare at the swirling liquid. His overall appearance placed him somewhere in his sixties. He was obviously very hale, judging from his recent swimming demonstration, but other than those two observations there seemed to be no more information forthcoming. The *Nemo's* crew exchanged questioning glances while the stranger continued to stare into his mug. Finally, Storm said, "I guess we should introduce ourselves. I'm Storm. This is Rory. He's a Navy doctor, and this is Smitty. He's really the one who saved you. You'd probably still be swimming if anybody else had been at the wheel."

The stranger raised his head at that statement, stood up to deliberately shake each of their hands, and then sat down again. "I am Chuck Von Stein. I'm very honored to meet all of you, and I thank you for your courageous assistance."

To Storm's thinking, Chuck didn't look like a man who was likely to take needless risks. He said, "You really took a chance, trying to get over the bar like that."

The older man placed both elbows on the table, held his head in his hands, and again stared into the mug of hot chocolate on the table before him. Without looking up, and with the same sadness in his voice the *Nemo's* crew had heard earlier, he said, "Gentlemen, sometimes, even to the most open and practical mind, this life just doesn't make any sense. I spent thirty years in electronics, paid my dues, saved up for my retirement, just wanting to have some good time in my remaining years with my wife."

"Marie?" Smitty asked, so tenderly as to surprise Storm.

Chuck raised his head up to look straight at Smitty. "Yes, Marie. Oh, we'd had a good life before, but now it was going to be different. We were going to get a motor home, see the 'States, visit the grandkids." Chuck stopped talking and finished off his hot chocolate. Then he rubbed his face with his hands and continued. "Two weeks after my retirement, Marie was diagnosed with a brain tumor. They couldn't operate. They couldn't radiate. They couldn't do chemo'. They couldn't do anything. A month later she was gone." Chuck paused another long moment and then said, "I guess today I just wanted to go sailing, and I really didn't care if I made it back."

Everyone in the cabin seemed to be at a loss for words. Smitty noticed Chuck's empty mug, and he bustled to make more hot chocolate, but Chuck stood up and stopped him. "No more, thank you. I've taken too much of your time already. I'd best be on my way."

The *Nemo's* crew watched their new acquaintance walk up the pier. With every step his figure seemed to stoop a little lower.

That had to be tough, Storm thought, imagining his own romantic breakups to be nothing compared to suddenly losing a spouse after a lifetime of marriage.

An hour later, the *Nemo* had been hosed down, wiped dry, and checked for damage, of which she had sustained none. Rory and Smitty had one of the shark monitors strewn across the mess table, and they debated about how to get it working again. Finding nothing else to do, Storm climbed to the flying bridge for some binocular sightseeing. On his first sweep of the harbor he spotted a familiar figure sitting alone in a dingy tied up to a mooring buoy. On the dingy was stenciled the name, *"Marie."* Storm lowered his binoculars. He didn't want to pry into Chuck's loneliness. Meanwhile, Rory's voice filtered up from the cabin below. "Look here. This striped thing-a-ma-jig looks like it's burned out."

"Yeah, and that's one of them modulating frigulators.

They're almost impossible to find."

"You just made that up."

"I reckon so."

"So, what do we do about it?"

"Deep-six the whole thing, and move to the next one."

Storm chuckled. Rory and Smitty were obviously navigating uncharted waters, but their conversation gave him an idea. He unlashed the inflatable boat from the top of the *Nemo's* cabin and lowered it over the side. He didn't break out the outboard motor but settled for oars, and in a few more moments he was stroking across the channel. Thirty feet from the *Marie's* mooring buoy he called out, "Hey, Chuck! Didn't you say you were into electronics?"

Chuck seemed to barely notice that he was being spoken to. Storm pulled up alongside the dingy, and he pressed the issue. "If you don't mind my asking, what kind of electronics?"

Chuck answered in a voice empty of emotion. "No, I don't mind. It was mostly research and development stuff, underwater acoustics and sonar. Stuff like that."

Storm could hardly believe what he was hearing. "I have to ask you something else, if I can. Did you ever work on any, let's say, sensitive projects?"

"It was all for nukes—subs. It was pretty hush, hush."

"You don't say?" Storm was liking his idea more and more. "Chuck, I have a proposition for you."

Chapter 27

Terry paced the wet planks of McDougal's Dock and checked her watch for what seemed the hundredth time. *Where were they?* An extra day had already been lost in Morro Bay while the newest team member had been gathered, and every minute the *Nemo* was overdue meant one more minute that Terry had to stew about how she would react when she saw Storm again. He was special, and the mere acknowledgement of that fact excited her, but it also perplexed her. She wasn't prepared to deal with a special relationship with any man, including Storm, at this particular time. She had to get her relationship with God put back together for starters, plus she had to fulfill a vow that she had made to Todd's parents.

Still...he was refreshingly attractive.

The fog became thicker and then turned to drizzle, as if Mother Nature was washing the last stains of a closed fishery from the docks upon which countless thousands of abalone had been unloaded. Terry turned the collar up on her coat and peered into the wet darkness. She was cold. She was wet, and she still hadn't figured out how she intended to greet Storm.

At last she heard the distant murmur of approaching engines. The sound grew steadily louder until finally a white boat materialized like a wraith from the gloom. To Terry's relief it matched Storm's description of the *Nemo*. She made the lines fast to the dock as they were handed to her, and she climbed aboard to meet the crew. "I am so sorry about Old Henry," she said, greeting Smitty first and giving him a hug as Mama Ho might have done.

"It's all right, Miss Terry. It ain't your fault."

"We'll find out what happened, Smitty."

Terry released Smitty and greeted Rory, to whom she gave what could be called a pat hug. A newcomer was next in line. Rory said, "This is Chuck, our new electronics expert."

"More in the realm of old electronics by now, I'm afraid,"

Chuck countered. "But I am extremely pleased to meet you, especially after hearing so many good things about you."

"The pleasure is all mine," Terry replied, shaking Chuck's outstretched hand and then glancing past him to Storm, who was climbing down from the flying bridge.

As Storm walked across the deck he fumbled for the right words to greet Terry. Even though he was surrounded by the rest of the *Nemo's* crew, he suddenly felt alone and self-conscious to be in the presence of the woman he had been trying not to think about for the last week. Why did she have to be so darned attractive, and not just physically? He noticed the droplets of fog glistening on her clothing. He tried to sound casual. "You look cold and wet. Did you bring your gear?"

"It's in my car," Terry answered in a tone that sounded neither hot nor cold.

So far, so bad, Storm told himself. The least he could have done was to have smiled and said "Hello, and how are you on this fine evening?" but, of course, he had mucked it all up. Oh well. Maybe it was for the best. He said, "Let's get your gear, and I'll show you your quarters where you can dry off. You'll have the whole bow cabin to yourself. It's got its own head, a locking door, the works."

They retrieved Terry's gear, and Storm led the way back into the *Nemo's* main cabin, where he and Terry were met by the entire crew.

"Yeeeeeess?" Storm said to Smitty, who seemed to be the leader of the pack.

"Tomorrow's Sunday, Skipper," Smitty said.

"True enough," Storm answered.

"And we've got a ton of stuff to do and no time to do it."

"Also true." Storm said, puzzled by Smitty's sudden penchant for stating the obvious.

"I just want to make sure I get to a church."

"I could pick you up, and you could come with me," Rory offered.

"There's a Mass in Newport at nine," Terry suggested. "How about it, Chuck, and you too, Storm?"

"I'll take a rain check," Chuck replied kindly, and now all attention focused on Storm, who suddenly felt like he was seated under a naked bulb in a bare room and being grilled on suspicion of purse snatching.

"I've got plenty to do already," he answered. "You guys go ahead without me, and I'll meet you all back here at one p.m." Storm wasn't exactly sure what he had to do tomorrow, but he was positive it would turn out to be plenty, so technically speaking he had spoken the truth.

The church issue settled, it was agreed that Rory and Storm would go to their homes, while Smitty, Chuck, and Terry would stay aboard the *Nemo*.

Rory's wife drove down and picked up Rory, and Storm readied himself to take the car that his parents had left for him earlier that day. The rest of the crew escorted him to the rail, and he climbed down to the dock but then he waited. There was no logical reason to be nervous, he told himself. The very worst thing that could happen was she'd turn down his offer, and he'd probably be better off in the long run if she did. That was it then. He had nothing to lose. Chuck and Smitty finally returned to the cabin, leaving Terry alone, standing at the rail and smiling down at Storm. Now, if he could only manage not to say something stupid.

"So, Terry, do you like fish?"

Terry laughed, and Storm glanced around for a place to hurl himself bodily off the dock and swallow seawater until he drowned.

"Do you mean to study, or to eat?" Terry answered, still laughing but now covering her mouth apologetically with both hands.

"Both. I mean, do you like to eat fish?" Storm decided it would be more productive if he first tied an anchor around his neck before hurling himself off the dock.

"Actually, I do like to study fish, but I also don't mind eating them. What did you have in mind?"

Storm's heart pounded as if he'd just swam a four-forty, and he had the sensation that a fishing bobber had somehow gotten stuck in his throat. He tried to sound casual. "If you'd like, I could spear some fish, and I have a never-fail fish recipe, and you could join me and my folks tomorrow night for dinner."

"I'd like that."

Storm's mind reeled like a drunken sailor's. He had just broken his first rule of confirmed bachelorhood by procuring himself a date. Well, he rationalized, trying to calm himself down, it wasn't a real date, because his folks would be there, and it would be more like a continuation of their first planning meeting with Rory. He said, "Then how about when I see you tomorrow back here, we firm it up?"

"That sounds good. I'll see you then." Terry gave him a little wave, and she disappeared into the cabin. Storm climbed the wet gangway from the dock to the parking lot, careful to not trip on a cleat, or anything else, and actually wind up in the water. He was a wreck, but he was an excited, happy wreck.

Chapter 28

The next morning Storm entered the water at Scotchman's Cove, a relatively untouched area of reefs and kelp beds located a few miles north of Laguna Beach. The cove was as close to a sure thing for spearing fish that Storm knew of locally. He had spear fished there for over twenty years, and more often than not he had brought something home worth cleaning.

He wore the minimum gear for hunting—wetsuit, weight belt, fish stringer, fins, mask, and snorkel. In his hands he carried his faithful *Arbalete*. It was a lightweight spear gun, powerful for its size, beat up from years of use, and irreplaceable. Three bands of surgical tubing propelled its steel shaft with the power of a ninety-pound bow, and in Storm's hands it was the ideal instrument to spear the elusive, sweet-tasting calico bass.

Storm picked his way through cobblestone shallows and then snorkeled sixty yards straight out to the main reef. There he methodically loaded the gun, giving the kelp forest time to accept his presence. When the ubiquitous senorita fish finally resumed their grazing, he hyperventilated and made his first dive. He reached the bottom easily at fifteen feet. With his left hand he pulled himself silently across the bottom. His right hand held the *Arbalete* pointed out in front of him with his index finger curled around the gun's trigger. All the while his eyes searched the kelp forest. Ninety seconds later he surfaced and repeated the process. Twenty deep breaths, hold, and dive. That was the drill he repeated silently and efficiently. Between dives he rested on the surface hidden in ribbons of *Macrocystis*, the seaweed more commonly known as "giant kelp."

For a diver like Cap Hanson using hookah, the giant kelp's flowing stalks and leaves could be a worst enemy, but in Storm's present situation they became a best friend, because they concealed him from the calico bass that he hunted.

Ironically, they also hid the calico bass from him, but that was where years of experience came in to play. The trick was to see what was actually there, because in the kelp forest the calico bass could hide right in front of a diver's eyes and not be seen until it was zooming safely away.

Storm dove halfway to the bottom and stopped. He hung motionless, staring into the forest, trying to discern the real from the shadow. From out of the kelp maze a calico bass appeared. It was at least a nine pounder, slightly to Storm's right, at his same depth, and partially hidden by kelp leaves.

Don't look at him!

Storm purposely turned his head in a different direction and tried to put the fish far from his mind. The last thing he wanted to do was telegraph signals through the water that he was on the hunt. He closed his eyes and turned, more like drifted, his body to the right until he figured his *Arbalete* was lined up with the fish.

He opened his eyes.

No fish.

Storm hadn't heard the fish bolt away, so he stared down the *Arbalete's* shaft and waited. As if by magic, the fish materialized into view, and Storm pulled the trigger, killing the fish instantly with a perfect shot through the backbone close behind the gills. As Storm slid the bass onto his stringer he promised himself to clean the fish carefully and bury whatever wasn't eaten in his mom's garden.

Ten minutes later he shot a smaller bass. It spooked at the last instant, causing his spear to hit it too high. The impaled fish dove for the bottom, getting itself, the spear, and the attached line totally tangled in the kelp. Storm followed it down, and he worked and worked all on the same breath before he could finally manhandle the entire tangled mess to the surface. For several minutes all he could do was breathe. Finally, he was recovered enough to string the fish, load the spear shaft, wrap the line, and pull back the three rubber bands. He was again ready to hunt, but now he debated. He had two good fish, and maybe it was time to call it a day. And besides, that last escapade had probably spooked every calico within a hundred yards.

As Storm floated on the surface contemplating his next move, a twelve-pound trophy bass materialized four feet directly in front of his spear with its head pointed straight towards him. The normally elusive calico bass, when presented to Storm in the head-on position, became a virtual sitting duck. Storm's right index finger tightened around the *Arbalete's* trigger, but then he carefully eased his finger away.

This one's a breeder, Storm told himself. With his right thumb he nudged the safety button forward on top of the *Arbalete,* making the gun impossible to fire. Then he slowly swam forward until the tip of his spear touched the big bass on the forehead.

"Get out of here, old timer," he thought to the fish. The trophy calico flicked its broom-shaped tail and zoomed away into the kelp, and the sound of its tail impacting the water zoomed Storm's thoughts back to his real reason for being in Southern California. Now, he was really finished fishing. He snorkeled towards shore, weaving through the surface kelp on autopilot, while his mind drifted to Simon Andrews, Cap Hanson, Todd Everett, and Old Henry. Meanwhile, debris stirred up in the shallower water by the surge had cut underwater visibility to fifteen feet. With the overhead sun reflecting off of every tiny piece of suspended debris, the immediate effect was like swimming inside of a snow globe that had just been shaken.

Storm suddenly stopped cold.

Directly in his path, partially hidden by kelp and blurred by the sun-sparkled haze, loomed the silhouette of an extremely large fish with a prominent dorsal fin.

There's nothing to fear, Storm assured himself. In these waters the great whites hung out further off shore, and he should know, because he was the expert, remember?

Neither Storm nor the big fish moved, and Storm told himself that in all his years of diving he'd never seen a great white shark at Scotchman's Cove.

The big fish now edged nearer, but became more concealed by the kelp than before, and Storm told himself that in all his years of diving he'd never known anyone, anywhere, anytime who had ever seen a great white shark at Scotchman's Cove.

The huge fish kept moving, inching close through the haze. Storm gripped the *Arbalete* with both hands and held it out in front of him as far as he could. His heart raced, and the muscles in his body tightened like giant springs. He suddenly remembered that the *Arbalete's* safety button was still pushed forward. Sweat formed behind his mask as he pulled the safety button back with his thumb. His gun was ready to fire, but then what? He envisioned the position of the big diver's knife that was attached near his hip on his weight belt. As soon as he fired the gun, he would go for the knife. If this were a great white that wanted a piece of him, he meant to give it the fight of its life.

The big fish slowly swam out of the kelp into clearer water, and Storm gasped aloud in surprise and relief. His great white shark had magically transformed itself into a huge *mola mola,* the harmless sunfish that looks like it's all head.

Some expert, Storm thought, lowering his *Arbalete* to his side.

He finished his swim to the beach, where he was now about to experience a certain, special recognition.

Considering the number of spear guns that were sold at dive shops, there weren't that many divers who could actually free-dive Laguna and come up with decent fish. As Storm walked on the hard sand near the water's edge he tried to remain detached while beach goers gawked and pointed at the two impressive fish swinging from his weight belt. The inevitable kid approached him to ask the inevitable question: "What kind of fish are those, Mister?" About then was usually when Storm began to think of himself as some kind of Tarzan. This time, however, he also wondered who might possibly be his Jane.

At the appointed time of one p.m. Storm climbed aboard the *Nemo.* "So, how was church?" he asked, figuring that he might as well broach the subject himself to get it out of the way.

"I went to Rory's church," Smitty answered. "It wasn't half

bad. You might have liked it, Skipper."

"I went spear fishing," Storm answered, trying to sound casual. "Got a couple of beauties. Saw a big *mola mola,* too. It was quite the sight." He neglected to add that he had just about swallowed his snorkel at the time.

"All nature declares the glory of God," Terry said, smiling.

Storm smiled back and nodded while he considered her statement. She had said something that, if true, validated the essence of creation itself, and he wondered if she had ever probed beyond the surface of those words. "It's not impossible that you're right," he replied. "So, you see, Smitty. I did go to church. It's just a different kind of church."

"Yeah, sure it is, Skipper, but the Good Book ain't wrong, and it says to remember the fellowship, or something like that anyway."

"Something like that," Storm replied in a voice that said he didn't want to offend, but now it was time to change the subject. He made a show of looking at the electrical equipment strewn across the mess table. Chuck had enthusiastically accepted Storm's proposition, and he had collected underwater microphones, tape recorders, speakers, an oscilloscope, and cords to connect the whole lot. Storm said, "It looks like you've wired us for sound."

"This might be a way for us to find out something. Maybe not, but maybe," Chuck replied. "I'll ask you all a question. Given the limited information we have, what's the one thing that might be considered a constant?"

"You mean besides the fact we don't know what we're doing?" Rory asked.

"Hopefully, we're doing a little better than that," Chuck countered. He continued, saying, "We have a sound. We have two recordings provided by Rory's secret source, our mole, as it were. I've made a new tape of them and edited it so the two special sounds on them play over and over. I'm going to play that tape right now, and while I do, you all watch the oscilloscope." Chuck played the tape; the sounds came over the speakers, and the oscilloscope screen flashed obediently. Chuck stopped the tape and said, "So, what can you tell me about the two sounds?"

"They sound pretty much the same, and they look pretty much the same, if you ask me," Terry said.

"And I'd say you're right," Chuck answered. "The two sounds are very similar, which means if the same thing made both of these sounds, especially at different times, then whatever that thing is, it has a signature. Let me show you something else." Chuck removed the cassette from the recorder and replaced it with another one. "This tape has different sounds that I've numbered one through five. It'll play all five over and over, always in the same order and starting with number one. Watch the screen and tell me which one of them you think is our sound." Chuck played the tape. The screen flashed accordingly, matching with the sounds in sequence. Three of the sounds were obviously not the right one, and the other two were a toss up. Chuck stopped the tape. "Well?" he asked.

Storm, Rory, and Terry chose sound number two, and Smitty chose sound number five.

Chuck said, "It's number two. That's the signature sound, and most of you picked it right out."

"What's number five, then?" Smitty asked indignantly.

"That was a toilet plunger, but it's very similar."

"Ahhhhhh!"

Chuck reached into his pants pocket and pulled out some change. "Here's the *Nemo*," he said, placing a quarter at the table's center, "And here are three inflatable rafts." He positioned three pennies equidistant from the quarter. "We set up three stations with underwater microphones...."

"We triangulate," Terry cut in.

"Essentially, yes. There's really nothing to it."

"Hold on a second!" Smitty said in a voice crowded with concern. "We're supposed to sit in an open raft in the hot sun all day and listen for a noise that lasts only a second, and maybe we can't tell what it is anyway? What happens if we sneeze, or if we have to use the head?"

Good old Smitty, Storm thought. Cutting right to the bottom line.

"We don't have to do that," Chuck explained. "We just set things up and then listen from the *Nemo*. We calibrate the recorders to respond only to the target sound frequency that we want and nothing else. When, and if, they do record something, we compare the signal strength, direction, and time. It won't be precise, what with the short distances and thermoclines and all, but it should be good enough."

"But how can you record something after it's happened?" Rory asked. "I mean, as soon as the recorders know they should record, the sound will be over."

"It's called digital memory. The main recorder will be on a five-second delay."

"You can do this?" Storm asked, both impressed and astounded.

"I think so. Get us a couple more rubber boats, and give me a day or two to round up the rest."

"How much is all this going to cost?" Terry asked.

"Maybe not much if we don't lose it or break it. I know a few useful people in this county."

Storm had seen and heard enough. "It all sounds good to me, especially since I haven't heard a better plan. What do you guys think?"

"I think we have nothing to lose," Rory replied.

"I agree," Terry added.

Smitty, meanwhile, appeared to be in deep thought.

"Is there still a problem, Smitty?" Storm asked.

"There sure is, Skipper. Now that I've seen how smart Chuck is with his fancy electrics, I'm wondering if we might surprise ourselves and really find something. If this thing's as bad as Cap thinks it is, that thought kinda' gets my skin crawling."

Chapter 29

But go your way, tell his disciples and Peter
that he goeth before you into Galilee....
(Mark 16:7)

Sometimes a plan turns out so well that a reversal of fortune seems inevitable, if for no other reason than to balance the universe. Such were Storm's thoughts during the dinner at his parents' house. His never-fail fish recipe had been an obvious hit with Terry, and she was making an obvious hit with his parents. If anything, they were enjoying her company even more than he was. Thankfully, his mom was on her best behavior and hadn't mentioned anything about mermaids or marriage.

Dessert followed dinner, and then Storm invited Terry to the back deck. The land had cooled, and the warmer ocean pulled at the air, sending a soft offshore breeze through the night. Storm purposely left the deck lights off, and with no marine layer to reflect the lights of Laguna Beach the deck remained dark. He was alone with Terry, but he was also hopelessly lost for words, so he remained silent and pretended to be absorbed in the tranquility of the evening.

That was partly true, he reasoned. He did enjoy the quiet of the night, but he dearly wished he possessed a better gift for small talk. Thank goodness Terry saved the rest of the evening by saying, "Chuck is going to need most of the day tomorrow. Smitty's in charge of food. Rory's getting the extra inflatables. I say we go to Leucadia, and you can taste some of Mama Ho's Natural Store fixings for lunch."

Storm was thankful that in the dark Terry couldn't see him take a deep breath before answering, "I'd like that. I'd like that very much."

"Good. Then it's a date, but if I'm going to be any kind of company I need to turn in early, so I should be getting back to the *Nemo*."

Instantly, the deck lights blazed on, and Storm's mom trotted out carrying a tray of coffee and cookies. "Nonsense, my dear," she said. "You're staying right here in our guest room. That way you can get an early start in the morning. You'll have your own private entrance, your own bathroom, the works. Come along now, and we'll get you some towels and things." She whisked Terry away and soon returned to find Storm sipping a cup of coffee and obviously waiting for her. He was not smiling.

"Mom, I can't believe you were snooping on us!"

"Snooping?" Don't be silly. I was merely coming out to see if you two wanted some coffee. How was I to know she was asking you on a date?"

"Well, even if you weren't snooping, your timing was suspiciously incredible."

"Mom's are like that, especially when they have grown sons who are looking for mermaids to marry."

The next morning, Terry and Storm checked in with the *Nemo* through the marine operator and were soon on their way south in Terry's station wagon. Halfway through Camp Pendleton, Terry pulled into a rest stop situated on a high bluff overlooking the ocean. They got out of the car and stood close to each other, looking seaward. The view to the horizon was unobstructed, and across the watery expanse Terry picked out a blue-gray streak that might have been the low profile of San Clemente Island, or it might have been only a fog bank. Either way, the sight took her back to that terrible morning on board the *Hope*.

"I've been scared in the ocean before," Terry said, "Like when I'm about to eat a really big wave, or when I'm wrapped up in kelp and low on air, but I've never had this weird fear I'm feeling right now. It's like some dark spirit that's been asleep for a long time has suddenly awakened." She shivered bodily and added, "This whole thing's giving me the creeps."

"If I take the wings of morning, and dwell in the uttermost parts of the sea; even there shall thy hand lead me, and thy right hand shall hold me," Storm said, still looking out to the horizon.

"That's from Psalms," Terry said, surprised. She took a step backward and faced him.

He turned towards her. "It's from Psalm 139 to be exact. Whenever I get scared in the water, I find those lines very comforting, that is, if I remember them in time."

"I was somehow under the impression that you didn't believe in God."

"I'm not sure what I believe about God, but I do appreciate the Psalms."

"Todd Everett's parents told me that Psalm 139 was one of his favorite Bible passages."

At the mention of Todd's name, Storm turned and stared out to sea again. He finally said, "I wish I'd met him."

They resumed their drive in silence. Terry struggled to find a way to bring up the subject of God again without seeming to be pushy. Storm beat her to it by saying, "Would you like to hear about Hancock's Paradox?"

"Hancock's Paradox? That sounds illuminating. Yes, I would very much like to hear about it."

"Ok, but if it doesn't make sense to you, don't feel bad. This illumination came to me one day in the shower, so it could be all wet. It goes like this. My human logic tells me that we can't exist, and yet, here we are."

A mile went by in silence as Storm seemed to be waiting for a response.

"That's it?" Terry finally said. "I guess I was expecting something a little more profound, or at least longer."

"Actually, it's packed with profundity if you take the time to think about it."

Terry just wanted the conversation to continue. "Maybe you could elaborate just a wee bit?"

"Sure I could. For starters we'll assume that we live in a cause-and-effect universe. Can we do that?"

"Yeeeeeess," Terry answered tentatively.

"Good. Following that assumption, if we could look back far enough we would have to find a very first cause, which in a cause-and-effect universe can't possibly exist. Therefore, without a first cause to start the whole thing rolling, what should exist is nothing, which in itself is a paradox. Are you still with me?"

"Uh, maybe, but keep going."

"Ok, take your best concept of a complete void, and then erase even that. What's left is what should be, or better put, what shouldn't be. There should be dimensionless, unfathomable emptiness. You just can't get something from nothing, and even God, by those terms, shouldn't exist."

"So how do you explain that we're here in my car driving to Leucadia?"

"The answer is simple, impossible, and also completely logical."

"I think you're going to simply and completely lose me."

"No, I think you'll like this part. Logically speaking, in a cause-and-effect universe, beings that are impossibly created from non-creation are necessarily dependent upon an uncreated being as a first cause."

"Hah!" Terry said, grinning. "Whatever it was you just said, you admitted it's possible for God to exist."

"It's more than possible. It's a logical probability. An uncreated entity that possesses the ability to create is the only logical explanation for the existence of anything. At least, that's how I see it in this universe."

"But if you believe that, why don't you believe in God?"

"Again, the paradox. There's just no way to prove God's logically necessary existence to my own intellectual satisfaction. I suppose I could pretend to believe, and maybe if I told myself enough times, I might almost talk myself into it, but in my heart of hearts I'd be a hypocrite. My problem is that if I say I'm a believer, then I want to mean it."

Terry groped for the right words. "You have to seek God to find him."

"Yeah, I can agree with that. I'd just like to see a little miracle or something."

"But didn't you just tell me that all creation is a miracle?"

"No, I said that all creation is illogical. It might well be a miracle too, but even if it is, it's a miracle that we're completely used to. I'd just like to see something a little beyond the normal human experience."

"I think God would like you to believe in him without him having to put on a show." As soon as Terry said those words she wanted to take them back. She glanced over at Storm, who was looking none too pleased, and she realized that she had just projected some of her own frustration onto him. She had goofed it up again. Here the conversation had been going along swimmingly, and she'd just thrown a dead fish into the pool. She said silently to heaven, "You see, Lord? I mess up every time."

"Why don't you let me help you?"

Terry stole a glance at Storm, who was looking out the side window. He hadn't said anything. Then what had she just heard? Or had she really heard anything? It was similar to when she had been at Trestles and had paddled out one more time and saved the Marine. Someone seemed to have talked to her then too. Whatever had happened, the question remained the same, and she didn't know the answer. Why didn't she let God help her? Maybe it was because her relationship with God had changed. The consuming fire that she had first known was now more like a smoldering wick. Since taking the job at Cal Ocean USA her prayer life had sunk into the abyss. She used to share her entire waking day in conversation with God, but now, besides an occasional thanks for a good wave, she was doing well to say her bedtime prayers. She drove on in silence, unhappy at how pale her light seemed to shine when compared with giants in the faith like St. Clement, and St. Andrew, and St. Peter, and so many others who had been persecuted and had even given their lives for preaching the gospel.

So unlike her.

"Help me, Lord," Terry inadvertently said in what sounded like a loud sigh.

"That was a heavy one," Storm said gently. "A penny for your thoughts?"

"I was just thinking about God, and faith, and St. Clement, and Andrew, and Peter.

"And Peter?"

"Yeah, him."

"Now, those are two words in the Bible that show the real heart of the man, Jesus."

"What two words?"

"And Peter."

Terry had no idea where this was going, but she wondered if her prayer had been answered. "How do they do that?"

"You know the story. Peter denies Jesus three times; Jesus is crucified, and poor old Peter is feeling like dirt. Three days later, a woman runs in hollering that Jesus is alive, and now Peter is feeling even worse than dirt, but here comes the good part. The woman goes up to Peter and tells him that an angel told her to tell the disciples, and him, singled out special by name, that everything's going to be fine. I imagine that Peter suddenly felt a whole lot better, and I just think that's cool."

Terry was flabbergasted. She had never noticed that particular detail as much as she had read the Bible. If Jesus could still love Peter, then he could surely love her in spite of her failures. And it took a nonbeliever like Storm to show her.

The big "Ho's Natural Store" sign came into view. As Terry pulled the car into the parking lot she heard Storm remark wistfully, seemingly almost to himself, "If only I could see an angel or something."

Terry spun in her seat. "How about talking to someone who maybe saw an angel?"

"That would depend on who I was talking to."

"Cap Hanson."

"I'd talk to him."

"All right!" Terry said exuberantly, and she prayed silently, "And, thank you!"

Terry led Storm into the store where Mama Ho immediately stopped whatever she was doing behind the counter and stepped out to greet them. Mama Ho hugged Terry and then stood back in apparent appraisal of Storm. "And is this handsome gentleman the new friend you mentioned?" she said, and Storm's face turned as red as a strawberry sea anemone.

"He sure is," Terry answered, not at all surprised by Mama

Ho's frankness. "Mama, meet Dr. Storm Hancock. Storm, meet Mama Ho."

"Dr. Hancock," Mama Ho said, ignoring Storm's outstretched hand and giving him a hug that almost lifted him from the floor. Storm gave a wide-eyed look to Terry who was obviously thoroughly enjoying herself.

"What a pleasure," Mama Ho said, finally letting go of Storm. "Come, sit down, and I'll get you something refreshing."

"Papaya smoothies," Terry whispered to Storm, as Mama Ho led them to a window table that looked out onto the garden. Mama Ho then called out the back door, "Tommy, someone special is here."

As predicted, Mama Ho soon placed two of the frosty drinks on the table. An Asian man wearing a straw hat entered the store. Storm stood up so quickly that he banged his knee on the table and almost spilled the smoothies. He shook hands with Tommy Ho and waited to sit until both of Terry's parents were seated.

Tommy Ho said, "Dr. Hancock, exactly what kind of doctor are you?"

"Well, for starters I'm not a 'doctor' doctor. I'm...."

"Papa, he's a specialist in tagging and monitoring great white sharks," Terry broke in, "and he's come to help Cal Ocean figure out what's happening at San Clemente Island."

Storm looked at Terry with astonishment plastered on his face. Tommy Ho asked, "Is it your opinion that the divers were taken by a white shark?"

"Not at all, and please, call me 'Storm.' We don't know what happened to the divers, but I'm fairly certain it has nothing to do with great whites."

Mama Ho said, "But it must have been an awfully big animal that killed Todd Everett."

Storm's grim face was answer enough, but he said flatly, "Yeah, it was an awfully big something."

"Then we'd better pray about it," Mama ho said. She reached out to Storm, who linked his hand with hers on his right and with Terry's hand on his left. Mama Ho closed her eyes and said, "Our Father in heaven, creator of all living things in the sea, please protect Storm and Terry and anyone else helping them as they seek to unravel these mysterious events, and we pray that whatever happens, it will be for your glory and honor. Amen."

Terry opened her eyes and wondered if Storm had experienced the same thrill she had just felt when she held his hand. She wasn't about to ask him, but she sure wondered.

Mama Ho said, "Why don't you two go down to the beach, and when you get back we'll have a real lunch."

Terry searched the house and found a pair of swim trunks that would fit Storm. They changed clothes, and then Storm seemed surprised when Terry asked, "What size duck feet do you wear?"

"Uh, extra large. Are we going snorkeling?"

"Nope, just swimming." Terry produced two sets of the blue fins, and then they drove the half mile to Moonlight Beach. The water beckoned, and they ran to meet it, putting their fins on at the water's edge and plunging through the surf. They were sculling in water deep enough that their fins barely touched the bottom when the first set of ridable waves rolled through.

"Going left!" Storm called out.

In classic bodysurfing form, with his arms and upper body forming an inverted cross, Storm sliced gracefully down the wave's face. Meanwhile, Terry carved her own white streak down the face in synchronization with him. They cut back through the bottom of the wave as it broke, and they surfaced together.

"Terry, you can bodysurf!" Storm exclaimed.

"You'd better believe it!" she answered, and for the next twenty minutes beachgoers were treated to a ballet of falling water and human forms as Terry and Storm caught wave after wave. They rode one last wave in, dried off, and returned to Ho's Natural Store where Mama Ho had prepared lunch.

"This is as good as Mom's cooking," Storm said, having cleaned his plate of the repast placed before him. "Mama Ho, you shouldn't have gone to the trouble."

"Trouble?" Mama Ho answered. She got up, swept his lunch plate away, and took from a nearby table a small plate with a piece of what looked to be home-made apple pie. She said, "I should always be blessed with this kind of trouble. Any friend of our Kanani is a friend of mine."

"Kanani?" Storm asked.

Mama Ho handed the plate with the apple pie to Storm. As he reached to take it, she said, "Terry's middle name. It means 'pretty one.'"

Storm's face took on a glazed look.

"Don't you like apple pie?" Mama Ho asked.

"Oh, yes, very much," Storm answered, recovering. "I just had a major case of *déjà vu.*"

After lunch, Terry led Storm on a walk through the garden. The only sounds were the crunch of their feet on the gravel paths and the singing of birds. The surrounding trees and plants seemed to absorb the noise from the road. Storm said, "There's a feeling of peace here that's hard to describe."

"It's a harmony of earth and spirit," Terry replied. "In Hawaii we call it *'lokahi.'*"

"And how does your Christian God fit in? Is he a part of *lokahi?*"

Terry prayed for wisdom. "Rather, *lokahi* comes from God."

"Hmmm. And what becomes of *lokahi* when things go terribly wrong, such as when mysterious diving accidents happen?"

"In times like that, we have to remember that everything that comes to us must first pass through the hands of our loving Father in heaven. Only then can we truly know *lokahi.*"

Had that been her talking? Terry asked herself. It certainly hadn't sounded like her. She wondered what Storm would think.

"We probably ought to be heading back to Laguna," Storm said.

Driving them north, Terry pondered her growing relationship with Storm. She liked him. She could see herself liking him even more, and she wondered if his not being a

Christian could pose a problem.

Chapter 30

Storm walked around the *Nemo* one last time and tried to stay positive. A tidy boat was a safe boat, but now the *Nemo* was loaded with two more inflatable rafts, a gasoline-powered air compressor, two-hundred pounds of electronic equipment, three sets of dive gear, extra air tanks, a battery-powered dive scooter, and enough food and supplies to last five people for two weeks. As hard as Smitty had struggled to find a spot to fit everything, the *Nemo* felt more like a salvage barge than the sleek research vessel Storm had put together.

There was probably nothing that could be done about it, Storm figured. He gave the command to let go the lines, and the *Nemo* pulled away from McDougal's Dock. Smitty soon joined him on the flying bridge.

"This is fine weather, Skipper," Smitty said, grinning at the marine layer that stretched unabated to the horizon.

"It looks a little gloomy to me."

"We abbers have a saying: 'If you can see Catalina from here, don't go.' If you do go, you're probably going to get slammed mid-channel by a northwester."

As usual, Storm was impressed by Smitty's copious supply of seafaring knowledge. He said, "Listen, Smitty, I have a special assignment for you. I want you to show Terry how the *Nemo* works."

"Me, Skipper? Don't you want to do that?"

"No, you're the best man for the job. You don't have to teach her how to dismantle the engines, but show her how to drive the boat, and anything else you think she might need to know."

"That shouldn't be too hard. You know, Skipper, when I first signed on with this outfit I had my doubts. I ain't never been on a boat where so many people had so much book learning, but I'm telling you right now you've got a top-drawer crew here."

"So, you're feeling a little better about the whole thing?"

"Sure, if you don't count that I'm as freaked out as a fly at a frog farm about meeting some fifty-foot, pre-hysterical shark."

In two hours the *Nemo* rounded the southeast tip of Catalina Island and its main town of Avalon. San Clemente Island loomed ahead, and Storm stood alone on the bow watching the island grow larger. A lingering cloud cover shrouded the island's mountain tops with a somberness that intensified Storm's misgivings of not knowing what he was doing.

But at least he was doing something.

He looked aft to see Terry at the wheel with Smitty sitting beside her. Smitty was right. Storm did have a good crew, and for that he was thankful, because he wanted to solve this mystery. He wanted to solve it for science, for his own curiosity, and for Todd Everett's family.

Two more hours and the *Nemo* was idling slowly past the northwest tip of San Clemente Island. Smitty eased her inside of Castle Rock and into West Cove—the first anchorage on the island's backside, and where the *Nemo* was planned to be anchored each night. Shortly thereafter, Terry experienced her first real sampling of Smitty's mess, featuring croissant tuna sandwiches with fresh fruit on the side smothered in a frozen banana-mango puree.

"Don't always expect this, Miss Terry," Smitty said, beaming, as Terry cleaned the last crumb from her plate. "When supplies run low I start serving weevily hardtack and coffee made from bilge water."

"Expect this most of the time," Chuck countered, his own plate licked clean.

Terry said, "Smitty, you must have been the best cook in the abalone fleet."

"Maybe so. That's probably why Cap's put up with me for this long."

"Oh, I'm sure there's more to it than that."

"You're right. It was more likely because of my good looks."

"I wouldn't sell myself short in that department either," Terry answered. "In fact, one day you're going to make some lucky woman a fine catch."

Smitty's face turned red as a cooked lobster. "I'd better get this galley cleaned up," he muttered, and he turned his attention to a cluttered sink. Terry scooted herself out from behind the mess table and headed outside, pausing momentarily to watch Smitty furiously wash dishes. "A fine catch," she said, and she pinched Smitty playfully on the cheek and scampered out of the cabin.

"Ahhhhhh!"

Lunch was cleaned up; the anchor was hauled in, and Storm eased the *Nemo* southward following the outside edge of the kelp. When the destroyer wreck became close, he nosed the *Nemo* into the floating tops of the kelp, shut off her engines, and let her coast to a stop.

"We're already a little into the restricted area, so this is as far south as we better go," he said quietly to the *Nemo's* crew, who were gathered with him on the flying bridge. Storm observed Terry carefully. She seemed to be holding up well considering what had happened the last time she had been here. "Is this close to where it happened?" he asked gently.

Terry nodded her head but said nothing.

There was no other boat in sight. There was no Navy activity, and there wouldn't be any abbers, legally anyway. The only sound was a slithering hiss whenever a swell rolled through the surface kelp. A hundred yards away, small waves broke silently against a pebbly beach, as if they too were fearful of disturbing the eerie stillness.

"Anyone for a swim?" Chuck's voice grated rudely into the quiet.

"That's not very funny," Terry answered.

"And that goes double for me," Smitty added. "In fact, I think I left the oven on at Cap's house. Maybe we should just motor back to San Pedro to make sure."

Instead, they motored back to West Cove, anchored, and went over their plan of action. Tomorrow they would begin listening from a triangle of positions, and for the next twelve days they would leapfrog in quarter-mile jumps up the shoreline. By then they would have covered the area north of the restricted zone. If they hadn't found anything, they would make a run to Catalina to stock up on supplies. Hopefully, the temporary restriction would soon be lifted, and they could work in the area where they most expected to find something. If the restriction wasn't lifted, they were determined to somehow work the area anyway.

That evening, Smitty served his Mom's meat loaf, sweet corn on the cob, and mashed potatoes and gravy. When the hot peach pie with vanilla ice cream came out, Chuck said, "What are you trying to do, fatten us up for the slaughter?"

"Enjoy it while you can," Smitty replied. "On a voyage like this you never know what's going to happen next."

"Now you sound like a prophet of doom," Rory said.

"I ain't no such thing. I'm just remembering that morning I was hauling in Cap's air hose, and he wasn't on the end of it. This ain't no game we're playing."

"You're right," Terry said. "This isn't a game, and we want to find out exactly what happened to Cap."

"And to everybody else," Storm added.

The next morning opened overcast, but the wind held off, making the first set up of the inflatable boats easier than it might have been. The inflatables were anchored to make a triangle, each one a hundred yards away from the *Nemo* and each one carrying an underwater microphone and a transmitter that would send any information to the *Nemo* for recording. The *Nemo* had its own underwater microphone. Chuck suggested they shoot for being set up by eight a.m. and picked up by six p.m., giving them ten hours of listening and also enough time to anchor at West Cove before dark. Once the system was up and running there was not much else to do but look forward to Smitty's lunch. The second and third day unfolded much the same way, and anticipation grudgingly gave way to boredom. The fourth morning, Rory's leave was over, and the *Nemo* ran around the end of the island to drop him off at Wilson Cove before setting up the listening posts. The microphones were barely in the water when Chuck removed his headset and announced, "We've got company."

In mere seconds a Navy-gray inflatable with an outboard engine sped out from behind a nearby point and made directly for the *Nemo*. This visit had been anticipated, and Storm was only surprised that it had taken this long in coming. As planned, Terry made the first contact.

"Good morning! How are you, today?" she said, all smiles, to the two sailors as the Navy boat pulled alongside.

"Just fine, Ma'am," answered the sailor apparently in charge. "I'm Ensign Cox. Could you please tell me what you all are doing out here?"

Terry was all charm. "Of course, Ensign. Come aboard, and we'll show you."

The ensign climbed aboard, leaving the other man in the inflatable. Terry made the introductions. "My name is Terry Ho. This is renowned shark expert, Dr. Storm Hancock, and this is our most valuable crewmember, Smitty, our cook."

"Pleased to meet you all," the ensign answered flatly. He studied Terry for a moment. "Have we met somewhere before, Ma'am?"

"Wednesday nights, 'Ask About Our Ocean.'"

"That's it; on TV."

"Come on inside the cabin, Ensign, and meet our last crewman, who'll show you what we're doing."

So far, so good, Storm told himself. He led the way into the cabin where he was surprised to find that Chuck had mussed his hair considerably and had perched his reading glasses precariously at the tip of his nose. A change of appearance wasn't part of the script they'd discussed in preparation for this meeting.

Terry said, "And this is our physical-science expert, Mr. Von Stein."

The ensign shook Chuck's offered hand, but his suspicions were obvious as he looked around the cabin at the odd mixture of electronic equipment and said, "This looks like some kind of listening set-up. What would you be listening to around a military facility?"

Here goes nothing, Storm thought.

"Pistol shrimp," Chuck replied enthusiastically.

Storm leaned against the galley counter for support. Chuck was straying further from the script by the second. What was coming next, a phony German accent? From behind the ensign's back Storm shot Chuck a wide-eyed look trying to signal him to return to the original plan. In response, Chuck began bobbing his body forward and backward reminiscent of a shorebird probing the mudflats.

"Pistol shrimp?" Ensign Cox said, obviously taken aback.

"Yes, my good man. Just listen."

Chuck turned a knob on one of the machines, and a sound similar to a crackling fire filled the *Nemo's* cabin. The oscilloscope responded eagerly to the increased volume by filling its screen with a blur of moving waves. Chuck, continuing to bob, explained, "What you're now hearing is the mating, and also territorial, call of the *Alpheus californiensis*, a small crustacean that inhabits the bottom. They make this sound with their pincers, the larger one of either the left or the right, pincer that is. You may have heard the sound yourself if you've done any local diving."

Chuck beamed at Ensign Cox as a teacher might at his star pupil.

The ensign seemed to have to pull his eyes away from the bobbing Chuck in order to return to his visual survey of the *Nemo's* cabin. "Can't say as I have," he said laconically.

Chuck, still bobbing, continued. "It appears that the shrimp perform this audio display nonstop at a constant frequency of snapping that varies by no more than one-tenth of one percent under normal conditions. Normal conditions, I say. It is possible, however, that during seismic activity, or I might even say, before seismic activity, the shrimp pick up vibrations traveling through the earth's crust, causing them to significantly alter the noise that you now hear."

Chuck turned the volume up further, causing the crackling sound to become difficult to speak over. He said loudly, "We can record the shrimp here for several weeks! Then, when we get back to shore we can compare our findings with the exact same time of recorded seismic activity on the San Andreas and it's outlying faults!" Chuck nudged up the volume again.

"Just a minute!" Ensign Cox all but shouted over the racket. "Are you telling me that these shrimp can predict earthquakes?"

"It's only a theory!" Chuck happily shouted back.

"I've heard it all now!" Ensign Cox shouted, and he bent down for a closer look at the oscilloscope. Meanwhile, Chuck turned the volume up even higher.

The ensign yelled up to Chuck, "Why do you have to be here? Couldn't you listen to shrimp at the mainland?"

"Oh, my good man!" Chuck yelled back, no longer bobbing but now rocking his body from side to side like a human metronome. "There's too much pollution! This study will only be valid if we use pristine, unpolluted pistol shrimp!"

Chuck lowered the volume back down to that of a crackling fire.

The ensign finished his examination of the oscilloscope, stood up straight, and hollered, "Is this....!"

He lowered his voice to normal.

"Is this a Cal Ocean Project?"

"They are funding us, yes," Terry charmed in.

Ensign Cox, still not looking overly convinced, said flatly, "Well, good luck with it." He strolled outside to where the inflatable was waiting with the other sailor. "You all want to be sure to stay out of the restricted area."

"We'll be sure to do that," Storm said. "Do you know when that restriction might be lifted?"

"No, Sir, but you can check with the Coast Guard weather report."

Storm, with Terry and Smitty, waved the Navy inflatable away and then entered the cabin. Chuck had dropped to his knees and was bent over laughing, with tears rolling down his cheeks.

"Pistol shrimp?" Storm asked. "What happened to our spiel about triangulation experiments? At least that had a shred of truth to it."

Chuck could barely talk. "Boring, boring," he finally said. "Besides, they are pistol shrimp. I figured you knew that."

"Of course I do, and I'm so glad to see that you're finally cheering up, but…predicting earthquakes?"

"You will note that I told the ensign that it was only a theory and nothing more."

"Then it really is a theory?"

"Of course it is," Chuck answered emphatically. "At least, it has been since I came up with it an hour ago."

Chapter 31

Fishbeck rattled his borrowed jeep down what was supposed to pass for a road. By now he had formulated at least two theories about his latest assignment. The first one was that he was cursed to be stuck on this two-bit-Navy-sandbox of an island.

It was partly his own doing, he needled himself. When his father had commandeered him to help Robins he should have put up more of a squawk, but now that he was here he was determined to be successful at the cost of sleep, comfort, and whatever idiot opinions commando-gung-ho Logan had of him.

"Logan!" Fishbeck said the name like a curse word and jerked the jeep to a halt at the base of a large hummock of sand and sage. Why should he give a flying leap at the moon about anything Logan thought, or anybody else for that matter? But he did care, and probably too much, he reminded himself, and he didn't know how to fix the problem. In the meantime, he placed most of the blame for his feelings of inferiority squarely on his family and their inflated expectations of him. He blamed his father, and he especially blamed his older brother–the good-looking family favorite who had gotten all the breaks.

"And all the girls," Fishbeck thought out loud.

He sat in the jeep and remembered bitterly how he had always worked harder than his brother for everything. Yes, he had worked harder than his brother, harder than commando-gung-ho Logan, and harder than that two-faced moron— Robins. He remembered the fights he had picked as a kid, and how he had usually found a way to win, especially when fighting some larger kid who had made fun of him. Yes, he had shown them, he remembered painfully, and he would show them now, and soon lots of things would change.

An ache in his hands caused him to look down to see that his fingertips had turned white. He slowly uncurled his fingers from around the binoculars dangling from his neck. He climbed out of the jeep and surveyed the hummock of sand. It rose at a gentle slope to eight feet high with a slight saddle at its top. If today went as planned, when he peeked his binoculars over that saddle he would have an unobstructed view of the *Nemo*.

"All the girls," Fishbeck griped again, crawling up the hummock's inland slope. Just below the hummock's top he lay down in a shallow depression he had scooped out the day before. He peeked his binoculars over the edge and steadied them on wooden slats that were the remains of an ammunition crate. Just as he expected, the *Nemo* had moved a quarter mile from yesterday's position and lay straight out from him, showing minimal activity, swinging on her anchor. He had been documenting her movements for the last week, and so far he had come up with nothing important. He had heard about the pistol shrimp.

Pistol shrimp! Fishbeck thought in disgust. Maybe they'd fooled that Navy squid who'd gone aboard, but they hadn't fooled him! He kept watching. A man emerged onto the rear deck, followed by a woman. That would be Dr. Hancock, and that would be Terry Ho, Fishbeck noted, observing the pair lean against the *Nemo*'s transom rail. They were close together, maybe rubbing shoulders, as if they were talking about something important, or maybe it was just because they were friends. Either way, Fishbeck was envious.

He had done background checks on the *Nemo*'s crew. Chuck Von Stein was an electronics nerd who had worked on sensitive projects years ago. The guy with the baseball cap was a nobody—a close to zero in the system. Hancock and Ho were another story, which was his second theory. He doubted that the published Dr. Hancock of shark fame had come to this desolate wasteland to listen to pistol shrimp with Cal Ocean's little princess. No, they were here for another reason, and he suspected it had something to do with the same reason that he was here. He would know more after tonight, because he had formulated a plan.

Late that night, on the rocky beach at West Cove a giant pile of driftwood that had been collecting undisturbed for a thousand years now concealed the furtive movements of a shadowy figure. Fishbeck peered out from the makeshift den that he'd created in the woodpile, and he frowned up at the quarter moon. He dearly wished the night were darker, but it would have to do. The *Nemo* was close, forty yards offshore, tucked in behind the north point of West Cove. Her lights had been out for over an hour, but in the moonlight Fishbeck could still easily make out her white hull against the background of the night. Ducking under a blanket, he turned on his waterproof flashlight, held up a small mirror, and positioned the light so he could see his reflection. He admired the fierce appearance he had created with camouflage face paint. If only commando-gung-ho Logan could see him now, he thought smugly. He checked the twist grommet securing his wet suit pocket to see that it was locked shut. Inside the pocket was a water-resistant microphone and transmitter that he would plant somewhere on the *Nemo's* hull.

Fishbeck was as ready as he would ever be. He left the shelter of the driftwood pile and stepped onto the pebbly beach. There was no wind or surf to mask the sound of his movement, and as he tiptoed through the loose stones, each footstep seemed to produce more noise than the one before it. By the time he finally reached the water's edge, he figured that everyone on the island couldn't help but know where he was and what he was doing. He sat down in the shallows, expecting the worst, but the *Nemo* remained dark and quiet. It was just as he expected. The people aboard the *Nemo* were typical, sophisticated softies unaware of anything but their own petty little selves. Reassured by the continued quiet, he put on his fins, crawled out into water deep enough to kick in, and started his approach.

Fishbeck wasn't wearing a mask and snorkel. He couldn't chance what moonlight there was reflecting off of a glass faceplate. Had he been wearing a mask and snorkel, and thereby swimming with his face in the water, he might have seen what was happening. As it was, buoyed high by his wetsuit, floating on his stomach with his arms at his sides and with his head out of the water and facing forward, he kicked stealthily towards the *Nemo*. He envisioned himself to be a jungle crocodile stalking its unsuspecting prey, and his confidence grew steadily as he passed the halfway point between shore and the *Nemo*. Then, he happened to look behind him.

This crocodile was stalking its prey with all the stealth of a strobe light.

Phosphorescence was the local term for it, though the liquid fire now outlining Fishbeck's every move had almost nothing in common with that particular chemical process. A more-experienced night diver might have remembered that Southern California waters were famous for the blue light produced by dinoflagellates—tiny organisms that possess the remarkable capability of bioluminescence. The slightest disturbance caused them to light up, and right now they were lighting up around Fishbeck by the millions.

Fishbeck's confidence was shattered. He turned for shore, but then he stopped swimming and just waited, holding his breath. Incredibly, the *Nemo* remained quiet. How could they possibly not see him? He remembered his reflection in the mirror. He had looked so heroic, and heroes didn't quit.

He pressed on.

Another minute and he reached the *Nemo*. He felt his way around her hull, but he didn't find a place for the bug where the *Nemo*'s crew wouldn't easily notice it. Finally, he decided to plant it on the underside of the swim step—the slatted platform projecting from the *Nemo*'s stern a foot above the waterline. He retrieved the bug from his wetsuit pocket, removed a plastic shield, thereby exposing an adhesive surface, and pressed it firmly to the swim step. His mission was completed.

Suddenly, he heard footsteps on the deck directly overhead. He crammed his body tightly against the *Nemo*'s stern and peered up through the slats of the swim step. Whoever it was leaned on the transom rail and seemed to be staring out into the night. Fishbeck heard a man's whispering voice. It was prayer, no, verse. He strained to hear.

All creation burns, a mighty wheel that turns,
And as our lifetime burns, we feel the turning of the wheel.
Into endless light, or into darkest night, we ride the turning,
burning wheel.

Momentarily, Fishbeck almost forgot his perilous situation. A poet didn't fit with any of his background checks. The whispering stopped. Fishbeck's neck ached from the position it was in, but he didn't dare move a muscle. The person above him continued to stare into the night. The pain in Fishbeck's neck became excruciating, and he clinched his teeth onto his tongue in an attempt to distract himself. He couldn't hold out much longer. In the nick of time, the mysterious person leaned out over the rail, as if looking into the water, and then turned and walked away, but not before Fishbeck had caught the silhouette of the man's head clearly in the moonlight.

The man was wearing a baseball cap.

For the next several days Fishbeck kept vigilance on the *Nemo* as she worked her way down the shoreline. Her routine didn't vary. She set up by eight, pulled down by six, and spent the night at West Cove. If those aboard her were finding anything, he certainly wasn't in on it. His bug had basically been a bust. There was too much engine noise when the *Nemo* moved, and when she was anchored the sound of water lapping against her hull and echoing under her swim step invariably drowned out any voices that he might have heard. The few times conditions had been absolutely perfect no one had been near the stern.

This morning, however, as Fishbeck reclined in reasonable comfort in a hollow of cord grass, he hoped for better results. The water was as calm as glass, and he listened expectantly through his earphones. The morning air was crisp, but in his grassy hollow the sun felt almost warm. He had trouble keeping his eyes open. Maybe if he closed them for just a moment.

He was so tired.

Voices.

Voices!

Fishbeck awoke with a start and trained his binoculars on the *Nemo*. Hancock and Von Stein were leaning against the stern rail, and they were coming in loud and clear.

"I'm surprised we haven't had a contact. I had the feeling we were on to a consistent behavior that would be repeated at least on a weekly basis."

"If it's something that even has behavior. We're assuming the source of the sound is alive and is maybe one animal, but our assumption could be way off."

"Maybe, but not likely. You're the biologist. I just manipulate electrons, but I can't get past that idea of yours that what we're dealing with is some kind of...."

Fishbeck heard a splashing sound, and the voices became muffled.

"Nooooo! Not now!" he moaned. He cranked up the volume on his receiver, but the signal had vanished, and he realized that his bug was on the way to the bottom. The last sound coming through was a crackling that reminded him of milk being poured over puffed-rice cereal. He was puzzled for only a moment before he figured the sound out.

It was pistol shrimp.

The next morning, as Fishbeck drove his borrowed jeep to the vicinity of the destroyer wreck, he rationalized that his bug hadn't been a complete wash out. It had confirmed what he had suspected. The *Nemo* was looking for the same thing that he was. He pulled the jeep up abruptly to the base of the large hummock. On the other side was a driftwood-covered beach. Outside of that was the destroyer wreck, and somewhere close by should be the *Nemo*. He hopped out of the jeep and scaled the hummock. Morning fog had made the sand wet and cold, but he dropped to his belly anyway and squirmed the last few feet until he could peek over the top with his binoculars. The *Nemo* was nowhere in sight.

Fishbeck scrambled down the dune to the jeep and gunned it back up the road to West Cove. The *Nemo* wasn't there either. Frantic now, he lurched the jeep cross country towards the airstrip that ran the width of the island. When his tires hit the concrete runway he stopped. Logan had given him specific orders to stay away from the runway, but it was the quickest way across the island. He had no choice. He floored the jeep for a mile to the runway's far end, and then he bounced his way out to the edge of a sandstone cliff. In the distance a white cabin cruiser was about to vanish into the fog. Fishbeck got his glasses on her just before she was swallowed up. It was the *Nemo* all right, and from the looks of her speed and course she was heading for Catalina, maybe even the mainland. She would be gone for at least a day, and that should give him enough time to do a little underwater research of his own. The scream of an engine being wound too high interrupted his thoughts, and he turned his head to see a jeep flying down the runway in his direction. He didn't dare do anything else but wait as the jeep screeched to a stop, and commando-gung-ho Logan jumped out.

Logan did not look happy.

Chapter 32

Storm cast a concerned look at Smitty, who scrambled down from the flying bridge and entered the cabin. One of the *Nemo's* engines had missed some beats a few minutes earlier as she cruised around the southern tip of Catalina Island, and now she was banging like a typewriter. From his perch on the flying bridge Storm could tell the instant that Smitty opened the engine hatch because of the loud misfires echoing up from below. He pulled both throttles to idle, and a minute later, Smitty's worried face appeared above the top rung of the flying bridge ladder. "Let's take her in on the port engine, Skipper. I'll check her out as soon as we're tied up."

Storm nodded to Smitty and shut down the starboard engine. At the Avalon Marina Chuck tied a bowline to one of the few remaining empty mooring buoys. Smitty soon popped up from the main cabin hatch clutching a piece of engine in his hand. "Here's the problem, Skipper," he announced triumphantly. "a worn out distributor shaft." Smitty held the offending part up proudly for all to see.

"Well, it doesn't owe us anything," Storm said. "I think it came original with the boat. I don't suppose you have an extra one in your bag of tricks."

"Afraid not, Skipper."

"Can we get one in Avalon?"

"If it were just the distributor cap or the rotor, we'd probably find something that would work, but a whole distributor assembly? I'd say our chances are slim to none, and Slim just left town. We can always try at the bus garage, and there's a small marine hardware store, but I wouldn't hold my breath."

The first time that the Avalon water taxi passed by the *Nemo*, Storm waved it away. On the taxi's second pass the entire crew was raring and ready to go. Smitty needed groceries and the engine part, and everyone else needed to feel solid ground under their feet. The *Nemo* was a comfortable boat, but after thirteen days of rubbing elbows she was getting a little small. Also, the fog had given way to sun, which made Avalon all the more inviting.

Once on shore, Smitty and Chuck set course for the bus garage. After a futile check at the marine hardware store Terry and Storm browsed the tourist traps that lined the waterfront. Smitty and Chuck found them again in front of a sweet shop. They had just bitten into opposite sides of the same candied apple. Storm chewed his bite as fast as he could while Smitty waited grinning.

"What's the verdict?" Storm finally asked, trying to sound all business.

"It's just like we figured, Skipper. We can't get it here. We'll have to go to the mainland, or we could have it sent over. Either way, we're stuck here for a least a day, maybe more."

"Wait a minute!" Terry said suddenly. "We have to get it on the mainland? Everybody stay put, and I'll be back in a flash." Terry ran down the sidewalk and disappeared around a sign with a picture of a telephone. Chuck remarked, "You know, sometimes that girl is just plain hard to figure."

"That's just a woman for you," Smitty responded.

"Yes, that is a woman," Storm muttered.

"What's that?" Smitty asked, grinning.

"I merely acknowledged that for once you were both right."

"Agreement from the confirmed bachelor," Chuck teased. "What do you think, Smitty?"

"What do I think? I think I'm not sure who's catching who, but I'd say they're both hooked."

Chuck laughed and added, "And she sure is pretty."

Storm answered them both with stony silence.

Terry returned, excited and in a hurry. "Smitty, what do we need, a distributor?"

"Yeah, but not just any one. Here, this is the best way." Smitty handed Terry a heavy object wrapped in a paper sack tied with string.

"Thank you. Storm, have you ever ridden in a seaplane?"

Fisher of Men

"No, thank goodness."

"Well, you're going to today. I'm taking you to see someone special. Smitty, we'll get your distributor. You and Chuck get the groceries, and we'll see you back on the boat tonight." She grabbed Storm by the arm. "Come on, Storm. We have to hurry if we're going to catch the plane."

Storm's fingers curled into the edges of his seat while water droplets raced across the inside of his window, and the cabin floor chattered like a washboard being played beneath his feet. To his relief, the speed of the landing seaplane rapidly diminished, and he felt reasonably assured that he was going to survive, at least until the return trip back to Avalon. The cabin door was opened, and he and Terry stepped out onto a floating dock in the midst of San Pedro Harbor.

"That was an E-ticket ride," he remarked as they walked away from the plane.

"And we get to do it again," Terry replied with a big smile.

"Don't tell me you enjoyed fluttering across the channel in that puddle jumper."

"I've checked the statistics. That plane is one of the safest ways to get to Catalina. That's hard data, Storm, your kind of faith."

"I'm not so sure anymore," he said thoughtfully.

"Do I detect a possible chink in your armor?"

"It's just that lately some things are happening that are hard to explain."

"Like '*lokahi*' for instance?"

Storm had been thinking about the Dall's porpoise, and Betsy, and how there seemed to be more to their behavior than what could be scientifically measured. "I wasn't thinking of that exactly, but I suppose it could be included."

Cap Hanson was waiting for them. On the drive to his home he stopped at an auto parts store for Smitty's engine part. Back in the car he said, "So, how's old Smitty working out for you?"

"The man's phenomenal," Storm answered. "I wouldn't be surprised if he could tap dance and play the violin."

"At the same time," Terry added.

"Yeah, that's kind of how I felt after he first signed on to the *Emerald*, and he hasn't stopped surprising me yet."

Cap pulled into a driveway next to the house with the fence of abalone shells. As Storm climbed the front steps he felt a comfortable familiarity. It was a blending of the *lokahi* that Terry had explained at Mama Ho's, and how he usually felt at his parents' house, and how he had felt that foggy evening when the *Nemo* had looked so cozy. He didn't entirely lose the feeling even when Molly Hanson flew out the front door and scooped him and Terry together into one big hug.

"It is so good to see you two again, and at the same time!" Molly exclaimed. She took a step backward to beam approvingly at the embarrassed pair. Cap, meanwhile, stood in the doorway rolling his eyes and saying quietly, "Molly, Molly, Molly."

Molly plied everyone with refreshments and finally got them settled in the front room to her satisfaction, which meant that Terry and Storm were seated close together on a couch. Cap looked at Storm and said, "Terry told me you wanted to hear my *Raven* story."

"*Raven* story?"

"That's the name of the boat I was on at the time."

"You mean when you saw an angel?"

"I didn't see an angel, but maybe I heard one. I'll just tell you what happened, and you can decide for yourself." Cap stood up. "It was like this."

"Not so fast, Cap!" Molly said. She had finally stopped bustling around and now made herself comfortable in the chair that Cap had just vacated. "Ok, Cap, Honey. Take it away."

Cap winked at Molly and started over. "It was December of '75, and we'd been diving the front side of 'Clemente up near Pyramid Head. A super-perfect, calm day suddenly blew itself up all to heck. Just like that we were caught in a Santa Ana gale, hard against a lee shore, and then one of our air hoses washed overboard and wrapped around the propeller. We were dead in the water and being blown straight for the rocks, and the only way to save us was for someone to go over the side and cut that hose free. I'll tell you right now, in all that commotion, with all the waves and currents, the idea of going over the side looked a lot like suicide. I'd heard of divers being swept clean away by the currents at Pyramid Head. Anyway, I was standing in the back of the boat, and I closed my eyes and said, 'What do I do?' That's what I said, those very words, and I said that prayer to every point in the universe."

Cap stopped talking for a moment as if to make sure that his audience was with him. Seemingly satisfied, he continued, "As sure as I'm talking to you right now, I heard a voice. It was a man's voice, and it said, 'It'll be all right.' At the same time I saw a picture in my mind's eye."

Cap picked up a ragged-looking Bible from the coffee table and opened it to a full-page painting. It showed Jesus standing in the bow of a boat, holding his hand up in the midst of a raging storm.

"This is exactly what I saw, this very picture," Cap explained. "It's Jesus calming the Sea of Galilee. You've all heard the story."

Cap continued, "Well, folks, I didn't believe what I was hearing, or what I was seeing, and there was no way I was getting in that water, but again the voice said, 'It'll be all right,' only this time I got zapped. This warm feeling started in my toes, and it flowed upward through my whole body. It was a feeling of peace, but it was so strong that I could hardly stand it. If there'd been a volume control on it I'd have been turning it down. I know it sounds crazy, but you just can't take that much peace all at once. It's like, if this is what it's going to feel like to die and go to heaven, then bring it on. We are talking no fear. None."

"Anyway, to make a long story short, I grabbed an old knife from the junk drawer, put on my mask and fins, and barreled over the side. I had that hose cut free in a heartbeat, and we were in good shape. The funny thing is that I'd had the ability to save us all along, but I'd just needed a kick in the rear to get myself over the side to do it. We motored on around Pyramid Head, and the only thing left after that was to try and figure out what in the world had just happened."

Cap sat down next to Storm on the sofa while his audience sat in thoughtful silence. Finally Storm said, "Whose voice did you hear, Cap?"

"I can't say for sure. Maybe it was Jesus. Maybe it was the Holy Ghost. Maybe it was the Father Almighty Himself, but I kinda' doubt all of that. What I'm really thinking is that it was my guardian angel. I guess it doesn't really matter. What's for sure is that I asked for help; I heard a voice, and everything worked out good. Pretty wild, huh?"

Storm's voice was contemplative. "Yeah, that's pretty wild, and if it wasn't you who was telling it I'd say that somebody'd been smoking something."

"He doesn't smoke anything unless he's trying to barbeque," Molly said jokingly. "Come on, Honey. Get yourself up, and give me a hand in the kitchen. You two keep yourselves company, and we'll have lunch in a couple of minutes."

Terry excused herself to find a bathroom, leaving Storm alone in the living room. In the sudden quiet he could hear the Hansons' muffled voices filtering from the kitchen.

"Did you see? Did you see?" he heard Molly's excited voice. "If it'd been dark we would have seen sparks flying between those two! Oh, boy! Oh, boy!"

"Now, Molly, be careful. Don't go pushing."

"I'm not pushing anybody! I'm just cheering from the sidelines!"

Storm couldn't believe that he had been that obvious. He certainly hadn't seen any sparks flying from Terry. Sure, she was acting friendly, but....

Lunch was over. Cap stepped out onto the porch where Storm was admiring the assorted flotsam and jetsam. Cap explained one interesting object after another but then became quiet when he came to a section of air hose that on his last dive had been pulled apart like so much twine. Finally, he said, "In all the years I was doing the abbing' I had my share of close calls, so I guess I know what I'm talking about. I'm going to say something to you, and then I'm going to shut up."

Storm was an experienced waterman in his own right, but

he figured that whatever the veteran diver wanted to say to him would be worth hearing. He had been profoundly impressed with what had happened to Cap. It was exactly the kind of thing he'd hoped to hear about from exactly the kind of person he'd hoped to hear about it from. He continued to admire the surrounding nautical decor, but he said, "I'm listening."

"Good. If you ever get in a jam, and you think this might be it. I mean if you really think you're about to buy the farm; you just pray. That's all you have to do. You ask God to help you, and if you mean it, he'll be there, and now I'm going to shut up. Let's see what those two women are up to."

The seaplane dropped from the sky like a wounded goose. Terry and Storm first caught the land shuttle, then the water taxi, and were finally welcomed by Smitty and Chuck on board the *Nemo*. Smitty had already filled the *Nemo's* larders for another two weeks. He quickly installed the new distributor and tested it to his satisfaction. All that was needed then was to fuel up, and the *Nemo* would be ready to head back to San Clemente Island. Smitty, apparently, had other plans, because he said to Storm, "If you two can go gallivanting all over God's creation while poor Chuck and me work our fingers to the bone, then we can decide that I'm not cooking tonight, and we're both taking the night off. That includes not driving the boat to 'Clemente."

"This isn't a mutiny is it?" Storm asked.

"Heck, no! It's an invitation to eat at my Aunt Emma's, and a chance for you to taste some good cooking for a change. Whatever I learned about food, I learned from her. You just all be ready to catch the water taxi at eighteen-hundred hours. Miss Terry, that means the little hand's on the six."

"You just make sure you're ready yourself, Mr. Smarty," Terry replied, and then she asked, "Storm, is being a comedian part of his job description?"

"I believe it comes with the package," Storm answered and then added, "Smitty, by any unfathomable chance, do you play the violin?"

"No, but I wouldn't mind givin' it a go-round or two."

Terry raised her eyebrows at Storm as if to say, "We can't expect the man to have done everything."

Smitty added thoughtfully, "I have tinkered a little with the cello."

Storm and the rest of the *Nemo's* crew soon learned that Smitty's Aunt Emma qualified for Avalon's version of local color, and that was in a town already known for colorful individuals. She had lived on Catalina Island for over forty years, twenty of which she had been the chief cook for one of the large cattle ranches on the island. Three times a day she had rustled up food for a dozen hungry ranch hands. Now that the ranch was long gone she still enjoyed cooking occasionally for an appreciative bunch of hungry people, which was probably why she seemed to be entirely pleased that Smitty had given her a call.

For Storm and the crew the evening was turning out to be both entertaining and informative. Aunt Emma seemed to have a story about everyone, with one of her favorites being about a ten-year-old Smitty coming home one day with his head stuck in a crab trap. She also stayed current with the local news, spending her mornings walking and talking her way through Avalon. The conversation finally drifted around to the *Nemo's* mission as Storm said, "Aunt Emma, have any of the locals mentioned the strange disappearances at San Clemente Island?"

"Oh, yes, there's been talk," Aunt Emma answered without hesitation. "Not all the time, but now and then someone will bring it up. They say there's a sea monster out there that no one's supposed to talk about."

Aunt Emma must have seen the surprise on everyone's face, because she explained, "People think we're isolated out here on our little rock, but that's not true. The abbers, the lobstermen, the Coasties', and even the Navy all finally wind up here. There's something strange going on, all right. There's even talk of some secret government guy snooping around."

Chuck said, "But if it's all a secret, how come you know so much about it?"

For an answer Aunt Emma held a finger to her ear and smiled.

Smitty piped up, "If Aunt Emma says it is, then it is. She knows everything that goes on out here. If someone wants to know something, they just ask her. Isn't that right, Aunt Emma?"

"That depends on what's being asked and who's doing the asking. Some questions are best left unanswered."

"Do you think there's a sea monster?" Chuck asked.

The room seemed to take a breath and hold it as it waited for Aunt Emma to answer.

"Heavens, no! There's no such thing. There could be some big, dumb animal doing what God gave it to do, but there's no monster."

Terry said, "Aunt Emma, what do you really think is going on out there?"

"I'm not sure," Aunt Emma said thoughtfully, "but I have a feeling we're going to find out sooner than later. It's just a feeling, but it's a strong one."

"That settles it, guys and gals," Smitty said confidently. "You can get ready for action."

"Now, you all are going to be very careful," Aunt Emma encouraged.

Storm caught Terry gazing at him. "Yes, very careful," he answered for everyone.

After dinner, Storm was in the kitchen helping himself to another cup of coffee when Aunt Emma entered the room and said "Here you are. I have something to tell you."

"Go ahead. It seems to be my day to be told things."

"I recently had a dream about someone I'd never met. I didn't know, until tonight, that the dream was about you."

"Is that good, or bad?"

"If I knew that, I'd tell you. Actually it wasn't so much about you as it was a message for you." Aunt Emma grasped Storm's hand with both of hers and carefully looked him in the eye. "The message is: Whatever it is you're looking for, you're going to find it."

"I guess that's good news," Storm said. "I'm just not sure exactly what it is I'm looking for."

Terry entered the room. "Caught you! Holding hands, huh?

Watch out for her, Storm. I hear she's got quite a few fish on the stringer already."

Aunt Emma laughed and dropped Storm's hand like it was hot potato. "That's because Smitty talks too much," she explained.

Storm said, "Aunt Emma was just telling me a dream she'd had about me."

"Really? Dreams play a big part in some of the best stories in the Bible. I hope this dream was a good one."

"I hope so too," Storm replied.

"Speaking of good things, you still haven't told me what you think about Cap's adventure."

"I've been giving it a lot of thought, and the safest thing to say is that I need to think about it a lot more."

Chapter 33

An eddy of Arctic air spun away from the main jet stream, squeegeed its way south around the North Pacific high, and then raced southeast towards the California coastline. At the same time, what was left of a tropical monsoon spiraled up the West Coast of Baja California. The two fronts collided directly above Fishbeck, and the mother of all squalls was born.

Fishbeck looked up at the sky with dread. Why couldn't he have picked a better day to make his first scuba dive in over a year? It didn't matter. He had to go diving today. The *Nemo* was away, and he had paid for that knowledge by suffering a royal chewing out from Logan. Besides, by accepting the added challenge of the raw weather, he could prove he was made of the kind of stuff it took to complete a mission, especially a mission that was in danger of unraveling.

But it wasn't his fault, he told himself. He was getting almost zero help from commando-gung-ho Logan, and his sponsor in this whole mess, Congressman Robins, acted like he couldn't care less. Plus, as Logan himself had said, he didn't have diddly-squat to go on, which was the only thing that Logan had ever said that had made a lick of sense. What he did have to go on were some third-hand accounts, some scratchy tapes, a couple of blurry photographs, and a chewed-up swim fin, that was now missing by the way.

Today, if he didn't take reckless chances, but worked within a calculated risk, he just might find out something of value. Stranger things had happened, and the risk was worth taking if it would help prove to his father and the other doubters that the poacher operation hadn't been a fluke.

On a chart Fishbeck had drawn lines between all of the suspected locations of the incidents. The center of the resulting drawing was just off of the destroyer wreck, and that's where he was going to dive on this stormy morning. Through early morning darkness he had maneuvered his borrowed jeep and a trailered rubber boat to the base of the large hummock. By the first gray light he had wrestled the boat and its outboard motor to the water's edge. Now, as he stood in the shallows, icy water probed at his ankles searching his wetsuit for a place to enter. He shuddered as words from Smitty's poem rang in his mind like a bell tolling doom: "Into endless light, or into darkest night, we ride the turning, burning wheel."

The dawn showed no signs of brightening, and Fishbeck felt nothing but cold and foreboding. Finally, with a face set like flint, he shoved the boat into deeper water, clambered aboard, and motored through a dark sea and sky to the point indicated by his chart. Fifty yards out from shore, in thirty feet of water, he shut down the motor and lowered the boat's small anchor. When he felt a sure connection with the bottom he calculated his next move.

Because of his lack of experience using scuba gear, Fishbeck harbored a realistic concern that he might accidentally suffer an air embolism in a moment of panic. A surfacing scuba diver always faced that dangerous prospect of expanding air rupturing the tiny air sacks in his lungs and releasing bubbles into his bloodstream. Fishbeck definitely didn't want that to happen.

He reviewed his rules for surfacing: look up, exhale, and follow your bubbles. In an emergency, if he managed to do any two of those three things, he should keep the worst from happening. If he somehow forgot to do the last two, the act of just looking up would clear his airway and allow the expanding air a safe pathway out of his body.

Fishbeck painstakingly checked himself over one last time. His mask was clear. His regulator was working. His air tank was full. The CO_2 cartridge in his buoyancy vest was brand new. His quick-release weight belt had been put on last, so it could be the first thing dropped in an emergency. He was as safe as he could be. He knew he was breaking a cardinal rule by not having a dive buddy, but that was out of the question. There was nothing more he could do to delay the inevitable. He put his snorkel in his mouth, held his mask tightly against his face, and tumbled backwards into the gray water. The sudden shock of cold took his breath away. He sputtered and coughed, and managed to fight his way into a facedown snorkeling position and grab hold of the anchor line. There, by force of will alone, he hung on. Finally, he was calmed down enough to look around. There was the anchor, thirty feet below, resting in a large patch of open sand. That was good. Fishbeck didn't want anything sneaking up on him from the surrounding kelp forest.

His initial plan was to go down the anchor line and never let go of it. Whatever he saw from there was what he was going to see. If he felt comfortable after that, he would venture further.

Look up, exhale, and follow your bubbles, Fishbeck told himself. He put the regulator mouthpiece in his mouth, and he let just enough air out of his lungs to decrease his buoyancy and begin his descent. A lone senorita fish darted out of his way as he inched down the anchor line.

Fishbeck wasn't in a rush.

Eight feet down, except for the light being dimmer than he would have liked and a surprising lack of fish, everything seemed fine. At twelve feet he passed through a thermocline, and colder water stabbed at his skin like icy needles as it found new ways into his wetsuit.

The light suddenly became dimmer.

An extra thick cloud must have covered the sun, Fishbeck told himself. The darkening gloom chipped away at his resolve.

He kept going.

Look up, exhale, and follow your bubbles.

Fishbeck was not calm, but he was in control. He descended feet first and tried not to think of what might be lurking out of sight beyond the sandy clearing. The bottom came up slowly. One more foot, and the tips of his fins would touch the clear sand. So far, so good. His fins touched down ever so gently, and the sand beneath them erupted.

Fishbeck wrenched on the anchor line, jackknifing his body upward and upside-down in one frenzied movement. Somehow, he resisted the urge to bolt for the surface. Through his half-flooded mask he saw a large guitarfish blast from its burrowed hiding place in the sand beneath him and streak away across the clearing.   It's all right! Fishbeck told himself. It's only a guitar...!

A gaping cavern rimmed with curved knives burst open from the ocean floor and sucked the guitarfish into it. The cavern slammed shut, and where it had been was replaced by an enormous mound of flesh.

Fishbeck clung to the anchor line, so frozen in terror that he was beyond any ability to move. On top of the mound of flesh he saw two huge eyes darting about independently, as if they were searching. One of the eyes stopped moving. It fixed upon him.

"Look up! Exhale! Follow your bubbles!" A voice in Fishbeck's mind screamed, as he clawed wildly for the surface.

Climbing the anchor line was too slow. Fishbeck abandoned it and thrashed violently with his fins. He broke the surface, hurled himself aboard the inflatable, and flung himself to the stern all in one motion. He yanked the outboard motor's starter cord, but the cord's stiff-rubber handle slipped through his wet fingers. He grasped it harder and yanked again. The motor started, and he gunned it, but instead of heading for shore, the boat made a nose-diving pirouette around its bow.

Fishbeck had forgotten the anchor.

He dove forward and slashed at the anchor line with his dive knife. The line fought him as if it were made of steel. It finally parted, and he dove aft and again gunned the boat for shore, hitting the rocky beach wide open. He threw himself over the bow and floundered up the slope on his hands and knees until he felt sure the creature couldn't follow. There he remained while lightening flashed, and thunder rocked his ears. Then came rain, and that's when Fishbeck noticed his own heavy breathing. The mechanical wheeze accompanying each breath warned him that something was terribly wrong.

Had he embolized?

His worst fears became all too real until he realized he was still breathing through his regulator.

The rain continued while Fishbeck slowly regained his composure. If it hadn't been for the guitar fish....

The fierce lightening seemed to be tapering off, but following every flash was a peal of thunder that caused Fishbeck to shut his eyes, and when his eyes were shut he saw that other eye, dark and unblinking, looking into his.

He sat in the rain, lonely, cold, and wondering what to do next.

The first crash of thunder ripped the *Nemo's* crew out of their sleeping bags.

"Holy jumping catfish!" Smitty exclaimed. He stood barefoot on the aft deck with a yellow slicker thrown on over his pajamas. Storm was the next crewmember on deck. Smitty said, "Skipper, the last time I seen anything like this was back in Biloxi, and I ain't never seen it here!"

By now, Chuck and Terry were also on deck. Do you think we should go ashore?" Terry asked.

"We're probably OK," Storm answered. "We're not the tallest thing around. Just to be sure, Smitty, would you lower the radio antenna?"

The *Nemo's* crew watched in awe as Avalon was rocked with a thunderstorm for the record books. Terry stood close to Storm. Without warning, a transformer on a pole at the base of the pier exploded in a blinding blue flash. In reaction, Terry jumped towards Storm, and he instinctively put his arms around her. Terry seemed to be over her start in a heartbeat, and Storm quickly let go of her, but the feeling he had just experienced didn't let go of him.

The thunderstorm rolled on, and Storm noticed that with every close flash of lightening Terry flinched. That was not good, he thought, because it made him want to put his arms back around her, and protect her, and be kind to her, and make her happy.

In other words, he was beginning to feel about Terry exactly how he had set out all along not to feel.

Chapter 34

The Navy swift boat was less than a minute away, throwing up a white spray as it planed in from the north end of the island. Storm jerked the binoculars from his eyes and rushed into the *Nemo's* cabin. "Logan's almost here!" he said excitedly. "Are you guys ready?" He was pleased to see that Chuck's hair was neatly combed, and that his glasses were tucked in his shirt pocket. Smitty said, "It's all set, Skipper. Chuck's promised to be on his best behavior."

Storm rushed back outside and watched the Navy boat pull alongside. Thanks to Rory's radio call this visit wasn't a surprise. Commander Logan had asked for a meeting on the *Nemo* and had told them that he would be bringing along a Fish and Game officer. From Rory's description, Logan was both someone to be counted on and someone on whom you didn't want to get on the wrong side.

Rory and Fishbeck boarded the *Nemo*. Logan took his time and seemed to do a visual survey of the *Nemo* before boarding and being introduced. He then showed keen interest in the electronic gear situated throughout the main cabin. Chuck gave a tour of the equipment, during which Logan nodded politely, while Fishbeck displayed an air of casual disinterest. Logan said, "Dr. Hancock, I'm told that your specialty is the monitoring of sharks, especially the great white."

"That's right," Storm answered, "and we have the monitoring equipment right here." Storm showed Logan and Fishbeck the underwater video port built into the *Nemo's* hull, and then he brought out one of the used monitors that had been reworked by Chuck. "These were designed with the great white in mind, but they should work on the blues around here."

"Then you are going to do some shark work?"

"If the situation allows."

"Of course, your pistol shrimp study comes first. I was just thinking that it might speed things up if you had access to the entire area."

Something in Logan's manner suggested to Storm that he'd just been thrown a piece of bait. Meanwhile, Fishbeck's disinterest seemed to be gravitating towards acute interest. "That could speed things up considerably," Storm answered carefully.

Logan looked pleased. "It's settled, then. You go anywhere you want, and if we need you to leave, we'll tell you." Logan clasped his hands together and continued. "As I've told Lieutenant Russell, I like to know about any studies being done by civilians on the island or in the water, and not just because it's my job to keep everybody safe. I don't mind lending a hand whenever possible, so if there's any material or information I can get for you, unclassified of course...." Logan laughed. He looked directly at Rory for a moment and then back to Storm. "You just tell me, and I'll put it where you can find it."

Storm measured his words. "Thank you, Commander. That's very helpful."

"But I would like something in return," Logan said, and Fishbeck's acute interest degraded into undisguised agitation as Logan continued on to talk about Liu Xin's upcoming visit, explaining at the end, "Liu is not a high-level diplomat, and as such he won't have a full entourage. For our part, it will probably be just him and one or two personal staff. He'll be staying aboard the yacht *Write Off,* but I'd like you to join the party. I want our Chinese guest to experience the *Nemo* with her scientific environment, her knowledgeable crew, and I'm not forgetting what Russell has told me about your cook." Logan looked kindly at Smitty, whose face reddened like a small-craft warning flag.

"Before you answer," Logan continued, "let me sweeten the pot. If you agree to help, it could be a feather in your cap for any further Cal Ocean research. The island is technically all restricted, as you know."

Fishbeck looked like he was about to blow a gasket. Logan gave him a look, as if to invite him to speak, but Fishbeck remained silent. Logan said, "So, how does that sound to you?"

"We'll need just a minute to talk it over," Storm answered.

He motioned to his crew, and they followed him to the bow. They faced forward, away from the windows. "Give me your thoughts," Storm said quietly.

"Logan's our mole," Rory responded.

"I wouldn't trust Fishbeck any further than I could throw him," Terry said.

"We'd finally get into the area where we thought we might find something," Chuck added.

Smitty had his thinking face on, and Storm wanted his opinion. "Smitty?"

"Well, Skipper, I could be wrong, but I think we should do like he says."

The look on Smitty's face told Storm that there was yet another issue. "Are you still thinking we're going to run into a fifty-foot great white?"

Smitty acted like he was embarrassed to respond. "Nah, Skipper. It ain't that. I just ain't never cooked for no Chinese diplomat."

The deal was made, and for the next week the *Nemo* worked and reworked a two-mile area around the destroyer wreck. Her crew listened through endless hours of territorial clicks of pistol shrimp but heard little else. Today was their last day before they would need to make a supply run to Catalina, and they had anchored a hundred yards straight out from the wreck. Another long day was winding down. The late afternoon sun stretched the *Nemo's* shadow towards the island's western shore. Terry lay on the bow, reading a copy of Treasure Island. Storm, tucked into the navigator's nook, fidgeted with his charts while he half-listened to Smitty and Chuck debate one philosophical point after another. Unknown to all of them, not far from the *Nemo*, a thirty-pound halibut was about to have its position changed on the food chain.

Chuck closed a book titled, Zen and the Unified Field Theory, carefully marking his place with a loop of electrical wire. "But, Smitty, just consider the sheer elegance, not to mention the mind-boggling ramifications of the idea. Imagine one, sublime equation that could unify gravity, electromagnetism, and the strong and weak nuclear forces. The possibilities are endless. Interstellar travel could be a reality. Why, we might even unravel the mystery of time."

"What you'll unravel is your brain," Smitty retorted. He plopped his Bible down heavily on the table and thumbed through it until he found a particular passage. "Here it is!" he said triumphantly. "You think your imaginary equation can explain how the universe ticks, but right here's the real answer, even though it's way beyond what anybody can understand, in this life anyways."

Chuck looked suspiciously at the open Bible. "I'm not interested in hearing some science-bashing, ultra-literal interpretation of Genesis."

"Oh, so you know Genesis, do you? Well, for your information, it's not Genesis. It's Exodus, and it is literal, but I don't know if your Zen-soaked brain could drop down out of the clouds long enough to understand it."

"I dare you to give me a try," Chuck taunted. "I double dare you."

"I will," Smitty said smugly. "It says right here in Exodus that Moses asked God what his name was, and do you know what God answered him?"

"I haven't a clue, but somehow I just know you're going to tell me."

"That's what I thought you'd say, Mr. Genesis expert. God said his name is 'I AM.'"

Chuck stared blankly at Smitty, who seemed to be waiting for a reaction. "That's it?" Chuck finally asked, looking disappointed, as if the spirited argument he had hoped for had just fizzled into oblivion,

Smitty seemed undeterred by Chuck's lack of enthusiasm. "You want elegance? You want mind-boggling ramifications? You just might try looking a little deeper into exactly what that means. I might add that this little chat between God and Moses took place over a thousand years before Socrates was even in diapers."

Chuck remained impassive, and as Storm observed quietly from the navigator's nook he realized that Chuck was stringing Smitty along for the sheer enjoyment of it.

"You still don't get it?" Smitty asked incredulously. "Do I have to spell it out?"

"Please do," Chuck said, smiling, as he waved his hand in mock invitation.

Smitty turned towards Storm. "Do you see what I mean about someone having too much book learning for his own good?" He turned back to Chuck. "It's like this, and do please try to focus. If God is 'I Am,' then he has to be the power behind 'what is.' His 'Am' holds everything together, but you won't be scratching an equation for it on a blackboard no matter how many pieces of chalk you break."

Chuck just shook his head and asked kindly, "Are you trying to push science back a thousand years, or are you simply saying we shouldn't even try to work out the problem in the first place?"

With exaggerated hurt, Smitty answered, "I'm just saying that science looks at what comes natural, and if it looked deep enough, which it can't, or maybe won't, it would someday have to look at what comes supernatural."

Storm was now thoroughly distracted from his work. He wondered if Smitty had ever read Thomas Aquinas. He wouldn't be surprised if he had, because the man had done about everything else. He said, "Smitty, you're sounding a lot like a Thomist."

"Actually, I'm Scotch Irish," Smitty answered with a grin.

Chuck suddenly held up both hands in a gesture asking for quiet. He pulled his headset over his ears. He hit buttons and turned knobs. He rewound a tape and played it again. On the bow, Terry rose from her book, as if she too had felt the sudden tension. She entered the cabin.

"What's...?"

Storm held a finger to his lips, and she joined him and Smitty in watching Chuck fiddle with his equipment. Finally Chuck took off his headset. The look in his eyes was more fearful than triumphant.

"I think we've got it," he said in a hushed voice. "Listen to this." He rewound the tape and turned on the speakers. The sounds heard were mostly the ubiquitous background crackling of the pistol shrimp, and then it happened, a sudden, powerful sound of water movement, like on the tapes, except much more formidable.

A collective chill gripped the *Nemo's* crew. Storm glanced at the cabin floor. What they had been searching for could be in the water only a few feet below them at that very second.

"How far away is it?" he asked.

"It's not far. Maybe a hundred meters, probably less." Chuck got up and led the way to the bow. He pointed to the destroyer wreck. "It's there."

No one spoke. There was no wind or surf, only a suffocating quiet that weighed down on the *Nemo* like a blanket. Storm stared across the glassy water to the destroyer wreck and struggled to remain objective. Had it been this quiet all day, or did it only seem different now? A pair of cormorants flew fast and low over the water in front of the *Nemo's* bow. Staccato puffs of air from their wings beat like muffled drums against the quiet and then faded away.

It really was unusually quiet, Storm decided. He was surprised that he hadn't picked up on it before. He had seen birds fly through the area, but he hadn't seen any of them land on the water, or dive in from the air, and there hadn't been any seals, or sea lions, or anything. There was only the sound of the kelp slithering beneath the *Nemo's* hull.

Five minutes later, Storm was suiting up, and Terry was on a roll.

"I don't like this!" she protested. "We said we'd stay out of the water! If we had a shark cage, maybe it'd be different, but we don't! You don't have a clue what's out there!"

"I'll be fine," Storm said, as he continued putting on his dive gear. "I'm not trying to put a monitor on the thing. I just want a look."

"You could be eaten alive, swallowed whole! Is that what you want?"

"Of course not. Excuse me a second." He called into the cabin, "What do you got, Chuck?"

Chuck had been working furiously, trying to pinpoint the sound exactly. "The direction's good, straight towards the wreck, but the distance is all messed up. It could be almost anywhere between here and the shore."

Storm turned back to Terry. "Look. I'm going to be careful. I'm going to stay near the surface. I'll have the scooter in front of me. If anything even begins to look funny, I can always hide in the kelp."

Terry's expression told him that she hadn't bought any of it. She looked angry. He said as tenderly as he could, "Tell you what. Pray for me. I could probably use it."

Terry didn't say a word. She checked Storm's tank valve, his pressure gauge, his regulator, and his weight belt, all the while saying nothing.

Then, Storm was in the water. He marked his course with the sun, waved to the crew, and descended to ten feet. The water was clear, and he had a good view of the kelp forest surrounding him. The kelp was not so thick that he wouldn't see something sneaking up on him from far away. He positioned the scooter in front of him. It was a torpedo-shaped device, three-feet long, with a handle bar on its propeller end. Storm squeezed the throttle on the handle bar and the battery-powered propeller whirred eagerly. He released the throttle and the propeller stopped.

He looked for his bearings. The sun was in one direction, and where he wanted to go was exactly the other way, but something was wrong. The more that he looked around him, the more that he noticed that there weren't any fish. There weren't any calico bass. There weren't any senoritas or blacksmiths. There weren't any opal eye, or anchovies, or kelpfish, or anything. It was as if everything that could swim away had done just that.

Storm double-checked his depth. Ten feet. That's where he wanted to stay. He had a growing feeling that to be near the bottom was dangerous. He put the scooter in front of him and gave it the smallest amount of throttle. It whirred quietly and pulled him gently forward. He picked his route carefully, staying partially hidden in the kelp but always with a clear view in all directions. He checked his depth again. He stopped, looked, and listened. There was only the crackling sound of the pistol shrimp.

It was time to get his bearings again. The scooter possessed slightly positive buoyancy, so he let it carry him gently to the surface. He had only gone about twenty-five yards. He waved to the *Nemo*. Everyone but Terry waved back. She was sitting on the bow with her head down. She looked as if she were praying. He descended back down to ten feet, turned away from the sun, and again motored slowly though the forest. He scanned every inch of the bottom, and it all looked normal except for the lack of fish. The bottom was slowly rising to meet him. He surfaced again. He was halfway to the wreck. Again, he waved to Chuck and Smitty, who again waved back. They were only fifty yards away, but they might as well have been across the ocean. He began to feel exposed upon the surface. He descended again and considered his options. His curiosity was being overcome by his survival instinct. How much further did he dare to go?

He would go another twenty-five yards and then see.

Twitch.

The bottom was coming up too quickly. Storm was still at a depth of ten feet, but now the bottom was only ten feet below him. The giant kelp of the forest had given way to large bushes of feather boa. He stopped behind a hedge of bushes at the near edge of a sandy clearing. The clearing was fifty feet in diameter and surrounded all around by thick feather boa. He reached a decision. He would go to the far side of the clearing and no further, at least not today. He kept his hand off the throttle and kicked gently with his fins. He eased the scooter, and then his entire body, through the hedge. He stopped there as his hunter's intuition ripped into full alert. He couldn't see it, and he couldn't hear it, but he somehow sensed that he had suddenly changed from being the one doing the hunting into the one being hunted.

A large shape streaked in from the side. Storm whirled to face the intruder, whipping the scooter around in front of him as a shield. A female sea lion rushed by him and then out of the clearing, and then she returned. She shot by him close, so close that Storm got a good look at the deep scars running the length of her tail flippers.

Matilda!

Terry had shown Storm the photograph, and a chill now ran through him as if he'd hit a sudden thermocline. What was Matilda doing, and why was she the only other living thing besides him that was down here?

The sea lion rushed at him, snapped her jaws in his face, and sped away.

Matilda! What are you trying to tell me, girl?

Storm sensed that she wasn't playing. It was almost as if she were trying to warn him, or maybe even trying to drive him away.

He didn't know.

Twitch.

Storm saw it, a fleeting movement behind the feather boa on the far side of the clearing. Matilda rushed at him one more time and then disappeared into the forest. He waited for her to come back, but she didn't. He was alone again.

Twitch.

Storm eased himself back into the cover of the feather boa bushes.

Twitch.

Whatever it was, he wasn't going to approach it from straight across the clearing. He would work his way around the edge.

Twitch.

Storm crept from bush to bush, until only one large feather boa separated him from the movement. Slow as drifting plankton, slow as an abalone crawls across a rock, he pushed the nose of the scooter through the bush.

Twitch.

It reminded him of an eel.

Twitch.

It had the same colors as the blob in the mystery photograph.

Twitch.

It was a lure.

The ocean bottom ripped open, and Storm heard *the* sound.

An irresistible suction snatched him towards a hellish gullet rimmed with ivory scimitars, and in that horrible instant he realized there would be no escape. In his mind's eye he saw himself as a child on the beach with his parents. He saw Rory bodysurfing down the face of a wave. He saw Terry praying on the bow of the *Nemo*.

As Storm was sucked into black oblivion, he heard a faraway sound that reminded him of his own voice: "If I take the wings of morning...."

Chapter 35

"Holy jumping catfish!"

Smitty bounded down from the flying bridge and into the cabin. Terry and Chuck were already there. Sweat beaded Chuck's forehead as he turned dials and rewound tape. The speakers had been turned up high during Storm's dive. They all had heard the electric whirring of the scooter starting and stopping, and then they had heard *the* sound.

"Where is it?" Terry asked frantically.

"In the exact same spot!" Chuck answered.

Terry shoved her way past Smitty and ran outside. When Smitty caught up with her she was already strapping on a scuba tank. "Miss Terry, wait!" he pleaded. "We don't know what's going on! Maybe he's not in trouble! For all we know, you could make things worse!"

"We can't just sit here and do nothing!"

Chuck joined them. "Smitty's right. What we need now is cool heads and calm deeds. First of all, how much air does he have?"

Smitty checked his watch. "Twenty minutes, give or take."

Chuck said, "Then I say we wait ten minutes. If we don't see him or hear him by then, we'll pull the anchor, and we'll all go looking."

Terry closed her eyes and took a deep breath. "All right," she capitulated. "We'll give him ten minutes, but then I'm going after him, and you can do whatever you want."

The minutes crawled by. "How long is it?" Terry asked for the umpteenth time, but Smitty didn't answer. He was afraid of losing Terry too.

Terry finally sprang to her feet. "That's it. It's been ten minutes. I'm going after him."

"All right, Miss Terry. We'll go, but let me drive," Smitty replied, and he scrambled up the ladder to the *Nemo's* flying bridge. Terry ran to the bow to pull the anchor. Chuck continued to listen with his headset.

The creature that had made the sound didn't belong here, but it was here, surviving, because it didn't know how to do anything else. It spent its life lying in ambush on the bottom, almost asleep, waiting for something to swim by. A would-be prey's movement would telegraph vibrations through the ocean water to minute sensory hairs along the creature's giant lateral line. Instantly, millions of ions would exchange places across an organic membrane. Involuntary muscle fibers would contract, and a modified dorsal fin would stand up and give a slight twitch, causing the eel-shaped lure at its tip to wriggle like a wounded animal.

Four feet below the lure, on the surface of the creature to which the dorsal fin was attached, two huge, non-blinking eyes would begin searching their watery surroundings, lifting the creature into a primitive, but highly effective, state of awareness. It would now attack anything that came nearby, because it was hungry.

It was always hungry.

Two decades earlier, when it was only sixty pounds of mostly head and mouth, the creature's remarkable journey to San Clemente Island began when it was hooked by an angler near the east shore of Chesapeake Bay. Locally, its kind was considered to be trash fish, but more and more of its species were being dished up under disguising names at seafood restaurants, and such was this animal's fate until providence stepped in. Right at the surface, as a gaff hook was about to end its life, the angler's line broke; the creature fled, and that's when it swam into a remnant of a fishing net. The remnant had one remaining float attached, which buoyed it up just enough to keep it adrift. One end of the net had snarled into a kind of a pouch, and it was into this pouch that the creature plunged headfirst. The fish's stout pectoral fins caught fast in the webbing, and no amount of violent thrashing on its part would gain it freedom. Then, with the tide pulling out and a nor'easter brewing, the net, along with its prisoner, was propelled from the shallows by wind and wave towards the deeper mid-channel.

The wind strengthened, and the seas came close together with their tops blowing off. It was not a day for a picnic on the water, but to the crew of the sea-going tug, *Algonquin*, it was all part of a day's work. The *Algonquin* was on her maiden voyage with a tow for the West Coast. The barge trailing four-hundred feet behind her was laden heavily enough that a ragged gash in its blunt bow rode completely underwater. The steel wound, having never leaked, had never been repaired or smoothed out.

From its woven prison the trapped creature felt the vibrations from the *Algonquin's* engines and propellers increase to a crescendo and then fade away to be replaced by a splashing sound created by the barge's bow thumping against the angry sea. A yard short of running the helpless creature down, the barge dove deep into a trough, and a weave of the net wedged into the metal gash as if placed by a hand. The rest of the net, along with its captive, swept back and downward tight against the barge's hull, pressed there by the steady eleven-knot pace of the *Algonquin*.

The tug and its tow proceeded south, averaging three hundred miles per day, and with each passing degree of latitude the water became warmer. By the fifth day a metabolic lethargy had set in, but the creature could still muster up a violent, however futile, few seconds of thrashing. By the seventh day the warmth of Caribbean water, plus the lack of food, had reduced the creature to a catatonic state. This fish, however, was no tuna—no greyhound of the sea designed for continuous swimming. To its advantage, this fish, though a particularly mobile individual for its species, had been designed for waiting.

The ninth day was spent passing through the Panama Canal. At times, the barge was completely still, and the net hung limp, yet it remained firmly affixed to the bow. There was little oxygen available to the creature in the warm water, and its ocean-bred body soaked up the poisonous fresher water like a sponge. No longer thrashing, not even moving, it clung to life.

Finally, the *Algonquin* entered the Pacific Ocean and

turned north, averaging three hundred miles a day. Midway up Baja California's long arm between Cedros Island and the mainland and in a vicious squall, a tremor coursed the length of the creature's body. The cold Pacific water, plus the violent shaking of the storm, had ignited a spark of life within the creature and had also awakened the one stimulus that might drive it to live. It was hungry.

It was very, very hungry.

Late afternoon on the twentieth day of the *Algonquin's* journey the barge was tied up to the Wilson Cove Pier at San Clemente Island. The following morning a crane lifted the island's new decompression chamber from the deck of the barge. The barge gave the slightest shudder, and the shred of net, after fifty-five-hundred miles of hanging in the gash, fell free. The net drifted away, and a dark object separated from it. Gently as a feather the object drifted downward in a languid spiral. From the bottom, twenty feet below, a sand bass warily watched the slowly sinking object. The sand bass's primal instincts were locked in a debate of whether to flee or freeze when it was inhaled.

Strengthened by food at last, the creature explored its new environment. With no natural predators, and with an abundance of food for the taking, the creature roamed and fed at will. It wandered deeper and deeper, and it grew larger and larger. For years it prowled the dark depths until it finally wound up on the backside of the island. More years passed until one day, prodded by an increasing demand for food to satisfy its massive bulk, the creature began to wander up the underwater slopes of the mountain that was San Clemente Island. Every day found it higher up the mountain, until finally it left the deep world of shadow, exchanging it for the sunlit, photosynthetic realm of the kelp forest and a whole new world containing Matilda and Storm and other unsuspecting prey.

Chapter 36

And God created great whales, and every living creature
that moveth, which the waters brought forth abundantly,
after their kind....

(Genesis 1:21)

Darkness.
The sound of bubbles.
Breathing.
Breathing?
Storm opened his eyes as if awakening from a dream. A net
of fringed, brown ribbons was plastered across his facemask,
blocking his vision. The ribbons told him that he was wrapped
up in feather boa, and the memory of the horror of his dream
instantly returned. He hung motionless in the kelp, daring to
move only his eyes, but he couldn't see anything because of the
kelp covering his mask. First one way, and then the other, in
the tiniest of position changes, he maneuvered his head until
his faceplate was partially clear. He was facing the sun, which
meant he had somehow gotten turned around. He closed his
eyes and tried to avoid sending prey vibrations through the
water. He turned slowly—as slowly as possible and still be
moving, turning the entangling kelp ribbons with him, until he
reasoned he was facing the same way he had been when he had
seen the horror. He opened his eyes and then bit his regulator
mouthpiece to keep from screaming.
The horror was right in front of him.
Storm didn't move. He didn't even breathe.
"Become one with the kelp!" His mind shouted silently.
Finally, he had no choice. He had to breathe, so he inhaled
quickly, and he exhaled slowly, hoping to make his bubbles
mesh better with the environment.
Five long minutes passed with neither the horror, nor
Storm, moving at all, and he gradually began to study the
creature for itself and not just as the terminator of his existence.

Really looking at it for the first time, he had to admit that the creature was both beautiful and terrible. It had a tremendous head, connected to a body that tapered abruptly to a long, fleshy tail. The creature's overall physique was of a banjo with fins attached, except that Storm's reeling mind estimated this banjo to be over twenty feet long. Its entire body was a mottled brown, but its color changed even as Storm watched, and he realized that the creature's skin was filled with chromatophores—those pigment-adjusting cells that conform to the color of the surrounding environment. Around the creature's edge, at the bottom of the slope formed by its broad back, a fringe of feathery projections helped it blend in almost perfectly with the ocean floor. Storm concluded that if the creature didn't move its eyes, its camouflage was close to flawless. Then he made the sobering observation that all of the creature's external features harmonized in symphony to draw unsuspecting victims to the feature now closest to him.

The mouth.

A fringe-covered gash stretched five feet across the creature's front end, and Storm realized that when that cavernous maw flew open, a cavity would be created in the ocean. Water would rush to fill the sudden opening and carry with it anything, or anyone, unfortunate enough to be caught in the stream. He also realized that it was only the tough ribbons of the feather boa tangled in his dive gear that had saved him from being swept to his death.

He couldn't expect to be so fortunate again.

"You are fearfully and wonderfully made," Storm thought to the creature. "Now, go away."

Ever so slowly, Storm inched his right hand down close to his side until he felt the hose leading to his pressure gauge. He focused on the creature's eyes to see if he could detect any interest coming his way. Seeing none, he slid his hand down the hose to the gauge and turned it towards him. It read one-hundred pounds. He must have been breathing harder than he'd thought. He could stretch that air for another five minutes, and then what?

"Please go away," he again thought to the creature.

Five more agonizing minutes passed with no movement whatsoever, and Storm was down to his last, hard breaths. He could tell that the creature was also breathing by the wisps of sand stirred up periodically from the ocean bottom behind the creature's gill openings.

Seemingly oblivious to Storm, the creature opened its mouth and spit out the scooter, which Storm had completely forgotten. The scooter looked scratched and dented, and with its slightly positive buoyancy it meandered slowly upward until it tangled in kelp just below the surface. Storm watched its escape with envy. The air was coming hard.

"Please, please, go away!" he thought to the creature.

It didn't move.

Storm hung on. His body began to cry out for air. From out of nowhere the words of Cap's advice ran through his mind. "If you ever think you're about to buy the farm...."

Storm closed his eyes. Even though he felt like the biggest hypocrite that ever lived, he prayed hard, "God! I don't mean any disrespect, but if you're real, and if you're hearing me, I've got a really bad fish problem here!"

This was it. Storm sucked the last, long breath from his tank, and he knew there wouldn't be another one. It was only a matter of seconds now before he would have to surface. The creature would surely see him, and it would all be over. The creature's eyes moved. Were they looking at him? A ripple ran the length of the fringe on the bottom of the creature's body, and then, like some monstrous underwater machine, the creature rose from the sea floor, hung suspended for a moment, and then swam directly at Storm.

Storm pulled his legs up. "God help me!" he screamed silently, as the full length of the creature's back brushed against his swim fins.

Then, just like that, the creature was gone, and so was Storm's air. He had to fight to not panic. First he unbuckled his scuba tank and squirmed out from under it. That freed him from most of the entangling ribbons of feather boa. He ripped away several kelp ribbons that had caught on the buckles of his fins. Finally, he had to undo his weight belt, because, impossible as it seemed, one kelp ribbon had found its way between the belt and his body. Free at last, he shot to the surface and hung there taking in huge draughts of air.

When Storm could do something more than just breathe, he looked towards the *Nemo*. She seemed tiny and miles away. She also looked like the place that he wanted to be right now more than any place else on the planet. He saw Smitty on the flying bridge, waving excitedly and shouting, and he saw Terry and Chuck rush to the rail. The scooter was floating right next to him. He tried the throttle. It still worked, and he gratefully let the scooter tow him back to the *Nemo*. The crew was waiting for him. Chuck and Terry were on the swim step to help him aboard. On the deck behind them Smitty hummed and danced a jig.

They pulled Storm up onto the swim step and slapped his back and hugged him. All the while, Smitty danced and hummed and wiped tears from his eyes.

"I saw it!" Storm remarked, when the celebration of his safe return had abated enough for conversation.

"You saw it? What? What did you see?" his crew all asked at once.

"It was some kind of angler!" Storm climbed over the railing onto the aft deck. "Smitty, get the little fish book, the one with the halibut on the cover."

Smitty hurriedly retrieved the book and placed it in Storm's trembling hands. "I guess I'm still a little excited," Storm apologized. He thumbed through the book. "Let's see, index, page one-fifty-nine." He stabbed the page with a wet, shaky finger. "That's it!" he exclaimed. "That's exactly what I saw, right there!" Storm shuddered visibly and handed the open book to Terry.

"A goosefish?" Terry asked incredulously. "You saw a goosefish?"

"No, I didn't see *a* goosefish!" Storm said excitedly. "I saw *the* goosefish! I saw the *mother of all* goosefish!"

Smitty took the book next and read aloud: "goosefish, *Lophius americanus,* up to four feet long and sixty pounds, Florida to the Bay of Fundy, swallows anything it can get in its mouth."

"You bet it swallows anything!" Storm exclaimed. "It tried to swallow me! It's as big as a truck! Heck! It could swallow a truck!"

"Are you sure it's a goosefish?" Chuck asked, taking the book next. "The book says sixty pounds."

"It's a goosefish all right, but it's big! It's huge! It has to be over twenty feet long! It must weigh tons!"

Smitty entered the cabin and returned with the plumber's swim fin that had the deep parallel scratches. He placed it on the deck next to the scooter. A few turns of the fin, and he had the scratches on it lined up with the scratches on the scooter. He said, "That settles one question for me, Skipper, but now I got two more. How'd the dang thing get here, and how'd it get so dang big?"

"Those are two questions we'll answer when we have a chance to study it."

"Who's 'we', Skipper?" Smitty asked animatedly. "You got a frog in your pocket? I'm staying miles away from that overgrown sardine!"

Storm had finally calmed down enough to laugh. He said, "What's the strongest thing we have on board?"

"We got some Costa Rican coffee with some of the burro still in it," Smitty answered with a grin.

"Make some of that, would you? And put some chocolate in it."

Chuck held up an underwater *Nikonos* camera. "I don't suppose you took a picture?"

"Are you kidding? I don't even remember having that with me."

"Well, we'll let you off the hook this time, but only because you were looking down the thing's throat and all."

"Yes," Terry said unhappily. "Almost all the way down."

Chapter 37

It was dark before the exuberant mood aboard the *Nemo* finally quieted for the night. It was a clear evening, and Terry found Storm standing alone on the flying bridge, looking up at a sky illuminated by thousands of stars. Storm remained quiet, drinking in the beauty of the night and the pleasure of her presence. She said, "I was afraid for you today."

He continued looking up. "I'm sorry. I guess I messed up good. That's what happens when my heart gets in front of my head."

Terry placed a hand on his shoulder. "I've done that more than a few times myself."

Storm covered her hand with his own. After the day's adventure, the tingle of excitement he felt from her touch surprised him. "Did you pray for me?" he asked.

"I did, the whole time you were down."

Storm gave her hand just the slightest squeeze. "Thank you. I think it helped. I think it helped a lot."

Storm was thrilled to be alive, and he was thrilled to be with Terry. At the moment, he wondered just how much those two events were connected. He removed his hand, as did Terry, but the tingle of excitement remained.

Terry said, "I guess the next question is: what should we do now that we've found our big goosefish?"

"I'd say the first thing we do is tell Commander Logan."

As Storm and Terry admired the stars, three-hundred-twenty miles to the north a question posed by Kim Yi took Congressman Kevin Robins by surprise, and he had to stop and think before answering.

Was there any deep diving at San Clemente Island? Not that he'd done anyway. He supposed the Nine Fathom Reef would suffice. It was certainly pretty enough, and the rummy dive tender who had first told him about the reef had said that black coral grew on its flanks down past the two-hundred-foot mark. Of course, Robins wasn't about to dive that deep to prove the rummy right. He opened his mouth to give his answer but shut it again, seeing that Yi had returned his full attention to the other person sharing their table and had launched into yet another diatribe.

"You say there must be dialogue between the East and the West, but what good is dialogue if nothing gets done? Has dialogue thrown the Western Imperialists out of Korea? Has dialogue kept my culture from losing its heritage and roots? Will dialogue keep Korea from becoming just one more American-Chinese puppet?"

Yi turned away from Liu Xin and glared across the table at Robins, as if still expecting an answer to his previous question.

Liu Xin spoke up instead. "There is an appointed time for everything, and in time all things are possible." Liu Xin bowed his head to Robins and smiled apologetically. "Please forgive my outspoken friend for his, shall we say, passionate display of patriotic zeal."

Yi appeared to ignore the comment about his lack of diplomatic tact. He replied hotly, "Time, yes. Surely there is an appointed time for useless dialogue to stop and for action to begin. Our people are hungry, and they are ripe for someone with courage enough to step forward and lead them."

Robins fidgeted in his chair. At least his dinner companions were polite enough to have their argument in English. He wondered if he had made a serious blunder in etiquette by inviting himself to dinner. With prior knowledge of their itinerary, and knowing that they would be dining in San Francisco tonight, he had recommended this restaurant and had mistakenly imagined that they would be pleasantly surprised when he showed up unannounced. Indeed, Liu Xin had welcomed him graciously, but if the looks that he had been receiving all evening from Yi Kim had been torpedoes, he would have already been sunk to the bottom several times over. If nothing else, it had been an eye-opener of an evening despite his present feeling of discomfort. Robins had followed the evening's conversation well enough to understand most of what Yi was driving at. Entire nations could be manipulated by using the right combination of force, misinformation, and above all, timing, but Yi's version of events would never unfold with moderates like Liu Xin standing in the way.

The dinner, such as it was, being over, Liu Xin said, "Congressman, it is a pleasant walk back to our hotel. Won't you join us?"

Before Robins could answer, Yi said, "I think we should take a taxi."

Robins couldn't figure that one out. It was only three blocks to the hotel, and there were a lot worse places to walk than in San Francisco's China Town on a crisp, autumn evening. Also, he hadn't appreciated Yi's treatment of him tonight, and he relished any opportunity to get back at him. He answered, "You're absolutely right, Mr. Ambassador. It is a lovely night, and I'd be honored to join you."

Robins glanced at Yi and felt an entire salvo of torpedoes bore into him.

Yi, Liu Xin, and Robins exited the restaurant and became three more of the bustling sidewalk throng, with Liu Xin leading the way.

They had traveled a block when Liu Xin turned down a narrow, brick alley lined on either side with large planters of bright geraniums. The alley looked inviting enough, Robins reasoned, and appeared to be more of a public walkway than an alley as it curved in a narrow crescent between the rows of buildings. The three diplomats had walked to the midway part of the crescent when Yi suddenly raised his hand, signaling them to stop.

"Did you see something?" Robins whispered, feeling a premonition of danger. Then he realized that it wasn't what Yi had seen, but rather what he hadn't seen. There were no other people in sight, and the immediate effect was a severe sense of foreboding.

"Maybe we should go back the way we came," Robins whispered.

At that moment, a man stepped out from a recessed doorway and stood in the middle of the alley, blocking their way forward. The man looked to be Asian, in his twenties, well built and basically the same size as Yi and Liu Xin. He wore blue jeans, a white t-shirt, and a bomber jacket. His hair was pulled back in a long, black ponytail. The man smiled fiendishly and hissed in a reptilian whisper, "You have money? We want money."

Robins was now absolutely certain that they should retreat back the way they had come. He turned to flee but froze in his tracks. Three more men, dressed exactly as the first one, were standing in the middle of the alley in that direction, blocking any escape.

Robins turned around again and saw another man come out of hiding to join the first one. This last one stood at least six feet tall and bore a wicked-looking scar that twisted from the orbit of his right eye to the crease of his mouth.

Five of them! Robins counted, all dressed the same and looking very dangerous.

Click!

A switchblade knife appeared in the scarcheek's hand and snapped open, catching the dim glow of city light on its stiletto blade. The sound of four more switchblades snapping open reverberated up and down the alley's canyon walls.

Robins stood frozen, petrified with fear. He did observe that Yi somehow seemed to be maintaining a much more relaxed body position than himself.

"Can't you hear?" the first man, and apparent leader of the group, hissed. With a defiant swagger he and the scarcheek approached to stand within arm's length of Liu Xin and Yi.

"We want your money, and we want it now!" the leader snarled, and he made a sudden lunge forward and swept his switchblade towards Liu Xin's face.

It never came close.

Like a coiled serpent, Yi shot to his right in front of Liu Xin, caught the wrist of the leader's knife hand with his own right hand, slammed his other hand into the leader's right shoulder and twisted down hard. The leader grunted in pain as he was thrown downward, and he grunted again at the impact of Yi's knee slamming into his chin. At the same moment, in a surprisingly quick move, Liu Xin delivered a crushing kick with the ball of his foot to the breastbone of scarcheek, who then tumbled backward gasping for breath.

Robins, at the first sign of violence, had regained some mobility. He dropped to the ground and crawled away, seemingly unnoticed by the attackers. He found a hiding place of sorts behind a large planter filled with geraniums. Meanwhile, directly in front of him, the battle raged on.

With the attacker's leader crumpled at his feet, Yi took advantage of Liu Xin's surprise move and spun like a buzz saw into the attacker that had been approaching him from behind. The two were soon locked in a desperate, grappling struggle across the alley bricks.

The last two assailants stalked Liu Xin. They had maneuvered him away from the relative safety of the alley walls and were trying to get on both sides of him at once. The three adversaries circled each other, the two attackers waving their switchblades in small circles while Liu Xin drifted in and out of various defensive postures. Just for a moment, Liu Xin seemed to concentrate on one of the attackers too long, enabling the other one to slip behind him. That seemed to be what they were looking for, because the front attacker suddenly waded in, slashing wildly with his knife, driving Liu Xin backwards into the attacker behind him. The man behind Liu Xin delivered a vicious downward stab, but Liu Xin chose that exact instant to tumble to the ground and into the man's legs, causing him to fall forward over Liu Xin and into the other attacker. Liu Xin's assailants both came down in a heap. Before they could regain their feet, Liu Xin delivered a hard chop to the back of the neck of one of them, bouncing his forehead off the alley bricks in the process.

From out of nowhere, Yi appeared and placed himself between Liu Xin and the last attacker.

By now Robins had seen enough. He raised himself from his hiding place, cupped his hands over his mouth and yelled as loud as he could, "Help! Robbery!"

Someone must have heard him, because the sound of running feet could be heard coming up the alley from the direction that they had first entered. The five attackers apparently had also seen enough, and they picked themselves up and fled in the opposite direction. A crowd of people and police immediately filled the alley. Robins pushed his way over to Yi and Liu Xin. He heard Liu Xin say, "Thank you for saving me, Kim. I didn't have anything left, and I believe that he would have bested me."

Yi wrapped a comforting arm around Liu Xin. "Did they hurt you?"

Liu Xin swayed on his feet, and Yi wrapped his arm tighter. Liu Xin answered, "No, I'm fine, just shaken. Let's just go to the hotel."

"Only as long as you're all right," Robins said.

"I'm perfectly all right, thanks to Yi Kim."

Robins looked at Yi, who met his gaze with a face that covered his feelings like a shroud.

The three shaken diplomats were driven to the hotel in a police car, and the simple evening that Robins had originally hoped for had lathered itself into a media three-ring circus. Robins put the best spin that he could on the situation, promising before the cameras that the fight against crime was at the very core of his political agenda. All the while, Yi continued to dote over Liu Xin like a mother hen would over her chicks, dividing his attention only to glower torpedoes at Robins. In turn, Robins studied Yi whenever he thought that Yi wasn't looking, and he pondered a question that the police detectives hadn't thought to ask. Had tonight's event been a genuine robbery attempt by some street thugs, or had an embarrassing and unfortunate accident been planned for Liu Xin? If it were the latter, Yi had put up one heck of a convincing fight, but that could have been because his plans had been interrupted by the presence of an uninvited guest. One thing was certain, Robins told himself. He had to be careful around Yi.

Real careful.

It was after midnight when the last of the media finally left, and the detectives were through with their questions. Robins arranged a ride in a police car, and, surprisingly, Yi offered to escort him from Liu Xin's room down to the street. As Robins sat down in the front seat of the police car, Yi dropped to one knee and said quietly through the open car door, "You never answered my question."

Robins stared at Yi, who knelt patiently on the sidewalk waiting for an answer. He was completely oblivious to what question Yi could be referring to. Finally, Yi said, "Is there any deep diving at San Clemente Island?"

Robins saw the barest upturn of a smile at the corners of Yi's lips, but the look in Yi's eyes was as cold as ice.

"Yes," Robins answered thoughtfully. "Yes, there is."

Chapter 38

Smitty balanced engines and rudder, holding the *Nemo* close to the Wilson Cove pier without actually touching it. A Navy MP spoke across the narrow gap of water to Storm. "I'm sorry, Sir, but unless you have a medical emergency or official business, this pier is restricted against civilian use."

"Is Lieutenant Russell at the chamber?" Storm asked.

"No, Sir, the chamber is closed."

"If you'll tell Commander Logan we're here, I think he'll want to see us."

"I can try to reach him, but that's all I can do."

"Tell him it's about 'Jonah.'"

Within minutes Logan and Rory were aboard the *Nemo* listening to Storm tell of his close call with the creature. The rest of the *Nemo's* crew added their own input as needed. Storm finished his story, and Logan walked out on the aft deck where the underwater scooter lay like a maimed seal. Logan knelt down close to it. He ran his fingers along the deep scratches running the length of its body. Finally, giving the scooter a pat as one might an old dog, he stood up and said to Storm, "You're telling me we have a goosefish. A giant, monster goosefish."

"It doesn't make any sense to me, either, but that's what it is," Storm replied, hoping that Logan wasn't writing him off as a complete lunatic.

Logan looked extremely unhappy. He walked to the *Nemo's* stern rail, and for several seconds he just stared at the water. Apparently reaching a decision, he finally turned and said, "Maybe I'm as crazy as you are, but if you say it's a giant goosefish, then that's what it is. I have only one question right now. Is it going to stay put for the next few days?"

Storm invited Logan back inside the main cabin and spread a chart across the mess table. "All of the known activity of the goosefish has taken place within four-hundred yards of the destroyer wreck. That's been over a three-month period, and that's what we might expect of the species. Goosefish normally aren't chaser hunters. Their natural method is to sit in one spot and ambush their prey. They don't swim fast, and they don't swim far. If this were a normal goosefish in its normal environment, I'd say the probability is that it'd stay put, but there's nothing about this goosefish that's normal."

"But your professional opinion is that it won't move?" Logan asked, piercing Storm with a penetrating stare.

"All I can guarantee about this animal is that it's big, unpredictable, and it's extremely dangerous."

"Hmmph," Logan said, obviously displeased. He bent low over the chart. "Liu Xin is scheduled to dive on the Nine Fathom Reef and then close inshore inside of Castle Rock. That's about five miles from where you saw your goosefish. What are the odds that the thing won't move five miles?"

Storm turned to Smitty and asked soberly, "What are the odds that the thing won't move five miles?"

"It's a half-dozen of one and five of the other on predicting anything about that messed-up mackerel, Skipper," Smitty answered promptly, as if he'd already been considering the question.

"And that's probably as good an answer as you're going to get," Storm said, turning back to Logan.

"You've made your point. There's no way to know, so here's what I want. Today is October first. Yi Kim is scheduled to arrive here tomorrow afternoon. On the morning of the third he wants to check out the dive spots, and I want the *Nemo* to be his dive platform. On October fourth Liu Xin makes his dives with Congressman Robins. That's the plan as it stands, but maybe we can change it. Tomorrow night I'm having dinner here at the pier with Yi and Robins on board the *Write Off*, and now I'm inviting you. In fact, bring another of your team with you to back you up, because I want you to tell Yi and Robins everything you just told me. If they've got any brains between them maybe they'll call the whole thing off."

"Can't you just call it off yourself?" Storm asked, hoping Logan wouldn't take offense.

Logan reached down and rubbed his leg. "Have you ever had the pleasure of dealing with Congressman Robins?"

"No, I haven't had that pleasure; at least I don't think I have."

"Well, I have, and as much as I don't like to, it's easier to work with him than against him. He can pull more strings than a piano tuner, and it's just possible he could make my life more miserable than he already does."

The following evening Smitty eased the *Nemo* up to the pier behind the larger *Write Off*, which was lit up like a church and seemed to be bustling with hired help. Storm and Terry walked the short length of pier between the two boats. Storm carried the dive scooter wrapped in a blanket like a small child. They were greeted at the *Write Off* by her owner and Rory who led them onto the aft deck. Logan, Yi, and Robins were already there with drinks in their hands. Logan said affably, "Dr. Hancock, Miss Ho, allow me to introduce you to our most important guest, representing the People's Republic of China, Mr. Yi Kim."

Without a word, Yi solemnly shook their hands.

Logan continued, "And it's my pleasure to introduce you to our other special guest, Congressman Kevin Robins."

"There's nothing special about me on this boat is there, John?" Robins said laughingly, winking at the *Write Off's* owner. He reached out and gave Storm a firm handshake. "Dr. Hancock, the man who studies everything from great white sharks to pistol shrimp, or so I've heard." The congressman beamed at Storm as if he were a long-lost, newly found, rich relative.

"From what I hear, you take quite an interest in the ocean yourself," Storm answered, silently wondering if he should have worn hip boots.

"Let's just say I appreciate the ocean for what it is," Robins replied, smiling. He turned to Terry, and in a tone so perfectly balanced that one couldn't tell whether they were being mocked or praised, he said, "What a delight to meet you in person at last, Ms. Ho. Whenever I feel a need to learn about our environment, I'm sure to catch your program on Wednesday nights. I find your presentations couched in language that even I can understand without having to run to a dictionary."

Terry's eyes blazed in the *Write Off's* festive lighting. "I do strive to keep the technical level low enough to be understood by the average fifth grader."

The *Write Off's* owner jumped into the conversation. "Why don't we all sit down to dinner. We don't have the famous Smitty's cuisine, but I think you'll all agree that I've enlisted a pretty good cook."

During the sumptuous and obviously expensive dinner, the rare moments that Yi spoke were with surprisingly American-sounding English, which he explained he had learned during his time at Berkeley. Terry, in tones reaching to melt some of the ice that seemed to describe Yi's mood, said, "Mr. Yi, I envy you and your opportunity to dive all over the world. You must find it very fascinating."

"It is fascinating," Yi replied, "But I find it even more fascinating that people can find time to dive for pleasure when so many more important matters are pressing on the planet and its people."

Seemingly undaunted, Terry tried again. "But isn't it true that you travel with Liu Xin in the interest of world peace? What could be more pressing than that?"

Yi's face flashed with a look of exasperation. "Yes, peace is always desirable in the long run, but what kind of peace, and on whose terms?"

Robins, who seemed to be enjoying the course of this conversation, joined in. "Now, now, Mr. Yi, if you start bringing up politics at the dinner table, I'm going to get indigestion. I promised you some great diving here, and that's just what you're going to get. We should all just relax and unwind and give the pressing matters of the world the night off."

Yi fired a full broadside of torpedo looks at Robins, who just grinned back at him and sipped his after-dinner liqueur.

"The congressman is right," Logan said, standing up. "We

should talk about the diving, because that's why we're all here. I'm going to ask Dr. Hancock and Miss Ho to tell you about something extraordinary happening at the island. I'm sorry to say that what they're going to tell you poses a real threat to the safety of Liu Xin and anybody else that dives here. Dr. Hancock? Miss Ho? Would you two please take it away?"

Storm stood up reluctantly, wishing that he could take it all far, far away. He surveyed his audience and wondered if they would believe him the same way Logan had. He also wondered about the noticeable absence of Fishbeck. Surely there was more going on than was being revealed. He conferred with Terry for a minute while Logan retrieved the scooter from the aft deck, unwrapped the blanket from it, and placed it in the middle of the table so all could see. It had been previously agreed that Storm would do most of the talking. Terry would back him as needed while trying to read Yi's reaction.

With as much detail as he thought necessary, Storm told about his encounter with the giant goosefish. He displayed positions on a chart, and he handed around the fish book marked on the goosefish page. He pointed out the scratches on the scooter, and he gave his professional assessment that it was impossible to predict that the fish would remain far to the south of the area where Liu Xin was scheduled to dive. He finished talking, and Yi stood up and made his reaction all too plain.

"Do you take us for such fools that we would believe this pack of lies? I won't begin to guess why you would sabotage Liu Xin's effort to encourage relations between our two countries, but I will file a formal complaint through Congressman Robins. I will also advise Liu Xin of your dishonorable action. He is an honorable man, and he will allow you to save face by continuing to accept the congressman's kind invitation. As for you, Dr. Hancock, I expect that you will have the *Nemo* ready to pick me up at nine o'clock tomorrow morning."

Yi marched out of the cabin without a nod, a "Good evening," or any of the other normally accepted forms of a parting acknowledgement.

"Mr. Friendly," Terry said, loud enough to be heard by

everyone present.

Robins, who had been poking at the scooter with a butter knife during Yi's tirade, and who was making no attempt to conceal his amusement, said patronizingly, "Ms. Ho, with all respect, what did you expect? I mean, even I had trouble following that one. You and the good scientist here spin this wild tale about, a what? A duckfish?"

"Goosefish!" Terry said hotly.

"Goosefish! Duckfish! What does it matter?" Robins said with a knowing smile. "You tell us you've found some kind of low-budget movie monster, but you have no proof except for some scratches on your battery-powered tadpole? No offense to your scientific scruples, but you are in the business of drumming up excitement for your new aquarium. I wonder if your giant goosefish couldn't be explained away by acknowledging that it's a product of some well-meaning, but overactive, imagination."

Terry strode across the room and stood in front of the much-taller Robins. "As for scruples, you'd do well to run to the dictionary and find out what that word means, because you don't have a clue!"

Terry snapped an about-face and stomped out of the cabin, snarling at Storm as she passed, "I'll be on the *Nemo!*"

Had the mutual disrespect now filling the *Write Off's* cabin been any thicker, Storm could have rolled it out flat and used it to wrap fish. He said to no one in particular, "I guess we'll be back here at nine o'clock."

On the other side of the island, at the same time the *Write Off's* dinner party was self-destructing, the goosefish was experiencing its own food-related problem. Up to this day in its life, everything it had eaten had either been spit back up or had found a way through its powerful digestive system. Now, a diver's knife—eight inches of Pennsylvania chromium steel— had gotten hung up only inches away from being expelled. Having survived over two months of fierce digestive juices and grinding, the blade was still intact and had lodged in such a position as to constantly prod the goosefish's flesh. To this end, the goosefish now suffered a malady experienced by all organisms that metabolize nutrients, from the tiniest bacteria to the greatest blue whale.

It was constipated.

The goosefish first tried thrashing its powerful tail for a few seconds in an effort to rid itself of the pain. The knife only prodded all the more. In reaction, the goosefish burst across the ocean bottom in a fifty-yard rush, causing all other life forms to flee or hide, but the knife only carved its way deeper. In a crazed frenzy, hour after hour, until the first rays of dawn began to illuminate the depths, the goosefish tried to flee from the pain in its underside. Finally, exhausted and ravenous, the goosefish didn't feel the pain any more.

The knife had passed.

The goosefish had traveled five miles.

Chapter 39

The category-three hurricane that Smitty had prayed would miraculously blow up overnight hadn't materialized, so at nine a.m. sharp the *Nemo* was dutifully waiting at the Wilson Cove pier to pick up Yi Kim. Smitty loaded Yi's dive gear aboard, and then Yi requested to be taken to the dive spots in the same order that Liu Xin would dive them tomorrow. Smitty decided that if Yi was still hot from the night before, he was doing a good job of hiding it. Even so, Smitty caught on early that if Yi was at the *Nemo's* bow, Storm could probably be found at the stern, and vice versa.

The *Nemo* shoved off for the Nine Fathom Reef, and thirty minutes later she was anchored in sixty feet of water above the reef's shallowest point. Yi then surprised everyone by saying he wished to dive alone. He didn't want a buddy diver, or anyone to show him around. Please, just tell him what to look for, and he would see for himself.

Considering the source of the strange request, Smitty didn't bat an eye. He figured it was Yi's show for the day, and as long as Storm didn't say different, he'd just go along with it.

No one on board the *Nemo* had ever dived the Nine Fathom Reef, but Smitty had tended hose there for Cap, which made him the resident expert on the place. He explained what he knew about the reef to Yi, who listened with what could only be described as strained politeness. Smitty finished by saying, "If you could wait about twenty minutes, we'd be getting into slack water. That'd make things a lot easier for you. The currents out here can get kinda' nasty."

"Thank you. I will wait," Yi answered politely, looking at Smitty with perhaps the slightest glimmer of respect.

Twenty minutes later, as Smitty had suggested, Yi was sliding down the anchor line. Terry and Smitty followed his progress by watching his trail of bubbles from atop the flying bridge.

"That Yi is one strange cat," Smitty remarked.

"And friendly too," Terry replied. She glanced at her watch and asked, "Shouldn't you be in the galley whipping up something special for our distinguished guest?"

"For him? Fat chance! Tomorrow, when the really big cheese comes aboard, sure. Today this guy gets peanut butter and jelly sandwiches. If he's real nice to me, I just might throw in some barbequed potato chips."

Yi surfaced after half an hour. He removed all of his dive gear except the Farmer John bottom of his wetsuit. Then, without commenting about his dive, he found a place on the bow to warm up in the sun. Storm kept busy in his navigator's nook surrounded by charts, and Chuck kept busy by strewing one of the shark monitors across the mess table. Smitty hauled the *Nemo's* anchor and motored her to the second dive spot—a shallow, kelp-filled cove inside of Castle Rock. Her anchor hit bottom in twenty-five feet of calm, clear water. True to his promise, Smitty served a lunch of peanut butter and jelly sandwiches but with two kinds of chips. After lunch, which Yi seemed to have thoroughly enjoyed, Terry again found Smitty on the flying bridge. "Better luck next time," she said in consolation.

"Ain't it the truth? Even when I try to cook bad, I cook good. How was I to know he was a peanut butter freak?"

"I bet there's a lot more about Yi that's freaky," Terry said quietly, bringing a finger to her lips and motioning with her head for Smitty to look aft.

Smitty raised himself slightly from the pilot bench for a better look of the deck. Yi was getting dressed for his next dive. "Yeah, there's another guy I wouldn't trust as far as I could throw him."

Terry said, "Even so, I suppose the polite thing to do would be for one of us to get down there and give him a hand."

Smitty rolled his eyes and scampered down the ladder to help Yi on with his gear. As before, Yi insisted on diving alone. The water being shallow and also as smooth as glass, Yi's progress could easily be followed by the trail of his bubbles billowing up from below. After what seemed a reasonably long time, Smitty checked his watch. Yi had been down for an hour. Shortly thereafter, Yi's bubbles streamed up the anchor line, soon to be followed by Yi himself. He snorkeled to the swim step and let Chuck help him off with his gear. Terry, who had again taken refuge with Smitty atop the flying bridge, took a second look at Yi as he climbed over the back rail.

"Look at Yi's face," she whispered to Smitty. "He's as white as a sheet."

"He looks fine to me."

"That's because you're melanin challenged, but I'm half Chinese, and I tell you that man is pale."

"Maybe he's just cold."

"But the water's not that cold. No, I think something scared him big time."

Smitty's eyes got wide. "You ain't thinking...?"

"The goosefish? I don't think so. He looks scared, but not that scared. Besides, it's supposed to be five miles away."

Smitty's face relaxed. "Yeah, you're probably right. Maybe he stuck his head in a hole and came face to face with a big moray eel. Cap always said they were thicker than fleas around here."

"Yeah, maybe. I wonder," Terry said, stealing another glance at Yi.

"Why don't you just go ask him?" Smitty said with a grin.

"Me? Ask Mr. Friendly? He doesn't talk to me, but he seems to like you. Maybe you should be the one to ask him."

"Yeah, right."

"So, you are going to ask him?"

"As a matter of fact, I think I will."

Smitty climbed down to the aft deck and approached Yi, who had removed all of his gear but his wetsuit. "Mr. Yi, how was your dive?" Smitty asked, friendly enough.

Yi's eyes held a vacant stare. "My dive? It was fine. It was just fine."

"Terry and I were just saying that you might have bumped into a big moray eel."

"A moray eel?" Yi became more animated, and he faced

Smitty. "Oh, yes, there was a big moray eel."

"I knew it!" Smitty said, slapping his knee. "Cap always told me there were some whoppers around here, but don't you worry none about that, Mr. Yi. They're not nearly as mean as their reputation. In fact, Cap always said there wasn't a moray eel alive he couldn't hand feed the very first time he saw it."

"Hand feed?" Yi suddenly seemed to become very alert.

"Yep. Cap said there was nothing to it. He'd just hold the food in front of them, and they'd suck it up like free hot dogs at a Dodgers game. Maybe you'd like to try it yourself, if you get a chance. "

Yi seemed to drift away into his own thoughts again. He said absently, "Yes, thank you. Maybe I will try it, if I get a chance."

Whatever had happened, Yi told them he was satisfied that the area was safe for Liu Xin to dive, and that he was ready to return to Wilson Cove, and thank you very much, and especially thank you for the tasty lunch. The *Nemo* obediently dropped him off at the Wilson Cove pier and then tied up at a nearby mooring ball.

Five miles down the coast another, much-smaller dive boat was calling it a day. Fishbeck had grown increasingly desperate and had mustered up the courage to look for the creature again. He had wrapped a camera in a plastic bag and paddled his borrowed inflatable out near the destroyer wreck. After two nerve-rending hours of hanging over the side of the boat with his face in the water, the only picture he had taken was of an insane sea lion that had caused him to nearly jump out of his wetsuit. When he was finally safe back on shore he agonized over whether or not he should try again tomorrow. That was the only day that he knew for sure the *Nemo* planned to be miles away. As he debated the issue he tried to console himself with the two positive conclusions that he had reached. The first one was that he had discovered exactly what it was he had come to this two-bit island to discover. The second one was that he had faced the creature, man to man, and had lived to tell it. No one, not the famous Dr. Hancock and his groupies, not commando-gung-ho Logan, and not the smooth-talking congressman could ever take that away from him.

If only he could tell somebody, but who?

Without real proof, he certainly couldn't tell Logan, and he wasn't ready to tell Robins. Hopefully, he would someday be able to tell his family, though he could just imagine what would happen. His mother would babble on about the mercy of God for providing the guitar fish, and his father would demand to know why he hadn't wrestled the monster to the surface with his bare hands. No, he wouldn't be able to tell them for a long time and not until he had found just the right spin for the story. At the moment he was leaning towards a "survival of the fittest" slant. The guitar fish had raced off in the wrong direction and had been eaten, but he, Fishbeck, had raced up the anchor line and had survived. That obviously made him the fittest.

But what if he never got a picture to prove what he had seen? And what if, in the meantime, the *Nemo* managed to stumble across the creature? And why hadn't he been invited to Logan's party last night on the *Write Off*? And why had Robins called him so cordially this morning, telling him to relax and take some time off?

Fishbeck sat down on the sand and stewed. He was as lonely and confused as on the morning he first saw the creature.

Maybe he should tell Logan and Robins.

He thought about it some more, and he decided to wait at least one more day.

Chapter 40

Storm shoved his Bible deep into the foot of his sleeping bag and looked at his watch. It was only six a.m. Even though the *Nemo* wasn't due to meet Liu Xin until nine, Smitty had been banging around in the galley for half an hour. There would be no more rest this morning, Storm figured, so he dragged himself out of his bunk. He probably wouldn't have slept the last half hour anyway. He'd been thinking about Aunt Emma's dream, Cap Hanson's advice, and Terry praying on the bow. He'd been thinking about the Dall's porpoise and Betsy and Matilda and how he wouldn't have dreamed of projecting anthropomorphic illusions on to those animals. Yet, each of them seemed to have communicated with him in a language understood only by the heart. All of which caused Storm to ponder the question of whether the recent events in his life were random, independent happenings, or was there a connecting thread weaving them together into some unknown whole?

It sure seemed like they were all connected, he concluded, but wouldn't such a conclusion require the taking of a leap of faith, since it couldn't be reached from the pure distillation of empirical data? Furthermore, wouldn't the very act of taking such a leap require a conscious desire? It would, he reasoned, and he felt his former convictions wavering as he fought off the temptation to take that leap. Then he wondered if that same temptation was nothing less than faith in its most embryonic stage.

"Rise and shine, everyone! It's a beautiful day in the neighborhood!" Smitty's voice resounded through the *Nemo's* cabin.

"What's all the ruckus about?" Terry mumbled, shuffling in from the bow cabin and finding Storm and Chuck already grumbling around a pot of Smitty's coffee.

Chuck said, "I don't know, but Smitty's acting strange. I

wouldn't get too close to him if I were you."

Terry plopped herself down next to Chuck, bumping him over a few inches in the process. Smitty poured her a cup of coffee and then returned to his busy galley. He whistled while he worked.

"All right," Terry said. "Something's up. What are we celebrating?"

The whistling ended, but only after building to a climactic, warbling crescendo. Smitty said, "Today's October fourth, the Feast Day of Saint Francis of Assisi, the guy I'm named after."

"Saint Francis? Isn't that the guy with birds in his hands?" Chuck said, looking around the table with a smirk on his face.

"That's my guy," Smitty replied matter-of-factly. "Gospel-preaching, soul-reaching San Francisco. He walked his talk better than most of us, I reckon."

"But what's the deal with the birds?"

Terry said, "He was into nature, huh, Smitty. He'd say things like brother sun, sister moon, brother wolf."

"Brother giant, man-eating goosefish?" Chuck asked sarcastically.

"Let's hope so, Smitty answered, as he placed plates of his usual gem of a breakfast on the table.

Storm observed the artful concoction before him and said, "Just a minute. If we're celebrating the feast day of a Franciscan, how come we're feasting on eggs Benedict?"

Smitty, holding a hot mitt in one hand and a spatula in the other, spread his arms apologetically. "Hey, am I ecumenical, or ain't I?"

"You certainly are that, though I would have better placed you in the Jesuit camp."

"You're just saying that because of my good cooking."

"Not at all. I'm saying it, because in your own Smitty way you are somewhat of a maverick."

"But he is a good-looking man who has tinkered with the cello," Terry added, smiling at Smitty, who was now rapidly reddening in the cheeks.

"What does any of that have to do with him being a Jesuit?" Chuck asked.

"Absolutely nothing," Terry answered. "But it sure matters to the single ladies at his church."

"Ahhhhhh!" Smitty turned his back to the conversation and noisily piled dishes into the sink.

At precisely nine a.m. the *Nemo* pulled up to the Wilson Cove pier. Rory, Robins, Yi, and Liu Xin were there waiting, and Storm figured that his day was now going to rapidly deteriorate. He forced a smile and stood with Terry on the *Nemo's* rear deck as his diving guests climbed aboard.

Robins led the boarding party, and he greeted Storm and Terry by pumping their hands as if they were big-time campaign donors. Then he wrapped his arms around them and steered them to the newest member of the group. "Liu Xin, these are our gracious hosts, Dr. Storm Hancock and his lovely assistant, Terry Ho."

Liu Xin said to Terry in heavily accented English, "Terry Ho, I have seen you on TV. I only wish you could come to my country to help my people appreciate their environment as much as you appreciate your beautiful California."

"That would be an honor and a pleasure," Terry replied, "and perhaps in time it might even be possible."

"You are quite right, Miss Ho," Liu Xin answered, smiling broadly. "In time, all things are possible." He nodded towards Robins, "And with the good congressman's help, in time it might even be probable."

Storm noted that the congressman's smile didn't waver during that exchange, though it perhaps looked a little more wooden.

With the guests and their gear safely aboard, the *Nemo* set a course northward around the tip of the island to her destination outside of Castle Rock. The day blossomed into a beauty with morning overcast breaking up, a slight breeze, and water clear enough that when Smitty let go the anchor he said he could see it hit the top of the Nine Fathom Reef.

The *Nemo* wasn't alone. The *Write Off* had followed them out and had anchored nearby. Two people on board the *Write Off* were dressed in wet suits and seemed to be busy with a substantial-looking amount of camera equipment. There were also three Navy divers in a powered inflatable boat hovering around the reef like bees in search of honey. From time to time, one of the Navy divers would go in the water for a short while and then climb back aboard. After several minutes of this activity they pulled up close to the *Nemo*, gave Storm a thumbs up, then buzzed away at high speed towards the shore. Storm appreciated the fact that Logan must have arranged all of that. He called down from the flying bridge, "How's she looking, Smitty?"

"She's hanging slack, Skipper. It's time to get 'em wet."

"Then let's get 'em wet."

The plan was for Liu Xin, Robins, Yi, and Terry to make the first dive. When the four divers were suited up in full scuba gear and assembled on the swim step, Liu Xin announced, "Let us dive together in the name of peace in the ocean named for peace." Without waiting for a response, Liu Xin took a giant stride off the swim step and was quickly followed by the other divers as he snorkeled to the anchor line.

Storm watched their progress from the flying bridge. Though Robins was the official host, it was evident from the moment the *Nemo's* guests stepped aboard that Terry was going to be Liu's preferred diving buddy. That was fine with Storm. As far as he was concerned, Robins and Yi deserved each other.

The divers disappeared down the anchor line, and an inflatable from the *Write Off* motored over close to where the divers' clouds of bubbles billowed up from below. One of the two wet-suited persons aboard the inflatable tumbled over the side wearing scuba gear and wielding a large underwater camera. That would be courtesy of Robins wanting more campaign footage, Storm thought cynically, and he wondered what other surprises were coming. With nothing better to do, he climbed down the ladder and discovered Smitty going bananas in the galley. Smitty explained excitedly, "Just before he suited up, Liu Xin said he'd like to try some Southern cooking. We ain't got no chicken on board, but if we had some fish?" Smitty looked at Storm hopefully.

Storm and Smitty walked out on deck and looked at the

clouds of bubbles breaking on the surface. Everything looked as if it were going smoothly enough. Storm said tentatively, "We have our inflatable in the water. I suppose I could run in to shore and maybe spear a calico or two, but I'm saying,'maybe.'"

"Maybe'd be a whole lot better than nothing at all," Smitty encouraged enthusiastically. "Tell you what. You go fishing, and I'll watch their bubbles. If you don't get something lickity-split come on back, and I'll try something else."

"You got a deal," Storm said, glad to have something to do other than just wait around. He gathered up his *Arbalete*, fins, mask, snorkel, and a fish stringer, and he climbed over the *Nemo's* side into the inflatable. He didn't bother with a wet suit. He would probably spend more time traveling to the island and back than he would in the water. He would either have some nice fish in a few minutes, or he wouldn't. He motored over to the island and tied the boat's painter to some surface kelp. His plan was to dive shallow and work the top ten feet of the kelp forest. He slipped over the side, hyperventilated, dove down, and grabbed onto a piece of kelp. He studied the forest, looking for the motionless shapes of the calico bass among the kelp stalks. Even though the pickings seemed a little slim, a six-pounder materialized in front of him as if by magic. Storm let go of the kelp and gave just enough kick with his fins to drift into range. He took a good shot, and he had the bass untangled and on his stringer before he reached the surface. He rested, reloaded the gun, hyperventilated, and dove again. This time he stopped very close to a ten-pounder. That would make more than enough for lunch, if he could just get a good shot. The bass gave Storm the head-on look, and Storm didn't hesitate. Within the next second, the bass was securely skewered and stone dead all at the same time. Storm quickly swam up to it and grabbed it to take it to the surface. At that instant, the corner of his eye caught something large approaching from behind. He whirled around and held the spear with the fish on it as far out in front of him as he could. Ten feet away from him, suspended in liquid space, was a Navy diver giving Storm an "OK" sign with his thumb and fingers. Meanwhile, Storm's heart tried to pound its way out of his chest. The diver removed his regulator mouthpiece and gave Storm a grin, and Storm then realized why he hadn't heard or seen the diver coming. The man was using a rebreather—a scuba device that didn't emit exhaust bubbles. Storm returned the "OK" sign and bolted for the surface and much-needed air. Five minutes later he had the two fish in Smitty's hands, and ten minutes after that the fillets were laying out on a piece of wax paper. Smitty worked furiously while the *Nemo's* divers filed up the anchor line and snorkeled to the swim step, where Storm and Rory waited to help them off with their gear.

"How was it?" Storm asked, as he lifted the heavy air tank from Liu Xin's back.

Liu Xin clambered onto the swim step and stood up. "Dr. Hancock, your ocean is beautiful. Your reef is beautiful, and my guide is beautiful." Liu Xin looked toward Terry, who was still in the water waiting her turn to climb aboard.

"I'd have to agree with everything you said," Storm replied, grinning at Terry, who was now blushing mightily.

Storm helped her off with her tank. She climbed up on the swim step, saw his wet hair, and said, "Did you go swimming?"

"I had to go inshore and spear some fish for Smitty."

"You speared some fish just while we were diving?"

"When you're good, you're good."

"Did you, by chance, go to the second dive spot?"

"I was close, but not right on it. Why?"

"I was just wondering if you saw anything unusual."

"There was a Navy SEAL who scared a few years off my life. Was I supposed to see something?"

"No, not really. It's just that when Yi got out of the water yesterday he looked like he'd seen a ghost. I was just wondering if you saw a big moray or something."

"Maybe he ran into a Navy SEAL. I just found out those guys can sneak around underwater even better than I can."

"I hope that's all it was."

Storm pulled the anchor himself while the divers dressed

down to their wetsuit Farmer John bottoms in preparation to warm up, eat lunch, and swap stories about the dive they had just made. Rory took charge of refilling the tanks, and Storm idled the *Nemo* to the second spot in a shallow cove inside of Castle Rock. The Navy inflatable buzzed by close while Storm was on the bow dropping the anchor. One of the Navy divers gave him a wave and a thumbs up.

In the galley, Smitty was making good headway on preparing his Southern meal, but he was losing the battle on keeping his galley neat. His usual culinary mode of operation when working in a tight galley was to clean up as he cooked, but not today. Today, one thing was getting pushed aside to make room for the next. In the midst of the melee, Chuck's recording equipment had been crowded on to a shelf above the mess table. The devices had been mostly forgotten during the last few days, but out of habit Chuck dropped a microphone into the water whenever the *Nemo* stopped. At the moment, the equipment was hidden from view under a pile of cookbooks.

The air compressor purred away outside. Animated stories about the previous dive saturated the *Nemo's* cabin and decks. Smitty clattered around in the galley. Amidst the commotion, Chuck's equipment remained unnoticed as it picked up the target sound, recognized same, marked the time, dutifully recorded all of that, and returned to its watchful sleep.

Chapter 41

Terry sat down next to Liu Xin and marveled at the presentation before her. It looked like Smitty had pulled off the impossible, serving up a lunch of fresh spinach salad with bacon bits and tangelo slices, deep-battered fillet of fish, corn on the cob, black eyed peas, and hush puppies—that most-southern deep-fried mixture of cornbread and onion. Dessert was hot peach cobbler with vanilla ice cream. The sumptuous meal made an obvious impression on Liu Xin, who said, "I think I shall leave Yi Kim here with you and take Mr. Smitty back to China with me."

The *Nemo's* cabin filled with laughter, with the loudest laugh coming from Robins. Yi only smiled coolly. He glared a salvo at Robins and said to Liu Xin, "But who would watch over you when you dive in strange and dangerous waters?"

"You are right, as usual," Liu Xin answered with a smile. "I should take Miss Ho with me also. I'm sure Dr. Hancock wouldn't mind loaning me his lovely assistant."

Terry said, "That sounds like a great idea! How about it, Storm?"

Storm turned beet red. "Well, uh...."

Liu Xin burst out laughing. "Dr. Hancock, please. Don't look so serious. Of course I would never take her away from you, though it would be a pleasure. Besides, what danger could I possibly face when Yi Kim is watching over me?"

"That's right," Robins agreed loudly, getting up from the table. "Now if you'll all excuse me, I have to get a little surprise ready. Go ahead and start your next dive, and I'll meet you underwater." Robins then boarded an inflatable from the *Write Off*, and it carried him straight to shore. What he was up to was anybody's guess.

Lunch would be allowed to settle before the divers would start gearing up for the next dive. In the protected, shallow cove there was no need to worry about currents caused by the tide, and the scuba tanks were still being filled. The divers and crew found different places to relax. Yi chose the flying bridge, laid himself down on the sun-warmed deck, and soon appeared to be asleep. Terry and Liu Xin sat close to each other on portable deck chairs on the aft deck. It was in the middle of a sobering conversation concerning human rights and the role of government when Liu Xin abruptly stopped talking. Barely turning his head he rolled his eyes upward toward the flying bridge. Apparently satisfied at what he had seen, he reached down to a swim fin lying on the deck near his chair. He glanced up again at the flying bridge and then wet his forefinger in water trapped in the foot pocket of the fin. With his finger he drew a small, shallow arch on the deck between his feet and Terry's. He then sat up and looked at Terry as if waiting for a reply.

Terry stared at the arch of water as if it were on fire. What Liu Xin had done was something she had heard about but had never expected to see, especially since she lived in a country where religious freedom was still pretty much taken for granted. She reached down, wet her finger in the same swim fin, and drew another arch, but upside down, connecting with the first one at one end and crossing it near the other. The completed drawing was the most elementary rendering of the Christian Fish. She raised her eyes to meet Liu Xin's, and he gave a slight nod in affirmation.

Suddenly, Terry had a thousand questions. What was it like to be a Christian in a communist country? Was the persecution as bad as they said? How had he become a Christian in the first place?

Liu Xin must have anticipated her thoughts, because he put a finger to his lips and mouthed silently, "Some other time."

Terry glanced up at the flying bridge. Yi looked to still be asleep, but had she just seen movement? It would be just like him to be watching them in secret. She said quietly, "How does Mr. Yi feel about that?"

Liu Xin's mouth smiled, but his eyes looked sad. He answered quietly, "Yi does not agree. He thinks I am an old fool."

Terry placed her hand upon his knee. "You are certainly

not a fool. You are a wise and good man."

Liu Xin just smiled with his sad eyes.

Terry looked up again. Yi was standing up. He grinned down at her and waved. She waved back, trying to look friendly, not trusting him for a second.

For the next dive, Yi insisted on being Liu Xin's diving buddy, stating that Terry had monopolized Liu Xin on the last dive, and that it was his turn. Now that Robins was mysteriously absent, Rory would complete the foursome and would be Terry's diving buddy. Yi then surprised everyone by producing from his gear a huge, Samson spear gun. Terry recognized the gun from her time helping at the dive shop. It was one of the most powerful spear guns that could be bought over the counter.

Storm chuckled in grim humor and remarked quietly to Terry as he helped her on with her tank. "If Yi thinks that pig sticker would be any good against the monster I saw, he's dreaming."

"Smitty and I think he's afraid of moray eels."

"Maybe so. Do me a favor, and just try to stay far away from him."

Now that the divers were away on their second dive, Smitty finally had time to clean up his galley, but he needed a break. He climbed up to the flying bridge for a look around, and what he saw caused him to run back down for a pair of binoculars.

"Would you look at that?" he cried out when he had returned to the flying bridge. "Robins has got himself some kind of submarine!" He handed the glasses to Storm, who then passed them on to Chuck.

A contingent of vehicles with trailers, inflatable boats, and wet-suited people had congregated on the pebbly beach directly inshore from the *Nemo*. At the moment, a sleek white craft was being floated from off one of the trailers and into the water. Near the middle of the boat, next to what looked like the cockpit, stood Robins.

"We got more company!" Smitty exclaimed, pointing north up the shoreline. Chuck turned the binoculars towards a dark-hulled boat, much larger than the *Nemo*, that was obviously making haste to join the impending operation. The approaching vessel had a long, low aft deck on which stood a substantial-looking crane.

"*Tuna Tail*," Chuck announced, reading the name on the vessel's bow.

Meanwhile, Robins had disappeared inside the white craft, closed the hatch, and soon was half submerged and heading towards the *Nemo*, with the camera boat from the *Write Off* following close behind.

"Must be making ten knots," Smitty observed, as the craft glided by.

The *Nemo's* crew could easily see Robins, who waved up to them just before the craft slipped beneath the surface, leaving a trail of bubbles.

"Pretty slick," Chuck commented. "I wonder if he could use a good electrical engineer."

"You'd work for that ...?" Storm saw the grin on Chuck's face and realized he'd just been had.

Smitty said, "Skipper, I keep telling you to take him behind the woodshed and whup' him some. I'd do it myself, but I can't learn him nothing."

The *Write Off's* inflatable boat tied up to some surface kelp, and a diver with a camera tumbled over the side. The *Tuna Tail* dropped anchor fifty yards north of the *Nemo*, and several inflatables buzzed out from shore to tie up with her. The show seemed to be winding down for the moment, so Storm ambled to the bow to catch some sun. Chuck grabbed a book and sat down at the mess table, and Smitty finally started to clean his galley. First he collected the leftovers. Then he washed the dishes and cooking utensils. Finally, he gathered up his cookbooks, which had wound up everywhere. He grabbed the last one, and he found himself staring at a flashing light on one of Chuck's machines.

"Chuuuuuuuck?" Smitty said, mildly alarmed, but figuring what he was looking at probably didn't mean much of anything.

"What's up, Smitty?" came a disinterested voice from

behind <u>Zen and the Unified Field Theory</u>.

"One of these gizmos of yours is blinking at me."

Chuck threw the book down and leaped to his feet. He saw the flashing light, and the color drained from his face. "Houston, we have a problem," he said tersely. He put on his headset, and his hands were a blur as he twisted knobs, rewound tape, and played it back. He repeated the whole process, then he looked wide-eyed at Smitty and said, "It's right under the boat!"

"Holy, jumping....!"

Smitty tore out of the cabin like a madman and raced to the bow. He found Storm stretched out on his back, dressed only in swim trunks. "Skipper, Wake up! Wake up!"

Storm opened his eyes. "I'm not asleep," he said groggily. "What's the problem?"

"We got a contact!"

Storm bolted upright. "What do you mean, 'a contact'?"

"I mean a contact! The goosefish! Right under the boat!"

Chapter 42

Storm raced aft, yelling as he ran. "Smitty, hit the diver recall! Chuck, get on the horn and call the Navy!" He reached the *Nemo's* stern rail where the inflatable was tied. He listened for the wail of the underwater siren, but all he heard was the slithering sound of the surface kelp and the pounding of his own heart.

"Smitty!"

"I'm hitting it, Skipper! It ain't coming on!"

Storm abandoned the idea of taking the inflatable. He opened a deck locker, pulled out a mask and a pair of fins, and ran to the nearest tank that had a backpack and regulator attached. The pressure gauge on the regulator read five hundred pounds. That would have to do, he told himself, and he flung the tank onto his bare back.

"Smitty, where are they?"

Smitty yelled back from the flying bridge. "I got 'em, Skipper! There's two sets of bubbles! One's straight off the bow, and one's a little to starboard!"

Storm pulled his mask and fins on and climbed over the rail. "Chuck, take the inflatable! If anybody surfaces, haul 'em in! Smitty, you're in command!"

Storm barreled into the water and powered down straight off the *Nemo's* bow. He quickly spotted the two sets of divers. Rory and Terry were nearest, kneeling on the bottom and looking at something that Rory held in his hand. He plummeted down on top of them, startling them with his sudden appearance. He gave them such an emphatic thumbs-up, surfacing signal they instantly obeyed him and shot for the surface.

Two down, two to go.

Eighty feet away Yi and Liu Xin were bobbing slowly across the bottom near some large feather boa bushes. Storm swam towards them at full speed.

Twitch.

Storm saw the lure, wriggling just behind a large bush of feather boa, but Yi and Liu Xin seemed oblivious and were actually moving towards it.

Twitch.

Storm ripped the water with his fins. Yi and Liu Xin continued to move in the wrong direction.

Twitch.

Storm was still twenty feet away. "Look out! Look out!" he screamed through his regulator, but his warning was lost in clouds of bubbles.

Twitch.

It couldn't be, but it almost looked as if Yi purposely shoved Liu Xin directly at the lure. Liu Xin stopped swimming and stared at Yi in obvious bewilderment.

Twitch.

Storm plowed into Liu Xin and wrapped him and as much of the feather boa bush as he could in an immense bear hug. In the same instant he heard *the* sound, and the water around them turned inside out. Like flags in an underwater hurricane, Storm and Liu Xin fluttered inches away from a nightmare mouth. Storm felt a jolt, then another one. The feather boa ribbons were breaking. "If I take the wings of morning!" his mind screamed.

The hurricane suddenly stopped, and Storm and Liu Xin flowed back gently in the opposite direction as the floats lining the feather boa ribbons brought everything back to vertical. Storm's heart pounded in his chest. He spit out the part of his mouthpiece that he had just bitten off, but he was still getting air. Liu Xin's mask was gone, but periodic clouds of bubbles told Storm that Liu Xin still had his mouthpiece and was breathing.

But where was the goosefish? It could attack again at any instant.

And where was Yi?

Storm didn't dare loosen his grip on Liu Xin and the feather boa, but he had to do something. They had come to rest in a position facing away from the goosefish, and it seemed easiest to turn himself and Liu Xin back towards the way they had first come. He kicked his fins ever so slightly, and then he saw Yi, ten feet away, with the Sampson spear gun loaded and aimed just over their heads.

Questions overloaded Storm's brain. Should they try to get to Yi under the cover of the spear gun? What if the goosefish attacked just as they let go of the feather boa? Hadn't he told Terry the spear gun was no match for the monster?

"What do I do?" Storm prayed, and suddenly he realized that Yi was not aiming over their heads at all. He was aiming directly at Liu Xin, and he was about to pull the trigger!

Storm yanked Liu Xin down hard and spun him around. At the same instant he heard the unique "clink" of a spear gun being fired. What felt like a mule kicked Storm in the back, and a searing pain ripped through his right shoulder. He somehow kept his grip on Liu Xin and the feather boa, and he spun them both around again in time to see Yi charging like an attacking barracuda. Sunlight glinted on the large diver's knife that Yi held out in front of him. A Navy diver was closing fast on Yi from behind, but not fast enough. Storm wrenched Liu Xin behind him, timed Yi's charge, and at the last instant kicked his swim fins in Yi's face, causing Yi to veer upward.

The shock from the shoulder wound now caught up with Storm, and he felt like he was drifting through a slow-motion dream. The Navy diver suddenly stopped swimming towards them. His eyes showed white behind his mask and were fixed on a point not far behind Storm and Liu Xin. "The goosefish is still there!" Storm's mind screamed silently, even as he saw Yi swoop down from above. Storm tried to spin Liu Xin out of the way one more time, but the tangle of feather boa ribbons bound him too tightly, and he could only watch and pray as Yi closed in for the kill, but then he heard *the* sound.

Masks, fins, and snorkels, ripped from their bodies in a tornado of water that tried to suck their very breath away. The feather boa stretched, and some of it broke, and then the tornado was over.

What was left of Storm's regulator was still giving him air. Liu Xin was still with him, and he too was breathing. Storm's mask was gone, and the saltwater burned his unprotected eyes, but that was nothing compared to the pain in his shoulder. He figured the goosefish must also have gone, because the Navy diver was now working to untangle him and Liu Xin from the feather boa. Terry, still in scuba gear, arrived to help. The spear shaft had gone through the tough plastic of Storm's backpack and into his shoulder, and she now steadied it carefully as Storm and Liu Xin finished getting untangled, and they all surfaced together next to an inflatable in which Chuck and Rory were waiting.

"Just stay put while I look at this," Rory instructed, seeing the spear shaft protruding four feet out behind Storm.

Storm waited patiently, with Terry gripping his hand, while Rory leaned over the inflatable's side and felt around for what seemed forever. Rory finally said, "OK, Stormy, the spear hit your tank, ricocheted into your backpack, went clean through that, and then into your shoulder. You were really lucky."

"You call this lucky?" Storm groaned.

"Yes. This thing has three huge barbs on it, but the tank and backpack slowed it down enough that they didn't reach your skin. If they had, we'd need to do surgery, but as it is...." Rory unbuckled Storm's backpack and tank and removed them straight back from his shoulder. The spear backed out with it, leaving a jagged puncture wound.

"That's good," Rory said, looking pleased. "Now let's get you to the *Nemo*, and we'll stitch this baby up."

Aboard the *Nemo*, Storm lay down on a makeshift mattress of wetsuits for Rory to do his work. Terry held his hand while Rory cleaned the wound, sewed it most of the way up, packed it with antibiotics, and taped a dressing over the top. Rory said, "You're going to have a great-looking scar. I don't want to close it all the way just yet. Let's let it heal from the inside out. You just need to stay out of the water for awhile."

"Yeah, like forever."

"Nah, just a week or two."

Rory finished his doctoring, and Storm sat up shakily. "Oooh, that hurts," he said, wincing and trying to find a comfortable position.

"Well, it should. It looks bad enough," Terry said.

From his sitting position, Storm counted the people on deck. He came up one short. "Where's Yi?" he asked, though he had a grim idea what the answer would be.

Liu Xin knelt on one knee to address Storm in a voice heavy with sadness. "He is gone, Dr. Hancock. Thanks to you, I am still here, but Yi was taken by that creature. I am ashamed to have caused you so much trouble."

Storm stared into Liu Xin's eyes. If there was ever one thing in his life he was going to be proud of, it was that he had saved this honorable man's life. He didn't know what to say. "You're ashamed?" he finally said kindly. "No, I'm the one who should be ashamed. I thought that thing was miles away."

Terry said, "Yi knew the goosefish was here. He ran in to it yesterday. I saw it in his face, but I didn't trust my own eyes."

Chuck climbed down from the flying bridge holding a small piece of tape. "Looks like our unfortunate friend found time to sabotage the diver recall. I wonder what else we'll find."

Liu Xin's face drooped in sadness. "I knew that Yi thought I was standing in the way of his dreams, but I misjudged his true loyalties. Because of that, his bitter life is over, but thank you again, Dr. Hancock. You are a very brave man."

Storm remembered his pounding heart, his prayer to God, his feeling of helplessness. "No, I'm far from brave. I'm just lucky, or something."

Smitty scampered out of the cabin. "Skipper, I've got Logan on the horn. I filled him in, but he wants to hear your voice. He's on his way out here."

"I guess I should talk to him," Storm said wearily. He put a hand on Terry's shoulder and let her help him up.

"Are you ready to stand?" Rory asked. "You've had quite a shock to the system."

"I'm all right. It just hurts like the dickens."

"We've got some Tylenol with codeine."

"Tylenol without codeine will be fine. Maybe after we're tied up for the night I'll take you up on it." Storm shuffled into the cabin and talked to Logan, who seemed mainly to want to make sure he had his facts straight and that Liu Xin was in one piece. Storm then thought he just might lie down for a few minutes. He sat down on a bunk, but Chuck said, "Before you pass out, take a listen to this."

"If you tell me you have another contact, you're fired."

"No, it's not that. Just listen."

Chuck turned up the volume on his machine. From the speaker came a slow, "tap-tap-tap... tap...tap...tap...tap-tap-tap." It repeated the same pattern over and over.

Storm said, "That, my friend, is an 'SOS.'"

Chapter 43

From the relatively safe confines of *Charlie*, Robins had watched the entire episode play out between Storm, Liu Xin, Yi, and the monster. The giant fish had inhaled Yi and then wandered off into deeper water with Robins following it to the hundred-foot mark. That was four times the depth he had ever taken *Charlie*, but it posed no problem, because she was designed to dive to five hundred.

The goosefish came to rest on a rocky ledge that dropped off sharply into deeper blue. The ledge lay just outside of the kelp forest, and Robins had a clear view of the creature as he eased *Charlie* down onto the same ledge at what he figured was a safe distance. From eighty feet away he took a studied look at the creature.

"Goosefish, you are some kind of piece of work," he finally said to the fish, acknowledging to it his own form of appreciation. "And now look what you've done. You've given me all kinds of options."

Although Robins was a hundred feet down, he wasn't worried about the bends, because he was surrounded by surface pressure in his bubble of clear plastic. His main concern was the quality of the air that he breathed and how much reserve of air he had at all times. He checked his instruments. Carbon dioxide was in the green, and his reserve air was at over ninety percent. The air reserve dropped quickest when used to blow ballast water or fire torpedoes. Otherwise, it just trickled into the cockpit to freshen the air.

Robins figured he had plenty of time, but he didn't enjoy being down that deep all alone, and he'd just as soon leave as quickly as possible. He told himself to get things right the first time.

The way he saw the picture, the Chinese had just lost a member of a peace delegation, and they would naturally be upset. On the other hand, they would probably appreciate the bargaining power the incident provided.

But what if he were to blow away the thing that ate their man? Couldn't that be construed as a form of saving face and give him an inside track during future negotiations? It could, he reasoned, and it could also show the fighting capability of his new submarine. Why, the entire scenario could wind up with him smelling like a rose.

Robins continued to study the goosefish, and he found himself appreciating it more and more. He would tell them that he had followed the goosefish in the interest of science, but it had attacked him for no apparent reason, and he had been forced to defend himself. He visualized the headline: "Congressman Wins Life and Death Struggle with Sea Monster!"

And what a monster! Robins thought, admiring the creature, and for just a heartbeat he considered the scientific and aesthetic values of keeping the goosefish alive, but then he envisioned the pleasure of breaking the news to Ms. Ho that her special goosey fishy wishy was all special deadsy wedsy.

Oooh, he would like that, he thought smugly.

Sure of his course, Robins reached down to the firing console to the right of *Charlie's* pilot seat. He pulled back a plastic cover, exposing four toggle switches. He flipped all four switches and heard the satisfying sound of air charging the launch pistons at the base of the two torpedo tubes. *Charlie* became silent again, and four green lights lit up on the console. According to the announced plan, Robins had elected to bring torpedoes on this first public excursion of *Charlie*, and he'd left the mechanical arms in San Diego. Without telling anyone, however, on the night before *Charlie* was to hitchhike on a Navy flight to San Clemente Island, he had slipped into her hangar, and on her two torpedoes he had substituted live, demonstration warheads in place of the dummies. He had originally hoped to unveil *Charlie* at the Nine Fathom Reef and possibly blow a chunk out of Castle Rock. It would have made fantastic video, but at the last second he had decided not to make *Charlie's* first ocean dive in that much open water.

But now, here he was, armed and dangerous, Robins

thought happily to himself, and everything was going to work out just fine. Granted, the demonstration charges were less than a five-hundredth as powerful as the real thing, but they still made a good bang, and he figured two well-placed shots should be more than enough to put one overgrown goosefish out of its misery.

Robins unfolded a sighting device built into the *Charlie's* front console until it was locked into position in front of his face. The sight was a simple sheet of clear plastic with marks on it and a bubble level. He merely had to line up the marks, the target, and sighting marks etched in the cockpit canopy. If he kept the bubble centered, he would hit what he aimed at.

Using *Charlie's* bow thrusters and tail, he lifted her off the ledge and began zeroing in. He marveled at how well she handled. It was all going to be so easy. The goosefish was even helping him by continuing to sit motionless like a sitting duck.

"Goosefish a sitting duck," Robins said, laughing. "Oooh, I like that, too." He flipped back another clear plastic cover to expose a red button marked with the word "Fire." With one hand he placed his thumb on the button. With the other hand he maintained *Charlie* in her hover.

"Goodbye, Mr. Goosefish, and Goodbye, Chicken of the Sea," Robins said smugly, and he pressed the button.

Nothing happened.

Robins was shocked. In all of the previous trials this had never happened. He struggled to maintain his target, and he pressed the button again.

Nothing.

Robins stabbed furiously at the button, again and again, until it finally got pushed below the surface of the console and became stuck there.

Robins cursed, and he slammed the sighting device back into its storage position. He let go of *Charlie's* controls, opened an emergency tool kit, and began undoing the fasteners that held the firing component of the console in place. *Charlie,* without guidance, settled back down gently onto the ledge, with her nose pointing out into deeper water.

The top of the console came free, and Robins turned his

head to check on the goosefish. It hadn't budged. "Just stay put, fish," he snarled. "I'm not near done with you."

Robins lifted the molded console top and immediately saw the problem. A fuse had been taken out of its socket and been taped to the console's underside. Alongside of it was taped a folded piece of paper. Robins ripped the paper from the console and opened it up. It was a note in the handwriting of Ed Mills, *Charlie's* transportation chief. Robins and Mills had butted heads throughout the entire length of the project, and Robins wanted him fired yesterday, or sooner. He read the note.

> Congressman,
>   Next time you change the warheads, let us know. The Navy wouldn't fly her out for us unless we did something to disarm her. We knew you'd find the fuse in your usual pre-dive check.

Robins, in his haste to launch *Charlie*, had not completed his usual pre-dive check.

"Mills, you idiot!" he roared, crumpling the note and throwing it to *Charlie's* floor. He ripped the fuse from the tape holding it and jammed it into place in its socket. Instantly he felt a double lurch, and the two torpedoes shot out into liquid space.

Robins had forgotten about the stuck firing button.

As he watched the two torpedoes hum merrily away into the deep he couldn't decide whether to foam at the mouth or go brain dead. "That's it, Mills!" he yelled. "You are gone! You are fired! As soon as I get to a...."

His words were cut short by the impact of his head slamming against the top of *Charlie's* cockpit.

Robins got a glimpse of a massive shape, and then *Charlie* was rolling and tumbling down the rocky slope. Robins hung on like a rodeo clown in a barrel as the goosefish rammed into *Charlie* again and again. Deeper and deeper they plummeted, with Robins screaming in terror.

Finally, apparently losing interest, the goosefish gave up its attack and leisurely swam back up the slope, leaving Robins and *Charlie* battered and bleeding.

Robins pulled himself to an upright position. His head was throbbing, and if he put his hand to the spot that hurt it came away bloody. That, and numerous bruises, seemed to be the extent of his injuries. *Charlie* lay on her side, surrounded by a landscape of jagged boulders. Her clear canopy was heavily scratched but seemed to be water tight. What concerned Robins most was the steady stream of bubbles pouring out from somewhere behind the cockpit. He checked his reserve air supply gauge. Its front had been smashed, but the needle read eighty percent. The depth gauge, assuming it was still working, read two-hundred-forty feet.

"OK, Kevin, get a hold of yourself," Robins said aloud to try and calm himself down. An inch at a time, he shifted his body and found that he was able to roll *Charlie* into a more upright position. That was a good start, he reassured himself. He tried *Charlie's* thrusters and tail. They were all dead. Meanwhile, the stream of bubbles continued to pour out. He checked the air reserve gauge, and he swore he could see the needle move.

Robins decided to risk blowing one of the ballast tanks. He turned a valve and heard the movement of air, and immediately he saw an increase in the bubbles streaming from *Charlie's* stern, but she didn't move. He shut the valve. He wouldn't try that again.

He wasn't done yet. He pulled a lever and slid the pilot seat aft. He removed four wing nuts and exposed a red D ring marked, "Emergency Only." If he pulled that ring, a sixty-pound weight would release from *Charlie's* hull, and nothing could stop her from rising to the surface. It would be an uncontrolled ascent, but anything seemed better than being stuck down here. He looked again at his reserve air. It was down to seventy-five percent.

Robins yanked the handle, and *Charlie* began to rise.

"I'm safe!" he cried in relief, and then *Charlie* pivoted upward on her tail and stopped.

Charlie's nose pointed straight up, and she was obviously trying to surface, but something was holding her. Robins could only figure that the forks of her tuna tail had somehow tangled themselves in the surrounding jagged rocks. He rocked his body from side to side and back and forth in an effort to free her, but she didn't move. He watched the bubbles stream away upward to disappear somewhere beyond the limits of the water visibility. The air in the cockpit suddenly seemed stale. Meanwhile, the realization sank in that no one knew where he was or even that he was in trouble.

He had never felt so alone.

Robins became motionless, listening to the sound of his breathing and the sound of the escaping bubbles.

He retrieved a pair of pliers from the tool kit, found a substantial piece of *Charlie's* molded interior, and he began to tap.

Chuck said, "All right, it's an 'SOS,' but who's sending it?"

Storm gave up completely on the thought of lying down, and he stepped back outside. The inflatables from the *Tuna Tail* were hovering over the dive site with their occupants alternating between scanning the water surface and peering into the depths. On shore, and on the *Tuna Tail* and the *Write Off,* people could be seen hurrying around in obvious distress. Storm instantly read the situation and mustered his crew and guest on the *Nemo's* stern. He said, "Robins is still down, and he's in trouble. Terry, start the engines and take the wheel. Smitty, pull the anchor. Chuck, get your headset on, and tell Terry which way to go. Rory, call the *Tuna Tail* and the Navy, and then fill air tanks."

Liu Xin said, "Dr. Hancock, what can I do?"

In the senior diplomat's face, Storm saw a willingness to try most anything. He put his hand on Liu Xin's shoulder. "You pray."

The *Nemo's* crew flew into action, and Storm wondered if this day could possibly get any worse. With Terry at the wheel, and Chuck telling her to turn left or right, the *Nemo* idled away from shore towards deeper water. In a few minutes Chuck called out, "This is as close as we can get with one microphone!"

"How deep are we?" Storm called from the back deck.

"Two-forty!" Terry called from the flying bridge.

"Smitty, drop the little anchor with the long line!" Storm called forward.

"I don't know if it'll reach the bottom, Skipper!"

"Drop it anyway! Let it all out! Rory, how are the tanks?"

Rory gaped open-mouthed at Storm, who by now had pulled his wetsuit on. "How are the tanks? Are you kidding? It's two-hundred-and-forty feet, and you've got a hole in your shoulder!"

Terry abandoned her post the instant she saw Smitty toss the anchor. She ran up to Storm and yelled, "What do you think you're doing?"

"I'm suiting up," Storm said calmly. "It's cold down there."

"No! You're not going anywhere! Wait a minute, and the Navy will be here!"

"Robins may not have a minute. Rory, how are the tanks?"

"We've got this full one and two more that'll be full in a couple of minutes, but no one goes to two-forty on a single tank."

"I've done it before," Storm said, and he strapped the full tank to his back.

"Oh, sure. You've been to two-forty on a single."

"Yes, in Micronesia, looking for black coral."

"This isn't Micronesia."

Storm ignored Rory's last remark. He understood full well the difference between a deep dive in the warm, aquarium-like waters of Micronesia and a deep dive in the cold, kelp-filled waters of California. He pulled eight pounds of lead from his weight belt to compensate for the great depth. He knew that his wet suit was going to compress more than normal and not be nearly as buoyant as usual. He looked towards the bow.

"Smitty!"

"I found the bottom, Skipper!"

"That's good. At least we have a line to go down."

"You can't go!" Terry protested. "I won't let you! It's too deep, and you're hurt! Wait for the Navy!"

"We can't wait. Robins could be out of air."

Storm reached up and touched the back of his hand to Terry's cheek. It felt soft and smooth, and more than anything he wished he could wrap his arms around her and tell her his full feelings. He said, "I need you to meet me at a hundred-and-twenty feet with an extra tank." He took his hand away, slipped his legs over the rail, and plummeted into the water. He heard Rory's voice yelling behind him. "You have five minutes bottom time! You hear? Five minutes!"

Storm descended as fast as his ears would equalize to the increasing water pressure. He powered down, letting the anchor line guide him. Down he plummeted, into a deep blue that seemed to have no end. He passed a hundred feet, and then he shuddered as a huge, sinister-looking shape materialized from out of the blue ether below him. To a diver descending alone in deep open water, the gigantic leaves streaming out from the singular float of bull kelp looked everything like some *Kraken* of ancient myth. Storm forced himself to breathe slowly as he continue to power down past the twenty-foot-long leaves, knowing that once he reached the bottom, he would be using the air in his tank nine times faster than he would at the surface. Below him, the deep-blue nothing faded into a darker deep-blue nothing, but he pressed on. As he passed one-hundred-fifty feet, three things happened. He saw what could possibly be the bottom coming into view below. He picked up the trail of bubbles streaming from *Charlie*, and he felt the first twinges of nitrogen narcosis. He continued down, following *Charlie's* bubbles, and the narcosis rapidly became worse.

"If I take the wings of morning..." He tried to repeat the Psalm in his mind.

The white shape of *Charlie* resolved plainly into view. Storm continued dropping. The water became colder and darker, until finally he was kneeling on the rocky bottom next to *Charlie* and suffering from narcosis unlike any he had experienced before. His depth gauge seemed to be in some kind of code. The dial rested on two-hundred-forty feet, but the exact significance of that number eluded him. He wasn't sure, but he thought it meant that he was dangerously deep, and that he had to get the heck out of there.

Storm studied his situation. Robins was gesturing wildly at him from inside *Charlie*, but he didn't have time to answer.

He had a problem to solve.

Charlie's tail was toggled in a crevice of rock, and Storm had to pull down on her and slide her tail out of the crevice. At least that's what he thought he had to do. Groping in the surrealistic dream of narcosis, he couldn't be sure. His bubbles sounded like small bells tinkling in four-four time whether he was breathing in or out. His head didn't feel attached to his body, and his anxiety level flirted with a feeling of panic.

"And dwell in the uttermost parts of the sea?"

Is that how it went?

He was so deep. Had he already been down too long?

Nothing made sense.

Extremely worried now, Storm pulled down on *Charlie's* tail and slid it away from him. Immediately, *Charlie* began to rise, and it dragged Storm with it. He must have done the right thing. Now if he could just get back to the surface before he ran out of air.

Wasn't that the problem? Running out of air was very dangerous, wasn't it? Yes, it was, Storm's befuddled mind reasoned, and that's why he had to hurry. His air was already beginning to come hard.

Charlie towed Storm upward, but it seemed so slow. He looked at his depth gauge. Two-hundred feet. Why was he still so deep? Was he going to get the bends? Was this submarine thing slowing him down? If only he could think more clearly.

The air came harder.

Storm saw a rope of some kind nearby and decided it was an anchor line. He followed the line upward with his eyes and saw three tiny figures far above him. One of them was smaller than the other two, and he thought he saw long flowing hair.

Was it a mermaid?

Storm was almost completely out of air, and this thing he was holding on to must be slowing him down. He let go of it and swam over to the line. *Charlie* rose faster now and quickly left him behind. There was no more air in his tank. He sucked the last short breath from it and struggled upward. The surface was still so far away.

The narcosis both blunted Storm's fear and caused his fear at the same time. He fought for the surface, kicking with his fins and pulling himself up the rope. He didn't want to die underwater.

Was this what it felt like to die?

A tunnel formed around his vision, and he powered into it, desperate, struggling. A moment before the tunnel collapsed into darkest night, Storm thought he saw the mermaid far above him coming his way.

Coming like an arrow.

Chapter 44

Air!

As much air as Storm needed coursed into his lungs, filling him with life. Accompanying that significant development was the gradual realization that someone was towing him upwards through the water.

Was it the mermaid? he wondered, remembering the tiny figure he'd seen plummeting toward him before everything had turned black. As Storm and his mysterious rescuer continued up through the hundred-foot mark, his narcosis, as was normal for the malady, left him instantly and altogether. He was suddenly stone-cold sober and completely functional, and not entirely surprised to find that his rescuing mermaid was Terry.

And wasn't that just like her? He had told her to meet him at a hundred and twenty, and she had come down to a hundred and seventy-five.

Thank God that she had.

That last thought caught him by complete surprise.

Storm and Terry reached the twenty-foot mark where Rory was waiting for them on scuba and holding another full tank under his arm. He showed Storm a message written on an underwater writing slate.

Stay here until I tell you otherwise!

Storm took the slate from Rory and wrote on it with the attached marker.

You're the doctor!

Rory left them with the full tank and returned to the surface with the empty one from Storm's back. Ten minutes later he returned with another full tank for Terry, and he motioned them both up to ten feet. They waited there another twenty minutes, allowing Storm to decompress until Rory came down for the last time and gave them the thumbs up signal to surface.

Storm rose gently up into the most glorious sunshine he'd ever seen. He removed the regulator from his mouth, and he breathed in the sweetest air he'd ever breathed. Terry surfaced right beside him, and if she hadn't had a regulator in her mouth he probably would have kissed her right then and there. He pulled himself onto the *Nemo's* swim step and marveled at how the *Nemo* had never looked so good, nor had Chuck, nor had Rory. Even Smitty's weathered mug looked good enough to kiss. Smitty helped him off with his tank, and he climbed over the rail onto the deck. Not far away, Robins could be seen standing on the *Tuna Tail's* rear deck as *Charlie* was being hoisted aboard.

"You probably won't even get a 'Thank You,'" Smitty remarked, jerking his head in the *Tuna Tail's* direction.

"You're just too cynical," Storm said, and he winced in pain as Smitty helped him off with his wetsuit jacket.

"You're right. You'll probably get a lovely form letter that's paid for with my tax dollars."

Rory joined them. "You! Crazy man! On the deck, now!"

Storm stretched himself out over a pile of wetsuits to let Rory take another look at his shoulder wound.

"This is just great," Rory said. "You've managed to undo everything I just did. If you don't stop acting like a hero this is never going to heal."

"Believe me. If Chuck tells you he hears something else in his headset, you have my permission to throw him overboard."

Smitty said, "You want some of that stuff with the burro still in it?"

"Yeah, and add some chocolate."

A Navy swift boat pulled up alongside the *Nemo*, and Logan stepped aboard. Storm, still laid out on the wetsuits, said, "Welcome aboard, Commander. We've been having a lovely time."

Logan looked very sour. "I just wanted to see for myself who's still here and who isn't. I would have been here earlier, but I had a bunch of SOGS on the island."

"SOGS?" Storm asked, suppressing what was perhaps

going to be his first smile of the day.

"'Save Our Goats Society.' They'd planned this meeting for months, and I couldn't miss it or they'd be all over me like grease on a hog."

Liu Xin said, "Commander, if it weren't for courageous Dr. Hancock, I would be dead, and perhaps the congressman also."

"That's what I've heard. I owe you one, Hancock."

Storm said, "I'm just sorry it all turned out so rotten. It's like everything we wanted not to happen did happen, and it's all going to come down on you."

"It's rotten alright, but don't worry about me," Logan said with a scowl. "If anybody's head is going to roll, I'll make sure it comes off the right shoulders."

"That still won't bring back Kim Yi," Terry said grimly.

"No, it won't, but I have to look at any bright side I can find right now. Liu Xin is safe. Robins is safe, and Yi will probably wind up as some kind of Chinese hero by the time things get spun around, and that brings me to something important. Things are going to get puckered up around here while this mess gets sorted out. I wouldn't ask you to do this right now if it wasn't absolutely necessary, but I need each of you to get off in a corner by yourself and write down everything that happened as best you remember it. It'll save a lot of heartache for us when the inquiry hits."

Smitty ran into the cabin and came back out with something in his hand. He said, "Commander, Sir, I ain't much for writing. Maybe I could just give you this instead." He handed over a videocassette.

Obviously surprised, Logan asked, "What's this?"

"Well, Sir, when I ran out of things to do to help, I opened up the underwater video port and started shooting."

"You videotaped what happened?" Logan looked dumbfounded.

"Yes, Sir. It's got the Skipper, and Mr. Yi, and the goosefish. Pretty much everything."

Logan slowly looked around at the rest of the *Nemo's* crew. Then he looked back at Smitty, and then he just smiled and shook his head. He turned to Storm. "I need you to grab a mooring at Wilson Cove, and we'll talk more about this tomorrow." He turned to Rory. "Is that alright with you, Doc?"

Rory nodded affirmatively and looked toward Storm. "He'll be fine, as long as we can keep him out of the water."

Logan shoved off in the swift boat. He could be seen looking back at the *Nemo*, shaking his head and smiling.

The next day, Logan was again on board the *Nemo*. The look on his face displayed an even mixture of sympathy and disbelief as he said, "Hancock, I'm going to tell you something that I don't just tell anybody. You've maybe got more guts than brains, but you've got yourself a hotshot team here, and you people don't need to prove a thing to me."

"Thank you, Commander, but I assure you we're not out to prove anything."

"And I believe you, so here's the way it is. Washington has finally got its priorities straight, and we're still in the budget. In three weeks this end of the island's going to be hopping again with SEAL training and your giant goosefish has to be either dead or gone."

"Then three weeks will have to be enough," Storm replied.

"I hope so. Look, I know the thing's an important scientific find, and I don't want it destroyed anymore than you do, but if it's not gone soon, I'll be gunning for it myself."

Terry said, "Can you tell us what happened to Fishbeck?"

"No. He disappeared, and good riddance, I say."

The eyes of the *Nemo's* crew grew wide, and Logan said, "No, no, he didn't get eaten. He just took off without saying goodbye, and I'm really hurt."

Logan left, and Storm gathered his crew around the mess table. "OK, hotshot team, if we're going to get some help with what we're trying to do, where do we start?"

"That's an easy one, Skipper," Smitty replied confidently. "The first thing we do is talk to Cap Hanson."

Chapter 45

As usual, Smitty had already been looking hard at the problem, and four days later Storm and company found themselves at Cap Hanson's house playing host to one of the more unlikely assemblages of characters to be found on shore. Over a dozen abalone divers and their crews, recently put out of work because of new environmental laws, had come together at Cap's invitation. Considering the abbers' tendency towards rugged individualism, a rather sociable party had shaped up when the time came to squeeze everyone into the front room for the real reason of the meeting. The lights were dimmed, and a slide of a goosefish was projected on a sheet that had been hung up for a screen. The anticipated comments quickly followed.

"That thing's been taking ugly pills!" one of the abbers called out, and the room filled with loud laughter.

"No, no!" called another. "That's Smitty before he got his teeth fixed!"

That got an even bigger laugh, and Smitty stood up and barked, "We got some serious business to do here, and if you smart-alecks could pipe down for a minute, you might just learn something!"

Smitty sat down amidst even louder laughter, and Cap stood up to take the floor. First, he introduced Terry, who gave an overview of the events of the last three months. When she talked about divers being killed, the jovial mood of the room plunged into sober thoughtfulness. Cap then introduced Storm as the resident expert on the creature, since he had encountered the goosefish twice and had lived to tell it. Storm told what he knew, emphasizing how it had been his entanglement in the feather boa, and Cap's attachment to an air hose that had saved him and Cap from being sucked into the fish's mouth. He wanted the abbers to know exactly how the creature captured its prey and how they could keep from being captured themselves. Such knowledge was imperative for what he was about to tell them next.

"We'd like you to help us catch it," Storm said matter-of-factly.

The room erupted.

"Catch it? Let's kill it!"

"It got Old Henry!"

"Let's send it back to hell where it came from!"

Almost everybody in the room echoed the same sentiment, with each one being louder than the last until Cap finally stood up again. He waited patiently until the last murmur died before saying, "You all know me. The dang thing tried to eat me too, so I guess I've got as good an opinion as anybody. Yeah, it got Old Henry, but we can't change that. I knew Old Henry about as well as anybody could. In fact, if it weren't for him, I might be paralyzed, or worse. Anyway, I also know he would probably feel the same way I do about this fish. It didn't know better. It's just a big, dumb animal. I'm not saying Old Henry couldn't be an ornery cuss at times, but he didn't have a mean bone in his body, not a revengeful one anyway, and I think he'd want us to hear what Dr. Hancock has to say, and that's all I'm going to say."

Cap sat down as arguments blew up like a sudden squall and raged throughout the Hansons' front room. For a moment it seemed that the abbers might actually come to blows, but the room finally quieted again as if a shaky truce had been reached. The Captain of the *Rainbow* finally stood up, glared around the room, and said in a growl, "OK, let's have it."

Storm stood up quickly. "You've already met Terry Ho, and you know she represents Cal Ocean USA and also K-EBB Television. What she has to say to you now is important for you personally."

"Thank you, Storm." Terry said, standing up to address a murmuring audience. "You gentlemen, and ladies, are commercial fishermen whose livelihood, rightly or wrongly, is being shut down."

To an undercurrent of grumbling agreement Terry pointed to the goosefish picture being projected on the sheet and continued, "But right here on our doorstep we have one of the most extraordinary biological finds of the century. Think of how it would look if the abalone divers of Southern California were instrumental in the live capture of this creature for scientific study and for the world to enjoy. I would personally make sure credit was received where credit was due, and I can personally guarantee you that whatever you did would make the news, and probably not just on K-EBB. This could do nothing but help you in the future."

From the back of the room someone called out, "So, how are we supposed to catch it? Use Smitty for bait?"

That was exactly the opening Storm had been waiting for to break the tension. Before the laughter in the room subsided he was standing up and outlining the plan. When he reached the part about attaching a shark monitor to the creature's back the question rang out, "Yeah, and what stupid fool gets to do that?" Another torrent of laughter flooded the room. When it finally died down Storm said soberly, "I get to do that."

The Hansons' front room became quieter than an underwater cave as, perhaps for the first time that evening, it sunk into the abbers' minds that Storm and his friends were deadly serious.

Chapter 46

In a sordid back-street motel Fishbeck coaxed a picture from the room's ancient television set. With a trembling hand he waved a nine-millimeter semi-automatic pistol at the figures on the screen. Because of the silencer attached to the end of the barrel he reasoned that one well-placed shot might not raise attention, but an exploded television set would be difficult to explain. The trembling of his hand calmed as he stuffed his simmering emotions down with a fist of willpower. No, he told himself. He wouldn't let blind passion drive him into doing some stupid, hothead maneuver. Rather, he would let that passion smolder, glowing hot without flame, powering his resourcefulness until he formulated a proper plan.

It was Wednesday night and time for "Ask About Our Ocean." Fishbeck carefully removed the silencer from the pistol and zipped it into a leather case. He slipped the pistol back into its shoulder holster, forced himself to sit down, and stared at the TV with diabolical interest and intent.

"Tonight, K-EBB is working on a breaking story about a series of deadly events that have taken place off our coast little more than eighty miles from downtown Los Angeles. During the last four months, in a drama unfolding more like a Jules Verne novel than reality, four divers have disappeared at San Clemente Island without a trace. Two weeks ago a Chinese diplomat invited to dive at the island by Congressman Kevin Robins was also killed in a tragic accident that appears to have involved a large, mysterious sea creature. To learn more, we now take you live to Newport Beach and a special segment of 'Ask About Our Ocean' with Terry Ho."

The picture on the screen switched to Terry standing on a dock.

"Thank you, Joan. I'm standing on McDougal's Dock in Newport Harbor, and behind me you can see veteran commercial abalone diver, Cap Hanson, preparing his boat and crew and getting ready to venture out with us to San Clemente Island to help solve this mystery.

"Joan, the large, mysterious sea creature you mentioned turns out to be a goosefish—a *Lophius americanus* in scientific terms. It's a fish that normally lives only on the East Coast and normally grows to about sixty pounds. This particular fish, however, is estimated to weigh in at several tons. We have no idea how a goosefish wound up in California waters or how it came to be so big. Those are just some of the questions Cal Ocean USA intends to answer with the help of people like Cap Hanson."

While Terry continued her narrative, the camera panned away from her and on to Cap and Smitty who were loading gear aboard the *Emerald*.

"Mr. Hanson is one of the few people who has actually encountered the goosefish and lived to tell it. We've enlisted his help in trying to locate the giant goosefish in hopes to capture it alive for study. Let's see if we can talk to him for a moment."

The camera followed Terry as she walked over to Cap, who stopped his work and appeared to be waiting for her. Terry said, "Cap, what does it mean to you that we try to find and capture this goosefish alive?"

"We need to catch it," Cap answered. "We sure don't want it hurting anyone else, but we also don't want to needlessly kill a one-of-a-kind animal that we don't know anything about."

"Well said, Cap," Terry replied, turning to face the camera which was now solely on her.

"Terry," Joan's voice asked off screen. "Is it speculation that this giant goosefish is responsible for the deaths of all four divers?"

"It's more than speculation, Joan, and the choice we now face is whether we should try to destroy the goosefish outright, thereby preventing further tragedy from occurring, or try to capture it and find out why, and how, it came to be here."

"It seems like capturing it would put an end to any danger it represents," Joan's voice said. "We certainly wish you all the best of luck. Just one more question before we break away. Why use commercial abalone divers? Wouldn't marine biologists be the people we'd expect you to enlist for help?"

"Joan, no people on the planet know the underwater landscape at San Clemente Island as well as these ab' divers. If we want to find an animal that's doing its best to hide, then these divers are our guys."

"Thank you, Terry," Joan said, as the picture switched back to her and stayed there. "And coming up: What's happened to the Dodgers? After this."

A cameraman gave Terry an OK with his fingers. She walked over to where Storm and Keith Stafford were waiting. "The cat's out of the bag, now," Storm said. "I hope we're doing the right thing."

"I think we are," Stafford said. "If we're going to get any support at all for the live capture of an animal this dangerous, we need to let the public in on the game from the start."

Storm pondered Stafford's choice of words. He hadn't told anyone about his reoccurring nightmare of being sucked down a giant gullet, and it wasn't going to be a game placing a monitor on the goosefish's back. He wasn't even sure if it was humanly possible. He'd gone over the problem a thousand times trying to come up with a plan, and the biggest hitch seemed to be that nobody had discussed his plan with the goosefish, and Storm wasn't sure how it was going to feel about the whole thing.

The morning after next, the *Nemo* was the centerpiece of a floating arrangement of abalone boats rafted together in San Clemente Island's West Cove. Thankfully, the Pacific Ocean was living up to her name as abbers from twelve boats received their final instructions and also some bolstering from Smitty's Costa Rican coffee. Swinging on her chain an anchor's scope away was Cal Ocean's research vessel, *Cormorant*. Her crew labored in the water pinning together the cage that, theoretically, would contain, and transfer, the goosefish to the mainland.

To the abalone divers that were gathered together on the

Nemo's aft deck, Storm finished his pep talk by saying, "Follow the plan. Be careful, and let's catch a big one for Old Henry."

The ab' divers began to disperse, but Terry surprised everyone by calling them back to attention. She climbed up to the flying bridge and announced, "If we want to do this job right, and we all want to come back safe, then we'd better pray about it."

From his short-term acquaintance with them, Storm couldn't say that the majority of the ab' divers were fervent believers, but as he watched them stop where they were and bow their heads, it struck him how the hope for a providential helping hand seemed to touch a nerve within them all. He bowed his head also. He could honestly have that hope too, he reasoned.

Terry said, "Almighty and eternal Father, creator of all things, including this great fish, we ask You to protect us, and it, from all harm this day, and we ask this in the name of Jesus, Your Son. Amen."

What could it hurt? Storm thought, as his own mumbled "Amen" mingled with all the others. He opened his eyes to see Terry smiling down at him. She looked pleased but not at all triumphant in catching him in a moment of shared faith. He smiled back.

The ab' divers shoved off and positioned their boats according to the diagram each of them had been given. Thirty feet apart, in a line stretching from the shallows to a hundred-twenty yards out, the divers hit the water. They began their search at the north end of the cove where Yi Kim had been lost, and they worked their way southward. The *Nemo* crawled in front of them, guiding their course and speed. Above each diver, their tender played their air hose extra tight, with the hose always having a wrap around something substantial. To avoid being becoming prey themselves, the divers were to stay twenty feet above the bottom at all times even if it meant swimming on the surface.

Storm and Terry, dressed in their Farmer John wetsuit bottoms, oversaw the operation from the flying bridge of the

Nemo. The nearest ab' boat to the *Nemo* was the *Emerald,* with Rory driving, Cap Hanson diving, and Smitty tending hose.

Exactly where he should be, Storm thought, watching how carefully Smitty played Cap's hose in and out, always keeping a wrap of it around the *Emerald's* bow bitt.

All morning long, the search line crept forward, giving the divers time enough to scan every square foot of the bottom as they looked for the camouflaged subject of their quest. The search stopped for lunch and then resumed. Twelve air compressors droned like a giant swarm of bees, and Storm, overly tired from the fierce pace of the last two weeks, was having trouble keeping his eyes open.

Three blasts of a nearby horn ripped him from his sleep.

"It's under the *Mermaid*!" Terry cried.

There was no doubt that somebody had seen something. Most of the boats had already stopped, and halfway between the *Nemo* and shore the *Mermaid's* diver hopped around on the bow of his boat waving his arms up and down as if he were trying to conjure up rain.

Storm felt his heart pounding as he hit the *Nemo's* diver recall button.

Cap surfaced and joined Smitty in one of the inflatables. Storm and Terry leaped in another one, and they all converged upon the *Mermaid.* Her diver was still dancing on the bow. When they pulled alongside he pointed his finger straight down in front of the *Mermaid.* "It's right there!" he croaked.

Storm stood up and waved his hands in exaggerated movements to signal everyone to shut everything down. One by one, every boat engine and air compressor quit running, until all that was heard was the slap of wavelets on hulls and the slithering sound of kelp.

Storm, trying to sound calm, said to the *Mermaid's* diver, "How deep are we?"

The diver shifted from one foot to the other as if the deck beneath his feet had become a bed of hot coals. He opened his mouth, but nothing came out. Storm waited patiently. The man had just run into the goosefish and had lived to tell it. That gave him the right to throw a full-blown, lathering fit as far as

Storm was concerned.

Finally, the man sputtered, "Twenty-five feet! The thing's as big as a house!"

Storm took some deep breaths, but it didn't seem to help slow down the beating of his heart. He turned to Cap in the other inflatable. "Are you ready to take a look at it?"

"Do I have to?"

It's either that, or we change our plans, but I'm not going to make anybody do anything they don't want to."

Cap looked extremely grim. "I guess I'm ready. If I don't do it now, I probably never will."

Storm put on his mask and snorkel and hung his face over the side. In the other inflatable Cap did the same thing. Seconds later, Storm jerked his face out the water and ripped his mask off. He suddenly felt like he wasn't getting enough air. Cap, meanwhile, had already ripped his own mask off, and he sat immobile in the other inflatable looking as if he were in some kind of psychological shock.

"Did you see it?" Storm finally asked.

Cap placed one hand over the spot his ribs had been bruised. "I knew it was big and nasty, but I didn't know it was *that* big and nasty!"

Ten minutes later, Storm looked intently at Terry, Cap, and Smitty as he went over the plan one last time.

"You absolutely have to see the dorsal fin standing straight up and its lure wriggling. That means the thing's watching the bait and not watching me. If the lure quits moving, or if the dorsal fin starts to sag, you absolutely must move the bait closer."

Smitty seemed to answer for everyone, saying, "We got it."

Cap looked green. "Can you do this?" Storm asked him.

"Just keep me out of the water, and I'll be fine."

"Good. Now remember, we'll have two minutes to do this from the time I go under, so we don't have to rush."

And if he believed that, he also believed in mermaids, Storm thought, but at least it sounded good, and it just might help everybody get things right the first time.

His eyes met Terry's. She didn't look happy, but she took

up a paddle and began moving the inflatable into position. Cap
and Smitty tied their inflatable to a patch of surface kelp
directly above and in front of the goosefish and began lowering
a thirty-pound yellowtail on a weighted rope. Terry and Storm
tied up twenty-five yards away to the rear, and Storm eased
over the side into the water.

Now, they all waited for Cap. When he had the yellowtail
dangling twenty feet in front of the goosefish, he lifted his
hand.

From the floor of the inflatable, Terry picked up a monitor
that had been specially modified by Chuck. She handed it over
the side to Storm. "He's got the bait in position," she said.

Storm looked longingly up at Terry. One of these days he
was going to have to tell her how he felt. "I guess it's time," he
said. "Don't forget to pray for me."

Storm hyperventilated, jackknifed his body, and sliced
down through the kelp, drawing on every dive he'd ever made
to get him through this one dive now. Quiet as sunlight he slid
through the water, sneaking towards the goosefish. The only
sound he heard was the pounding of his own heart.

"If I take the wings of morning...." The Psalm ran through
his mind.

Twitch.

The movement jumped out at Storm from fifty feet away
and stopped him cold. Waves of fear rushed over him, and he
envisioned his nightmare as clearly as if it were playing before
him on a movie screen.

He couldn't do this. There was no way he could do this.

He watched as the yellowtail dangled twenty feet in front
of the lure, and the goosefish's dorsal fin stood straight up.

"And I dwell in the uttermost parts of the sea...." The
Psalm continued in his mind.

Twitch.

Storm willed himself to move closer. He'd already been
down thirty seconds. He was supposed to have a minute and a
half more, but he hadn't counted on the wild pounding of his
heart. This was not at all like tracking down a calico bass.

The dorsal fin sagged, and Storm stopped again. He was

only twenty feet away from the goosefish's tail. The yellowtail dangled closer, jerked up and down, and the dorsal fin sprang back up.

"Even there shall thy hand lead me...!"

Twitch.

Storm kept his eyes glued to the goosefish's lure and crept forward. He felt the first pangs of needing to breathe. He stopped ten feet behind the tip of the goosefish's tail. He couldn't go any further.

The dorsal fin began to sag.

Storm was almost out of breath. He knew he would never be able to try this again, and yet there was no way he was going closer.

The yellowtail suddenly moved within ten feet of the monster's jaws, jerked up and down in a frenzy, and the goosefish's dorsal fin sprang back up.

"Thy Right Hand Shall Hold Me...!"

Twitch.

"Now!" Storm's mind yelled, and he swept in over the goosefish's tail and hurtled towards the twitching fin. Halfway there he veered downward and pressed the monitor hard onto the goosefish's broad back. He felt the monitor's adhesive take hold, and he spun around to make his escape.

Then, he heard *the* sound. The water around him contorted like a tortured, living thing. Storm flailed uselessly, as if he were swimming in air instead of water. The current ripped him backwards, out of control, towards the goosefish's mouth, but before he got there he slammed into the goosefish's upright dorsal fin. His body wrapped helplessly around it, pinned there as a leaf in a gale.

Then, the gale ended, and Storm streaked away. His chest ached, and every cell in his body cried out for air, but he continued out and away before veering upward. He hit the surface like a breeching whale, and then he didn't stop swimming until he had hauled himself back into the inflatable with Terry. There he lay, wheezing like a bellows.

"It's on," he gasped.

Terry's reply was to fire up the inflatable outboard engine

and speed back to the *Nemo*, which again had become the center of a raft of boats. As they maneuvered through the throng and pulled up alongside, Chuck ran to the rail and held up two thumbs. "We're in business!" he said exuberantly.

Storm felt giddy after having cheated the goosefish again. He bounded to the top of the flying bridge to announce through a bull horn, "Did you hear that everybody? The monitor's on and working, and we can track the goosefish from a distance! No more of this looking down the throat!"

At least not for all of you, he thought soberly. He still had one more job to do.

He continued, saying, "This next part's going to take a little time to set up, so everybody warm up, relax, come over for coffee and cake, and stay close. We'll try to get moving again in an hour."

Storm sat down on the pilot's bench to catch up with himself. The morning had been too much of a blur already, and he was afraid he might miss something important. Somebody could still wind up being eaten, and more than likely it would be him. The first part of the plan had worked. The monitor was on, and Chuck could track the goosefish wherever it went, at least until the monitor came off. The next part of the plan was just as dangerous and maybe even more so. Storm needed a clear head, but as he analyzed the events of his last dive, he couldn't help but remember how a Psalm in his mind had seemed to help him and also how he had felt as he had looked up at Terry just before she had handed him the monitor. He suddenly found himself thinking about God too much, and Terry too much, and he didn't have any empirical data to guide him with either relationship. He gazed around at the raft of abalone boats. The divers were having themselves a regular party. He'd better get things rolling before they ended up partying too much for his own good.

Storm and Terry sped their inflatable back to the *Cormorant* where the cage was ready and floating in the water. The cage was no more than several pieces of aluminum tubing pinned together into the shape of a box. Buoyancy cylinders were attached to each corner of the box, and a fiberglass faring was attached to the front. Nestled underneath the faring were two large bottles of compressed gas. All but the bottom bars of the cage were now pinned together.

Dr. Frank met Storm and Terry at the rail. "I think we're ready," she said, as Storm and Terry climbed aboard.

"I need to go over the plan with the abbers again," Storm said, "but first; are you still planning to do this? I'm telling you one last time we can find someone else."

Dr. Frank's face took on a look of determination. "Thank you, but it has to be me. If the thing winds up dead because of my calculations, then it should be me who gets the blame. All I ask is that you don't let it eat me."

"Just be sure your safety rope is secure and snug at all times. If you can't be sucked forward, you can't be eaten."

"In theory."

"Well, yes, in theory, but at least we have several events to support that theory."

"Yeah, real, raw, empirical data," Terry said cynically.

"You don't much care for this whole thing, do you?" Dr. Frank remarked.

"I just get tired of Storm trying to get himself swallowed. Why does it always have to be him?"

Storm said, "Nobody else is crazy enough. Well, now there's also Dr. Frank."

"Yeah, and I used to think she was smart," Terry said without humor. "Shows what I know."

A boat chugged into view from around the north end of the island. She was the charter dive boat *Pieces O' Eight.* On the many large cameras visible on board her were the call letters of at least four TV stations, including K-EBB.

"We'd better talk to them before they get too close," Terry said.

"Yes, and let's have you do all the talking," Storm replied.

"Why is it always me who has to do the talking?"

"Because that's your specialty. You're the ocean-answer person, and I'm just a crazy shark hunter."

"No, you're not crazy; you're hardheaded, and you worry me sick, but you're not crazy."

As Storm sped the inflatable on an intercept course with the new arrival, he wondered if he might actually have a chance with Terry.

The *Pieces O' Eight* coasted to a stop, and Storm pulled the inflatable alongside. Terry stood up and held on to the larger boat while she addressed the people now crowding the rail above her.

"Hi, everyone. We're at a super-critical moment, and I can't talk now, but if you'll go down near those other boats and stay just outside of the *Nemo*, you'll get plenty of footage, and in a few more minutes you'll get more than you dreamed of."

That must have sounded fair enough, because the *Pieces O' Eight* chugged on as directed, while Terry and Storm sped to the *Nemo*.

On board the *Nemo* they found Chuck zeroing in on his prey, locating the goosefish by using only the swinging of the *Nemo* on her anchor line. Chuck pulled his headset off. "The critter's moved, but probably no more than fifty yards, and it's still close to shore in shallow water."

Storm said, "Well, we're way past the point of common sense, and I still haven't been swallowed. I guess it's time to gather the troops."

Chapter 47

As Storm went over the plan with the abbers for one last time, it sounded almost too simple to work.

The *Nemo* would lead the way to the goosefish. The *Cormorant* would tow the cage into position. Storm and Dr. Frank would knock the goosefish out. The abbers would lower the cage over the goosefish and slip the bottom bars underneath it. The cage would be raised and towed to the mainland, and everyone would live happily ever after.

Either that, Storm figured, or his nightmare would come true, and he'd wind up being sucked head-first down the creature's throat.

All too soon for Storm, the *Cormorant* arrived, towing the cage, and the abalone divers dispersed themselves back to their own boats. With Smitty at the helm, the *Nemo* hauled anchor and idled south, waving her nose back and forth like a shark following the scent of blood. Chuck was homing in. He suddenly held up his fist and cried, "We're on top of it!"

The *Nemo* coasted to a gentle stop, and Smitty held her in position using the engines and rudder. The dive boats positioned themselves in a hundred foot circle around her, eased their anchors over the side, and shut down their engines. When their divers and tenders were ready, Smitty eased the *Nemo* forward, and the *Cormorant* snuck in behind her until the cage was directly over the target, then the *Nemo* and *Cormorant* also eased their anchors over the side and shut down their engines.

The next move belonged to Storm and Dr. Frank, who had gathered in full scuba gear on the swim step of the *Cormorant*. Rory methodically attached body harnesses to both of them. Two strong lines were then passed down which Rory attached to the harnesses. "Make sure these have at least one wrap around a cleat at all times," Storm called up to the line handlers aboard the *Cormorant*. "Two wraps would be even better." He turned to Dr. Frank. Her face was as pale as death.

"How are you doing?"

"I'm fine," she answered, looking anything but fine.

The *Cormorant's* crew next handed down a long fiberglass pole, and then a strange apparatus came over the transom rail. It was a specially designed, biodegradable cylinder around which had been molded a papier-mâché sculpture of a tuna. Rory attached a line from the nose of the fake tuna to the end of the long pole. He attached another line to the tuna's tail. All was prepared, and it was now just a matter of nerve.

"Are you guys ready?" Rory asked.

Storm said, "Ready as I'll ever be. How about you, Doctor?"

Dr. Frank just nodded.

Cap and Terry pulled alongside in an inflatable. Storm looked down at Terry. Her long, black hair was pulled back into a pony tail, the same as when he had first seen her on what seemed to be a lifetime ago that morning at Cal Ocean USA.

She sure is pretty, Storm thought, and he wished this whole adventure were over and he could get on with his life, including finding out what was going to happen between him and Terry.

But when would it be over? And for that matter, what was he even doing here? It all seemed to have started because he had autographed a magazine. Maybe if he hadn't done that, Todd might still be alive, and this whole mess wouldn't have happened.

Of course, he knew that wasn't true, and besides, he couldn't go back, so he might as well get on with it. Through his face mask he saw Terry mouth the words, "I'll be praying for you," and she paddled herself and Cap fifty feet astern of the *Cormorant* and stopped. Cap put on his mask and snorkel and hung his face over the side. He would be the signal man for the rope handlers. He raised his head up and said grimly, "We're right over it."

Storm and Dr. Frank eased themselves off the *Cormorant's* swim step and into the water. Rory handed Storm the long pole and then handed Dr. Frank the line that was attached to the fake tuna's tail. In theory, if the cylinder's design worked properly, and if Dr. Frank yanked on that line hard enough, the cylinder would rupture and release its contents.

Storm switched to his regulator, as did Dr. Frank. They had to move quickly, because from the moment the fake tuna hit the water, there would be only ten minutes before the whole thing would melt and come apart at the seams. They had only one fake tuna.

The line handlers aboard the *Cormorant* let out slack, and Storm and Dr. Frank began their descent. Straight down they drifted to twenty feet deep, and then they stopped. On the bottom, ten more feet down and fifty feet in front of them, the giant goosefish lay leering up at them with a devilish grin.

Storm closed his eyes, and the creature's leering grin was replaced by a scene from his nightmare. He was only a heartbeat away from dropping his weight belt and shooting upward like a Polaris missile. Somehow he opened his eyes and forced himself to look at the creature. His scientific side reasoned that its leering grin was nothing more than his own unreasonable anthropomorphic projections onto the creature's immobile anatomical features.

Yes, that was it, Storm reassured himself. The goosefish couldn't actually be grinning at him.

He shuddered as the goosefish's grin seemed to grow even more fiendish.

So far, so bad, Storm thought, and he turned to Dr. Frank to see if she was doing as poorly as he was. A geyser of exhaust bubbles poured from her regulator. Storm guessed that she was churning through her air at sixty breaths per minute, and maybe even faster. At that rate she could hyperventilate and pass out, or she could run out of air and pass out. She might even manage to do both at the same time.

That does it, Storm thought. He was going to get them both killed. The best thing he could do would be to leave the goosefish alone, tell everybody to go home, and he would become a door-to-door brush salesman.

Then, remarkably, Dr. Frank gave Storm an emphatic nod with her head and the "OK" sign with her free hand.

They proceeded.

Storm telescoped the pole to its full twenty-foot length. Then he led the way, holding the neutrally-buoyant, fake tuna as far out in front of him as he could. He pointed the pole straight at the goosefish and crept forward through the water. All the while Dr. Frank stayed glued to his hip and continued to chug through her air like a steam engine.

Storm inched closer to the creature. His heart pounded like a pile driver in his chest. He changed course away from a direct head-on approach, hoping to escape at least some of the suction. He stopped again, still ten feet higher than the creature but now only thirty feet away. A drop of sweat dribbled into his eye. He blinked furiously to remove it, and the goosefish's dorsal fin snapped to attention.

Twitch.

Storm turned his head slowly to look at Dr. Frank. She looked back at him with eyes that showed more white than color. An almost constant stream of exhaust bubbles poured from her regulator. To Storm's amazement, she emphatically nodded her head again. He slowly turned his head back to the creature.

Twitch.

Storm knew it was absolutely now or never. "God, help me!" he cried silently, and he raised his arm and swept it forward in a dramatic gesture to let Dr. Frank, Cap, Terry, the rope handlers, and anybody else that might possibly be interested, that he was going to go NOW!

Twitch.

Storm aimed the fake tuna for the center of the creature's mouth, screamed like a wild man, and charged. Dr. Frank, still stuck to Storm's hip like glue, screamed and charged with him.

The creature's cavernous jaws flew open. Storm's face mask ripped away, and it and the fake tuna disappeared down the gullet of his nightmare. At the same moment, Dr. Frank threw her entire body into one mighty pull on the line attached to the tuna's tail.

The next instant, they were both streaming backwards through the water, hauled by their safety ropes back to the swim step of the *Cormorant*. Hopefully, enough nitrous oxide to send the entire abalone fleet higher than the *Nemo's* radio antenna had just been introduced into the goosefish's gills.

Dr. Frank's respirations had slowed to a mere forty times per minute.

"Well?" Storm asked.

Dr. Frank wheezed something unintelligible. Then she took the regulator out of her mouth and peeled off her mask. "We.... We didn't get eaten!"

Cap's head was in the water. Storm called out, "What do you see?"

Cap pulled his head up. "By golly, Storm, it might have worked! The dorsal fin's down, and the thing's not moving!"

"Untie me!"

Storm turned so Dr. Frank could detach him from the harness. He picked up her facemask and tried it on. It wasn't a perfect fit, but it would do. He snorkeled out to the inflatable that held Terry and Cap and then stared down at the goosefish. It lay still as a statue, but that meant nothing. Being still was how it captured its food. Storm snorkeled as far as he could away from the fish and still keep it in sight, and then he descended on scuba. He crept across the bottom, approaching the fish from its tail. Even though the creature remained motionless, danger seemed to ooze from its every pore. Storm crawled to within ten feet. The dorsal fin remained flat.

He inched closer.

Here we go again, he thought, and, ever so gingerly, he reached out and touched the creature's flesh with his bare hand.

Storm shot upwards, breached the surface, and yelled, "Let's do it!"

Divers already in position on either side of the cage barreled into the water and plummeted down. They cut any kelp stalks that might get trapped as the cage was lowered and floated them out of the way. Meanwhile, Storm and Terry let air out of the cage's buoyancy cells, and the cage began to sink. The divers guided it down over the fish, slid the bottom bars underneath it, and pinned them home. In ten minutes the cage was complete. Dr. Frank uncoiled hoses from the nitrous-oxide tanks nestled beneath the front faring and placed the hoses' free ends into the creature's mouth. She cracked open the tank valves, and as soon as she saw bubbles escaping from the creature's gill vents she motioned Storm to raise the cage. Storm did a quick swim around, and then he and Terry used scuba tanks with filler hoses attached to put air back into the cage's buoyancy cells. The cage rose slowly to the surface. Twenty minutes from the moment when Storm had broken the surface, the giant goosefish and its custom cage were bobbing gently just below the surface of the peaceful Pacific.

The abbers surfaced in a state of revelry. They jumped and hollered from boat to boat as if they could hardly believe what they had just done. Storm didn't blame them, because he could hardly believe it himself. He climbed aboard the *Nemo*, grabbed a bull horn, and announced, "That was unbelievably, incredibly fantastic! Watch the six o'clock news tonight, and you'll all see yourselves on TV!"

Having mentioned the news, it was now time to accommodate the news. The *Pieces O' Eight* tied up to one side of the *Cormorant*, the *Nemo* to the other side, and the ab' boats tied up everywhere. For the next hour it seemed that anyone breathing surface air was interviewed at least once, and probably twice. The only person apparently not enjoying themselves thoroughly was Dr. Frank, who said she just wanted to get going. In the meantime, she doted over the goosefish like a new mother over her baby, and she found that the only way to escape from being interviewed was to stay on scuba underwater.

Storm finally told the news people that it really was time to get a move on for the well being of their new charge, but the *Nemo* would be traveling slowly and would be available for boarding at any time. The *Nemo*, having been with the project from the beginning, was to have the honor of bringing the goosefish in. The cage's towing bridle was transferred over to her from the *Cormorant*, and the tedious journey began. The *Pieces O' Eight* chugged off to try to make several deadlines, and the abbers raced away to either Catalina or the mainland, hoping to see themselves on the six o'clock news. Except for the *Cormorant* acting as escort, the *Nemo* was left alone to her five-knot pace.

The plan was to travel nonstop, but as the afternoon wore on, and the two boats pulled even with the western tip of Catalina Island, Smitty climbed up to the flying bridge and said, "Skipper, if you don't mind me saying, there's two things that are going to happen. The wind is going to howl from the northwest, making for steep following seas and rough towing, and poor Dr. Frank is going to turn into a frozen zombie if we don't get her out of the water and away from the cage."

Storm was always interested in Smitty's opinion. He said, "Do you have a suggestion?"

"Yeah, Skipper. I think we should turn right and tuck into Emerald Cove for the night."

"As usual, you're way ahead of me," Storm replied. "We will turn right, but I'm putting you in charge of getting Dr. Frank back on board."

After brandishing a large knife and threatening to cut the cage adrift, Smitty finally did get Dr. Frank aboard and warming up over some hot soup. By then, the *Nemo* and *Cormorant* were anchored in snug to Catalina Island. Chuck hooked up the *Nemo*'s television. The day's adventure led off K-EBB's newscast.

"Would you look at that?" Smitty said. "You guys are regular movie stars. All you need is some fancy sunglasses."

Then Smitty's picture filled the screen, and his face turned as crimson as a "red-right-returning" buoy.

"You're looking pretty manly there, yourself, Smitty," Terry said. "And I bet those women at church are watching."

"Aaaahhh!"

The next morning broke calm with a lifting fog, and the *Nemo* and her escort set course for Redondo Beach, Cal Ocean USA, and the Big Lagoon. At a steady five knots, Storm estimated their arrival to be around two in the afternoon. Dr. Frank, as expected, rode herd over the cage, but at least now she was riding in an inflatable boat tied alongside, and she only went underwater for periodic checks on her patient. The marine layer cleared, and the first helicopters arrived, and from then on at least one helicopter was over the *Nemo* at any given moment. At lunch time, and still ten miles away from Redondo Beach, the first boat from the mainland met them. She was an ocean-going speedboat that pulled alongside and deposited Keith Stafford's secretary onto the *Nemo*. "I thought I'd better come out here and give you a warning!" she said in an excited voice. "There's a big crowd gathering to meet you even as we speak!"

"Is that good, or bad?" Smitty asked.

"It's good! It's real good! Just be prepared for anything and everything! This thing is really taking off!"

As if to emphasize her point, one helicopter sped away and another one replaced it, coming in low and hovering a few hundred feet overhead. "Expect a lot more of this!" Stafford's secretary said loudly over the noise. "I'm going over to the *Cormorant* now to pick up Keith. Keep smiling, wave at the cameras, and good luck!"

Storm watched the speedboat pick up Stafford and then roar away.

"Smitty?"

"I know, Skipper!" yelled Smitty, who was already inside the cabin. "You want the coffee with the burro!"

The little convoy was five miles out of Redondo Beach when the first pleasure boats showed up. At one mile out, an armada of everything that could float surrounded the *Nemo*. Big, small, slow, fast, wind, power, or paddle, it had ventured out to meet her. Terry, having just shuttled back to the *Nemo* after one of her frequent visits to Dr. Frank at the cage, joined Storm and Chuck on the flying bridge.

"How's she doing?" Chuck asked.

"Breathing easy, heart rate steady, appears to be asleep."

"No, no. I mean Dr. Frank."

"Oh, her. That's different. She's about to have a cow, twins maybe. She wants to turn down the nitrous, but she's afraid to do it with all the hubbub."

"You can tell her that we're almost home," Storm said. "In less than an hour we'll be at the Big Lagoon."

Terry delivered the message and then returned to the flying

bridge. The Redondo Beach Pier was now coming into plain view. It seemed to have a lot more color to it than its normal drab. Smitty bounded up the flying bridge ladder with a pair of binoculars in his hand. "It's people!" he exclaimed. "The pier is covered with people!"

As Smitty continued to watch through the binoculars, a giant banner unrolled across the front side of the pier. Smitty read aloud, "Redondo Beach Welcomes Goosey!"

"Well how about that?" Smitty said, handing the binoculars to Chuck.

"'Goosey.' I like it," Terry said.

"It seems a little cutesy sounding to me," Chuck countered, "especially for something that's eaten at least five people, and that's just counting the ones we know about. There could be even more for all we know."

"Chuck, we need the people to like her."

"It's a 'her,' for sure?"

"That's Dr. Frank's latest guess, so you see? 'Goosey' is a perfect name for a lady."

"It's not only a 'her.' Now, it's a lady," Chuck said cynically.

"Well, it sounds like a good name to me, Miss Terry," Smitty said, loud enough for Storm's benefit. "Just don't let the Skipper hear you speaking that 'lady' stuff when you're talking about a big, nasty fish."

If Smitty was hoping for a laugh, Storm didn't give him one, because he was getting more uneasy by the second. He eased the *Nemo* around the breakwater and edged her through the nautical traffic jam towards the slip that connected with the Big Lagoon. He hadn't counted, but the crowd appeared to be in the thousands. Terry stood near him, scanning the scene with binoculars. Storm said, "I don't like the looks of this. I'm worried about somebody getting too close or falling in at the worst possible time."

Terry lowered the binoculars from her eyes. "I'm not worried at all," she said with a knowing smile.

"What do you have, some kind of woman's intuition?"

Terry kept smiling and said, "Trust me."

To Storm's relief, when he finally brought the *Nemo* to a halt just short of the slip, the crowd situation was under complete control. A group of marines wearing field camouflage uniforms had created a safe perimeter around the slip and the pier above, and they were politely, but firmly, keeping the area clear.

Terry grabbed a bull horn and called out, "*Semper Fi,* Second Platoon!"

In reply, the entire group raised a collective fist and shouted, "Ooo-raahh!"

Storm gaped at Terry in wonderment. "You know them?"

She smiled at him and said smugly, "Fan club."

As thousands of tightly-packed spectators watched from above, Goosey's cage was nosed into the slip and snuggled up against an underwater gate. The gate was opened, and Cal Ocean divers unpinned the front of the cage, sliding the front pieces and faring away until nothing remained between Goosey and the Big Lagoon but a fifty-foot tunnel.

Goosey didn't move.

Meanwhile, Dr. Frank looked close to having a nervous breakdown. Storm escorted her into the *Nemo's* cabin and sat her down. "Tell me exactly what's happening," he said gently.

"What's happening is that Goosey's been knocked out for a whole day, and she's not coming out of it. I turned the gas off over an hour ago, and she hasn't woken up. If she doesn't move soon, we could lose her."

"Not to worry," Storm said. "Wait here."

Actually, Storm was as worried as Dr. Frank, but it wouldn't help to let her know that. He retrieved his faithful *Arbalete* from his gear locker and returned to the cabin. "I'd do this myself, but I have orders to stay out of the water. Just give Goosey a jab in the tail with this, and then stay clear of her prop wash."

Dr. Frank put on scuba gear and entered the water. She swam around to the back of the cage, stuck the *Arbalete* through the cage bars, and gave Goosey a jab with the spear point.

Goosey didn't move.

Storm called down from above, "This is a big fish. You've got to give her a big jab!"

Dr. Frank poked Goosey again, hard.

Perhaps it was because the giant fish remembered the recent pain of the diver's knife in the same general vicinity, or perhaps it was that she woke up from her drug-induced slumber with a start, but for whatever reason, Goosey ignited like an underwater rocket and swept through the tunnel and into the Big Lagoon with such force and horribleness that some of the waiting onlookers fainted. It was, after all, the first glimpse the public had gotten of Goosey, and for some of them the shock of seeing such a monster must have been too much to take.

Monstrous though she was, Goosey instantly became a smash hit, even doing nothing, which was what she was now doing in the deepest part of the lagoon, sixteen feet under water and directly beneath the observation deck of Cal Ocean's seafood restaurant. Three-hundred people, two of whom were presently being revived, had crammed into that tight space for Goosey's first, official public appearance. The majority of them were thrilled, exhilarated, and downright proud to have such a monster in their midst.

To those people watching her from above, Goosey looked wonderfully terrible.

To Goosey, those people above her looked wonderfully like food.

Chapter 48

"Would you help me talk some sense into these people?" Terry read the note that Storm had just passed to her.

They were guests at a Cal Ocean USA board meeting, and Keith Stafford was wrapping up his argument on why Goosey should be returned to the wild.

Terry understood why Storm was so agitated. It was him, after all, who had almost been eaten by Goosey, and not just once. If anyone had a right to an opinion about Goosey's freedom, it must certainly be Storm. She patted him on the knee, wrote, "Wait for the right moment," on his note, and passed it back. She worried that in his obvious frustration, he might speak too harshly and at the wrong time to help his argument.

Looking across Cal Ocean's board room, Stafford could hardly miss seeing Storm's sour expression. Stafford continued unabated, "In the last six months over a million people have come to Cal Ocean USA for a glimpse of Goosey, and I can say with reasonable assurance that the Goosey exhibit promises to be an ongoing, dynamic, and educational success. I'll just mention right now that the suggestion about a 3-D movie experience in which the viewer is swallowed whole is only a suggestion, though I do agree that Dr. Hancock's idea of calling it the 'Jonah Experience' is right on."

Chuckles filled the room, and Storm squirmed in his seat. Terry patted him on the knee again. She felt sure that Storm would get an opportunity to speak his peace.

Stafford continued, "Goosey is healthy, and we've taken enough blood and tissue samples to keep us busy for years. Her physical presence is no longer necessary for us to continue further study. The time is rapidly approaching to release her in a location where she should be able to survive, where we'll still have the means to locate and monitor her, and where she shouldn't pose a threat to human life. The policy at Cal Ocean

USA has always been to release an animal back into the wild whenever possible, and we believe that prevailing wisdom impels us to adhere to that policy."

Stafford smiled at Storm. "I believe that Dr. Hancock has something to say."

Storm glanced at a new note that Terry had just written. "Take your time, and remember to smile." He didn't feel like smiling, but he was willing to try as he said, "I admire and agree with Cal Ocean's release policy in most cases, but this is different. We are not talking about releasing a sea lion, or a dolphin, or even a killer whale. We're talking about turning loose a known man-eater. We don't know her habits. We don't know her movements. We don't know if she might migrate. We don't even know how she got here or where she came from. Six months ago I hoped that Goosey was going to stay in one spot, and I was wrong. She traveled five miles overnight, and a man was killed. Why, when, and how far Goosy travels are things we just don't understand, unless somebody in this room can tell me how she got here from the East Coast."

"But we don't know that she even came from the East Coast," Stafford interrupted.

"You're making my point for me," Storm replied. "We don't know if she was born here, or if she swam here, or if she was transported here, and until we figure that one out it's a big mistake to let her go."

Storm looked more frustrated than ever, and Terry could hardly blame him. She appreciated Keith Stafford, but right now she felt as if Storm might as well be talking to a brick wall.

"I appreciate your opinion, Dr. Hancock," Stafford replied, "But I would respectfully disagree. Should we go to the last habitations of the lion and tiger and put every large cat in a cage? Should we go to Alaska and round up the last grizzly bear? Should we capture every white shark in the ocean? Of course not! Cal Ocean's mission statement clearly states that it is desirable that predators should exist within their natural environment and in a natural relationship with their prey, even though human encroachment sometimes puts the humans themselves at risk."

Storm spoke without an invitation, "Yes, but your mission statement refers to natural predators and their natural prey. For all we know, Goosey is not an all-natural product, and therefore she can't have a natural prey. I haven't any data to prove it, but I strongly suspect that her aberrant location and huge size is somehow the direct result of human impact. If that's true, then she isn't subject to the normal Cal Ocean policy of release to the wild, because she is not a normal product of that wild."

"But isn't your argument reaching into the realm of speculation?" Stafford countered. "And I ask that as a straight question to a respected colleague."

Storm glanced again at Terry. He wore a look of futile resignation. With her eyes she tried to say to him, "Keep cool."

He said, "It's speculation to think we can turn a killer like this loose without suffering some unintended consequences. We don't know enough about Goosey to let her go. If I'm wrong, nobody gets hurt. If you're wrong...." Storm paused, and he looked as if he were remembering an unpleasant experience. He continued, "If you're wrong, somebody could wind up being served for lunch, and I've been there, and it's not very nice."

Terry patted Storm encouragingly on the knee. She had voiced her own reservations about setting Goosey free, but she leaned more towards a hope and prayer that everything would work out for the good.

Late that evening, working in her office, Terry neatened the piles on her desk and wondered if she would ever catch up. She could hardly complain. Thanks to Goosey, for the last twenty-four weeks she had been busier than a moth in a mitten doing exactly what she loved most, which was educating the public about the wonders of the ocean. At the same time, by steadily retrieving her prayer life from the abysmal depths where it had languished of late, some of the spiritual fire from her youth was being rekindled. As for her becoming a fisher of men, however, she wondered if that particular part of her life would continue to be channeled into an eddy swirling nowhere.

As long as Goosey had been the focal point to bring Storm and her together on a daily basis, it had been relatively easy to steer clear of the sensitive subject of Storm's relationship with God. Now that Goosey was probably going to be set free, Terry was forced to ask herself, maybe for the last time, if she was willing to risk jeopardizing her relationship with Storm by taking a bold stand for her faith. As always, in her heart of hearts, she knew exactly what she was supposed to do, but could she do it?

Terry telephoned Cal Ocean's security office to inform them that she was heading for the employees' parking lot. She turned out the lights of her office, locked her door from the outside, and briskly walked down the empty hall in the direction of the parking lot. Concerning Storm, her mind was finally made up. First thing in the morning, she would talk to him about her faith. She would take the bold stand.

"Tell him now, Terry."

Terry froze in her tracks. Had she just heard someone speak, or had she just felt a voice somewhere inside her mind? She looked down both directions of the hall. There was no one in sight, and all of the nearby offices appeared to be empty. She was reminded again of that day so long ago at Trestles when she had paddled out just one more time. It was a similar feeling, strong, but just a feeling. She looked at her watch. It was past eleven. Storm was probably long gone and asleep aboard the *Nemo*, and she was so tired that she just wanted to get to her apartment and collapse. She resumed her walk to the parking lot. Tomorrow morning, no matter what, she would talk to Storm about God.

She stopped again, carefully listened for a moment, and resumed walking.

Chapter 49

I sought the Lord, and He heard me,
And delivered me from all my fears.
(Psalms 34:4)

Storm flopped his body down on a bench in front of a maintenance kiosk near the Big Lagoon. Cal Ocean USA was officially closed on Mondays, but after this morning's meeting, at which Storm had voiced his mostly unwanted opinion, more than five thousand visitors had been allowed into the park for a peek at Goosey. Storm hadn't counted, but he felt like he'd talked to them all. He was glad to see the sun finally set and the last group of visitors trek out the front gate.

Storm wasn't surprised that after six months people still couldn't seem to get their fill of Goosey. She was, after all, such a magnificent beast. Goosey books, Goosey toys— anything having to do with her seemed to be in a state of mass proliferation. Even Congressman Robins had joined the band wagon by introducing a bill to name Goosey as California's State Sea Monster.

But why not? Storm thought. It was all for a good cause. He only hoped that something bad, now turned good, wouldn't turn bad again, which he feared could happen if Goosey were set free.

Storm leaned back against the bench and stared blankly towards the Big Lagoon. Between him and the water was a sturdy, head-high, electrified fence that had been erected around the perimeter of the giant pool containing Goosey. The fence was built to keep the overly curious, including Cal Ocean staff, a safe distance from her dangerous jaws. Through the growing darkness and the wires of the fence Storm couldn't see Goosey, but he guessed she was probably sulking in her usual spot down at the shadowy deep end. She only ventured from there for food, or when Betsy the killer whale was allowed into the lagoon to give her some exercise.

Actually, Storm didn't try to see Goosey. He didn't want to see Goosey. He had rarely looked at her since the day she had entered the Big Lagoon. When he was giving his highly popular talks at the restaurant overlook deck, or when he was at the Big Lagoon's underwater windows, he averted his eyes from looking at her. Maybe it was because he'd looked down her gullet enough times already. Maybe it was because his nightmare, while occurring less frequently, had taken a new twist in which he was trapped in the Big Lagoon with Goosey, and he couldn't get out. Maybe it was because he had finally found an underwater animal even more dangerous than great white sharks. Maybe it was all of those things.

Storm didn't know.

He didn't look at Goosey.

As Cal Ocean USA prepared to sleep for the night, orange shadows cast by the security lighting ushered all but a few remaining staff people out of the park. Storm had already said "good night" to Terry at her office, and he had been making his way to the *Nemo* when he had stopped at the bench. Getting up again, he left the Big Lagoon, circled around Betsy's tank, and let himself out the dockside entrance. He needed to think, and that meant walking the docks.

Storm wandered aimlessly, letting the docks lead him where they would. By all rights, he shouldn't even be alive, he told himself, barely noticing the boats and their names, and as that weighty reflection dogged his unhurried steps, another thought hounded him for attention. Throughout his clandestine sojourn through the Bible, the scriptures had constantly reiterated that all creation gives witness to a creator. Storm found that argument to be both elegant and simple—two classic attributes of good science. In fact, he found it to be almost too elegant and too simple. It was too good to be true, and yet it dovetailed so snugly within his own "Hancock's Paradox."

He wandered the docks for over an hour and finally found himself back at the *Nemo*. Without thinking, he climbed up the ladder to the flying bridge and lay down on a bench seat. He stared up into a clear sky as a cool breeze brushed his cheeks. The wind reminded him of Cap's angel story. Something special had happened to Cap that wintry morning, and there was no denying it. Maybe something like that had happened to him too. Several times in the last few months it seemed that a providential hand had nudged him just enough in one direction or the other to save his life. How could he explain that in a way sufficient to satisfy his scientific logic? Not through facts and figures, that was for sure.

Good old Smitty was probably right. There was no equation that could explain God.

Storm continued his upward gaze. In the eastern sky, through the glow of the harbor lights, he could barely pick out one of his favorite constellations. Backyard astronomers might have seen Cygnus the Swan soaring through the Milky Way, but Storm had always known it as the Northern Cross. It was a cross he saw tonight and not a swan. It was a cross that intertwined itself with everything that had happened to him since he'd first become involved with this Goosey adventure. It was a cross now leading him rapidly to a crossroads, and that prospect frightened him. He lay on the bench and weighed the arguments that might sway him either way. Could this unseen God, who perhaps created everything that existed, have actually come to earth as a man and let himself be killed on a cross? And all just to get people like Storm to heaven?

That'd be one heck of a God if it were true, Storm figured. It'd be the kind of God that he'd like to know.

But if God were that good, why be afraid to follow him?

Storm knew the answer to that question. He had always known the answer. He figured it was the same answer that everyone had facing that question.

He was afraid he would lose his independence and freedom.

Was he willing to risk that much?

Storm stared upward at the Northern Cross, and for the first time it appeared to him that the horizontal cross beam was bending down, almost as if it were supporting a great weight. The scriptures said that the man from heaven had taken upon himself the sins of the world. That would be a heavy load, Storm reasoned, perhaps heavy enough to bend even a heavenly cross.

The breeze died to nothing, and the water in the harbor smoothed into a reflective mirror. The normal night sounds quieted until Storm could almost hear the cry of his seeking heart.

Why did it have to be so difficult? Storm asked the night.

With all of his soul Storm wanted to know the truth about God, but he had another fear, a terrible fear, far more terrible to face than the possible loss of his freedom.

What if he took the plunge and gave himself up to this mysterious God?

What if he surrendered all and asked the man from heaven into his heart?

What if he got down on his knees and prayed for healing and forgiveness and to start his life anew?

What if he did all of that, and nothing happened?

What if he did all of that, and it turned out that God really wasn't there?

Storm feared that most of all.

But if that were the case, then what was the point of anything?

Storm took a deep breath, slid off the bench, and knelt on the *Nemo's* deck. He was going to take the plunge. He was going to risk the fear.

He needed to know.

He closed his eyes and prayed, "All right, God, you win. Take all of me, the good, the bad, everything. If you're who you say you are, then I want to know you and everything about you—the whole nine yards."

Nothing.

Storm opened his eyes and talked things over with himself. He hadn't been entirely honest, and he knew it. He was remembering a time when a wild-eyed maniac had grabbed him by both lapels and had spat out, "Do you know Jesus?" Storm had always believed that one could tell a person by his friends, and if that loony was a friend of the man from heaven, well....

Storm sighed heavily. He just couldn't do it. Terry had told him that to become a Christian required a total surrender, but there was no way he was going to become some kind of whacko Jesus freak.

He had been so close.

Again, Storm looked up at the Northern Cross, and a painful emptiness seemed to be burning its way outward from the center of his body. He whispered aloud to the night sky, "What do you want from me?"

Of course, Storm knew exactly what God wanted from him.

God wanted all of him.

As Storm knelt agonizing on the *Nemo's* deck, he suddenly couldn't seem to get enough air. His heart began to pound as if he were running away from his nightmare, and yet he knew that there was no running away and that there was no escape. There was only one way he was going to know about God for sure.

He bowed his head.

"All right," Storm said again, quietly. "All right, God. You can have me, even....," he hesitated.

How much did he want this?

He continued, "even if it means I become a Jesus freak."

The next instant, time seemed to stop. Then, as refreshing as summer rain, and as life-giving as the sun, Storm felt an overwhelming peace pour through him. Like a lost Rembrandt in the hands of a master restorer, the years of grime and dirt were peeled away from his soul until all that remained, kneeling in stillness on the *Nemo's* flying bridge, was Storm Hancock, seeker, finder, and beloved child of God.

Storm opened his eyes as if awakening from the most restful sleep. He touched his arms, his hands, and his chest. He touched his face. Something about him was different. He was the same person, and yet he wasn't the same person. The *Nemo*, the harbor lights, the water, all astounded him as he suddenly felt a physical connection to the entire universe. He looked up at the Northern Cross, and he could almost feel the pulsating heat from its stars surging through him. He realized that everything he was seeing was all one big plan, and he had suddenly become a part of it, and then he realized one of the best parts of all.

He didn't have to become a Jesus freak.

Storm looked at his watch. It was almost eleven, but maybe Terry was still in her office. She'd been working late these last nights. He'd take a chance. He rushed up the docks from the *Nemo*, and his timing was perfect to meet a security guard at Cal Ocean's dockside entrance. He was let in, and he hurried past Betsy's tank and around the Big Lagoon.

He stopped.

In the orange glow of the security lights, he saw a shadowy figure within the enclosure, standing on the deck between electric fence and the water. Whoever it was appeared to be staring toward the Big Lagoon's deep end.

Storm walked closer until his toes were almost touching the fence. "Who's there?" he said in a friendly voice. By now he was on a first name basis with almost everyone connected with the park.

"Well, well," the mystery person said in a mocking voice, still facing the water. If my ears don't deceive me, I'm being paid a visit by the famous Dr. Storm Hancock."

Storm didn't recognize the voice right off, but he had an uncomfortable feeling that he'd heard it before. The person turned around, and Storm found himself staring down the barrel of a pistol with what looked like some kind of silencing device. The gun was held by a gloved hand. The gunman moved closer to the fence and into better light.

Fishbeck!

Fishbeck smiled devilishly in the orange light. "Poor Dr. Hancock, always meddling in other people's business. I had planned to perform this little operation by myself, but you've forced me to have to do it with your assistance."

He's lost his mind! Storm told himself.

Fishbeck motioned at Storm with the pistol and said, "Please, Dr. Hancock, climb over the fence and join me."

"I can't. It's electric," Storm said, stalling for time to collect his wits.

"Oh, no, I've taken care of that," Fishbeck replied, and he touched the muzzle of the gun to one of the fence wires. There were no sparks or any other indication that the current was flowing.

"See?" Fishbeck said, grinning, and aiming the gun at Storm again. "I've turned it off."

Storm glanced at the maintenance kiosk. The controls for the fence were inside. Was the kiosk door ajar? In the dim light he couldn't be sure. He looked back at Fishbeck.

"Oh, yes, I can pick locks, too," Fishbeck said, motioning with the gun towards the kiosk. "In fact, there's a whole lot of things I can do that aren't appreciated. Now, climb over the fence."

Storm looked down the gun barrel and hesitated. Maybe he should make a run for it. From what little he knew about guns, he knew that most people couldn't hit the broad side of a barn with a pistol, let alone a moving target.

Fishbeck said, "If you're thinking I don't know how to use this thing, think again. I was runner up three years in a row at the state championships. Now, climb over the fence, or I will shoot you, and no one will hear it."

It seemed to Storm that Fishbeck had gone crazy enough that he just might shoot. He had no choice but to follow orders and try to buy time. He gingerly touched a fence wire with the tip of his finger. He didn't get shocked. Slowly, warily, using the wires of the fence like rungs of a ladder, he climbed up and over and stood on the deck, facing Fishbeck.

The cool breeze had come up again, sending ripples across the dark water of the Big Lagoon. Storm didn't look at the water, but he could almost feel Goosey's presence. He knew that she was down there watching.

She was always watching.

Fishbeck waived the gun in a cavalier manner, saying, "Thanks to your rude interruption, I have to change my plans, but maybe it's all for the best." Fishbeck bent down and picked up a long pole that had a cylindrical device attached to one end. "Take this!" Fishbeck commanded, handing the pole to Storm.

Storm grasped the pole. Maybe he could use it as a weapon. "What am I supposed to do with it?"

Fishbeck took a step backward, and aimed the pistol at

Storm. "You really don't know?" he sneered. "This, Dr. Hancock, is a bang stick. You do know what those are for, don't you? They're used to kill sharks, except this one was made special for Goosey. Plant the end of this baby between her eyes, and the explosive charge in it will blow a hole in her skull as big as a basketball."

Despite his fear, Storm was genuinely puzzled. "Why would you want to do that?"

"Why?" Fishbeck said in agitation. He aimed the gun at Storm's face. The gun, the hand holding it, and Fishbeck, all seemed to tremble together in a fit of emotion. Fishbeck's voice quavered as he said, "For your information, I discovered Goosey before any of you, but did I get the credit? No! It was the famous Dr. Hancock who gets the credit! It was the famous Dr. Hancock who gets the glory! The famous Dr. Hancock even gets the girl!"

Then, so quietly that Storm barely heard it, Fishbeck muttered, "Just like my brother."

Fishbeck's hand stopped trembling, and he lowered the gun to his hip but kept it pointing at Storm. "Get in the water."

Storm was incredulous.

"Wait! Wait a second!" he pleaded. "It doesn't have to be like this! If you found her first, then fine! We can tell the world!"

"No! It's too late!" Fishbeck said vehemently. "Now, get in the water!"

"I can't get in there with Goosey!"

"Of course you can," Fishbeck said, lowering his voice and taking on a sarcastic tone. "You're Dr. Storm Hancock, the famous diving hero, remember? I'm even giving you a fighting chance. You've got the bang stick. All you have to do is get Goosey before Goosey gets you. I was going to kill her myself, but now that you're here, I can only watch."

Fishbeck reached into his shirt pocket with his free hand as if he were making sure that something was there. Apparently satisfied, he brought his hand back out again. He aimed the gun at Storm's chest and said coldly, "I'll give you to the count of three. If you're not in the water by then, a nine-millimeter custom-packed load will put you there."

Fishbeck's hand began to tremble again, and then his entire body. He took another step backward, leaned against the wires of the electric fence as if to steady himself, and aimed the gun at Storm's face.

"One!"

Storm couldn't think. He slowly sat down at the edge of the Big Lagoon. He had the bang stick. Could he somehow get into the water and maybe swim to the other side and get away from Fishbeck? He looked towards the shadowy end of the pool. He couldn't see Goosey. Maybe he could fend her off long enough to actually get away, but what if he couldn't? Could the bang stick really save him? What if it didn't work?

Any way he looked at it, his nightmare was about to come true.

"Two!"

Storm lowered his body into the water as slowly as he could. He didn't know what else to do. "God, where are you?" he cried out silently from the depths of his soul. He turned towards Fishbeck, who now held the gun with both hands, so perfectly aimed at Storm's face that Storm felt like he was looking down a big, dark tunnel.

"God help me!" Storm prayed aloud.

"Three!"

Fishbeck suddenly convulsed as if every muscle in his body had gone berserk. In one, violent contortion he catapulted himself across the deck and plunged past Storm into the Big Lagoon. In the same instant, Storm hauled himself out of the water and jumped to his feet. Even as he did, a massive, dark shape wriggled from out of the shadows of the deep end.

Fishbeck seemed to be disoriented. He splashed and floundered helplessly eight feet away from the side of the pool.

"Fishbeck, swim! Here!" Storm yelled. He held the bang stick out for Fishbeck to grab. He saw Goosey's dark form racing towards them along the bottom.

"Fishbeck, grab the pole!" Storm screamed, but Fishbeck ignored him and continued to flounder.

Storm saw his nightmare becoming real. It was all here, the

Big Lagoon, Goosey. All that was left was for him to be sucked down her gullet. He watched helplessly as Goosey surged up from below like some leviathan of old.

Rage and frustration ripped at Storm's soul. "There's nothing more I can do!" He yelled at heaven.

He had faced the source of his nightmare too many times already. He could not face her again.

Goosey swept upward, her mouth open, her prey helpless before her.

"The wings of morning!" Storm screamed, and he leaped into the Big Lagoon and planted the end of the bang stick right between Goosey's eyes.

Chapter 50

Storm dragged himself out of the Big Lagoon. He still held the bang stick, the one that hadn't worked. He ran a finger across the device at the end of the stick and discovered the threaded hole that would have held the detonating mechanism. He saw the mechanism itself on the deck near where Fishbeck had been leaning against the fence. He figured that's what had been in Fishbeck's pocket, and it was all clear now. Fishbeck had counted on Cal Ocean USA's opening tomorrow morning and finding a non-working bang stick covered with Storm's fingerprints, and Storm gone and presumably eaten. Fishbeck had originally come to kill Goosey, but had altered his plan on the spot to let Goosey kill Storm.

"Ahhh, Fishbeck," Storm said bitterly, looking towards the deep end of the Big Lagoon where Goosey had returned with her latest catch.

He heard footsteps, and he turned towards the kiosk to see a familiar-looking figure running towards him. Terry stopped just on the other side of the electric fence.

"Are you OK?" she asked in a voice shaking with fear.

"Thanks to you, yes."

"I didn't know what else to do. I came looking for you to talk about God. I saw you in the water, and I saw Fishbeck with the gun. I thought he was going to shoot you, and all I could think of was to turn the fence back on."

"You came looking for me at midnight to talk about God?"

"Yes."

Storm looked up into the night sky. The Northern Cross seemed to be burning even brighter than before.

A May northwester blew the tops off whitecaps and made it cold on deck. The people on this deck, however, found the weather invigorating, gorgeous to behold, and definitely not bad enough to delay a schedule. As for the crew of the ocean tug, *Algonquin*, today's weather was just part of another day's work, though they were sure to keep a sharp eye on the special cargo shackled to the *Algonquin's* fantail. That special cargo consisted of a custom-made fiberglass tub in which sloshed one giant goosefish to be delivered alive to the Osborne Bank. She would be released over an underwater ridge that rose within nineteen fathoms of the surface. The ridge, fished by party boats but never dived, was one crest on the same range of mountains whose highest peak formed Santa Barbara Island seven miles to the north. It was expected that Goosey would find abundant food there, making it improbable that she would have cause to probe the deep canyon between her and the island. To the other compass points, the bottom dropped off even deeper. Barring the most unlikely rambling, Goosey would be isolated, though with Goosey nothing could be taken for granted. For that reason, and for possible future study, she had been fitted with a special collar around her tail that would reflect sonar waves and make her relatively easy to locate.

The passengers on board the *Algonquin* made up Goosey's send-off party. The *Nemo's* crew was on board, plus Cal Ocean staff, Cap and Molly, Sheriff Jim, and a K-EBB camera man. They all wore matching sweatshirts that read, "Goosey Gang," compliments of Congressman Robins, who had apologized in advance for missing the trip, although no one on board could remember having invited him.

The *Algonquin* coasted to a stop in what looked to be the middle of the ocean. Dr. Frank did a last check of Goosey's vital signs. Apparently satisfied, she opened a valve, and one end of the fiberglass tub lowered hydraulically. Moving deliberately, Dr. Frank then loosened four latches on the end of the tub, and water began spilling from the tub onto a wide, fiberglass ramp that sloped into the ocean over the *Algonquin's* transom. Dr. Frank had only to throw one last lever, and Goosey would slide out like a bar of soap. She put her hand to the lever but then took it away and turned to Storm who was standing nearby. "You caught her," she said to Storm. "You get to let her go."

Storm stood next to Goosey's tub and reluctantly rested his

hand on the lever. With just a pull of the hand, so much would be finished, and some things would be just beginning. He didn't agree with letting Goosey go, and it was only because of Cal Ocean's solemn promise to keep close tabs on her that he was able to join the others on the *Algonquin.* He looked across the deck at Terry, huddling with the rest of the Goosey Gang to keep warm. Yes, Storm thought to himself. So much could be finished. Is that what he wanted? He prayed silently, "Well, God, you've pulled me through enough times already. I guess I'm not going to quit on you now."

He said to Dr. Frank, who had been waiting patiently, "Are we ready?"

Dr. Frank nodded. "Any time you are."

Storm pulled the lever. The tub's end gate dropped, and Goosey slid into the water. At first she floated just beneath the surface as if she were checking out her new surroundings. Then, in her awkward way, she wriggled downward until those aboard the *Algonquin* saw only the blue gray of the Pacific Ocean in spring. Immediately, Chuck stuck his head out of the *Algonquin's* cabin. As usual, he was wearing a headset. "Sonar reflection is A-OK," he called out with a grin.

Storm stared into the depths long after Goosey had dropped from sight. "Well, she's gone," he finally said flatly. He wasn't sure how he felt about that. Relieved, he supposed, and strangely saddened.

The Goosey Gang retired into the cabin and started a penny-ante poker game, leaving Storm and Terry huddled together, seeking shelter from the wind behind the now-empty tub. They stood silently, scrunched together, watching the *Algonquin's* wake trail away like a long, white veil, until the spot where Goosey had been released could only be imagined. The closeness of Terry had become so familiar to Storm that he was loathe to let it go. Her touch, her voice, even her smell; how could he just walk away from all of that? He couldn't. He wouldn't, he told himself. Maybe women were nothing but trouble, but the kind of trouble that Terry provided was something he didn't want to live without.

Again, he had come to a frightening crossroads. Should he

tell her how he felt, and risk losing her, or should he just go on as usual, holding back and never knowing for sure what he could have had? He looked up into the windy blue sky. His heart pounded as wildly as it had any time in the last few months.

"Well, God," he prayed silently. "Here we go again."

He turned to face Terry at exactly the same time she turned to face him, and they both laughed. He put his hands on her waist. Now, if he could only manage not to say something stupid.

"So, Terry, do you like fish?"

Terry laughed again, and Storm realized just how much he enjoyed hearing that.

She answered, still laughing, "Do you mean to study, or to eat?"

"I mean, do you like fish enough to maybe go steady with a guy who also likes fish?"

Terry stopped laughing. She put her hands on Storm's shoulders. "When you say steady, how steady do you mean?"

"God, help me do this right," Storm prayed with all of his might. He said, "Steady enough to last forever."

There was no turning back now. Heart pounding, adrenaline raging, he took the plunge. "I love you, Terry, and I'm asking you to marry me. I'll do my best to love you even more and take care of you and be kind to you...." He didn't know what else to say.

Terry looked intently into his eyes. The wake of the *Algonquin* stretched ever longer. Finally, she said, "I would like a long engagement—at least a year."

Storm's eyes grew wide. "Does that mean 'yes'?"

"Yes, that means 'yes'! I love you, Storm, and I will marry you!" Terry gave Storm a quick kiss on the lips.

"Well, praise the Lord!" Storm cried out, and he swept Terry up from the *Algonquin's* deck and spun her around.

Terry, squealing and laughing through tears of joy, also cried out, "Yes! Praise the Lord!"

Storm laughed, and he spun her again. Meanwhile, Smitty, ever alert and curious to a commotion on deck, peeked his head out the cabin door, and then the Goosey Gang poured out onto the deck and joined Storm and Terry in the laughing and the hugging and the tears of joy.

And the *Algonquin,* faithful as ever, carried them home.

The End

Breinigsville, PA USA
21 March 2011
258036BV00001B/1/P